"I hardly need your advice," Ainsley scolded him in return, every word pushing her flesh against his. Almost as if . . . as if *she* had just kissed *him*.

But this wasn't kissing, she assured herself. This was merely a new form of arguing.

Anticipating his next contradiction, she angled her head for closer contact and Reed growled in response. The low, primal sound sent an unexpected thrill rushing through her.

"It would be a waste of breath to tell you anything," he said, fitting his other hand over the curve of her cheek to cradle her face. "Even if I wanted to say that your lips are soft and plump and more luscious than wine-poached pears, I wouldn't."

Then he tilted her head back to cement his argument. Opening her mouth with his own, he nibbled gently into her flesh, tasting the seam of her lips without hurry. The slow, thorough exploration caused her eyes to drift closed.

Her senses centered on the firm, enticing pressure of his mouth, the delicious rasp of his tongue. A wanton mewl tore from her throat, hungry and needy and urgent.

The unguarded sound brought her to an uncomfortable admission . . .

She might be kissing the enemy.

By Vivienne Lorret

The Misadventures in Matchmaking Series

HOW TO FORGET A DUKE
TEN KISSES TO SCANDAL
THE ROGUE TO RUIN

The Season's Original Series

"THE DUKE'S CHRISTMAS WISH"
(in ALL I WANT FOR CHRISTMAS IS A DUKE
and A CHRISTMAS TO REMEMBER)
THE DEBUTANTE IS MINE
THIS EARL IS ON FIRE
WHEN A MARQUESS LOVES A WOMAN
JUST ANOTHER VISCOUNT IN LOVE (novella)

The Rakes of Fallow Hall Series

THE ELUSIVE LORD EVERHART
THE DEVILISH MR. DANVERS
THE MADDENING LORD MONTWOOD

The Wallflower Wedding Series

TEMPTING MR. WEATHERSTONE (novella)
DARING MISS DANVERS
WINNING MISS WAKEFIELD
FINDING MISS MCFARLAND

The Rogue to Ruin

Misadventures in Matchmaking

VIVIENNE LORRET

AVONBOOKS

An Imprint of HarperCollinsPublishers

Lyrics from "The Lass of Richmond Hill," by Leonard McNally and James Hook, public domain.

THE ROGUE TO RUIN. Copyright © 2019 by Vivienne Lorret. All rights reserved. Printed in the United States of America. No part of this book may be used or reproduced in any manner whatsoever without written permission except in the case of brief quotations embodied in critical articles and reviews. For information, address HarperCollins Publishers, 195 Broadway, New York, NY 10007.

First Avon Books mass market printing: August 2019

Print Edition ISBN: 978-0-06-268552-0
Digital Edition ISBN: 978-0-06-268553-7

Cover design by Amy Halperin
Cover illustrations © Jon Paul Ferrara
Cover photograph © Michel Legrou/Media Photo

Avon, Avon & logo, and Avon Books & logo are registered trademarks of HarperCollins Publishers in the United States of America and other countries.

HarperCollins is a registered trademark of HarperCollins Publishers in the United States of America and other countries.

FIRST EDITION

19 20 21 22 23   QGM   10 9 8 7 6 5 4 3 2 1

For Toni, Isabelle, and Abbey. I was blessed the day you joined my family.

Acknowledgments

Sometimes it takes a village, a miracle, and a mobile office.

As with every story, the expedition to Ainsley and Reed's happily-ever-after encountered a few bumps and surprises along the way. And I'd like to thank the people who shared the journey with me.

Many thanks to my editor, Nicole, for your patience and helpful insight. To my agent, Stefanie, for being ready with a quick word of support and advice. To Pam, Kayleigh, and the entire (wonderful) Avon team for everything you do. And to the incomparable Jon Paul Ferrara, Amy Halperin, and Michel Legrou for the stunning artwork on the cover.

Hugs to my friends—our Saturday morning chats and cups of caffeine refill my soul. And extra hugs to Cyndi for being this book's first reader and for sending impatient emojis when I didn't get pages to you quickly enough.

I also want to thank my readers for welcoming these characters into your hearts, for sending emails and leaving comments, and, most of all, for your warm smiles whenever we meet.

Unending love to my boys—my heroes, my heart.

Because of you, I am truly blessed.

The Rogue
to Ruin

Prologue

Autumn, 1825

This wasn't the first time Reed Sterling had a pistol aimed at him, and it likely wouldn't be the last. Though until now, he'd never seen one brandished by such a prim bluenose.

From the doorway of Sterling's, he studied the chestnut-haired figure standing in the pallid morning light in St. James's. She wore a plain straw bonnet, situated squarely on the crown of her head, and a tailored fawn walking dress that covered her from throat to footpath.

As the owner of a gaming hell, Reed had a knack for getting a sense of a person straightaway. This woman, for example, likely imagined that her unadorned self was hardly worth notice and easily forgotten.

She couldn't have been more wrong.

He was wholly aware of her, and it had nothing to do with the weapon in her grasp.

There wasn't a single embellishment in her attire. No baubles, feathers, or even embroidered cuffs. And yet, his attention was fixed like a child's who'd spied a brown paper package with his name on the card. And all he could think was, *I wonder what's inside all that clever wrapping.*

A pair of brownish-gray eyes narrowed at him. "Surely *you* are not the owner of this gambling establishment."

At the slight rasp in her voice, his flesh tightened over his frame, pulse thrumming. "I am Reed Sterling."

The fringe of her black lashes bunched together. "Impossible. A man of such a reputedly successful business would have a degree of distinction."

"Carry a walking stick?" he offered, stepping down to the pavement. "Quizzing glass on a chain?"

"Something of the sort. In the very least, he should be graying at the temples."

Reed scrubbed a hand through his ungrizzled brown hair, still damp from his daily sparring exercises.

She followed the gesture, scrutinizing him the same way he had done to her, her gaze sweeping over his form. The only difference was that her cheeks colored as if she'd never seen a man in his shirtsleeves before. And when he grinned, she flushed deeper.

"Why, you're not even properly attired," she chided in a scandalized whisper. "Surely you do not always receive calls in such a state."

"I was informed that you rapped rather impatiently on the door and demanded an audience without delay. Though the lad neglected to tell me that you intended to shoot me."

"*Shoot you?* Of all the absurd—" Her eyes widened slightly when she glanced down to the dueling pistol and frilly white handkerchief in her grasp. Then, with nothing more than a casual turn of her wrist, she pointed the long blackened barrel at the ground instead of at his heart. "This isn't what it seems. I merely carried the weapon over in my reticule because I knew it belonged to one of your drunken patrons. But do not worry yourself for it isn't loaded. I made certain of it. And the percussion cap is absent as well."

"Know a lot about pistols, do you?"

He watched, amused as she awkwardly began to slip

the handkerchief through the engraved trigger guard and around the checkered grip as she continued.

"When I discovered the heinous thing this morning, I skimmed through a book in my uncle's library. I had to ascertain if it was safe to remove from our doorstep. We live *there*, you see."

Reed's gaze did not follow her gesture to the stately townhouse across the street, adorned with pristine white pillars and box windows that had been void of candlelight until a sennight ago. "I already know who my neighbors are, Miss Bourne."

"You know my—" She broke off, her full lips parting. Then, she straightened with a jerk as if he'd just pinched her bottom instead of merely saying her name. "You should not address me as if we are acquainted. We are not. Nor are we likely to be formally introduced at any social function."

"Because common blokes like me don't get invited to the high-society parties you lot attend?"

Those lashes bunched together again. "Because I am certain that I do not share any amusements with a man who promotes lascivious activities like imbibing in liquor, gaming, dueling—"

"Not dueling," he said firmly, feeling a muscle twitch at his jawline. After his own father was killed in a duel, Reed had a supreme distaste for the practice. In fact, he spent a good deal of his nights trying to keep his more hotheaded patrons from *demanding satisfaction* over insignificant slights. "It's a coward's way to hide behind a pistol. Real men know how to settle a score fairly."

"An educated man might use *words* to reach an amicable understanding with another. However, I do not imagine that is the preferred method of the owner of a gambling establishment."

Actually, it was. As far as Reed was concerned, a man in his line of work had to be skilled in the art of mollifying and mediation. But he didn't feel the need to explain himself to Miss Bourne. He'd let her think what she liked. Besides, he was enjoying how easy it was to get a rise out of her.

"*Using words?* Now, where's the sport in that?" He chuckled at the way she huffed, all smug and superior, even as her curious gaze dipped to the open neck of his shirt once more. "I tell you, nothing excites a mob of dandy, silk-pursed aristocrats more than the prospect of betting on blood sport. Every time I get these duel-at-dawn gents to step into the ring for a few bare-knuckled blows instead, it's good for business."

She paled visibly, her mouth set in grim disapproval. "You encourage . . . pugilism in your establishment as well?"

"Aye. I was a prizefighter, you know," he announced with a carefully humble expression, expecting her to look down the length of him with renewed interest. His former title fascinated most women, no matter if their blood was aristocrat blue or common red.

He waited for her eyes to flit over him, for her mouth to soften. But after a beat or two, and her expression remained unchanged, it became apparent that Miss Bourne was not like most women.

Reed shifted, straightening his shoulders. As a fighter, he was still considered something of a legend. Men from all over England knew his name. And the fortune he'd earned helped him open Sterling's. In fact, that was what set his hell apart from others and put him on par with clubs like Brook's and Boodle's. He offered everything under one roof—betting books, fine food and liquor, a private silk-covered room for a gent and his paramour, high-stakes gaming at the tables, *and* ring-side exhibitions.

Sterling's was truly a man's world.

"I also give lessons to the patrons who can afford it," he added proudly, but wished he'd kept quiet. To his own ears, he sounded as if he was trying to impress her.

She sniffed with disdain, extending the handkerchief-tied pistol that dangled from her fingertips. "How thrilled you must be to teach violence to other men."

When he took the weapon, she immediately smoothed her hands down her skirts as if the thought of touching him sickened her. So it was like that, was it?

"My family and I are at an unfortunately close proximity to this"—she paused to draw in a breath, her cool gaze flitting over his shoulder to the open doorway—"institution."

He untied the handkerchief, then balled it in his fist before offering it back to her.

She wrinkled her brow. Then, somehow, she managed to tug the dainty square free without the barest contact, and so swiftly that the finely stitched seams left a burning trail along his palm.

Watching as she tucked the lace down into her glove, he wondered if it was still warmed by the heat of his fist. He hoped it was. He wanted her to imagine that she was only a scrap of lace away from the bare hand of a common man.

"What is unfortunate to some might be fortuitous to others," he said. "There are many who would enjoy living so near Sterling's."

"That is not the case in my circumstance, I assure you. And I would prefer it if you would keep the midnight carousing of your patrons to a dull roar and ask them not to litter on our doorstep."

"If you don't wish to live here, Miss Bourne, then take other lodgings. I'm certain that the duchess can find someone else to rent her townhouse, or even to buy it outright."

Her chin snapped up. "How dare you speak of my patroness in a familiar manner, as if you share an acquaintance. It is because of you and your seedy establishment that the estimable Duchess of Holliford was forced to abandon St. James's and now lives in Mayfair. Her Grace has been the kindest and most generous person my sisters and I have ever known and I will not stand for any such casual references."

Miss Bourne was a fierce one, to be sure. All prim and proper on the outside, but with the heart of a warrior.

The sight of those flashing eyes and castigating mouth had Reed's pulse thrumming once more. Against his better judgment, he wondered what other passions might be lurking beneath such a tempting, haughty veneer.

"If it wasn't for Her Grace," she continued, "my family would never have been able to embark on our new venture. We plan to run a business from the townhouse, you see."

He smirked. "Is that so?"

"Indeed. The Bourne Matrimonial Agency will doubtless become the *ton*'s premier establishment. We open our doors a fortnight from today. There's even an advertisement in *The Post*."

His amusement faded as the look of smug certainty settled over her fine features. Apparently, this wasn't a jest.

Suddenly, his mind's eye flashed with a vision of hoity-toity society women traipsing along the footpath with their frilly parasols and clucking their tongues at his patrons for drinking, cursing, and gambling to excess.

That would be bad for his business.

"And what would this *agency* do, exactly?"

"Simply put, we are matchmakers. Or rather my uncle, Viscount Eggleston, is. My sisters and I will assist him in taking the applications of our clients and in finding prospective spouses for them."

Reed choked on a laugh. Why had he worried for a single instant over such a foolish enterprise?

"That's a new trick for husband hunting. Your uncle *pretends* to play matchmaker, then, while taking down the names of the most eligible bachelors in London, he just happens to find wealthy, titled husbands for each of his nieces."

"You are wrong, Mr. Sterling. The purpose of the Bourne Matrimonial Agency is to serve others. To promote worthy ideals like honor and respect—things I'm certain are foreign to a man whose primary goal is to introduce wickedness to the world."

"I cannot take full credit for all the wickedness in the world, or even in London. It's been around much longer than either of us. That's how I know *my* estimable establishment will outlast yours."

When her dark winged brows arched in challenge, a thrill shot through him, heating his blood. That inner warrior flashed in her eyes, so close to the surface that he wondered what it would take to unleash it completely.

"It is the prideful man who will fall to his knees the hardest," she said.

He leaned in, just a bit, and lowered his voice. "Not when he fixes his attention on what matters."

Her cheeks colored again, but she didn't back down. She set her hands on her hips as if to make herself larger. "Mark my words—the Bourne Matrimonial Agency is here to stay."

"You and your sisters will be married off and gone in six months."

"Proof of how little you know of your new neighbors."

"I know that three highborn young women wouldn't have moved to London unless they intended to find themselves three highborn gentlemen to marry."

"Wrong again, Mr. Sterling."

Miss Bourne didn't bother to elaborate. Instead, she turned on her heel with a snap and confidently navigated through the morning traffic.

Reed watched her go, admiring the swish of her plain brown skirts. And by the time she safely reached the other side, any lingering concern that this matchmaking agency would jeopardize Sterling's success was laid to rest. There wasn't a doubt in his mind that Miss Bourne would take a husband and lose interest in her business within six months. Perhaps even sooner.

Chapter 1

"Her way was clear, though not quite smooth."
JANE AUSTEN, *Emma*

A Year and a Half Later

Scrutinizing the white-glazed sign on the outer door, Ainsley Bourne absently worried the corner of her thumbnail. Her livelihood depended on these freshly painted words.

> *Welcome to the Bourne Matrimonial Agency.*
> *For exceptional matchmaking services,*
> *please enquire up the stairs.*

Was this enough to spark curiosity and entice passersby? She knew something had to change or the family business would fall into utter ruin.

The flesh of her brow knitted in doubt. Perhaps she should have underlined *exceptional*. And was it her imagination or did *please* sound a bit beggarly?

Until this moment, she never realized what a needy word it was. Slanting to the right, *please* even resembled a crawling thing, the *e* dragging the rest of the letters along like a dog that had left something foul on the parlor rug, the looped tail of the *p* trailing behind.

"Botheration," she huffed, wondering if there was enough paint left in the pot. Had she actually gone through seventeen drafts, six sheets of paper, a jar of ink, three brushes, and a permanently splattered apron just for this? A costly endeavor.

Frustrated, she lifted the red ribbon off the peg for her eighteenth attempt.

The agency may be hard-pressed for clients, but she was not about to grovel. If people refused to seek a happy union based on trust and respect, then she felt sorry for them. What did it matter to her if men wanted to marry empty-headed ninnies? Or if women chose men of questionable character, only to end up heartbroken and abandoned like her mother . . .

A cold chill tumbled through Ainsley. She hesitated, wavering one-footed on the threshold.

"I know I can depend upon you, dear. You've always been the strongest of us all," her mother had once said.

More than ten years had passed since Heloise Bourne-Cartwright's death, but Ainsley could still hear their last conversation. Still feel the grip of the frail hand that had squeezed her own.

Expelling a soul-deep sigh, Ainsley set both feet on the ground and hung the sign back up. Then, she adjusted the ribbon until it was equal lengths on either side. There.

Who knew? It might make a difference. At the very least, she could give it until the end of the day to see if any monumental changes would happen. Just a smallish ravening horde would suffice.

"And perhaps the *ton* will suddenly see the agency in a new light and stop believing that we are only interested in making matches for ourselves," she muttered under her breath, her inner cynic rising to the surface.

Though with her two younger sisters, Jacinda and Briar, now married to their once-best clients, Ainsley could hardly fault society's presumption.

And yet, that was last year. It didn't explain why there was still a lull in new applicants.

After all, they'd survived the initial wave of mean-spirited gossip when Uncle Ernest first started the agency. And when Jacinda had married the Duke of Rydstrom, there was speculation regarding their methods but also a good deal of interest. Then, Briar's marriage to London's most rakish bachelor, the Earl of Edgemont, had brought in a handful of the curious and more adventurous clients.

In Ainsley's opinion, the fact that they remained open proved that they intended to stay that way. But the frightening truth was, they were only months away from closing their doors for good, and no one knew but her.

She didn't have the heart to break the news to her family. All she wanted was to make the Bourne Matrimonial Agency a sweeping success. Well that, *and* to fill the family coffers with more coin than moth wings.

After everything they'd overcome already, this year's Season should have brought the change they needed. So then, why weren't there scores of eager debutantes and young bucks seeking their services?

Ainsley believed she knew the answer.

Because there was one thing the agency couldn't overcome—their location.

Turning away from her own sign, her gaze settled on another across the street. Sterling's—the bane of her existence.

How was a respectable matchmaking agency supposed to succeed with such an unsavory establishment just steps away?

At first glance, the pale gray brick corner building was stunning in the morning light, regal even, with three stories of arched windows polished to a mirror-like finish. Such a façade might deceive some poor, naive soul into thinking that it was respectable. Or even that the name, chiseled into the stone hood molding above the door, represented a sense of long-standing permanence. But it was all an illusion created by the owner, Reed Sterling.

The former prizefighter belonged in London society as much as a bear belonged at an afternoon tea. He was unmannerly, unrefined, and untamed.

During their first encounter, he'd granted her an audience while attired solely in his shirtsleeves and snug-fitting breeches. He hadn't even attempted to cover himself or to apologize for his near nudity. He'd been perspiring as well. His deep mahogany hair had been tousled into damp waves that curled at his temples, the thick cording of his throat exposed for all the world to see, and the open neck of his shirtsleeves revealed a rise of heavy muscle swathed in dark hair. Why, he'd looked positively primitive.

It still made her blood hot simply thinking of his audacity.

Reaching up, she lifted the fine chestnut-brown tendrils off the nape of her neck and felt the cool relief of the spring breeze. Then, the man himself appeared in his doorway, filling it with uncivilized brawn.

He must have sensed her ever-fixed animosity aimed in his direction.

Without even glancing at the broom-toting chimney sweep passing in front of him, or to the rambling traffic of carriages, drays, and hackney cabs between them, his gaze cut directly to Ainsley.

She lowered her arms. Her pulse kicked shamefully at the sensitive flesh of her throat, and all she wanted to do was turn around. But there was no point in that. He'd already caught her staring in his direction. To look away now would be an admission of guilt, a white flag of surrender—which was something she would never, *ever* give to Reed Sterling.

Even from this distance, she would lay odds that he wore his usual half grin, his mouth curling up where a tiny scar notched his upper lip near the corner. When he inclined his head, her stomach did a strange little flip, seating itself directly beneath her lungs, making her breaths come up short.

The symptoms of pure abhorrence, she was sure.

Instead of offering her nemesis a greeting in kind, she snubbed him with a sniff. Only then did she turn around to deal with her daily chore—cleaning up the filth that traveled from his doorstep to hers.

All manner of handbills for boxing lessons, hazard tournaments, and dancing ladies littered the whitewashed steps. If only his wealthy patrons were as eager as his rubbish to make it inside the agency.

Of course it was doubtful she could make viable matches for any of them. Rogues and wastrels were not the sort of men she would recommend to any woman. But she wasn't above taking their money. In fact, if Mr. Sterling—the devil himself—should like a subscription, she would even take his application.

After all, as the most practical member of the family, it was her responsibility to keep the agency in candles and coal. She did what had to be done. If it were up to Uncle Ernest, he'd spend every farthing on the endless list of women he wooed, as the bills from the flower shop and confectioners could attest.

Issuing a sigh, Ainsley bent down. Rain had come and gone in the hours before dawn and the handbills were plastered to the steps. She had to peel off the pages, one by one, and drop them into the rusted rubbish bin she brought out each morning.

Dark runnels of ink coasted down the sloped stair tread, leaching into the hem of her burgundy day dress. Silently, she gave Reed Sterling a piece of her mind.

She was just inching backward when she heard a familiar jaunty whistle. And the sound was closer than she would have liked.

Glancing over her shoulder, she spied Mr. Sterling crossing the street between a carriage heading in one direction, and a horse cart filled with fragrant flowers bound for market.

They swerved to avoid him, his tune muted beneath the jangle of rigging, sharp whinnies, and shouted cursing. But he did not alter his strolling pace. In fact, he took a second to bend down and pick up a stray primrose, twirling the butter-yellow blossom between his fingers.

Pinched between such large, brutish digits, the dainty stem didn't stand a chance. And before she could stop herself, she wondered how much damage hands like those might do to a woman's slender throat.

An icy shiver rolled over her, a dark memory stirring in the corner of her mind like a sticky cobweb disturbed by a draft. But she closed the door on it before it could take hold.

She was no longer the weak, pathetic young woman she'd once been. That person lived in a small hamlet in north Hampshire. Her reborn, stronger self lived in London and was determined to make the family matchmaking business a success.

She found solace in that, if nothing else.

Straightening, she watched Reed Sterling step onto the pavement and into the long shadows in front of the agency. He stopped whistling, his broad mouth frowning as he openly studied her countenance as if she were a Captain Sharp at one of his tables.

She kept a mask of impassivity in place. Whatever cards she held, she'd keep to herself.

Boldly, she stared back into the most peculiar eyes she'd ever seen. His irises were near perfect spheres of dye-dipped indigo, all except for one smudge in the left eye and *only* the left. That strange top quarter portion appeared singed to a bright copper color, like an ember that refused to cool.

An ember that might catch fire at any moment.

Ainsley could almost feel the heat of it warming her cheeks. But that was silly, of course. The discoloration wasn't anything more than a form of heterochromia—a term she'd learned shortly after they'd met, finding it among the pages of a medical journal at the lending library.

It always made her feel more centered and in control when she could define something she didn't understand. This was especially true in matters concerning Reed Sterling.

"I believe you're on the wrong side of the street, Mr. Sterling. You won't find anything of interest over here."

If there was any confronting to be done, she would prefer to be the one to do it.

He held her gaze for a moment without responding, then turned to squint at the front of her family's rented townhouse. "Wouldn't be too sure. Had to stroll over to see what my prim and proper little neighbor hung on her door, didn't I?"

Her stomach, which had been seated high beneath her lungs, suddenly dropped at the sound of his gravelly, uncultured drawl, her skin drawing tight over her frame. It was the queerest sensation. Why it happened whenever he was near, she could not fathom.

Her inner repulsion working its way to the surface? *Most likely.*

She abhorred him and everything he stood for—all manner of savagery and unabashed wickedness.

Doubtless, he awoke with a checklist of sins to complete by the end of each day. He'd begin with gluttony, breaking his fast with a dozen coddled eggs and an entire loaf of toasted bread. Then he'd slather each piece with honey, so thick it would overflow and drip down his chin.

She slid a cursory glance to that part of him, over the square edge of his jaw, and past a small red nick over the shadowy endysis of whiskers lurking beneath the shaven skin.

Her gaze strayed to the bare expanse of his neck. Of course, his cravat was absent. Again. She shouldn't be surprised to find a sticky amber-colored droplet resting in the hollow beneath the protrusion of his Adam's apple. Regrettably, the errant thought caused her mouth to water, her tongue tingling with an imprudent craving for sweets.

Ainsley swallowed. "No, you certainly did not *have* to, because the sign is of no concern of yours. Besides, you're not even respectably attired for venturing out of doors."

He dismissed her comment with a mocking sideways glance. "Unlike you, I didn't inherit my grandmother's wardrobe, complete with an array of neckerchiefs and brooches. I think you might have a new one for every day of the month."

She stiffened. "Hardly. I wore this the day before yesterday."

"You're wrong." He faced her again, speaking with a conceited degree of certainty that abraded every nerve in her body.

"*Wrong*, indeed! I should think I would know better than—"

"Two days ago, you railed at me for the snuff box you found on your doorstep," he interrupted. "And *that* neckerchief was the color of milk and it had a wavy sort of edge."

Absorbing his declaration, she dimly lifted her free hand and splayed her fingers over this morning's pale lace. Drat! He was correct. She'd worn the white silk with the scalloped edge that day. But what sort of man was he to take note of such a small detail?

Gathering ammunition against his enemy, even by way of criticizing her attire? *Undoubtedly.*

"It is a *fichu*," she corrected, enunciating the word clearly. "And I dress to demonstrate the respectability of my position. Being a matchmaker is an important occupation. A client's quality of life is dependent on what I do."

He crossed his arms over his chest, the primrose disappearing into his fist. "A real man knows how to find his own woman. All you haughty Bournes are just playing at games you don't understand."

A buildup of exasperation burned the inner lining of her lungs. She held it at bay, letting it come to a full boil before she unleashed it upon him. She'd heard enough of Mr. Sterling's opinions on her profession in their previous—almost daily—encounters to know that he loathed her as much as she did him.

He seemed to think that her life was an endless array of privileges. As if all she had to do each morning was to fling off her coverlet and a team of servants would swoop in—bringing order to her life, balancing the accounting ledgers, finding a way to pay her uncle's debts *and* have enough to put food on the table and fires in the hearths. He had no idea of all the sacrifices she'd made over the years.

"Whereas you dress as if your occupation were at the docks, unloading barrels of ale, one under each needlessly burly arm," she hissed.

But she made the mistake of letting her attention drift along his throat, to the dark springy curls above the open neck, and over to the bulge of muscle straining the sleeves of his coat. Doubtless, if she compared his arms and her thighs, side by side, she would find that their circumference was the same. It was almost tempting to untie her garter ribbon and measure him, right then and there. He would have to remove his coat, of course, and . . . and . . .

Somehow, she lost her train of thought.

When she met his gaze again, he grinned, the notch at the corner of his mouth mocking her. "You don't seem too offended by the sight of me. Those eyes of yours are greedy things this morning—they've gone dark and hot as fresh coffee."

"Hardly likely," she said, her voice oddly hoarse as if she'd just woken from sleep. She cleared her throat. "I'm certain they are still just as brown as they have always been. No more, no less."

Again, he shook his head and took a step toward her, crowding her. "No. They're usually brownish-gray and silky looking, like an otter's pelt."

The nerve of him for comparing her eyes to an animal! Of the two of them, he was most certainly closer to crawling around on all fours.

And did he have to stand so close? At once, her corset felt too tight, her skin too hot, her fichu clinging to the vulnerable skin beneath the modest neckline of her bodice.

She took a step back. "For your information, I was merely noticing that you have a cut on your jaw. You should tell your valet to sharpen the razor for next time. And if I'm fortunate, he'll press a little harder on your jugular vein as well."

"You'd like that, would you?"

"Immensely."

He cocked a disbelieving dark brow over that copper-scorched iris. "I don't have a valet. I'm not some pampered fop that needs someone to wash and dress me."

The image he conjured—him in the bath, dripping wet—was not one she particularly wanted flashing inside her mind. When it did she felt her lungs react, hitching in one steamy breath. She made an awkward move to cross her arms over her chest, only to realize she still held that dripping handbill.

She had the urge to fling it directly at the open neck of his shirt. "I beg to differ."

"Are you offering, then?"

"Of course not. I'm merely pointing out that a man of two and thirty ought to know how to see to those matters himself. Somedays I even wonder how you manage to make it out of your be—"

She stopped abruptly, her cheeks catching fire. He was steering this conversation onto unfamiliar avenues, taking control of the ribbons. She didn't like it one bit.

His grin widened slowly, his eyes looking warm and drowsy as they dipped to her lips. He chuckled when she pressed them together.

"My *bed*?" He looked as smug as a bull let loose in a pasture full of milk cows. "I'd wager that's not all you wonder about me."

"Clearly, you've received far too many blows to the head in your little boxing exhibitions. It knocked all the sense out of you, *if* you ever had any in the first place."

She cast him a flinty-eyed glare, but he missed the effect by turning away, angling toward the stairs.

"If I had any sense left, I would've bought this house from the duchess before you moved across the street. Every day since has been pure hell." He expelled a breath and bent down, swiping up a number of soggy handbills and tossing them into the bin.

Was he cleaning up, then? This was a first. As far as Ainsley knew, his only skills consisted of leaving messes for someone else to tend and bludgeoning men inside a boxing ring.

Though, grudgingly, she admitted that he must be something of a good businessman, for there was a queue of carriages out front every evening. She'd heard that he had all manner of depraved enticements to lure the wayward through his doors. All for a price, of course.

She had a feeling that, with Reed Sterling, everything came at a price.

Absently, she watched him drag a large hand over the stone tread. Between his shoulders, the black wool of his coat tightened into long horizontal furrows, his collar rising to trap thick curls of brown hair. She had a peculiar impulse to reach down and free them.

Puzzled, she shifted her attention to the topiary beside her, lifting her gaze to the top of the evergreen spire. "If I had my way, I'd run you out of business. Close the doors of Sterling's forever."

There. That ought to get a rise out of him and have him storming off across the street. There was nothing he loved more than his precious gaming hell.

But he had the nerve to chuckle at her instead. "You seem to forget that I was here first. Yet, even after you met your unsavory neighbor, *you* still chose to live across from *me*. Why is that, by the by?"

There hadn't been another option—she'd had to escape Hampshire. Her life had depended on it. Though only Uncle Ernest and she knew the reason. They'd even shielded Jacinda and Briar from the full truth.

No one needed to know about Ainsley's shameful secret.

Gradually, she became aware of wetness leeching through to her stocking. Looking down, she saw that she'd squeezed the handbill dry until it was like a stone in her fist. She dropped it into the bin and shook out her skirts where the muslin had turned a dark, angry red.

Not wanting to let on that she'd been woolgathering, she issued a hollow laugh and evaded his question. "Are you worried that I spend my day plotting to steal your depraved clients and turn their minds to the wholesomeness of matrimony?"

Hmm . . . actually, that wasn't a terrible notion. She could start a campaign to save the floundering family business— *Subscriptions for all Sinners.*

And if it took money away from that despicable gaming house, then all the better.

"You're hardly a threat to me, and I never said anything about marriage being *wholesome*. It's a cruel business, what you do, taking people's money before you rob them of their souls." Straightening to face her again, he had the nerve to cluck his tongue, the scar on his upper lip practically winking. "And you do it to your own kind, too. For shame, Miss Bourne. I guess that makes my gaming hell the more respectable business. After all, at least I'm honest about cheating the snobbish prigs that walk through my doors."

She gasped . . . or tried to . . . but outrage clogged her throat. Was he calling *her* the thief? How dare he! For a moment, she couldn't say a word. She just stood there, staring at the challenge in his mismatched eyes, her mouth agape like a freshly caught trout.

The blackguard took her silence as an invitation to goad her. "You can't even deny it, can you?"

"I am," she croaked, recovering. "Your half-brained assessment is the furthest from the truth. You prey upon people who are weak in spirit. Your currency is sin, whereas mine is sanctity. I should hardly call us alike. When our times come and our lives are at an end, you and I will be standing at opposite gates and I will have a lovely view of the ones encrusted with pearls."

"Ah. So *that's* why you're here, then—to bring salvation to London? Well, you might be onto something. I'm sure many of the clients you marry off will be on their knees, praying for death by the end of the first year of their life sentence. You're a veritable queen of torment."

He laughed up to the heavens, throat exposed, a hearty rumble rolling out of his broad, burly chest.

The sound seemed to vibrate the air inside her own lungs, spreading out in tiny tingling pulses through the rest of her body. She wanted to chafe her hands over her skin to quell the provocative sensation. Cover her ears. Run in the opposite direction. Do anything to rid herself of it.

"If you abhor the idea of matrimony so much, I have to wonder why you even dared to cross the street to stand so near our door. You are welcome—nay, *encouraged*—to leave at once." With an impatient swipe of her hand, she pointed across the street.

"You're the one who invited me," he said with a shrug, amusement still tucked into the corners of his mouth.

She scoffed at his unbelievable amount of hubris. "I did no such thing."

"I don't know what else you'd call it. Every morning I see you gazing at my building, and at night you skim over each window before locking your door. Well, it's as clear as the pert nose on your face that you can't stop thinking about me. All day long. And doubtless all night long as well."

He studied her closely, challenging her to reveal something in her expression. But there was nothing to see. She made sure of it by holding perfectly still. She didn't breathe. Didn't flutter a single eyelash.

Even so, he grinned wickedly as if he'd caught her stuffing cards up her sleeve. "Don't worry, Your Highness, it will be our secret."

Then, without warning, he lifted his arm.

She only caught the movement out of the corner of her eye. Instinctively, she flinched, her hands raising in defense, the ghost of an old wound emerging from the crypt.

Reed Sterling went utterly still.

He frowned once again, his brow furrowed into corrugated rows. Then he took a step back and carefully opened his hand. And there—still unharmed in his grasp—was the tender primrose.

Mortification slapped her hard, stinging her cheeks with heat. She wanted to die right then and there. Disappear. Put the rubbish bin over her head and pretend she was invisible. But all she seemed capable of was to stand there and hope he hadn't noticed her reaction.

His gaze held hers with almost brutal intensity as if he were peeling away the layers of her memories and he could see them for himself. Then, all at once, those mismatched eyes lit with keen understanding. And there was no mistaking the quick flash of pity that followed.

No, no, no. She hated the tremor of vulnerability that tumbled through her, dropping like a wind-battered nest from the highest branch of a tree. And she couldn't leave it this way—with him believing he knew something about her. With him having the upper hand.

Ainsley needed to regain a sense of control that had slipped.

"I detest primroses. Simply abhor them, if you must know. And filthy street primroses, well, they're even worse." Waspish lies tumbled out of her mouth in a rush as if she possessed Jacinda's talent for bending the truth, and perhaps even a flare for the dramatic like Briar. She only hoped she was putting on a convincing show. "You weren't about to give that wretched thing to me as a sort of . . . peace offering between us, were you?"

He remained quiet, her comments turning stale in the air between them. In that moment, she thought she'd failed.

Then he inclined his head and tossed the flower aside.

Wiping the palm of his hand against his coat, his gaze swept over the façade of the townhouse as if it were a puzzle to solve. "Peace between us? Not likely. We'll be at odds until our dying breaths. Then I'll go to my gate and you to yours, and we'll finally be free of each other."

He might have been reading the words from a poorly written script for all the bland intonation they held. The necessary hard edge that such a declaration demanded was absent.

It left her unsettled.

She preferred to keep them always on the same footing—abhorring each other. So she quickly added, "Oh, I don't plan to wait that long to be rid of you, Mr. Sterling. I have every intention of running you out of business within the month. It's something I should have done from the very start."

This time, it was just the right nerve to flick.

Those eyes swerved back to her, his jaw tight. "And how do you propose to do that, Miss Bourne? Call upon your new brothers-in-law, the duke and the earl? Have them do your fighting for you while you watch from the window, eating sugared grapes?"

"Of course not. I need no man's assistance to succeed," she said, ire prickling as she crossed her arms. "Just wait and see."

"And now you've confirmed my suspicions—you do like to dream of me. In fact, you're dreaming right now."

He gave her a once-over, that smug grin of his returning. She hated the sight of it.

His low chuckle was the last straw and she narrowed her eyes. "I loathe to shatter your grand illusions, but I only think of you when I find rubbish on my doorstep."

"Well then, that doesn't give me an incentive to have it cleaned up, now does it?"

He gave her a mocking bow, pretending to doff a hat he wasn't wearing. Though if he had been, she would have delighted in stripping it from his grasp and stomping on it.

She watched him strut away, heedless of the traffic that had to swerve around him. And soon he was on his side, and she on hers.

Normally, she would be content with that. But not today.

Reed Sterling had seen her flinch. What were the chances that he would simply forget about it?

Chapter 2

*". . . and I was excessively shocked indeed! I would
not have Mr. Knightley know any thing about it
for the world!"*

JANE AUSTEN, *Emma*

Reed stormed into Sterling's and slammed the door with
enough force to cause a thunderclap to echo around him.
The resulting gust stirred the burgundy brocade drapes
that swathed the windows on either side and, for an instant,
bright morning light gilded the hell's dark interior. It shim-
mered in the haze of acrid cheroot smoke lingering like
a fog in the black-marbled foyer. Then the fabric settled,
entombing him in the familiar shadows that matched his
current mood.

Ainsley Bourne was the most provoking . . . impossible . . .
and bloody maddening woman he'd ever met!

Fists clenched at his side, he strode into the main hall.
The gas lights were turned low, the eerie blue light flickering
over the paneled walls, empty tables, and upended chairs.
He stalked toward a long serpentine mahogany buffet where
a tray with a single leftover glass of whisky waited.

One of his men must have been distracted by a woman
and neglected to take this to the kitchen.

*Oh, the enticements of the fairer sex. Every man's ul-
timate downfall,* Reed thought bitterly as he downed the
biting liquor in one swallow. He hissed from the burn of it,

then expelled a pent-up growl. "Do I look like a man who would strike a woman?"

Apparently so, for Ainsley Bourne had cringed when he'd lifted his hand. There'd been no mistaking it.

"Hardly. Then again, I know you better than most," a gruff, incongruously cultured voice said.

Reed turned to see his man-at-the-door emerge from the narrow corridor that lead to the hazard room. "I didn't realize you were still here."

Ambrose Finch was a giant of a man, forced to walk in the center of the arch or else knock his block-shaped head against the filigreed plaster molding. He kept his black hair trimmed razor close, while sporting a full soot-whiskered beard. Though justifiably heavy-footed, he did not lumber, but moved with efficiency and confidence. And it was well-known that, in his fighting days, a single blow from his ham-sized fist could lift a man out of his boots and fell him like a tree.

He was an intimidating specimen, to be sure. Yet, in order to maintain Sterling's exclusivity, it was imperative to have such a formidable man guard the door.

Finch bit down a yawn. "'Tis the nursemaid's day off. With the little one still teething, my wife and I have an agreement that I nap for one hour, return home, then she naps for four while I watch the girls."

"You could always hire another nursemaid with the money we earn here."

"Quite true, but Trudie prefers to live without extravagance. She fears that I would step back into the ring if anything happened to Sterling's."

Reed chuckled at the absurdity. "She needn't worry. Sterling's will be here for ages, even long after we've gone."

"Regardless, she frets over seeing me hurt again." He flashed a grin and pointed to the gap where his upper canine tooth had once been.

Reed had done that during their last bout, knocking him flat. It was his first step toward the fortune he now possessed and the legacy he would leave behind one day. "She'll never forgive me for that, will she?"

"Oh, she likes you well enough, I suppose. After all, we both gained our prizes during those exhibitions. You won money by the fistful, and I won her. It was after that very match when I asked her to marry me."

"And you've been moonstruck ever since."

"It is a fortunate man, indeed, to be stricken by such madness," Finch said, eyeing Reed with the shrewdness of longtime friends. "'Tis certainly preferable to finding it at the bottom of a bottle."

Reed set the empty glass upside down on the tray. Having experienced what men were capable of after a few too many drinks, he never had trouble limiting himself to one every now and then. But he certainly didn't mind it when his wealthy patrons were lost in their cups, and loose with their purse strings.

"It's late for me, as you know. I'm usually abed by dawn and this might help me sleep before we open again this afternoon."

"And does your belief that you will be *unable* to sleep have anything to do with your encounter with Miss Bourne?"

Reed slid a glance to his all-too-perceptive friend. "Watching through windows, were you?"

"Merely drawing the curtains closed," Finch replied, lifting his heavy brows in mock innocence. "It sparked my curiosity to see you crossing the street to her, when it is usually the other way around—her haranguing you for the filth, the noise, or something along those lines."

"I was ready for it, too. Ready to shock her with my plan to hire young Billy to see to the rubbish each day." Reed had imagined seeing her tight, scornful mouth fall slack with astonishment and her diatribe to sputter to a halt. He would have relished that moment. He'd even shaved for it, put on a fresh shirt, too. And made sure to leave his cravat behind because he knew it would get under her skin to see him without being *properly attired*. "But then she turned away and set about the chore herself."

"Robbing you of the satisfaction."

Reed shrugged. "I just went for a stroll. That's all. We exchanged glancing verbal blows as we always do, goading each other. But then she"—he scrubbed a hand over his jaw, worrying the pad of his thumb over the nick—"looked at me like I was going to . . . As if *I* was capable of . . ."

He couldn't finish. The words were too abhorrent to speak aloud.

As a boy, he'd witnessed his own mother getting a drubbing by her second husband, a prig of an aristocrat with a sense of entitlement. And Reed had always felt responsible for the suffering she'd endured. After all, it was because of him that she married Lord Bray in the first place.

A new widow, Mum had been managing the tavern on her own. Still considered the fairest beauty in the county, there was a line of men wanting to step in and help her by way of marriage. But she never gave any of them the time of day.

Lord Bray, a regular traveler to the inn, saw this as some sort of contest. He flashed his charlatan's smile and offered a fine future for her son and any other children she might have during their *arrangement*.

Doubtless, Bray expected accolades for being a magnanimous noble. A regular hero of the moment. But Mum didn't see it that way. Refusing to be any man's mistress, she gave him a flat setdown in front of a roomful of sniggering men.

Then, for reasons known only to Bray and the many pints he'd drunk, he'd offered to make her his wife instead. And she'd accepted.

Reed's stomach still turned at the thought. He'd never forget the way that Bray smiled as he beat her, leaving her to cower in the corner as he reminded her that he'd married *beneath his station.*

Reed had been a runt at the time and too scrawny to do much about it, but that hadn't stopped him from trying. Usually he got a slap across the face before the blighter went off somewhere else to get pissed. But the last time Lord Bray had something else in mind.

The servants were off for the afternoon on St. Stephen's Day, and the carriage house was empty. Bray had caught Reed feeding a stray puppy, which he'd kept against orders to the contrary. Enraged, his stepfather started kicking the helpless, yowling creature. When Reed tried to stop him, Bray turned his fury on him. And for a fop, he'd sure known how to land plenty of rib-cracking blows.

Reed had been doubled over and spitting up blood when Lord Bray reared back to kick him, too. That was when Finch showed up—an orphaned stable boy, big as a man at ten years old—and knocked Bray onto his entitled arse.

But Bray had taken exception to the assault on his *noble* self and reached into one of the carriages for a loaded pistol kept under the bench. Reed had had just enough time and strength to push Finch out of the way.

They'd saved each other's lives that day. As a prize, Reed had won a friend for life, and a scar on his shoulder where the ball had grazed him.

The puppy had not survived, however, and neither had Lord Bray. That very day, he'd left for his mistress's house only to find her with another man—her husband, as it turned out. Bray had been killed in a field of honor the following morning.

Honor, indeed.

Even after his death, Mum's spirit had been so broken by the abuse that she'd rushed into two more abysmal marriages while Reed had been away at university. And his own beatings hadn't stopped with Bray.

The sons of aristocrats had taken exception to him sharing the same room and board with their lofty selves, and thought to teach him a lesson. Every single day.

But Miss Ainsley Bourne didn't know any of that. No, she'd sooner believe that he was a monster, capable of striking a woman. And why, because he was a commoner and former prizefighter? Because he offered lessons and sparred to keep fit? Did she think that because he ran a gaming hell, he lacked any semblance of right and wrong?

"Whatever Miss Bourne thinks, it matters not," Reed said to Finch.

His friend made no effort to conceal his dubious expression. "Clearly."

"All that concerns me is the future of Sterling's. I wouldn't waste my time thinking about some hoity-toity matchmaking agency."

Reed was still trying to leave his mark and amass a fortune. If there was one lesson he'd learned from his father's untimely death, it was how quickly dreams could end. Not only for oneself, but for everyone who depended upon you.

"And yet, here you are, with your thoughts on—" Finch's reply was cut short, his wary gaze darting down to the floor.

Reed followed his gaze and saw a white-and-gray piebald cat. "And what are you doing out of my rooms?"

"I shouldn't be surprised if that *devil's spawn* picked the lock," came Finch's contemptuous response. "I caught her in the kitchen earlier. The instant I told her to jump down from the worktable, she looked directly at me and then nudged a glass off the edge, shattering it on the floor. I'm convinced that she knew precisely what she was doing."

Winding a trail of pale fur over Reed's dark trousers, the cat lifted her head and blinked one green eye as if to say she was completely innocent. Her other eye was a cloudy blue, bisected with a diagonal scar that ran from the top of her fist-sized skull to her jaw. Part of one ear was gone as well.

He'd found her a year ago, half-starved in the back alley. She'd scratched him up good for the first few months, daring only to show her face when he brought food. But he'd been patient, and gradually she'd warmed to him enough that she'd come inside, and even slept beside him most days.

Still, she was a skittish thing, finicky when it came to allowing anyone to pet her. So he always waited for her signal, which she gave him now. Stretching up with a single paw, she sank her claws into the leg of his trousers. And into his flesh as well.

Chiding her with a *tsk*, he reached down to dislodge those razor points and scooped her up into the crook of his arm, running a hand down her silky length.

Tucked against him, she purred contentedly. "Surely not. My clever cat would never cause mischief. You must have frightened her."

When his friend rolled his eyes, Reed laughed, knowing the truth. She was a wicked little minx when she wanted to be.

"Perhaps if you gave her a name, we could scold her and train her."

"The last time I tried that, she didn't come near me for a week. Has a temper, this one," he said, scratching behind her good ear. The weight of her head fell slack with bliss in his palm. "She prefers 'Cat' to anything else. And besides, she's already trained. Fetches all manner of things and brings them to my office."

"Dead things," Finch said, frowning with distaste. "Yet another of those disgusting traits cats have."

"Maybe if you didn't treat her like some misbegotten stray then she'd warm to you, too."

Abruptly, she leapt out of Reed's arms and landed directly at Finch's feet, pausing there to clean her paws, *or* ready her claws—one could never be too sure.

"She'd sooner scratch out my eyes."

When she twitched her tail, Finch took an automatic step back, watching warily until she sauntered off.

Issuing a malcontented grunt, he walked to one of the door panels hidden in the walls. Behind it was a narrow corridor, meant for keeping watch over the patrons at the tables. Finch also kept his overcoat in this one. He shrugged into it as he added, "Though you should take some of your own advice."

"What do you mean?"

"With Miss Bourne. You treat her as if she is the sole representative of the class you abhor so much."

"And why not? She sees me as nothing more than a common-born brute, who'd dared to infiltrate society and rub elbows with the upper crust."

"Though you're not concerned in the *slightest* what her opinion of you might be."

"That's right," Reed said with a hint of warning.

Finch chuckled and reached inside to remove his hat from one of the pegs. And for such a large head, it was a considerable hat. "Though it could be that her reaction had little to do with you in particular. She might have been uncertain about standing next to any imposing man on the pavement. It's happened to me more often than not."

"She's never shrunk away from me before. Never been afraid to confront me about the rubbish. Never been afraid to speak her mind, either. No, this was different. This was . . ."

His words trailed off, his thoughts quick to recall the way she'd recoiled and raised her hands.

Could it be that her true opinion of him had finally slipped through the cracks? Or was there more to it?

There had been an unmistakable flash of fear in her eyes that he'd never seen before. And damned if it wasn't eating at him to know the reason.

Reed didn't like the dark suspicion that began to brew in his mind. It left an acidic taste on the back of his tongue.

"I know that look, Sterling," Finch said, pausing at the door. "You need to stop right there before it goes any further. She isn't another stray you need to rescue."

His friend teased him often about the people Reed hired to work for him. Most were those who didn't have anywhere else to go, or those who'd been kicked in the teeth one too many times. But this wasn't the same.

Reed stared back at his friend, keeping his expression impassive. "I know that better than you. Miss Bourne is as domesticated as they come. An uppity, headstrong, little pampered housecat."

Proof of that was in the way she'd turned her nose up at the primrose. What made it worse was that he'd actually intended to give it to her.

What a fool he was! She would have tossed it directly into the gutter.

"Be sure you remember that." Finch opened the door to the blinding morning light. Then, from the pavement, he hailed a cab and headed home.

As the dingy yellow coach rumbled out of view, Reed's gaze drifted to the Bourne Matrimonial Agency, already forgetting his friend's warning.

AINSLEY SAGGED against the door inside the white-marble foyer. She couldn't catch her breath. Her pulse hammered at her throat as if she'd just escaped the Tower of London with the crown jewels.

Yet it wasn't The Sovereign's Scepter in her grasp. It was something far more damning, should anyone discover it.

Warily, she looked down and opened her hand, unfurling one finger after another. And there, lying against her palm, was the discarded primrose.

Whyever had she picked it up the instant he was out of sight?

A mere whim? *Laughable*. She wasn't an impulsive sort. In fact, she mulled over things quite fixedly, as the corner of her thumbnail could attest.

A keepsake, then? *Ludicrous*. Ainsley hadn't pressed a flower in ages.

Though . . . it *was* tempting. At one time, it had been her favorite hobby. She'd often collected flowers alongside her mother, who'd told her that every perfect blossom was a gift to be admired.

When she was young, Ainsley had agreed. She, too, always looked for perfection, especially in herself.

Yet as she'd grown older, she discovered that the most beautiful ones were different from the others—not quite symmetrical, missing a petal, or even bruised and trampled underfoot. She believed those deserved admiration just as much as the others. Perhaps even more. And by the time she'd reached four and twenty, she'd had quite the beautifully bedraggled collection.

Then, one day, that had changed.

The reason still managed to chill her skin, so she chose not to think about it. She was a firm believer in shutting the door on painful events and unpleasant memories. Even so, her heart still ached when she thought about the day she'd thrown out most of her collection. Nearly every bloom, every memory of warm, sunlit afternoons with Mother . . . Gone.

In fact, the only one she'd kept was a single bluebell pressed between the glass frame that hung on the wall in her office upstairs—the flower she'd picked the day Mother had died.

And now, a stray primrose.

Tracing the fragile nick in one of the petals, she did her best not to recall how perfectly sheltered the blossom had been in Reed Sterling's hand.

She failed miserably.

How could such a hand have been so tender? It didn't seem possible. Prior experience had taught her that men who dabbled in pugilism were seldom gentle. And it was that ingrained knowledge which had resurfaced, against her will, this morning.

She'd flinched, and she wished she could shut out this memory as well, but she couldn't this time. Because Reed Sterling had seen her.

Now, every time she closed her eyes, she could see him staring back at her, suspicion and curiosity sharpening his gaze. Missing nothing.

It worried her that he would think on this more than was necessary. The same way he had with her fichus. *Honestly, what man notices such a trifling thing?*

Her pulse gave another panicked jolt. She didn't want Reed Sterling puzzling over anything regarding her, especially not from this morning. The secret she and her uncle kept was so damning that it would ruin the agency's reputation, not to mention her own.

Though it was clear that her neighbor had been just as surprised by her reaction as she. After all, there hadn't been a single instance when confronting him on his own doorstep that she'd ever acted afraid of him.

Because she wasn't, not really. Though admittedly, she was a cautious person in general. In her opinion, no matchmaker worth her salt should trust too readily.

Therefore she was going to do what any sensible person would do. She was going to forget about the primrose.

Then she was going to do something to ensure that Mr. Sterling never thought about this morning again. In fact, she would do whatever she could to rid her life of Reed Sterling and his unsavory establishment altogether. The only problem was, she didn't know how.

At least, not yet.

Chapter 3

"She was, in fact, beginning very much to wonder
that she had ever thought him pleasing at all; and
his sight was so inseparably connected with some
very disagreeable feelings, that, except in a moral
light, as a penance, a lesson, a source of profitable
humiliation to her own mind, she would have been
thankful to be assured of never seeing him again."

JANE AUSTEN, *Emma*

"*You're dawdling again, Ains,*" *Nigel huffed in exasperation.* "*We can never go on a walk without you stopping to
pick flowers.*"

"*But you know it was something I always did with my
mother.*"

"*Perhaps when you were a little girl and given to childish
flights of fancy.*" *He chided her with a reproving chuckle,
brushing the posies from her grasp as he placed her hand
on his sleeve.* "*There. Now you're all grown up, just the way
a man expects his betrothed to be.*"

*Ainsley frowned down at the blossoms lying in a tangled
heap on the path. Yet, knowing that Nigel's mood tended
toward petulance without the slightest warning, she tried to
be understanding.*

"*Cannot a newly betrothed woman enjoy the sight of
pretty things?*" *She laughed lightly and slipped free of his
grasp to retrieve them.*

He made a sound, something between a hiss and a growl. Then with a quick jerk of his hand, he reached out and snatched her wrist, yanking her upright.

She gasped. "Nigel—"

"I told you to leave them." His features were hard, his complexion blotted the bright red of the berries on the maythorn hedgerow lining the garden. "Don't try to make a fool of me by disobeying. The only flowers you're going to have are the ones I give you. Do you understand?"

No, she didn't. Her main concern in that moment was in trying to pry his fingers from her wrist. But he only gripped tighter, cutting off the blood flow to her hand. Her fingertips felt as if they might explode from the pulsing pressure. "You're hurting me."

He looked down, and his expression altered again. A disconcerting smile curled his lips as he peeled his fingers away, one by one, revealing the red-violet impressions he'd left behind.

"Look what you've made me do, Ains. All those boxing lessons must have made me stronger than I thought. But if you would have listened and done the proper thing, then none of this would have happened. And look at my sleeve. You've stained it with your flower stems. Am I supposed to take care of your mistakes now, in addition to putting up with your disrespect? Is that how my life is going to be?"

He was so convincing in his ire that Ainsley felt a renewed rush of panic and confusion. Had she caused this by thinking only of herself? By being childish?

"Forgive me," she said in haste, eager to put their relationship back to where it was a moment ago. "I'm sure I can brush that out and there won't be a stain."

He tsked her, almost fondly, and lifted her hand to press a kiss to the marred flesh. "There's a good girl. Let's put all this behind us. It's my own folly that I'm so fond of you, for no other man would put up with your immaturity. Then

again, I've always had a good deal of tolerance for imper-
fection. But don't worry, Ains, by the time we wed, I'll turn
you into a right proper wife."

Ainsley gasped awake. She clawed at the coverlet, kicking to be free. To escape.

Everything was dark around her and it took a breathless
moment to orient herself.

Then she heard the sounds from outside—the crunch of
carriage wheels on cobblestone, drunken singing, revelry,
and laughter—and suddenly she knew where she was.

Sitting up in bed, her heart pounded so hard she thought
it would escape the cage of her ribs. She curled her knees to
her chest, telling herself it was just a dream.

Then she shook her head in self-derision. "So much for
believing you could shut out those memories for good."

She knew exactly who to blame for this, too. Reed Sterling.

If it wasn't for him, then she never would have done the
unthinkable.

The unpardonable.

The very thing she'd warned herself against.

She'd pressed the primrose.

☙❧

LATER THAT morning, Ainsley found herself pacing the
floor of her office.

Normally, the Pomona green room was a place of solace.
Surrounding her were the furnishings from the Hampshire
cottage where she'd lived with her mother and sisters for
sixteen years. The cream-upholstered chairs from the parlor.
The rosewood table from the hall. The oil landscape above
the mantel from the morning room.

On any given day, she could look around and feel a sense
of permanence—of sameness—that both comforted and
grounded her.

This was especially true of the book lying in the center

of her blotter. *Emma* had been Mother's favorite, and she'd gifted a different volume of the strong-minded matchmaker's story to each of her daughters shortly before her death. Ainsley kept it here, where she spent most of her time, and it always served as a good reminder of her purpose.

Until this moment.

Now, the book was a veritable Pandora's box.

Knitting her fingers, she slid a wary glance to the red leather tome. A fringe of vellum peeked out from between the pages, tempting her to have one more look of the butter-yellow petals. But to do so might unleash all manner of chaos in her life.

No, it was best to leave it alone. Or to get rid of it for good.

Yet just as she reached out to slip the vellum free and toss it into the fire, she heard a cheerful greeting from the doorway. "Good morning."

Guilty, Ainsley jerked her hand back. She swung around to see her youngest sister skirt sideways into the office, carrying a tea tray just above the slight swell of her midriff. "Briar, you shouldn't be carrying such things in your delicate condition."

"Fear not, mother hen, it isn't heavy," she tsked, her cornflower-blue eyes rolling toward the ceiling. Clearly, she was still unaware that worrying about the family came second nature to Ainsley.

Abandoning her own task for the moment, she hurried across the rug. "Here. Let me have this."

Briar expelled an exasperated puff of air that displaced the pale curling tendrils from her forehead. Even so, she relinquished the overladen tray. Then, taking a step to the glossy maple wood bureau, she lowered the hinged platform. "I cannot manage to leave or enter a room without someone offering their assistance. With four months to wait until the blessed arrival, I'm not ready to retire to the country. Yet I suppose I must. Especially if everyone sees me as an un-gainly elephant plodding around in a day dress."

"Hardly. You are the portrait of beauty and grace as always. It's simply that you have far too many people who love you and want to dote on you."

Briar grumbled as she arranged the cups and saucers. "Even Nicholas is forever offering to rub my feet if I so much as walk ten paces, and I always give in. Anyone would if they knew how exceptional he is with his . . ." Her words trailed off, a pink blush coloring her cheeks.

"Oh, the trials you endure," Ainsley said with a small laugh, hoping to hide the reprehensible—but unmistakable—twinge of jealousy that speared her.

At one time, she'd had dreams of such a husband who would care for her and offer support whenever it was needed. But those had turned to nightmares with Nigel.

When their betrothal had ended, she'd been left with the irrefutable knowledge that she would never marry because she would never be able to trust again. Not even herself. After all, it was her own mind that had foolishly led her astray.

"My first husband was just the same when I was in a delicate way," announced another voice from the door. "Wouldn't think a rake could be so gentle and sweet, but . . . *ah* . . . he was the finest of men. My very own knight in armor."

Ainsley and Briar turned to see Mrs. Teasdale saunter into the room as if she belonged there. As if she were a member of the family. Yet Rosamunde Teasdale was merely a client of the agency's. One day she'd shown up with her knitting, stating her desire to find a bride for her son and a new husband for herself, and never left.

That was nearly a year ago. Since then, she'd become something of a fixture, much to Uncle Ernest's dismay. At any given moment during the three days a week the agency hung the knocker on the door, one might catch a glimpse of her wandering the halls, trailing yarn behind her. This was usually accompanied by Uncle Ernest darting into rooms to avoid her *and* her garish attire.

Today's frock was a bright ocher color that any woman of fifty—and a widow four times over—wouldn't dare. Though somehow it matched her brash personality and highlighted the sorrel brown of her hair, detracting from the heavy threading of silver.

"No knitting today?" Ainsley asked, steering the conversation away from the topic of Mrs. Teasdale's perfect first husband. Even a matchmaker could stomach only so many romantic tales of marriage in one morning.

"Left it in the parlor. I'm making tiny booties for Briar's little lord of the manor, and for—"

"You think it will be a boy?" Briar interrupted, a hand splayed over the tender protrusion.

"Of course," she said with a matter-of-fact nod, gesturing with the teacup and saucer that Briar had just handed to her. "You're all in front, the same way I was with my boy. Girls are in the hips, the way your sister carried her little Emma. I've made a pair of booties for her as well."

"I'm sure Jacinda will be delighted," Ainsley lied. Those knitting creations were often perplexing and as mismatched as . . . well . . . as Reed Sterling's eyes.

At the thought, she felt an unwarranted rush of heat climb to her cheeks. She averted her face to avoid notice, but just in time to see the middle sister—the most observant of the three of them—enter through the connecting door of the adjoining office.

Though thankfully, Jacinda appeared distracted. Not to mention a trifle winded.

With the back of her hand, she pushed a lock of auburn hair from her brow. Her robin's egg–blue eyes glowed with warmth, her cheeks flushed. "And why, precisely will I be delighted?"

"Because I'm making booties for Emma."

"Oh, lovely. Something to look forward to, then." Jacinda turned to take her cup of tea from Briar and all but swallowed it down in one gulp.

Ainsley scrutinized her sister, taking note of her unusually wrinkled green taffeta. "Why are you so out of breath? If you are feeling unwell and that is the reason you are late, then—"

"Never been better," she answered with a secret grin before helping herself to a scone. "Actually, I've been here for a spell. But Mrs. Darden wanted to see Emma and time must have gotten away from me."

"Your sash has come untied," Briar said, tugging at the loose end of the dark gold ribbon.

"Has it?" Jacinda glanced over her shoulder and, catching sight of it, her ears colored. "Well, I did step away from the kitchen for a moment to fetch something from the linen closet and since it was on the very top shelf . . . Crispin had to assist me."

Briar hiccupped a laugh, her eyes bright and knowing. "Husbands are quite helpful in closets."

"Indeed, they are," Mrs. Teasdale agreed with a dreamy sigh. "Why else would I have been married four times? Though none were quite as passionate as number one. Reformed scoundrels make the best husbands."

At seven and twenty, Ainsley was not clueless about the subject matter. She knew that married couples engaged in certain activities that resulted in children, but the subject did not hold her interest.

She'd never been a particularly passionate person. For the most part, she kept her emotions subdued as well.

As the oldest, she'd never had the luxury of being brokenhearted when Father abandoned them, or scared when

Mother never left her bed again. No, for she had sisters who needed her and a house to manage as well. From the age of twelve she was seeing to household matters that her melancholic mother could not. Living in London and traveling abroad, Father had stopped sending money to pay the salaries for the servants, forcing them to find other positions. This also left Ainsley, her younger sisters, and Mrs. Darden to see to the house and gardens. There had not been time for daydreaming.

Much later, after they'd lived with Uncle Ernest for a number of years, Ainsley had met Nigel.

Even then, she had not been plagued with any ardent hungers. She'd simply been looking forward to having someone help her look after the estate and her sisters. And during the few stolen kisses she'd shared with him, he'd expressed greater fondness in criticizing her efforts than in the intimacy itself. It did not take long before she'd lost all desire to engage in the activity.

"Oh, Ainsley, it will be so wonderful when you are married, too," Briar said, her eyes glinting like a beam of sunlight reflecting off the tip of Cupid's arrow.

Ainsley squelched a cold shudder as she lowered down into the rose-tufted chair behind her desk.

"You could marry my son," Mrs. Teasdale said and—sadly—not for the first time. "He's rich enough, to be sure, and even handsomer than his father had been."

The three sisters exchanged a glance. None of them were entirely certain that the man even existed. He'd never set foot inside the agency. Instead, Mrs. Teasdale had filled out an application for him, listing his given name as Lancelot and leaving the majority of the other answers vague.

But still . . . Lancelot Teasdale? If such a person existed, Ainsley felt sincerely sorry for him. He must have been teased mercilessly as a child.

"I'm certain he's wonderful," Briar interjected brightly, carefully sinking down into one of the cushioned bronze chairs. "Though if he doesn't suit, there's always Lord Hull-worth. He's quite handsome and with a fine income."

"And he is also one of our few clients," Ainsley reminded. "Therefore, he is strictly forbidden fruit."

Why her gaze chose to drift down to the book at that moment, she didn't know. The fringe of vellum seemed to wink at her and say, *"Have another look. You know you want to . . ."*

Abruptly, she straightened and cleared her throat before she continued. "Which was something the two of you conveniently forgot when finding your own husbands. If I were to marry him it would all but stitch a burial shroud over the agency. In fact"—she made sure to keep her expression impassive—"I believe it would be best if I did not marry at all."

Her sisters scoffed simultaneously as if it was the most ludicrous jest they'd heard.

Mrs. Teasdale, however, took the news rather hard. She issued a gasp of distress, turning pale as she lowered the cup to her saucer with a clatter. "But you must!"

Ainsley shook her head in placid disagreement.

"If you do not," Mrs. Teasdale continued, and with more vehemence than was warranted, "then you'll only confirm the rumors in society. Why, everyone thinks you're waiting for the next duke or earl to walk through your doors. You have to set them straight by marrying a commoner. And start having children without delay, too. Then before you know it your agency will be teeming with new clients."

Clearly the woman had spent far too much time at the agency and had succumbed to overblown romantic ideals.

"Have a scone, Mrs. Teasdale. I believe those are honey almond, my favorite." Ainsley gestured to the escritoire, hoping that their conversation would end there.

Unfairly, Jacinda chose that moment to chime in. "She might have a point. Though your husband shouldn't have to be a *commoner*. Perhaps a younger son without a title, or an officer."

"Oh, yes!" Briar was quick to add her exuberance. "A wealthy young man with a romantic soul, who brings you flowers. You were always so fond of those."

Again, Ainsley's gaze dropped to the book. Her thoughts veered to Reed Sterling and a frisson of something akin to panic scurried through her, hot and tense. Discretely, she placed an accounting ledger over the book.

But it wasn't enough distance for her liking. So she stood and stepped away from her desk.

"That was long ago. Besides, I have my hands full of business matters, accounts, and so forth, not to mention dealing with that . . . that"—she drew in a steadying breath—"heathen across the street. If you want to blame anyone for keeping clients away from our doorstep, it's Sterling's gaming hell, and the rubbish that is forever littering our doorstep."

"Perhaps you should tell him to take care of it," Mrs. Teasdale said calmly. Apparently having recovered herself, she was busy piling jam, marmalade, and clotted cream on her saucer like a painter's palette.

"I've mentioned it countless times to that oaf—yesterday morning, in fact—and he all but vowed to make certain our stairs remained forever enrobed in handbills. So, in return, I told him that I plan to run him out of business within the month."

And if she could just figure out how, she would do it this very day. Unfortunately, she couldn't think of a single thing. What could make a man give up his business? His life's pursuit?

The problem was, Reed Sterling wasn't just any sort of man. He'd fought—quite literally—to earn the money to open his gaming hell, and now his establishment played host to some of the wealthiest gentlemen in London. Which made him even more of an obstacle in the path of her own goals.

He was her nemesis in every way and—after their latest encounter—she was desperate to find a way to be free of him.

Mrs. Teasdale let out a bark of laughter. "You didn't."

"Never doubt it. Ainsley's dealings with Mr. Sterling are always rather heated." Jacinda snickered, a mischievous glint in her eyes.

Ainsley slanted her sister a hard stare but Jacinda only grinned, adjusting her sash.

"What we should do is litter his doorstep with *our* hand-bills," Briar said, absently nibbling on a slivered almond.

"I would consider it, if I could guarantee they wouldn't simply end up over here again," Ainsley said, willing to do anything at this point. Yet there was one glaring problem. "There isn't money in the budget for printing fees. I've had to cut back on our advertisements as well."

And her sign hadn't made a bit of difference, either. There'd been no ravening hoard—either great or small—clamoring through their doors. If only the *ton* were as curious as Reed Sterling had been.

Jacinda's amused countenance turned serious. "We could always help with that. Crispin's aunt Hortense has been rather generous."

"That isn't fair," Ainsley said. "We each agreed when we started this venture that the Bourne Matrimonial Agency must stand on its own merit. How else can we determine if we are doing the good we'd intended when we began?" She shook her head, vehement. "Only when the accounting ledgers have more credits than deficits can we prove that our methods are sound. If we do not earn the money our-selves, then we would be the frauds Mr. Sterling accused us of being."

Mrs. Teasdale huffed, her mouth set in a grim line. "Did he actually say that to you?"

"Indeed, he did. He said we're only playing at games we don't understand."

Jacinda set her hands on her hips. "The nerve of that overinflated, knuckle-dragging—"

"—lout!" Briar added, her soft voice rising.

"That boy needs to be taught a lesson," Mrs. Teasdale hissed. When they murmured their agreement, she started speaking in an excited rush. "I think our Briar is onto something with the handbills. I've got a friend at the printer's and he owes me a favor, a two-dozen-handbill-type favor. So, it won't cost a farthing."

Ainsley opened her mouth to say that the Bourne Matrimonial Agency would not take charity, but Mrs. Teasdale forestalled that with a wag of her finger and continued.

"I won't take no for an answer. And it just so happens that I know someone on the inside of Sterling's, too, which means we could put them right under Mr. Sterling's nose. Neither he nor his customers will be able to escape them."

"But will that be enough? I think we should infiltrate his establishment with one of our own," Jacinda interjected, her eyes gleaming with determination.

Sometimes, Ainsley found her sister's quick ideas toward subterfuge a bit alarming. "We are not sending one of our own. Uncle Ernest is really the only man among us and . . . well . . . you know how dreadful he is at cards."

The sisters murmured their agreement. They loved their uncle, but he lost his coin about as easily as he lost his heart, which was saying quite a lot. This was just one more reason to eradicate the problem in their midst.

Sterling's would have to close for good. Reed Sterling would have to seek his fortune somewhere else, which was fine with Ainsley.

"No, no. The handbills will be just the thing." Mrs. Teasdale absently brushed the scone crumbs from her fingertips, a smile lurking in the corner of her mouth. "The patrons of Sterling's won't like advertisements for matrimony at their club. None of them want reminders of their obligations to hearth and home. They'll take one look at the owner and think he's gone soft."

"It could work," Ainsley mused, a sudden stirring of expectation in her veins. "Once they stop seeing Reed Sterling as some sort of god of manliness, they'll start seeking their entertainments at other clubs."

"Mr. Sterling would lose business," Briar added on a breath.

And best of all, Ainsley thought, he would be too distracted to ever think of the way she'd flinched again.

Jacinda stepped forward, excitement marked in her quick breath and the impish delight in her expression. "You'd start a war."

Yes, indeed. A war Ainsley planned to win.

"Mrs. Teasdale, how quickly can we make this happen?"

Chapter 4

"A piece of paper was found on the table this morning—(dropt, we suppose, by a fairy)—containing a very pretty charade . . ."

JANE AUSTEN, *Emma*

Late the following afternoon, Reed returned to Sterling's after visiting his mum.

His ears were still ringing from her harping on him to *"Stop dillydallying. Take a wife and give me grandchildren before I'm cold in the grave."* Otherwise, he would have noticed the strange silence that greeted him inside the main cardroom straightaway.

Though soon enough, he caught sight of the nine men in black-and-silver livery shifting to stand at attention, and several attempts to conceal smirks.

Something was clearly amiss.

A dozen carriages waited outside for the knocker to be hung on the door. These first patrons who arrived before dusk were typically his most loyal—the *greeks* who were well schooled in the arts of gaming and the *pigeons* they brought in the hopes of plucking a few golden feathers to plump their own purses.

His men should be at their stations, polishing brass fixtures or readying trays with whisky and port. Not standing around as if their livelihood didn't depend on Sterling's continued success.

Reed was creating a legacy that would live beyond him—the prizefighter who'd come from nothing to establish London's most elite gambling club. He hoped that there would be a time when a young boy, coming from nothing, would hear this story and know that he could achieve anything he wanted, and that no obstacle was too great. But that wouldn't happen unless everyone beneath this roof put in effort, every single day.

Reed's gaze raked over his men, stopping on the large, barrel-chested Teddy. The former pickpocket had a round boyish face and sandy blond curls, but had never developed the ability to look innocent when he wasn't. That had been the only reason Reed hadn't called the guard to arrest him when he'd chosen the wrong man's pocket to filch.

"Well?" Reed asked, knowing he wouldn't have to say more before Teddy spilled the contents of his soul.

Before Reed had his answer though, Finch strode into the room, agitation marked in every step. "Your cat is about to lose another one of her lives."

Pushing his query to the side for the moment, Reed felt a quick grin tug at his mouth. "What did she do this time?"

Scowling, Finch furiously patted his pockets. He only grew more cross when his finger slipped into a narrow slit, cut into the lining of his coat. "She stole the ribbon I bought for Trudie."

"Seems like that's not the only thing stolen around here," one of the men muttered. A few snickers followed.

Reed's attention veered back to Teddy and then to the lean, ebony-haired man beside him, who couldn't hide the laughter glinting across his piercing, ice-gray eyes.

"What's this about, Raven?"

Like Teddy, Raven claimed only one name. According to the story, the headmaster of the foundling home where Raven was raised had given him the name for the odd bird-shaped birthmark he bore on his shoulder. Though, as far as Reed was concerned, it suited him because he was as quick-witted and as sly as his namesake.

He'd met Raven three years ago, finding him bloodied and broken near the docks and left for dead. Other than that, his origins were a mystery. Raven didn't talk about his past, but the matter had never given Reed cause for concern. He'd proven his loyalty time and again, working diligently and honestly. Those qualities mattered more than anyone's class or birthright.

Beneath high cheekbones and a Roman nose, a smirk bracketed one corner of Raven's mouth. "There's a bit of thievery afoot. As far as the gents and I can figure, a match-maker must've stolen your heart."

All at once, the room exploded with laughter. A raucous wave rolled through the room, starting low and then ending with loud knee-slapping guffaws.

Reed kept his own expression unreadable. As far as he knew, Finch was the only one aware of his most recent en-counter with Ainsley Bourne. So to the man standing beside him, he muttered through his teeth, "Is there something you would like to tell me, old *friend*?"

"I haven't a clue," Finch answered. "I've been dealing with your miscreant cat since I arrived."

Reed looked back to his men. "Very well, I'll bite."

From behind his back, Raven produced a pair of hand-bills, displaying them like a winning hand of vingt-et-un.

Lacking his usual degree of patience, Reed strode forward and snatched them out of his grasp.

On the page a cartoon depicted a brutish man holding a bulging bag of coins and leering at a frightened bride and groom. Underneath the tableau it read:

Do not be swindled at cards and table games. Take the best gamble and win the prize of your life at the Bourne Matrimonial Agency.

Reed felt his jaw fall slack. Was *he* supposed to be this villain, then?

He gritted his teeth, knowing there was only one person who would dare such a trick—Miss Ainsley Bourne.

That privileged little minx! How dare she sneak in through his doors to plant her propaganda and insinuate that he was a crook.

I have every intention of running you out of business.

Apparently, that hadn't been an idle threat.

He was incredulous. Incensed. And . . . strangely enough, a bit awed by her audacity. So, Miss Prim and Proper had let a bit of her warrior out, hmm? He wished he could have seen it for himself.

"How's your neck, Sterling?" Raven quipped, egging on the merriment in the room. "Feeling the tug of the marriage noose?"

Reed grinned, but in a way that made Raven's smile falter. "And why would you think that?"

"It's just that it seems to favor the agency across the street, and not so much Sterling's. You wouldn't allow it unless you were . . . um . . . smitten, so to speak."

Reed growled. The last thing he needed was to have anyone associate his gaming hell with the Bourne Matrimonial Agency. Men did not come to Sterling's to be reminded of marriage; they came here to escape it. They wanted plenty of sport and high-stakes gambling in the hazard room. And they would quickly find their amusements elsewhere if the thrill of those pleasures were dampened by feminine nonsense.

Proof of that was in the low turnout Sterling's had experienced when the agency had first opened.

To overcome it, Reed had held a raffle—a lottery, as it were—putting up a thousand pounds of his own money. Thankfully, business had recovered in short order, and all had gone smoothly ever since. But now this.

Reed didn't know how Miss Bourne managed to get past the door, but damned if he wasn't going to find out.

He scrutinized each one of his men, looking for signs that they had been part of this scheme. Had they been charmed by her soft brown eyes? Under the spell of the throaty rasp in her voice? Done in by the tantalizing curves in schoolmistress wrapping?

Yet not one appeared to be glazed eyed with lust. All the better for them.

"A clever trick, to be sure." Finch laughed, gaining Reed's attention as he moved around the room. After gathering the rest of the handbills, he handed the small stack to Reed, his brows inching higher with significance. "Obviously someone is trying to get a rise out of you. I only wonder who it might be. An old opponent, perhaps? Someone you once bested in a match?"

Suddenly, Reed understood what Finch was trying to do—remove the Bourne Matrimonial Agency and Miss Bourne from this entire episode.

Not only was it bad for business, but it would do neither of them any good to have their names linked. The truth was, there wasn't just his reputation to consider, but also hers. Ainsley Bourne might never think it of him, but Reed did have a code of honor—one that would never allow a woman's name to be dragged through the mire.

"Whoever he is, he's trying to insult your manhood," Teddy said, eyes as round as sovereigns. "Do you think he'll challenge you to fight as well?"

The room went quiet, everyone's attention snared. Teddy likely didn't know how brilliant he was.

Reed dragged his knuckles along his jaw as if in deep contemplation. "It could be. And if I ever find out who this man is, I might have to settle the score."

Whispered speculations were already running rampant, listing Reed's former opponents. Especially the last, Lord

Savage, who'd been very vocal since his defeat, always challenging Reed to a rematch, calling him a coward.

Soon enough, every one of his men was convinced that Lord Savage was responsible.

Good. The handbills were all but forgotten. Though, should any rumor about the incident leak by accident—Reed slid another glance to Teddy—the patrons would only wonder if Reed planned to enter the ring again as a fighter instead of an instructor.

For years, many men had tried to bribe him and goad him—even at gunpoint—but Reed had always kept a cool head and worked every situation to increase the interest in Sterling's. It was a lesson he'd learned from his father, who'd run a busy tavern.

Only fight when it matters, son. Use your noggin first, and save your fists for when it's the only way.

And so, when Reed finally earned enough prize money to open Sterling's, he'd stopped fighting.

"Raven, if you find any more of these, burn them," Reed said, tucking the stack into the inner pocket of his coat before he left his men to prepare for the evening.

He went upstairs to his office. Then, closing the door, he stalked toward the window and stared at the townhouse across the traffic-snarled street. A slow grin lifted one corner of his mouth as he thought about a visit he intended to make later this evening.

So, a certain haughty matchmaker believed she could steal into a hell and leave a few handbills without confronting the devil?

"Well, Miss Bourne, I'm afraid you're wrong about that."

BY THE time Ainsley returned to the townhouse after dinner at the Duchess of Holliford's that evening, she was exhausted. And the last thing she'd wanted to see was the queue of carriages lined up in front of Sterling's. It served as a reminder that the agency had never had such a problem.

The traffic was so thick, in fact, that she'd had to have the driver drop her at the garden gate, and she'd come in through the servant's entrance.

Well, one thing was for certain, she would be glad when Mrs. Teasdale delivered those handbills. Though when, precisely, that would occur remained a mystery. Rosamunde had merely stated that she'd take care of the matter with utmost haste.

It couldn't happen soon enough.

Ainsley stepped into the kitchen, greeted by the yeasty aroma of freshly baked bread. Mrs. Darden was brushing the loaves with butter. The beloved family cook was dressed in her nightclothes, a shawl draped over her thickly rounded shoulders, her grizzled hair tied into curls with strips of linen.

Her plump cheeks lifted when she spotted Ainsley. "You're home early, dear. Another headache like last week?"

"Not exactly. I simply had to leave for my own sanity." There was no need for excuses or pretense with Mrs. Darden.

"Did Her Grace introduce you to another gentleman?"

"Yes, and again under the guise of improving our client list." The duchess was not the subtlest of would-be matchmakers. Though until recently, these weekly dinners had been part of Briar's schedule. But after her marriage, the duty reverted to Ainsley.

In all honesty, she couldn't fathom how her sister had managed to endure this week after week without committing murder.

Ainsley began yanking off her gloves, finger by finger. "This evening, I met Lord Berryhill. The pretentious stuffed shirt had the gall to say—and mind you, this was before I had known him a full minute of my life—that I would be better occupied with children to look after. And he actually looked pleased with himself, too, grinning with those beaver teeth of his as if he'd spoken the words every woman longs to hear. As if he expected my response to be 'Oh, yes, my lord. Please rescue me from the life I have chosen for myself and confine me to the childbed.'"

Mrs. Darden didn't rail at the injustices that women faced, or even purse her lips in commiseration. Instead, she hid a yawn with the back of her hand. Though, in truth, she'd heard a similar diatribe last week and the week before, so Ainsley was not too bothered by this lackluster response.

"Perhaps if you told Her Grace that you've no intention of marrying, or ever having children of your own, she would stop introducing you to new gentlemen."

Ainsley frowned. "It isn't as if I've made a declaration *against* marriage. Not completely."

"Haven't you?"

"Well, perhaps I have. But is it any wonder? After all, there is my age to consider. And the agency, of course," she said in self-defense. "A lot of men are threatened by a woman with a profession. I should need to find a man who valued my time and my goals as much as his own. And . . . well . . . there isn't one of those out there."

"You've looked, have you?"

"I've been busy." Ainsley slapped her gloves into her bonnet, not particularly caring for the doubting lift of Mrs. Darden's thin brows. "Just because we haven't had any clients lately, doesn't mean I'm not constantly working on ways to draw them inside our doors."

The cook yawned again. "Of course, dear."

"And I'm an aunt, now, don't forget. I need to keep my schedule free in case Jacinda might have need of me. Not to mention, Briar in the future. And there is Uncle Ernest to watch over. Right this very instant he is wooing Lady

Broadhurst at the duchess's dinner. Someone will have to keep him from spending the remainder of his fortune on flowers and comfits, and to remind him to rest after he stays up all night writing sonnets."

Mrs. Darden tutted, though not unkindly. She even shuffled closer and patted Ainsley on the shoulder. "Such a list. I don't know how you bear the burden. Even when you were just a mite of a girl, you always managed everything around you." Then she sighed heavily before turning away toward the corridor that led to her compact but cozy room. Through another yawn, she continued her gentle reproof. "But somewhere along the way, I don't think you ever learned how to have a jolly time. Let down your hair, every now and then."

Ainsley scoffed. "I enjoy amusements. I do. I . . . read. In fact, I just started this ridiculous novel about a gloomy castle and a curmudgeonly duke and . . ."

It was no use. She was talking to an empty room. Mrs. Darden had gone back to bed and there was no one to argue with.

"I know how to be jolly," she muttered and stalked out of the kitchen.

Head high, Ainsley began her nightly rounds of checking the locks on the ground floor windows and the garden door. She wasn't about to let this evening cause her any more agitation.

She'd already had enough on her mind since her encounter with Reed Sterling the other day. Ever since, she'd been distracted and somewhat unsettled, much like a repotted plant struggling to take root in new environs. She didn't like it. And she couldn't wait until her plan to run him out of business took effect.

Everything would be right again as soon as he was gone from St. James's, and gone from her thoughts.

After snuffing out the majority of the sconces, but leaving enough light for her uncle's return, she walked briskly down the main hall. As was her habit, she would check on the state of things outside the townhouse one last time before she locked up for the night.

Yet when she opened the door, it wasn't the gaming hell she saw looming across the way, but the owner himself.

On her very doorstep.

Ainsley startled, her heart rising to her throat. "Mr. Sterling!"

"A man could set his watch by you, Miss Bourne," he drawled, his broad mouth slowly spreading in an uncivilized grin.

The sight of him—all tousled hair, raffish opened collar, and mismatched eyes—caused a perplexing jolt to trample through her, setting off every nerve ending in a series of voluptuous tingles. She didn't know what to make of it.

She wasn't accustomed to seeing him in the evening hours. Darkness accentuated the rough-edged lines of his countenance, casting shadows beneath his heavy brow, hewn cheekbones, and square-cut jaw.

Admittedly, he was handsome in a raw, brawny sort of way . . . if one were inclined to admire such traits. Which, she assured herself, she was not.

"Now isn't the time for paying calls." She stepped back, intending to close the door in his face.

"I never took you for a coward. You cannot even own up to your actions, but prefer to hide away in your little palace instead."

She bristled, anchoring the door with the toe of her shoe, then peered at him through a narrow crack. "I have done nothing from which to hide."

"I've a pocket full of handbills that proves otherwise."

Handbills! So soon? Ainsley didn't expect them to be printed already. In fact, she had yet to see one for herself.

"So you've come to confront me. Is this what you want—to rail at me face-to-face?"

Only now, she realized that she hadn't had a proper amount of time to worry over this eventuality. She still had a bit of thumbnail remaining on her right hand.

"Can't be certain." He shrugged, his midnight tone edged with unabashed wickedness. "Now that you asked, I want to know what my other options are."

His dye-dipped gaze coursed over her in a thorough sweep from head to hem as if he could see every bit of her through that small seam in the door. Another disconcerting thrill plucked every one of her nerve endings like harp strings.

She took a step back from the source. "There are no other options."

"'Twas only a jest, highness. Don't get your neckerchief in a twist," he said with a dismissive shake of his head as if he'd never imagined her in a more salacious sense.

Strangely—quite strangely, indeed—the notion irked her. Was she so cold and undesirable? So distant that even the rogue next door could find nothing appealing about her?

Hmph. "State your business, if you please."

"We have a matter to settle. It seems to me that—"

Before he could continue, a blur of white darted between them, squeezing in through the door. A creature of some sort. Ainsley had just enough time to catch a glimpse of a bedraggled gray tail as it scurried around her skirts and into the foyer, trailing a length of crimson ribbon.

She didn't shriek but took an automatic step to follow, hoping the animal wasn't hurt. Then she remembered the door and turned to close it.

"Deuced cat." Reed Sterling nudged the door wider, wedging a shoulder inside.

Ainsley held fast. "What are you doing? You cannot come in here."

"That's *my* cat."

"Impossible. A man like you cannot have a cat. A vicious, rabies-infested wolf, perhaps."

His brow flattened. "Yes, yes. We both know your opinion of me, but she stole a ribbon from my man and is likely frightened. So, will you let me in or not?"

Chapter 5

"... she will never lead any one really wrong; she will make no lasting blunder; where Emma errs once, she is in the right a hundred times."

JANE AUSTEN, *Emma*

So, will you let me in or not?

Ainsley pulled the corner of her mouth between her teeth, mulling over all the possible ramifications. The midnight caller, however, did not wait for deliberation.

Reed Sterling elbowed the door wider. Then he crossed the threshold, watching her closely as if anticipating her argument.

He'd never set foot inside the agency before. Sure, he'd stood on the doorstep a time or two, but he'd never been right here, underneath the same roof. And the instant he closed the door behind him the air thickened, permeated with the spicy scent of his shaving soap and the natural heat of his skin.

Now the spacious marble foyer seemed to shrink to intimate proportions. Strangely, even her clothes felt tighter.

She shifted, not knowing whether to stand apart or to stand her ground. "You hardly gave me a moment to answer."

"I've learned that, when you have any real objections, you voice them straightaway."

Glancing past her and toward a flash of moon-white fur darting between rooms, his shoulders lifted in an offhanded shrug. The neck of his shirt parted to expose more of his throat, the heavy protrusion of his Adam's apple, and the hollow niche underneath.

Did the man never wear a cravat?

Her gaze drifted to the horizontal ridge of his clavicle, following the line until it disappeared beneath the linen. Absently, she wondered what it looked like when it reached his shoulder. Did the bone end in a knobby protrusion the way hers did, or was it enshrouded in thick ropes of muscle?

An intriguing question, but one she dared not seek the answer to. She couldn't very well ask *him*, after all. And she could just imagine the appalled expressions on the attendants of the circulating library. *Might you direct me to the nude etchings in your collection? Preferably the ones depicting large, strapping males.*

Ainsley cleared her throat. This would be one instance that her curiosity would be left unresearched and unsatisfied.

Still, she couldn't seem to halt her study of this subject. She noted how the golden glimmer from the sconce drifted over the wavy locks of his dark hair and softened the shadows on his countenance. Beneath his strained brow, his eyes hinted at a genuine concern that surprised her.

In this light, he didn't look capable of pummeling other men with his fists. Even if that was precisely what he did and, by all accounts, excelled at, too.

She reminded herself to keep that thought foremost in her mind. "The fact of the matter is, I didn't invite you inside. A moment of careful consideration doesn't imply approval or a welcome with open arms."

It was a mistake to mention her limbs, for he took the opportunity to study them. And everything else about her, from her sheer silk-net fichu to the ruffled hem of her ivory gown.

Her skin reacted, warming, drawing taut, puckering with

sensitive gooseflesh. His blue gaze settled on her face, the scorched iris smoldering as it flicked over her mouth.

The pulse on the side of her throat quickened. Was he thinking of kissing her?

At once, her lips felt plump as peony blossoms before the first bloom. She pressed them together, gently biting down on the tender flesh to keep them from opening.

A smirk teased the scar on his upper lip. "All I want to know is if you can use those arms of yours for anything other than fanning yourself."

Ainsley stiffened. Clearly, there was no need to worry that he would make any untoward advances. Which was excellent news, of course. After all, every solid inch of this man was built for strength and power. A mere touch of his hand would likely shatter her bones into dust.

So why, in heaven's name, had she let him in?

Hiding her inner confusion, she adjusted her fichu firmly about her shoulders, making certain no part of her was exposed. "I can manage to use them to find one cat."

"You? Aren't you going to ring for your servants instead?"

"Being the lowborn scoundrel that you are, I'm certain you are unaware that, in respectable households, many servants retire early because they must awaken early."

"Have them buttering your crumpets at dawn, do you?"

Argh. "You're impossible."

Fully prepared to end this search and be rid of her odious neighbor with utmost haste, she turned on her heel and spotted a blur of white and gray. The only problem was, the cat was heading up the stairs.

Botheration! This was going to take longer than she wanted.

Crossing the foyer, she noted that he kept pace beside her. "I don't suppose I could convince you to stay here."

"I don't suppose you could," he said, taking the stairs with her.

Ainsley hoped to find his cat at the very top so that she could send Mr. Sterling on his way. Perhaps over the railing with a quick shove.

Then again, she likely wouldn't have time to drag the corpse out of doors before her uncle came home.

That thought gave her a bit of pause, but only for Uncle Ernest's sake. There was no telling what he would think to find her alone with a man, and well after business hours.

Then again, her uncle needn't worry. Clearly, Reed Sterling saw her only as the gatekeeper to his cat and nothing more alluring. Which was perfectly fine. She preferred to be seen as forbidding. The idea of being the object of his carnal appetites didn't appeal to her.

Not in the least.

Reaching the top of the stairs, and now more ill-tempered than she'd been at the bottom, she picked up a lamp from the marble-topped demilune table against the wall and began her search.

"Our offices are on this first floor. Earlier, I closed most of the doors aside from my own office, so it should take nothing more than a cursory glance down each corridor."

"Keeping all these beeswax tapers burning must cost a pretty penny," the interloper said with an undisguised note of disapproval. "That's no way to run a business. You should switch to tallow or use oil."

She sniffed, not appreciating the advice. "Our clients don't like the scent of tallow, and oil smoke stains the wallpaper."

"Then why bother keeping them lit at all after business hours? Unless . . ." He paused. "Miss Bourne, are you afraid of the dark?"

There he was, goading her again.

Having no intention of answering, she continued her course. She would hardly tell *him* that it gave her peace of mind to see down the length of the halls, beyond the straight-backed chairs and slender tables alongside the doors, to account for every single shadow.

However, when she glanced over, she caught him scrutinizing her with the precision of an artist tracing her silhouette on vellum. So she gave in.

"I cannot fathom why it should matter to you, but I have a system. I extinguish the flames floor by floor before I retire," she admitted. "Regardless, it is better for our search. Though if my uncle were home we should be quicker, still. I daresay, we could locate the cat solely from the sound of his sneezing. He is dreadfully allergic."

"Your uncle is not at home?"

The note of censure in his voice plucked a string of alarm in her. She should not have made such an admission.

Facing him, she held the lamp between them, eying his hard-set features carefully. "He will return at any moment."

"And when he does"—Mr. Sterling growled, raking a hand through his hair with an impatient swipe of his large hand—"only to discover a man alone with his unmarried niece, what then? Will he raise the alarm and call the guard? Or will he call the vicar instead?"

Understanding the reason for his irritation, she expelled a breath that stirred the flame. "Ah. I see that you are familiar with some of society's strictures—though clearly not the ones regarding proper attire—but fear not. You won't be forced to marry the forbidding spinster across the way. No one here is set on fleecing you of your fortune. Rest assured, if my uncle returned to find your hulking form lurking about in the dark, he'd likely shoot you before you could even announce yourself, thereby saving you from a lifetime of untold misery."

It wasn't true in the least.

Uncle Ernest was a terrible shot and never comfortable with such a weapon. He excelled in fencing, stating on more than one occasion that he preferred the romance of a rapier to anything as boorish as a pistol.

Still, she had a point to make.

Leaving Mr. Sterling to ponder his fate, she moved toward her office. And there she found the cat sitting in the recessed window seat, absently pawing at the ribbon.

The creature lifted its scarred face, beseeching her with the slow blink of one green eye and a plaintiff *"Meow."*

Without delay, Ainsley set down the lamp and crossed the room, scooping up the solid but scraggly cat. "Oh, you poor dear."

In response, the animal burrowed closer, purring almost instantly as she rubbed her head against Ainsley's fichu. There was nothing she detested more than to see suffering of any sort. Though it was quite evident from the well-healed scars beneath her fur that her injuries had occurred some time ago.

Ainsley cuddled her, softly stroking her patchy fur. "What would you say to a nice dish of cream, hmm? I'm sure Mrs. Darden has some in the larder."

"That'll be enough. Give her over," Mr. Sterling said with an impatient gesture, crowding the doorway. "It took a long while for me to earn her trust, and I'll not have you undermining my efforts by spoiling her more than I do."

"With the way she's been mistreated in the past, it's no wonder she doesn't trust easily. Why, just look at her. Anyone can see that she requires tender care. I can hardly believe she could ever be comfortable with a rough and burly man like you."

"Are we still talking about the cat, highness?" he asked, stone-faced.

Recalling her noticeable flinch the other day, she felt the shameful heat of a blush rise to her cheeks. Why had her nemesis, of all people, borne witness to such a reaction? She swallowed down a vulnerable twinge in her throat.

He drew near and reached out, albeit slowly. Yet watching his hand close the distance, degree by degree, she felt herself tense and clutched the cat like a shield.

"I wouldn't hurt her, not for anything," he crooned.

Caught unawares by the unexpected warmth in his voice, Ainsley's gaze darted up to his. At once, she was ensnared by the tenderness and understanding woven through those dye-dipped spheres.

She didn't know what to make of him. Her thoughts were being pulled in two different directions. While she should be terrified of a man who'd made his fortune with his fists, she was also conscious of being helplessly, mortifyingly— and she would never admit it aloud—*drawn* to Reed Sterling.

Achingly uncomfortable with this fraught awareness, she held her breath as he crowded near. His movements were slow and patient as if he saw her as a wild animal— dangerous and needing to be approached with great care.

Yet if anyone was wild, it was he.

"If she truly belongs to you then, pray tell, what is her name?" she asked tersely, hiding her discomfiture over the new way he was looking at her.

"Doesn't have one. I've tried to name her a few times, but she tends to let me know straightaway when she doesn't like it," he continued, his voice a low, soothing drawl. "Prefers 'Cat' to anything."

"But she deserves a name, one that is special and is just as strong and obviously resilient as she is."

His mouth spread in a slow grin that hinted at a challenge. "Then give her one."

Ainsley's gaze slipped to that nick on his upper lip. Absently, she wondered what it would feel like against her own.

The thought startled her, cheeks growing hot. Even her lips felt warmer. Whyever would she wonder something like that?

Clearing her throat, she looked down, watching as the cat extended a foreleg to him. In turn, he took hold of the paw. And seeing that big burly hand tenderly stroke the offering with the pad of his thumb, Ainsley couldn't help but remember the way he'd protected that primrose.

The creature in her arms purred audibly, the vibrations so strong that they affected the beating of her own heart, sending it racing.

"Chloris," she said after a confused moment, her thoughts in complete disorder. "Her name should be Chloris, as in the Greek goddess of—"

"Flowers," he finished for her and cocked his chin. "Not *all* the sense has been knocked out. There's still a bit of the university swimming around in this empty skull of mine."

Ainsley shifted her feet on the carpet, the harsh slights she'd delivered to him on occasion ringing like a gong. "I never said you were a dimwit."

"And I never called you a prude."

Oh, very well, so they'd each exchanged a fair number of jabs.

"Nevertheless, we were discussing her name. Chloris is perfect because I've always thought flowers were rather resilient, coming back each spring even after the harshest of winters."

He stared back at her, head tilted in scrutiny. "All except for primroses. You detest those, as I recall."

"Yes," she amended quickly, "except for those—*sss!*"

Ainsley hissed smartly as a sharp claw sliced across the thin skin on the top of her hand. The cat suddenly leapt out of her arms then stole out of the room, still trailing the ribbon.

"Apparently, she doesn't prefer *Chloris* to *Cat*, after all."

Glancing down to the thin red mark, Ainsley moved to follow the creature before Mr. Sterling had the opportunity to mock her.

But he blocked her path.

"Here. Let me have a look."

"There's no need. It's only a . . ." Her words trailed off as his bare, blunt-tipped fingers closed over her wrist, gently but startling nonetheless. "A scratch."

Shock quivered through her. Reed Sterling was touching her—*and* she was letting him!

Admittedly, during moments of weakness and errant curiosity, she had often wondered what this might feel like. But only abstractly, of course, as one might wonder what it would be like to bathe in milk like Cleopatra. It wasn't to be *done*.

And yet . . . it was happening.

"Hmm," he murmured, gently ascertaining the severity of this insignificant wound.

The warmth of his skin seeped into hers, his broad palm nestling the frantic throb of her pulse. Callused fingertips dragged lightly over her skin and her body gave way to shameful tingles, every nerve ending exposed and wanton.

She never expected it to feel so decadent. So illicit. She shouldn't be surprised if she started to purr. Surely this was the reason society frowned on ladies and gentlemen touching each other with familiarity unless a severed limb were involved.

His hands were capable and seasoned, with long thick fingers and nails trimmed to the quick. The knobby protrusion of knuckles showcased nicks and scars that told a violent history all on their own. And yet, every touch was surprisingly tender.

Even so, she should withdraw and reprimand him soundly for taking such liberties. She was appalled that she didn't.

And shame on her for letting her fingers relax, curling ever so slightly over the sturdy mound at the base of his thumb.

Thankfully, he didn't seem to notice. Nor did he pause in his study.

Singularly focused, he bent his head, his breath coasting over the thin upper layer of her flesh. The heat of it seemed to penetrate places where it couldn't possibly reach, collecting in humid patches beneath the fine cambric against her skin.

At once, the air in her office seemed stiflingly hot. She felt both overdressed and underdressed. She was torn by simultaneous desires to shed some clothing while donning others.

The notion produced the strangest vision of herself wrapped in a coverlet while being completely naked underneath. Her breath quickened.

She caught the scent of him, her nostrils flaring on hints of warm spice and an earthy aroma—a subtle but potent mélange of salt, sweat, and undeniable masculinity. She should be disgusted by it. Instead she found his fragrance utterly—disconcertingly—appealing. So she dragged in another reckless lungful, her eyelids growing heavy.

Anyone would feel trepidation to stand this close to such a large, imposing figure. And yet, it wasn't trepidation she was feeling. It was something else entirely. Something foreign and new.

"It doesn't appear the cat broke the skin, but . . ." he said, his midnight timbre setting her pulse off-kilter.

"Yes?" she whispered, her throat dry. "Do you see something else?"

He shook his head, his touch careful as if he thought she was made out of blown glass and susceptible to shattering. "It's just that . . . you have the softest skin imaginable."

A hot shiver tumbled through her. Inanely, she stammered out a response, "I use a b-balm at night with rosehips and almond blossoms."

He murmured an appreciative sound that rubbed a raw place, deep inside her body. A place she hadn't even known existed until this moment.

Then, lifting his head, he winked at her, grinning. "I never would have guessed someone so thorny in demeanor could feel like this. I always thought you'd be covered in thistles."

All at once, Ainsley felt like a fool.

He'd only been teasing her. The cold, harsh realization brought her back to her senses.

Tugging her hand free, she purposely brushed it down her skirts. "Well, you're just as rough and barbaric as I thought you'd be. I could hardly stand your coarse pawing."

He eyed her with the expertise of a jewel cutter sizing up a paste gemstone, and issued a mocking laugh. "Is that why your cheeks are so red, highness? Because you could *hardly stand* the touch of a man?"

Ignoring him, she swept past him and out of the room, glad that he did not stop her.

Her nerves were worn thin, frayed from the upheaval of the past few minutes. She hated this never-ending sparring. It was exhausting. But was there another way?

No. They were either to be at odds, or to be nothing at all—a fact she should well remember for future encounters. Fortunately, there wouldn't be many of those to endure once he was gone from St. James's for good.

With a weary sigh, she rounded the corner but stopped abruptly.

The red ribbon was halfway up the stairs.

Ainsley's stomach dropped. She would have to search for the cat in the family's private rooms. And Reed Sterling would follow, whether she liked it or not.

Chapter 6

⌒

"... it might be wise to let the fancy touch it
seldom; for evil in that quarter was at hand."

JANE AUSTEN, *Emma*

Reed mounted the stairs after Miss Bourne, brooding over
his unpredicted outburst. Had he actually marveled over the
softness of her skin aloud, like a besotted cub who'd yet to
cut his milk teeth?

He had, *damn it all.*

Of course, he'd responded by putting up his guard with
a jest, forestalling any blow she might strike against him.
Their previous encounters had proven that Miss Bourne
could flay a man's ego with a single lash of her tongue.

As expected, she'd acted the injured party, insulted that
he'd dared to touch her highborn self. And yet, there had
been moments when she hadn't been offended or repulsed
at all.

He'd heard the rasp in her breath. Watched her lips part
and plump with color. They turned the deep hue of wine-
poached pears—one of the few sumptuous delicacies he'd
never been able to resist. Was it any wonder he'd been
tempted to take a bite?

He could have made a meal out of her.

The signs of attraction were there. He'd noticed the precise instant when she'd let her own guard slip, her hand
curling softly over his, her eyes dark and inviting. Yet he

also knew—beyond a shadow of a doubt—that Ainsley Bourne would sooner fling her precious fichus into the nearest fireplace than admit she'd felt anything other than supreme loathing.

All the same, he could still feel the perfection of her skin. White and warm as swans' down. Soft and silken as fresh snow. Reflexively, his hands curled on emptiness. The pads of his fingertips pulsed with the need to touch her again. To discover *all* the places where she was soft and warm.

He could still smell her, too. Every indrawn breath was rosehips, almond blossoms, and thorny Miss Ainsley Bourne.

Bloody hell. He was more than half-aroused walking up the stairs behind her. The tailor cut of his clothes did nothing to disguise the heavy outline of his cock, bloating the fall front of his trousers.

This certainly didn't bode well should her uncle return home and catch him in such a state. Thinking of that, Reed made an adjustment so that he was better concealed.

He approached the inner sanctum of the Bourne family with caution, his senses alert, his pulse drumming as he stood at the base of the narrow, arched corridor.

Ahead of him, Ainsley Bourne cast a wary look over her shoulder as she flitted in and out of the bedchambers on either side. To soothe her nervousness, he held back, keeping a good distance between them.

There was always something between them—class, profession, animosity, frustration. Yet when his bare hand had been on hers, there was *something* there, too.

Reed tucked that thought away for the moment, then proceeded at a measured pace.

His steps were muffled on the tightly woven runner as he passed gilt-framed landscapes flanking either side of the hall. The further he went, there was one thing that stood out from his surroundings. The stillness. Every sound was muted—the shush of her skirts, the occasional creak of the floor. Even the air in this private, untainted space seemed reverent, like the hush of a cathedral when the choir takes a breath before they sing.

A queer sort of tension filled him at the thought, his lungs tight. He took it as a reminder that he didn't belong here, where the rooms were dressed in hand-painted silk paper and costly oil paintings, floors draped with thick Persian rugs and topped with imported furnishings.

Doubtless she hadn't lived a day without such luxuries in her life. Hadn't been brought up in a house so small that the only sort of kitchen was a hook above the hearth and a pail of water on the floor.

Of course Reed's father had always planned to buy a big house and to make the tavern a grand coaching inn. But those dreams had been cut short that day of the duel.

A traveler had come to the tavern—one of the many pompous aristocrats to stop on the way through Knightsbury.

The fop had issued a slight to another, insults had been exchanged. Then came the challenge—pistols at dawn. Having no companions with them, the slighted lord had asked Reed's father to be his second. Since Dad was the kind of man to feed the poor with the last food from his own cupboard, he'd agreed.

Mum had later said that he'd wanted to force an apology, but Dad's attempt was futile.

The duel commenced, and a misfired shot had gone straight to his heart.

That event was the cornerstone for Reed's determination to make something of himself while he was alive to do so.

Distracted by the memory, he caught himself staring at one of the ornate tables, too narrow and delicate to serve a real purpose. It seemed more like an altar, hosting a slender vase filled with flowers and bits of greenery. Above it hung a painting of sheep on a windswept hillside. A little stone hut with a thatched roof stood in the distance, looking almost idyllic. Highborns would likely think so, imagining the romance of such a setting. They wouldn't think about the stench of sheep dung blowing in the tiny window and caking the boots of the people who trudged those hills every day.

That was the difference between them, he thought. Well, one of the many.

"I imagine you miss your quiet country life," he said, needing to disrupt the silence that was starting to unnerve him.

Two doors down, Miss Bourne scoffed. "*Quiet*, indeed. With a constant list of tasks to be done, Jacinda knocking about and getting into mischief, and Briar singing or plunking away on the piano, our cottage was hardly ever quiet.

"If anything, I miss the noise," she continued with uncharacteristic verbosity. "Especially of late, with my sisters married and seldom here unless . . ." Her words trailed off as if she realized she was rambling and revealing more about the inner workings of her mind than she'd ever done before. "Oh, never mind all that. I'm sure it's of little interest to you."

She was wrong about that. From the day they'd met, he'd wanted to unwrap her. Not only her prim and proper clothes, layer by layer, but all the thoughts she kept buttoned up as well.

And he would no sooner admit any of that than she would to being lonely without her sisters here.

Besides, that wasn't how things worked between them. She liked doling out waspish retorts, and he liked shocking her to a crimson blush.

"Ah, so the truth comes out at last," he said, his tone dripping with the smugness he knew she despised. "All the times you've stormed across the street, pretending to rail at me for the noise of my patrons, was actually an uncontrollable desire to see me in my shirtsleeves again."

Stopping in the corridor, she cut him a narrow-eyed glance. "Once more you are assuming that I find an absurd sort of pleasure from our encounters when the reality is, I would have preferred it if we'd never met at all."

"Believe that all you like, highness."

She bristled and stormed off into a room at the end of the hall.

Instead of emerging after a few seconds as she'd done before, she lingered. It was long enough for him to suspect she'd found his cat. Though after making his way to her, he wasn't prepared for the sight that greeted him.

Peering into the last room, Reed saw prim Miss Ainsley Bourne on her hands and knees, searching beneath a glossy mahogany tester bed swathed in deep blue silks.

He went still in the doorway. As she reached under the heavy wood frame, his greedy eyes roved over the pale fabric of her dress, molding over the curve of her hips and the perfect delineation of her heart-shaped bottom. Every muscle and appendage in his body gave a lush kick, spurring him forward, pulse swift and insistent.

It took no effort at all for his mind to flood with carnal thoughts. It never did with her.

Thinking of how incomparably soft she was, he imagined what her delicate, private skin would feel like to caress. His fingers ached to discover the answer, the tips prickling as he gripped the door molding. He drew in a breath to steady himself, only to catch a familiar fragrance that nearly buckled his knees. *Rosehips and almond blossoms.*

The sweet, tempting scent was stronger, more concentrated here. Without a doubt, this was her bedchamber.

Scanning the room at a glance, he noted a slender wardrobe with every garment tucked out of sight. The only adornments within these four walls were those of the essential—yet elegant—variety, like the ormolu clock on the mantel, the ornately carved walnut dressing screen in the corner, the small chest at the foot of the bed, and the marble-topped vanity with a brown jar resting beside a smooth-handled brush and dish of hairpins.

Biting the inner wall of his cheek, he forced himself not to imagine her sitting there, brushing her hair every night before bed. Instead he turned his attention to the far wall and focused on the gold-tasseled tiebacks for the brocade curtains. But as he studied the tall window, a disgruntled sort of amusement nearly had him laughing like a madman.

Her bedchamber overlooked Sterling's. Not only that, but the rooms directly across the street—on the very floor and corner—were his own. This was too much!

Miss Bourne and he were even more intimate neighbors than he could have known. It was like sharing the same space, with him sleeping days and her the nights.

And now he wondered how he was ever going to be able to enter his own chamber again . . . without thinking of hers.

"Ah-ha! I've caught you at last," she said as she wiggled and stretched, her voice like raw velvet, stroking a place low inside him. "*Drat!* Come back here, you naughty thing."

Reed cursed under his breath. He'd just entered some sort of hell, he was sure of it. But he'd had his fill of torment for one night.

Ready to end it, he strode into the room and kneeled down on the other side of the bed. Sure enough, he found the cat, absently cleaning her fur and stealthily keeping just out of Ainsley Bourne's reach.

"Oh, you remind me of Seymour," she said on a strained breath, fingers wiggling to reach the cat, the space only just too narrow to fit her body. "He even had your coloring. But he only hid beneath my bed during thunderstorms. Well, or whenever Jacinda and Briar tried to put him in a dress."

"You had a cat when you were younger?"

Her eyes rounded when she caught sight of him, their gazes locking beneath the bed. She took his crouched form in at a glance, assessing the threat within her midst.

"I'm not a lecher, no matter what you might think. I'm only trying to thwart the cat's escape so that we can both end this night. Sooner rather than later. After all, I don't want to get shot by your uncle."

Though if Eggleston even knew how to load a pistol, let alone fire one, Reed would strip down and shout the child's rhyme of "Wee Willie Winkie" in the middle of the street.

Expelling a breath through the barest opening of her mouth, she nodded but with obvious reluctance. Then she resumed her task but kept an eye on him all the same. "Seymour was our dog, actually, or at least I called him by that name. Jacinda and Briar referred to him as Mr. Fluffington."

"Poor beast. A far from noble moniker."

"I always thought so, too. After all, how was he to know that he was a valued part of our family without consideration to his sense of self-worth? Names are very important in that regard."

"Hmm . . . I sense a lecture coming forthwith about how I have failed to name this cat," he teased.

"Well, it is the least you could do."

"Actually, calling her 'Cat' *is* the least I can do."

"Quite true," she said with a surprised laugh, then quickly muffled the rich throaty sound by biting her lip.

It didn't make a difference, however. He'd heard it all the same, and that small break in her composure made his pulse accelerate again. And he wondered what it would be like if she were so at ease with him that she laughed all the time. What would it be like if her head tilted back and her eyes became heavy lidded and glistening from joy as she gazed at him . . .

Abruptly, Reed shook himself free of the wayward notion before it took hold.

The cat stretched out, rolling to her side to bat his hand. But Reed was done playing. He was ready to take her by the scruff and haul her out.

Crawling toward the bedpost, he reached under, shoring his shoulder against a bedside table. But then a scrap of apricot-colored lace brushed across his cheek.

He went deathly still as if facing a viper. One wrong move and he was done for.

Unable to look away, he stared fixedly on that lace, noting the gathers of a slender cuff and a length of whisper-thin fabric that peeked out from beneath a pillow. A sleeve, he determined. The sleeve of—*he swallowed*—her nightdress.

All at once, his determination to keep a tight rein on errant thoughts broke free and sped away with reckless abandon. The liquid beats of his heart descended in the thick rush, pooling low and heavy in another surge of arousal, one hundred times more potent than before.

He drew in a breath, so heady he could taste it on his tongue.

The idea of Miss Prim and Proper wearing this bit of frippery filled his mind. It would be transparent, just a veil over her body, displaying every curve, every swell, every shadow. And her hair would be down, too, draped all silky-like over her shoulders as she brushed it.

He wondered how long it would be when she took the pins out and unwound that tight coil. Long enough to cover her breasts? Would it feel like silk in his hands, or falling across his face with her straddling him, gazing down into his eyes as she sank down onto his . . .

"Caught you," Ainsley breathed from the other side.

Reed jolted, guilty. Then he realized she was talking to the cat.

A lengthy minute elapsed before he was able to stand and follow her out and down the corridor. He had to blink several times, the vision in his mind as clear as a memory.

Viper or no, it seemed that the lace had bitten him all the same.

He walked woodenly down the two staircases toward the foyer, trailing behind as she crooned to his cat, telling the cretin that she was clever and pretty but very, very naughty.

An affectionate reprimand, the likes of which he would never hear. Not the common son of a country tavern owner.

No, she would save her tender words, her laughs, and her smiles for a nobleman from a fine family, and together they would look down their noses at the likes of him. Reed had always known this. Though why he gave it a passing thought, he couldn't imagine. Perhaps it was the nightdress venom working through his veins, slowly poisoning him.

As he descended the last few treads, his cat eyed him with an arrogant twitch of whiskers, lid half-closed in bliss as she was being nuzzled and petted while draped over Miss Bourne's shoulder.

He frowned, disgusted to feel the slightest bit of jealousy. Over a cat.

Miss Bourne lingered near the bottom of the stairs, casting an uncertain glance toward the door and then back to him. "It is time for you to leave, Mr. Sterling. I'm sure you are as eager as I to bring this ordeal to an end. However . . . I should hate for anyone to notice you departing, especially at this hour."

"I could leave by way of the servant's entrance if your highness prefers."

"I was going to suggest the garden."

She huffed, her exasperated breath lifting the fine chestnut tendrils that curled against her brow. They must have come loose during their beneath-the-bed search. And only now, as he stood near her, did he notice the bit of fluff there as well.

"You have a feather," he said, moving closer.

"I do?"

This time, she didn't flinch when he lifted his hand. Then again, he was much slower and held her watchful gaze all the while, reassuring her.

She held stock still as he sought the white downy bit amidst the fine silken locks and slipped it free without fuss. And without lingering either—which proved the more difficult of tasks.

Pinched between his fingers, he showed the feather to her as proof. She nodded, then abruptly took a step back and thrust the drowsy feline out at arm's length, its tail swishing like the pendulum of a clock, head lolled to one side. "Here is your cat."

Now of course a gentleman would have made the exchange without any unnecessary contact. But Reed had no intention of passing up an opportunity for one last tantalizing touch. So, as he reached for the cat, he fumbled a bit on purpose. Thankfully, the boneless creature made bobbling the exchange more convincing and Ainsley was forced to draw closer.

Slyly, his fingertips brushed her impossibly soft hand, the underside of her wrist, the quick thrumming of her pulse. Her breath caught and a new blush stained her cheeks.

Again she took a quick step back, covering that tender spot on her wrist. It seemed she was always shielding herself in some way or another.

His gaze briefly strayed to the way she pressed her lips together, hiding them, and then further down to the gathers of fine netting tucked into her bodice. How many times had he lain awake imagining her parting that silly frippery instead, revealing the milk-white skin beneath, inch by inch?

Too often. Yet even on the hottest days, she always held herself tightly together.

Except for that one moment when she'd flinched.

"You're not afraid of me this time," he said, circling around the question he'd had since their last encounter.

Frowning, she searched his features as if suspecting him of wearing a clever mask and she was trying to find the string that held it in place. "Mr. Sterling, I hardly know what to make of you this evening."

"It's the cat, isn't it?" He expelled a dramatic sigh of understanding. "As the owner of a loathsome gaming hell, I should have preferred a rabies-infested wolf but they were in short supply in the middle of town."

She averted her face, but not before he saw a smile tucked into the corner of her mouth. "A pity for you."

"And for you as well. Just imagine how quickly you could've been rid of me if I'd been bitten."

"Well, you could take a trip to the country and wave around a hunk of raw meat to see if you have any luck."

"There's a thought." He tried not to laugh, but it was damnably difficult. "How kind of you to always think of me, Miss Bourne. Even . . . when there *isn't* rubbish on your doorstep."

She slanted him a glance as she picked up the lamp and began to walk toward the shadows at the back of the house. "Plotting the demise of your business hardly signifies."

"To my way of thinking, it all puts a betting chip on my side of the table."

"With a philosophy like that, it leaves me to wonder if your prizefighting success is mere rumor. Perhaps you considered it a victory whenever an opponent decided to appear for the match."

He chuckled. "There was a bit more to it, highness. Contrary to what you might believe, not just any club-fisted oaf can enter a ring and come away with the purse."

The instant the words fell from his lips, regret settled in. Now he was thinking about how she'd cringed the other day.

And so was she. He felt the air change between them. Their static charge suddenly turned stale and silence followed.

The succinct clip of her soles on the hardwood floor slowed until he could count them one by one. Fifteen before she spoke again, her voice quiet. "Considering your reputation, you must have been skilled. I have to wonder why you gave it up to teach lessons and run a gambling establishment."

It seemed that every accomplishment he'd made and everything Sterling's represented were the cruxes of what would always be between them. The insurmountable barriers.

"Lots of reasons." He shrugged and kept his tone conversational, not wanting to reveal his frustration. "There were, and are, too many fools out there who believed I was the Goliath to their David and set out to prove something, only to get hurt. Pugilism isn't about pain—either being the giver or the receiver—but about endurance. And only those with even temperaments make it as far as I had done."

"I should think that"—she swallowed, her complexion stark—"rage would assist a man in such a situation."

"Only weak men fly into a rage," he said quietly, watching the subtle shift of candlelight and shadows on her delicate features.

He'd had experience reading people enough that he could see white-eyed wariness, her gaze flitting to the hand he kept curled around his cat and then up to his eyes.

Yet what had him fighting to maintain his own composure was her nearly imperceptible nod of agreement. That was the answer to the suspicion he'd never wanted confirmed.

Ainsley Bourne had witnessed a man's rage before.

The cat stirred in his grasp, mewling for affection. Not realizing he'd gone tense and still as a headstone, he settled her against his shoulder, petting her as he continued. "That's why weak men will always lose in the end. A patient man, on the other hand, will take time to learn his opponent if he wants to succeed."

She stopped at the terrace door and faced him. Her gaze searched his, her brow knitted in concentration as if she expected there to be an examination on this subject. "Was there never a time that you were afraid? Or thought that you would be beaten and injured during one of your exhibitions?"

"Aye. Especially during the last few," he answered honestly. "In my prime, I was lightning quick. Then years of bare-knuckled body blows took their toll, and I started to notice how slow my hands had become. It was only a matter of time before someone else did, too. And once an opponent learns your weakness . . . well . . . you're done for."

Her study of him altered with this admission, a light of understanding flickering in her gaze. "A lesson I shall remember in the days to come."

"Still going to rid St. James's of me, are you?"

"Never doubt it." All at once, a smile bloomed on her face, unexpected and stunning.

His breath stalled, seizing as if he'd taken a blow to the gut. He felt lightheaded, not quite himself. She'd never looked at him this way before—her face glowing and her eyes glinting with impish delight.

It was like stepping directly into the fantasy he'd had upstairs a moment ago.

"Besides," she continued when he was unable to form words, "I hardly have much choice in the matter. It is either your business or mine. After all, we cannot continue to live on opposite sides of the street. Our mutual loathing would never permit it."

She sounded so resolute that he couldn't argue with her.

"Then I welcome you to do your worst," he said when she opened the door. Stepping out into the cool night breeze helped him come back to his senses. "But you're going to have to do a far sight better than handbills."

"Oh, I shall," she countered with a smug arch of her delicately winged brows.

The threshold between them was now a line scratched in the dirt.

"Best make quick work of it then, if you still expect to have me gone by month's end like you'd promised. After all, in this game of ours, it's now my turn and I won't play fair."

"And *I* will find your weakness, Mr. Sterling."

Dimly, as she closed the door, he worried that she wouldn't have far to look.

Chapter 7

"She knew the limitations of her own powers too
well to attempt more than she could perform with
credit . . ."

JANE AUSTEN, *Emma*

I won't play fair.

Those four words had been a plague upon Ainsley for the
days that followed.

Anticipating heaps upon heaps of handbills, she'd checked
the doorstep too many times to count but found nothing. Not
even the usual amount of rubbish.

Suspicious, she'd walked the footpath in front of the
agency looking over every inch of the façade. Still, she'd
found nothing amiss and spent far too much time glaring
at Sterling's. On more than one occasion, she'd caught the
owner standing in his doorway with his shoulder propped
against the frame, facing her direction. Then, casual as you
please, he would incline his head and disappear back into
his den.

Just what was he plotting?

Ainsley didn't know, but his lack of retaliation was wearing on her nerves.

Strange as it seemed, part of her wanted him to do *something*, if only to keep her mind from venturing back to their
last encounter. To those imprudently pleasant and intimate
moments alone with him.

"That is a dreadful habit, my dear," the Duchess of Holliford said with fond reproof from across the low table in her lavender parlor.

Realizing she'd been gnawing the corner of her thumbnail, Ainsley sat up straighter and lowered her hand. "Terrible, I know. Forgive me."

The duchess nodded, her cheeks creasing like frail vellum when she smiled. A woman in her later years—though she would never divulge her true age—she wore her dove-gray hair in a flawless twist at her crown, the jewels dangling from her ears matching the teal green of her wizened eyes. And, albeit small in stature, she was large in influence on matters of decorum and respectability in society.

"It's perfectly understandable to be distracted with the agency floundering the way it is," the duchess said, not unkindly, her voice warm with affection.

Ainsley felt a stab of guilt that Reed Sterling was occupying her thoughts more than the family business.

Keeping this a secret, she responded with her own nod of disappointment. "We have not had a successful match since my half brother married Miss Prescott last Christmas. The worst part is that the agency cannot even take credit because it was nearly all Mr. Cartwright's own doing."

John Cartwright was her half brother, indeed, but her junior by only two months. Their father, Michael Cartwright, Lord Frawley, had kept two families for years. And when Heloise Bourne-Cartwright discovered his illegitimate offspring, her heart had broken and she'd never recovered from her melancholy.

The scars left behind by loss and betrayal were the primary reason that Ainsley had never sought to contact either her father or his other children. Recently, however, she'd warmed to the idea of inviting these estranged siblings into her life. She'd even started to exchange letters with John and with a much younger half sister, Amelia.

As for her father, Lord Frawley had not lingered long—or faithfully—with his second family either. Consequently, there were other siblings scattered about here and there as well.

Father had reached out to her a few years ago, sending a missive with an absently worded enquiry about her, Jacinda, and Briar, but Ainsley never responded. She'd buried the hopes she'd once had and the hatred she'd felt toward him long ago.

"But you have other clients," the duchess said, breaking into Ainsley's musings. "Lord Hullworth is such a handsome specimen, too. Have you made any progress with him?"

"I have introduced his lordship to several young women, but he was not enticed enough to court any of them. I daresay he is quite busy this Season, playing escort to his young sister."

"He would certainly make an advantageous match," the duchess remarked, tapping her fan against the arm of her chair. "And on that topic—"

Ainsley knew what was coming. Drawing in a breath, she steeled herself for another attempt of the duchess's matchmaking. Like her sisters and Mrs. Teasdale, the duchess was absurdly determined to see her married.

They were all going to be disappointed.

"—just the other day, I met a gentleman in the park who had perked his ears at the mention of your name. I daresay he's quite keen for an introduction."

"Perhaps Your Grace could convince him to apply to the agency instead."

The duchess pursed her lips in displeasure. "It will only be once you are married that these rumors of the *convenient matches* for the nieces of Viscount Eggleston will disappear. Then the *ton* will be all too eager to become clients."

Ainsley had traveled enough down this avenue of the conversation, so she carefully steered away from it. And what better way than to throw Reed Sterling under the carriage wheels?

"To me, it seems the larger issue is the agency's proximity to a gaming hell. After all, it was Your Grace who said that you moved to Mayfair because of the den of iniquity at your doorstep."

The duchess splayed her fingers over her bosom, penciled brows inching higher in pleased surprise. "Did I say that? A clever turn of a phrase, if I do say so myself."

"Indeed," Ainsley hesitated. Then after a moment of deliberation, she decided to tell the duchess of her plan. "For that very reason I've declared war on Mr. Sterling, taking steps to ensure that his patrons will choose another gambling establishment. By the time I am finished, his business will fail and he will be forced to close the doors for good."

The duchess studied her from over the rim of her blue-and-white Nanking teacup. "And does Mr. Sterling know of your plans?"

Ainsley nodded, absently nibbling an almond biscuit, worrying away the outer edge. Once again, her evening interlude with Reed Sterling and their parting words consumed her thoughts.

Just what could he possibly be plotting?

"You've ensnared me in a state of suspended curiosity. Pray tell, how did he take your declaration?"

"With far too much amusement, if you ask me," she said, taking out her hostilities on the biscuit. "He appeared neither threatened nor inconvenienced by my efforts. In fact, he even claimed that this was a game between us and that it was his turn now. Can you believe his audacity?" She huffed, dropping the crumbled remains of the confection on her plate. "Though as of yet, he has done *absolutely* nothing. I cannot help but wonder what could be taking him so long to retaliate."

Likely, he was studying her, just as he'd admitted to doing with every opponent who'd fought against him. It never occurred to her that a man with undue patience could be so . . . so maddening!

"But is it a game, my dear, or is it war? In the latter, you never wait for your turn." The duchess punctuated this comment with the rasp of cup to saucer, her cheeks creasing with a grin.

Ainsley let out a breath of relief, feeling her shoulders relax. "I'd hoped Your Grace would understand."

"My dear, I was married to a duke for the better part of forty years and that man loved to irritate me beyond belief. If anyone should know a bit about war, it is I."

The notion of pairing marriage with war gave Ainsley pause, a shiver racing down her spine. "Then again, perhaps I should not have done so. After all, I cannot be unquestionably certain of his temperament."

The duchess tsked. "I would never have allowed my precious girls to live there if Mr. Sterling had not proven himself to be even-tempered. Granted, he is rough around the edges, but I had my solicitor look into his background quite thoroughly, and there was not a single account of Mr. Sterling fighting another man unless it was for money. Therefore, I say to let him laugh and think this is a game. But you, my dear, will be the one laughing in the end."

"I wish I was as certain. Thus far, my efforts have not been grand—only a small number of handbills made it inside his establishment."

"What a delight!" the duchess cheered.

"Unfortunately, I have since learned that all the handbills were turned into tinder for the fire." Mrs. Teasdale had been just as disappointed as Ainsley and her sisters, too.

Clearly, she would have to think of something not so easily extinguished, or so easily mocked by Reed Sterling.

. . . you're going to have to do a far sight better than handbills.

Frowning, she could almost hear his condescending drawl. What did the man expect, after all? That she would wallpaper his . . . establishment with . . . advertisements . . .

A rush of tingles skittered through her and she asked, "Would Your Grace happen to have that collection of *La Belle Assemblée* magazines?"

"Of course." Rising from the chair, the duchess bustled to the other side of the room and withdrew a stack from the drawer of a polished Pembroke table. "Are you planning to educate Mr. Sterling's patrons on more wholesome pursuits? Remind them of their obligations? I'm sure there is an article on deportment as well, for there always is. Ah, yes, here it is."

Ainsley's excited gaze skimmed over at least a dozen issues. This could work. And honestly, there was too much at stake for her to stand around like a ninny, waiting for him to fire the next shot.

"I'm certain Your Grace is familiar with the epidemic of bills and placards pasted over every shopfront and window?"

The duchess clucked her tongue in disgust. "Simply dreadful. One cannot shop anywhere without being bombarded with advertisements."

"And wouldn't it be terrible if the windows of Sterling's resembled a ladies' shop, with pastel prints and pages on the importance of ruffled hems? I should think that the owner could not so easily dispense of those."

The duchess grinned and clasped her hands to her bosom. "What a splendidly devious mind you have, my dear."

❧

THE FOLLOWING morning, Ainsley stood in the shadows of the foyer, peering through the sidelights as she waited for Mr. Sterling's man-at-the-door to leave in his hackney coach. She'd spoken with the towering Mr. Finch on several occasions when she'd gone there to complain to his employer. He'd always met these requests with more amused curiosity than ill-tempered sternness. Even so, she did not want to risk a confrontation this morning, for that would ruin her plan.

In fact, she did not want anyone inside Sterling's to be aware of her maneuver for at least several hours. By then, surely, all of London would have come to gawk at the windows of her nemesis.

When the carriage trundled out of sight in the patchy fog that shrouded the street, she lifted the hood of her cloak. Then—armed with a stack of papers, a small pail of wheat paste, a wooden-handled brush, and a broad grin—Ainsley Bourne started a war.

Chapter 8

"Now there would be pleasure in her returning—
Every thing would be a pleasure."

JANE AUSTEN, *Emma*

A loud rap sounded on the bedchamber door. Reed growled in warning and squeezed his eyes shut tighter.

Thanks to his encounter with Ainsley Bourne, and his newfound knowledge that the windows across from his chamber were hers, he'd been hard-pressed to find sleep this week.

But that didn't mean he was done trying.

"Sterling." The knocking continued. "There's a matter—"

"*Sod off.*" Rolling to his side, he sealed the pillow over his head.

He couldn't stop thinking about how soft she was. Silky as rainwater rushing over his fingertips. Or perhaps more like that bit of downy feather he'd taken from her hair, or even scented powder, so fine it might have dissolved into nothing.

He wanted to touch Miss Prim and Proper all over. Hear the whisper-soft sound of her gasp as he explored underneath all those layers, unwrapping her slowly, seeking all the right places, feeling her arch against his hand . . .

The incessant knocking came again, banging hard enough to rattle a picture on the wall, interrupting a near-perfect—albeit foolhardy—fantasy. He threw the pillow off his head and sat up, hard as an obelisk, and glared at the door.

"Unless Sterling's is on fire, I suggest you leave immediately and let . . . me . . . sleep."

A creak of hesitation shifted on the floorboards in the corridor. "It isn't on fire but just as bad as all that."

Reed expelled an exhausted breath through his teeth, scrubbing a hand over his face. He recognized the low voice as Raven's, who wasn't one to bother him unless the matter was dire. "What is it, then?"

"Vandals, by the look of it. They've pasted pages all over the windows."

"Preposterous. There isn't a man in London who'd dare." Yet the instant he made the declaration, he felt a prickling at the back of his neck. "Pages of *what* precisely?"

"I dunno. I just got back from spending the night with a couple of the girls at Miss Molly's and found a crowd gathered, so thick I had to come in through the back."

Naked, Reed stalked stiffly over to the window and yanked open midnight-blue curtains to see the crowd below. Even carriages stopped to have a gawk. His suspicions grew only stronger when he glanced across the street to a certain matrimonial agency.

Down a few floors, the front door crept open and a face peered out for a second. A pleased-as-punch grin lit up a familiar countenance before the door closed.

His eyes narrowed. *Why, Miss Ainsley Bourne, just what have you done this time?*

If AINSLEY had known how much fun it would be to wage war on her neighbor, she might have done so when she'd first arrived.

Grinning, she felt like skipping back to her office. But she refrained, choosing instead to swish her skirts from side to side, like a bell peeling a celebration chorus.

So Mrs. Darden didn't think she knew how to have a bit

of fun, hmm? Well this was far more enjoyable than any fusty dinner party or parlor game.

After climbing the stairs to her office, Ainsley sat down in the rose-tufted chair behind her desk and hummed a happy little tune. She didn't even care that she was essentially ruining the melody through her off-key efforts.

All that mattered was how she had bested Reed Sterling.

Scores of servants and laborers traveled this road on the way to the market or the shopfronts where they worked. And from the look of things, every one of them was gawking at the windows of Sterling's.

The owner likely wouldn't even be aware of it for hours to come. After all, the man had to sleep at some point, did he not? And by the time he learned of her subterfuge, word would have already spread throughout London that the former prizefighter had gone a bit soft. Sterling's certainly would not be considered a club for any hardened sinners, wastrels, and rakes. No, indeed. And the exclusive invitations he sent to the *ton*'s elite would no longer be held in high regard.

Smiling to herself, she opened a ledger, ready to double-check the accounting figures. Before she uncapped the ink, however, she heard the front door open and close succinctly.

Her first thought, of course, was of Reed Sterling and a frisson of wariness mixed with her excitement. Would he come in without knocking?

She glanced at the clock and instantly decided against it.

It was far too early for a nocturnal creature to be about. And it would be odd if it were either Jacinda or Briar, for they never arrived an hour before they opened for business. Since they married, they were more apt to run an hour late, instead. Though it could be Mrs. Teasdale. She was always here early—though usually by way of the kitchen door—to have a chat with Mrs. Darden and discover what scones they'd be having on any given day.

Yet, the more Ainsley listened, she decided that the purposeful footfalls climbing the stairs were not at all like Mrs. Teasdale's. They sounded heavy, like a man's.

"Uncle, is that you so soon? I thought you'd just left for your walk."

When there was no response, that frisson shot through again. Was Reed Sterling coming to confront her already? This was not part of the plan. She'd wanted her sisters and uncle around her for this. It was safer that way.

Not because she was afraid that he would be overly cross with her. No indeed, for she believed he was a man who appreciated a worthy opponent. The reason she wished for her family to be near was because, with an audience, he was less likely to have any reason to touch her. Or to remark on the softness of her skin in that low drawl that made her tingle all over.

Her pulse quickened at the memory, her breath stuttering. "Mr. Sterling?"

He did not answer. But she supposed he was just the sort of unmannerly person to simply stride directly into her office. So she stood and smoothed down her skirts.

She would meet him in the hall, she decided. After all, there was no reason to be in a confined space where the appealing scent of his shaving soap would permeate her every breath. And besides, she would rather have the advantage of being only half a head shorter, instead of allowing him to tower over while she was seated at her desk.

"Mr. Sterling, if you are here to discuss—"

Ainsley's throat closed before she could utter the last words. It wasn't Reed Sterling standing outside her office.

It was the monster from her nightmares. Her former betrothed.

Chapter 9

"—and now it had happened to the very person,
and at the very hour, when the other very person
was chancing to pass by to rescue her!"

JANE AUSTEN, *Emma*

"Are you not glad to see me, Ains?" Nigel Mitchum smiled, his tone all politeness and affability.

For a moment, Ainsley could only stare in disbelief. Her stomach roiled as flashes of their last encounter flooded her mind—the bitter argument, his bruising grip and sudden weight upon her, his forearm pressing against her throat, the cruel hand wrenching up her skirts . . .

And like then, she was essentially alone. Mrs. Darden was in the kitchen and Ginny was at the market.

Trapped in a strange hinterland between that encounter and this one, she could only stammer a response. "Wh-what are you doing here, Mr. Mitchum?"

"Come now, I will always be *Nigel* to you."

She hated the blatant familiarity of his tone, his practiced charm. Only she knew how changeable he was. How quickly the vilest and cruelest words could spew forth without much alteration in his countenance.

It was painful to admit how pleased she'd once been to be on the arm of such a handsome man with his tall, athletic frame and trim nut-brown hair. But that pleasure faded.

She'd come to dread the crunch of his carriage wheels in the drive of her uncle's house in Hampshire, the sharp sound of his knock, and the hard, methodic steps he would take from the foyer to the parlor.

And now he was here in London.

When she didn't respond, he tutted. "Living in a fancy house in London, and you're suddenly too important to receive a call from me, is that it?"

"Of course not."

Instantly, she despised herself for placating him as she had always done. But the edge to his tenor and the coldness in his gaze sent an icy chill down her spine. She even caught herself backing up a step.

"Then, what is it? Are you still angry that I broke our betrothal to marry someone else?"

That wasn't what had happened at all. Then again, he'd usually found a way to twist the facts of things to shed a far more complimentary light on himself.

When she'd first noticed this flaw in his character, she'd tried to understand it. She'd believed that he'd had to tell these white lies in order to boost his own ego because he was raised by such critical and demanding parents. Foolishly, for a time, she'd wanted to rescue him from that lack of affection in his parents' house by showering him with compliments. But the kindness was not reciprocated. In fact, the more of it she gave, the more he'd required.

By the end, she could not even so much as have a displeased tone without him flying into a rage.

"I did hear of your marriage," she said, knowing that it wasn't wise to keep him waiting for a response.

The same week she'd moved to London, she'd learned that Nigel had eloped with the seventeen-year-old daughter of a cleric in the neighboring village. The scandal it caused eclipsed the sudden end to their lengthy betrothal. That was likely what he'd intended so no one would look too closely at the reason. Not because he'd thought he was in the wrong, but because he could never admit to failure.

For the first few months of his marriage, Ainsley had always kept the girl in her prayers, until finally deciding to put Nigel and everything associated with him out of her mind for good.

Standing mere paces away, he tilted his head in scrutiny as if searching for a shred of jealousy to satisfy his ego. Then his smile turned into a self-congratulatory smirk, clearly mistaking pity for envy.

"Did it bother you to know that you were so easily replaced?" He did not wait for her answer but continued on, forever in the mood to hear the sound of his own voice. "Grace was so young and pretty, so adoring and obedient—all the things a man wants. All the things a man deserves."

Ainsley swallowed down the bile rising to the back of her throat. *"Was?"*

"Died in childbirth, both her and the girl, nigh on a year now."

"My sympathies," she rasped, sorry for the end of such a short life, and sad for whatever pain the girl had suffered.

He nodded, adopting a solemn frown. Yet he was quick to recover, mouth curling upward as he dusted his hands together.

"At least I'm out of that wearying obligation of mourning. Now that I'm a man of the world once more, I thought I'd move to London and see what all the *fuss* was about." His voice gained a sharper edge. He slowed his speech as well, enunciating every word, gradually growing louder as if he were standing on a pulpit. "After all, you seem to like it so much that you never thought to return to Hampshire. The tenants living on Viscount Eggleston's estate tell me that your uncle has no intention of returning."

"You . . . you went back to the house?"

"Of course. I felt it was only right to renew my addresses to you once I was free to do so. As I recall, you were quite keen to be Mrs. Mitchum once upon a time." His gaze skimmed over her dress with sickening familiarity. "Quite keen, indeed."

Ainsley was going to be ill. Had he truly convinced himself of entirely different events between them?

She took a step back only to encounter the doorframe of her office. "I'm afraid that won't be possible."

He snickered as if she'd made a jest. "I don't see a ring upon your finger, Ains. And there haven't been any banns read for you either. Not that I've heard . . . well, not since they read my name along with yours. I still have the page with our announcement. The way I see it, we're still betrothed in the eyes of the church."

But she was sure that Uncle Ernest had taken care of all that before they'd left for London.

"I—I have an understanding with someone. A man. He—he'll be here any moment," she stammered in a rush of self-preservation.

Nigel sobered—altered—with alarming speed. It was clearly the wrong thing to say.

His mouth flattened to a straight line as he took a hard step toward her. "And did you know this *man* in Hampshire? Is *he* the reason you left me without a word and looking like a fool?"

"No, I met him when I came to London." She hardly knew what she was saying. Acute panic rushed through her in shrill, icy waves that buzzed in her ears. Her limbs froze in place, heavy and useless like they'd been once before.

She thought she'd left this cowardly version of herself in Hampshire. Where was her stronger self now?

"Well? Who is he?"

Only one name rushed to the forefront of her mind. Only one name held the power and strength she was lacking in this moment but wished she possessed.

"Reed Sterling."

Nigel eyed her skeptically. "Reed Sterling, the prize-fighter?"

"Mmm-hmm," she murmured with a tight nod. "Reed Sterling, indeed. But, of course, he's far more than a mere prizefighter to me."

She hoped she sounded convincing. Even more than that, she hoped her neighbor would never know that she'd used his name to save herself.

Ainsley should have known better.

In the very next instant, as if she'd spoken his name into a genie's lamp, Reed Sterling slowly appeared. It wasn't possible, but there he was, ascending the staircase, step by step, at the end of the hall. She blinked, dumfounded, breathless, and wondering if he was an apparition conjured by desperation.

Yet the instant his gaze fixed on her, she knew he was real. She felt it in the quick thrumming of her pulse and in the way her skin grew taut, shoring up her frame.

"Did I hear mention of my name, highness?" He flashed a knowing grin.

Dear heavens, he'd heard her. At once, her cheeks grew hot. She'd breeched a level of acquaintanceship, hitherto un-breeched, by using his given name and intimating that they were . . . well . . . *drat.*

What was she going to do now?

She swallowed, wondering if it was actually possible to die of embarrassment. "You did, indeed."

Out of the corner of her eye, she saw Nigel glance over his shoulder, not once but twice. He straightened, shoulders back, chin jutting as if to make himself appear taller and broader. But no amount of posturing could ever make him as virile as Reed Sterling.

She was sure very few men were.

Her neighbor's lips cocked in a familiar smirk as he approached. But his gaze was sharp, too, alert in a way that left no doubt he was assessing every nuance of the situation—Nigel's close proximity, her fisted hands and locked arms.

Reed stopped at her side, close enough for her to feel the heat rise from his body. Strange as it was, his presence comforted her.

"Then it's rather serendipitous that I should arrive at precisely this instant to make the acquaintance of . . ."

"Mr. Mitchum," she supplied.

The gentlemen exchanged cursory nods, each sizing up the other.

Again, Nigel puffed out his chest. "You know, I once employed a sportsman who studied pugilism under the venerable Gentleman Jackson."

Reed said nothing to this, but glanced at Ainsley. In the strained silence that followed, she knew she was expected to say more. But the last thing she wanted was for Nigel to know that the imposing figure beside her wasn't her intended.

"Mr. Mitchum hails from Hampshire and dropped by to pay a call on an old . . . acquaintance." Nerves constricted her throat as she kept her tone achingly, ingratiatingly polite. "But with all of London beckoning I should hate to delay his explorations."

"'Old acquaintance,'" Nigel chided with a laugh, his mouth twisting into his usual self-aggrandizing grin. "Ains, you are being modest for the sake of the stranger in our midst. There is no reason to keep the fact of our betrothal a secret."

She could never depend on Nigel to leave when he was asked. "*Former* betrothal."

He turned to Reed, and like a trained actor on the stage, Nigel applied his friendly *everyman* eyeroll and lifted his shoulders in an offhand shrug. "She always has the tendency to be overly dramatic. So full of herself, making up stories . . . and stringing other men along. Though it is good that I am here to make you aware of the situation before your small *understanding* with my Ains took an unfortunate turn."

She straightened, her bones no longer filled with dread but with anger. How dare he make her seem like an empty-headed nitwit! And did he actually believe that he could force her into an agreement simply because there was an audience present?

Reed turned the full force of his attention on her and she feared he would mock her. Yet when she looked into those indigo eyes, she was surprised to find understanding.

She should have known. He'd always had this innate ability to read her, whether she liked it or not.

And now, he lifted his brows in an unspoken question as though he was willing to assist her, but only if she agreed.

Forgetting for the moment that everything with Reed Sterling came at a price, she felt her head wobble in something of a nod, giving him permission.

As if that was all he needed, Reed turned to Nigel and began with a swift verbal uppercut. "If Miss Bourne was interested in your attentions, wouldn't she have remained in Hampshire?"

Nigel's gaze flashed with instant fury. "I don't think you have any—"

"And as for our *small understanding*, as you put it, I'm afraid you're mistaken. It's rather large," Reed cut in with another jab. "In fact, I asked her to marry me."

All the air rushed out of her lungs at once. She felt like a flattened bellows. Dimly, she wondered if it was this difficult for his boxing opponents to keep up with him in the ring.

And yet, she had asked for his assistance . . .

Still, she barely managed to croak out a response. "And I said *yes*."

"Without any hesitation whatsoever." Reed glanced down at her and, this time, with a roguish grin tucked into one corner of his mouth. Then his hand—his *slow hand*, as he'd put it the other night—was terribly quick to settle into the small of her back and draw her against his side in a demonstration of possession.

She should've been thoroughly disgusted by such a primitive display. After all, how dare he insinuate that he had laid claim to her!

Yet instead of revulsion or ire, a disconcerting thrill shot through her. Every pulse inside her body jolted at once, thrumming to life in a rush of tingles. More confusing was the peculiar sense of comfort she gained from this highly improper near embrace. She even settled her hand lightly over his lapel, trying—but failing miserably—not to notice how solid he felt. It was like being pressed against a wall of warm contoured granite.

"Of course, you asked my uncle's permission first," she added without looking at Nigel, but kept her gaze locked securely on Reed's. "Remember, *dearest*?"

She nearly cringed at the awkwardness of the endearment.

"How could I forget?" he asked, amusement glinting in his eyes. "Eggleston is drawing up the contracts today. As a matter of fact, I dropped by to talk to you about where we'll live. I imagine you'll want a fine house like this one with lots of servants to butter your crumpets."

She gave his chest another pat, a little harder this time. He was enjoying this a bit too much. Therefore she decided to give him a taste of his own medicine. "You know very well that I could be content in a tiny cottage without any servants. As long as we have each other, that is all that matters."

His breath stalled for an instant, and he went completely still. Well, all except for the hard thumps rising beneath her hand. Then he blinked, and something altered in his expression but she couldn't quite put her finger on it.

"We should talk about this more in private," he murmured. Then he slanted a glance to Nigel in a way that made it patently clear that he was unwelcome. "Though of course, I don't mean to rush you out the door, Mr. . . . *Winkle*, was it?"

"Mitchum," Nigel corrected through clenched teeth, reddish-purple color rising above his cravat. He speared Ainsley with a dark look that sent her stomach roiling in panic. "I'll come back to finish our discussion at a more convenient time."

Reed shook his head, covering the hand that she'd thoughtlessly curled over the lapel of his coat. "That won't be necessary. You've said all you needed to say this time around. But if there's anything else, you can tell me on our way to the door. Or, better yet, come over to Sterling's across the street. Then you and I can have a . . . chat."

Before Reed stepped apart from her, his fingers brushed lightly over hers. And though she would never admit it aloud—not even in the privacy of her own rooms—she had the disturbing desire to take hold of his hand and keep him at her side.

Then he remedied that desire in short order when he turned his head and winked at her. "Try not to miss me too much while I'm away, highness."

REED STARED at the figure storming off down the pavement, filled with a deep dislike for Mr. Mitchum. He'd met too many of his kind before, all charm and arrogance on the outside with a twisted core of entitlement and wrath on the inside.

After his childhood experiences with Lord Bray, Reed had learned to spot the signs long ago—the self-satisfied grin, the need to condescend to others, the unmistakable flash of fury when challenged, and the constant flow of horse shite spewing from his lips.

Had Mitchum actually tried to proclaim that the stern, reserved Ainsley Bourne tended to be dramatic? That was as ridiculous as saying Finch tended to wear frilly dresses and prance around town in a bonnet.

"Ignorant prig," Reed muttered and closed the door. He slid the bolt for good measure.

If he'd learned anything about Mitchum's type, he knew he'd come back around, needing to settle the score. Though men like him usually didn't want a fair fight. No, they liked to pick on those who were smaller and defenseless.

At the thought, tension knotted the muscles in Reed's neck and shoulders as he looked up the marble stairs toward Ainsley's office.

He didn't like that she'd been alone this morning, unguarded. Where were her servants? Her butler standing sentinel at the door?

Looking around at the rich surroundings, he saw no one move from room to room with a feather duster. And the sounds of footsteps—of people going about their chores—were absent, too. Only the sweet aroma of freshly baked pastries let him know that someone was in the kitchen, and likely it was that cantankerous cook, Mrs. Darden.

But where were the others?

Reed frowned. Recalling the instant he'd seen the unmistakable pallor of fear in Ainsley's face, he'd wanted to murder Mitchum on the spot. And since Reed prided himself on never losing his temper, that was an unexpected awareness.

That impulse had grown stronger when she'd sought his

reassurance, fixing her gaze on his as if her life depended on it. *Him* of all people. The very enemy she was attempting to run out of business.

That frailty had been his undoing. He'd been possessed by a reckless desire to hold her, to comfort her, and to make her feel strong again. And from their innumerable encounters, he'd learned that the surest way of catching a glimpse of Ainsley's inner warrior was through their usual banter.

So he'd overstepped the boundaries of their *mutual loathing*—as she liked to call it—and declared that they were getting married.

He was surprised the words had come out so easily. After all, claiming an intimate association with wholesome Miss Matchmaker could hardly bode well for his business.

In all honestly, he'd expected her to put up a fuss and correct him. Or in the very least, remove his hand from her lower back. It was only when she'd relaxed against him and had gone along with his story that something primal had torn through him.

He'd wanted to grip Mitchum by his scrawny neck for causing her even a moment of fear. The reason didn't matter. She could have told him that her former betrothed had done nothing but kill a spider in front of her and Reed still would have enjoyed ripping the limbs off Mitchum's body, one by one.

Yet he knew her fear stemmed from something greater . . . Something that might have given her cause to flinch reflexively when she saw a man raise his hand.

You know, I once employed a sportsman who studied pugilism under the venerable Gentleman Jackson.

Recalling what Mitchum had said, Reed growled low in his throat. *Damn.* No wonder Ainsley had loathed him from the very beginning.

Well, that was going to have to change. With Mitchum sniffing around, Reed wasn't about to let Ainsley be caught alone again. And since her uncle obviously did not employ reliable servants to stand their posts, someone would have to step in—or *overstep*—and hire someone.

Now Reed just needed to convince her to let him handle everything.

A wry grin tugged at his mouth as he mounted the stairs. This ought to be interesting.

Chapter 10

"It appears to me the most desirable arrangement
in the world."

JANE AUSTEN, *Emma*

Ainsley hoped that Reed Sterling would conveniently leave
the agency when he escorted Nigel out. She didn't want to
answer any questions, or to be confronted about the posters
she'd pasted either. That would have to wait until she was
more herself.

Unfortunately, the genie's lamp that had granted her
previous wish did not hear her this time.

Mr. Sterling returned to her office. His intense gaze settled on her, his features hard and immovable as granite. It
was the look he always wore whenever he claimed to know
something about her. Her spine stiffened.

"Just so you know, I did not ask you to come to my rescue."

"Didn't you?" He crossed his arms over his broad chest
and arched a single smug brow.

Leaving her desk, she stalked toward him, ready to
send him on his way. "See here. I know how to take care
of myself without any interference from the likes of you."

"Is that why you told your *old acquaintance* that we have
an understanding?"

"Well . . ." She stopped near the edge of the rug to smooth
her skirts, trying to come up with a good answer, or at least
one that made sense. But she couldn't.

"Using the name of the gaming hell owner you loathe was a rather curious choice. After all, you might have picked any one of your highborn clients or a family acquaintance instead."

If only she could have thought of someone else. Anyone at all. But his had been the only name in her mind, as if every other man had been erased.

She swallowed down a rise of discomfiture. "That would have been unethical."

"And the lowborn bloke across the way could hardly be bound by ethics," he said evenly.

"You're making too much of an insignificant slip of the tongue."

"Have my name on your tongue often, do you?"

Honestly, the man could turn every conversation into something untoward. "Perhaps I did take a *miniscule* liberty by using your name, but it was the most convenient way out of my predicament. It shouldn't matter to you one way or the other. It changes nothing."

"Oh, it changes a good deal of things, you just don't know it yet." He eyed her shrewdly, seeming to size her up. "Both of my professions have required that I see a bit more than people think they're showing. I can spot a left hook before an opponent lifts his arm, and a Captain Sharp the instant he walks through the door. I can see who's betting their last farthing and has nothing to lose but their self-respect. In other words, highness, I can spot trouble when it's brewing."

"An impressive list of skills, to be sure," she said blandly, but shifted from one foot to the other, unsettled. "Though I can see no reason whatsoever why you should feel the need to tell me this."

"Because you'll need to resign yourself to seeing me more often. Not just out on the pavement either. *And* I'm going to find you a reliable man-at-the-door."

There was that hard-set look again. He believed he knew

something she didn't. Or something that she wasn't prepared to accept—like the possibility that Nigel might return.

Her heart hammered against the wall of her ribs, panic setting in. She would much rather believe that Nigel would stay away, especially now that he was aware of her association with Reed Sterling. If she couldn't convince herself, then how would she sleep at night?

"No, you most certainly will not," she said, adopting a false show of bravado as she marched forward. "As I said, I will see to this matter on my own. Now, if you would shake hands with me to accept my gratitude for your assistance, we shall put this entire affair behind us, and you will be on your way."

Ainsley didn't know what compelled her to offer her hand. Shooing him out the door and closing it firmly behind him was what she'd intended. Yet the wrong words tumbled from her lips. Then her body followed the command. And by the time she thought about withdrawing, it was already too late.

Reed Sterling unfolded his arms and reached out, closing his hand over hers.

At the first touch, a small tremor escaped through her fingertips, disappearing into his secure grip. Her breath caught. Tantalizing warmth engulfed her, stirring a current of vibrations beneath her skin.

Was it possible to develop a craving for someone's touch? Strangely, that's how it felt—as if she'd had this inexplicable emptiness gnawing at her, and it could only be satisfied in one way.

Wordless, she looked to him for an answer to this puzzle but noticed that his attention was fixed on their shared grasp, on the tanned blunt fingertips that drifted over her pale skin. Once again, she marveled at how such a large labor-roughened hand could be so gentle, yet exude such power beneath the surface.

"I almost convinced myself that I'd imagined how soft you are."

His words were so quiet, so secret and low, she wondered if he meant for her to hear them at all.

With infinite care, he turned her hand over, exposing the lines of her palm. Then the pad of his thumb stroked the sensitive flesh. Her fingers curled reflexively, tingles burrowing deep. It tickled a little, too. But she didn't stop him from tracing a path to the underside of her wrist, to the pulse fluttering beneath the ivory skin.

Her stomach shifted, clenching sweetly as he circled the tender throb. His touch was maddeningly light, methodical and mesmerizing. And she held her breath, unable to look away.

Inexplicably, her pulse slowed to match his lazy sweeps. Her quick beats turned sluggish and heavy, radiating to a place in her middle, thudding low and liquid. She'd never felt anything like it.

A whisper of warning advised her to slip free. And she would, most assuredly. But first, a need for understanding demanded her to indulge for just one more minute.

Experimentally, she arched her wrist—a subtle shift against his callused flesh. He inhaled raggedly, the stuttered sound surprisingly vulnerable. In that moment, he did not seem like a rogue bent on scandalizing her, but simply a man who was as shaken by the contact of their joined hands as she was. And just when she was anticipating another loop, circling around the tender pulse, he brushed his thumb softly over the center swell instead.

This time, Ainsley gasped. Unexpected pleasure surged through her, lush and heated. And when he did it again, she pressed her knees together, flooded with foreign sensations. The word *desire* whispered in her mind but she refused to acknowledge it. She knew, without a shadow of a doubt, that she didn't possess a passionate nature.

"I—I think that should settle matters sufficiently," she stammered, carefully avoiding his gaze.

She tried to slip free ... well ... mostly. Her smallish tug was a feeble effort that didn't result in her freedom. Her lack of conviction made it far too easy for him to slide their hands together—a twining of fingers, the nudge and stretch of the webbing in between, the intimate press of palm to palm.

Then suddenly he was closer, standing in her breathable space. Only she couldn't breathe at all. And worse, she was helpless against the enticing pull of warm pleasure that kept her hand in his.

"The way I see it," he drawled, the deep sound tunneling deliciously through her, "using my name was like playing on house credit, and a handshake just isn't enough to satisfy the debt."

"It isn't?"

She lifted her face only to find his heated gaze on her lips. Her pulse accelerated again like a clock wound too tightly. A frantic tension coiled in her midriff. She took a step back, but—*drat it all*—she realized that she was still holding his hand, practically tugging him along.

"If you're thinking a ... a kiss would settle things, then I'm afraid you're wrong. You won't find any satisfaction from my lips."

"Wouldn't be too sure about that."

Reed crowded her slowly. One boot moved forward, then the other, corralling her. He seemed to be allowing her to get used to him. But that was an impossibility. She could never adjust to the way her pulse reacted when he was near. And he was close enough now that she caught the clean, spiced fragrance of his shaving soap. The delectable, intoxicating scent filled every breath. She might very well suffocate.

And he shouldn't look at her that way either. It made her lips feel plump and heavy, far too full to hide between the press of her teeth.

"It's true. I'm not a person who is . . . inclined toward such activities." She tried to sound forbidding, but her voice came out in a rasp, her throat dry.

"But not everyone has a mouth like yours—a mouth made for kissing."

His husky murmur excited that low throbbing pulse. And when he leaned in and grazed his warm lips across her cheek, a strangled sound rose in her throat from the startling pleasure of it.

"It's far too wide," she whispered in a rush.

He tucked a lock of hair behind her ear and lingered, his fingers slipping through the wispy tendrils at her nape to fit perfectly against her skull. Then his mouth skimmed across her other cheek. "You're wrong about that."

"There's also that plump part in the center of my upper lip that gets in the way."

"This part here?" His lips swept lightly over hers and drew her gasp into his mouth.

She nodded, still unwilling to accept the fact that Reed Sterling's mouth was on hers, the heat of his breath on her tongue. "I've been told it makes the experience quite unpleasant."

It was a mortifying admission, but these were desperate circumstances. She didn't think she'd be able to survive the humiliation if two men professed that kissing her was awkward and unpalatable. Especially not this man.

"Before you trust anyone's opinion"—he nipped the tender reprimand against her lips—"consider the source."

"I hardly need your advice," Ainsley scolded him in return, every word pushing her flesh against his. Almost as if . . . as if *she* had just kissed *him*.

But this wasn't kissing, she assured herself. This was merely a new form of arguing.

Anticipating his next contradiction, she angled her head for closer contact and Reed growled in response.

The low, primal sound sent an unexpected thrill rushing through her.

"It would be a waste of breath to tell you anything," he said, fitting his other hand over the curve of her cheek to cradle her face. "Even if I wanted to say that your lips are soft and plump and more luscious than wine-poached pears, I wouldn't."

Then he tilted her head back to cement his argument. Opening her mouth with his own, he nibbled gently into her flesh, tasting the seam of her lips without hurry. The slow, thorough exploration caused her eyes to drift closed.

Her senses centered on the firm, enticing pressure of his mouth, the delicious rasp of his tongue. A wanton mewl tore from her throat, hungry and needy and urgent.

The unguarded sound brought her to an uncomfortable admission . . .

She might be kissing the enemy.

And she would take this shamefully wondrous moment to her grave. No one could ever find out. Right now, she just wanted a sip or two more. A last lingering taste of Reed Sterling.

Rising up on her toes, she gripped his lapels, keeping him close. Reed took a breath. Then he deepened the kiss, nudging into the dewy heat of her mouth. And she was shocked by her own eager welcome of his flesh, tangling her own with his.

She never knew kissing could feel like this. So basic. So raw. There was no anxiety brimming in her stomach, but only a tightly coiled heat that she was quickly learning to like.

With Nigel she'd felt as if she were enduring a chore, knowing that he would list his disappointments in her poor performance shortly thereafter. Yet, somehow, Reed made her feel as if kissing her was as essential to him as breathing or eating . . . and that he intended to feast on her lips for hours, days, until there was nothing left of her.

Ainsley feared she might enjoy being consumed by him. A bit too much. In fact, she was feeling like a cannibal herself, drawing the salty essence of his tongue into her mouth like a woman half-starved. She wondered if she would ever get her fill of him.

But there wasn't time to find out, she thought absently. They didn't have hours, or even minutes. They were standing in her office and apt to be discovered at any moment.

Unwilling to let her lapse be witnessed by anyone else, she placed her hands over his, preparing to extract herself.

Regrettably, she became distracted and fascinated by the texture of his skin. The hard knobs of his knuckles. The crisp hairs near his wrist. She had the reckless desire to know what he felt like everywhere, underneath his clothes, her hands coasting over his bare flesh . . .

That thought shocked her back on her heels. What in heaven's name made her think of doing that?

Breaking the kiss, she panted for breath. "We—I mean, *you*—shouldn't have done that."

Apparently unwilling to let her get too far, he gently wrapped her in his embrace, her folded arms the only barrier between them. He drew her close, his hand drifting up and down her back as if she were a wild creature that needed to be soothed. "I disagree. *We* should conduct all our arguments this way."

A sense of otherworldly euphoria kept her from slipping free. She felt drowsy, as if she'd been fed a sleeping draught, lulled by the hard thump of his heart beneath her palms. She blinked at the Pomona green walls around her in bewilderment. Had she actually kissed Reed Sterling?

Yes, her lips answered, full and tender skinned as overripe plums. Her mind boggled at this staggering awareness.

She never abandoned all self-restraint. Indulgence was not in her nature.

Confused, she could think only about how her actions had been wrong in countless ways. Lines had been crossed. Rules had been broken.

"Those rules no longer apply to us," Reed said, his lips pressing warmly to her temple.

She hadn't realized she'd spoken aloud. Or even that, somehow, her fingertips had found the open collar of his shirt, weaving into the dark, fascinatingly springy hairs. She really ought to stop doing that. And she would, of course. In the next minute or so . . .

His cheekbones were tinged with the burnished flush of exertion. She'd seen him this way many times before, whenever she'd interrupted his boxing exercise to reprimand him. But from this point forward, she would not be able to see this high color without remembering their kiss.

Ainsley's gaze drifted to his lips. When his tongue licked a lingering trace of dampness at the corner, her breath caught. He was tasting her, she thought dazedly. And his hungry gaze locked on her mouth as if he intended to devour her in one lusty bite.

A rush of heady, insupportable delight flooded her. Giddy, she swayed against him, shamefully clinging like muslin to wool stockings.

What was happening to her?

Whatever it was, it was his fault! He'd done something to her by breeching a barrier that should have been left alone. And it was vital that things returned back to normal.

"Of course the rules apply," she said, her voice raspy and tight as the sensations of pleasure and panic warred within her, her breath coming in ragged gulps. "Even more so now. We need to put everything back the way it was. The way it should be between enemies."

"But we have an understanding," he teased, though his voice was almost too deep to be mocking. And yet, he had to be amused, laughing inwardly at the prim spinster who'd developed a taste for a scoundrel.

"You know very well that we do not."

His hand slid to the tension gathering in her nape, his fingertips working in wonderfully tantalizing circles. Oh, she wished he wouldn't do that.

And she wished he'd never stop.

"Then kissing you again would be . . ."

"Strictly forbidden," she admonished, trying to sound firm. To think rationally. And not let her eyes drift closed on a blissful sigh. "This never happened. Is that clear? We'll both go about our daily business—or nightly, in your case—and never think on this episode again."

His lips curled in a slow, wicked grin. "I'm afraid I can't do that, Miss Bourne. When it comes to kissing you, I hope it happens again and again. And again."

A heated shiver tumbled through her, curling her toes in her sensible half boots. "Well, it won't."

"Care to wager on that?"

No. No she wouldn't. Right then, she wasn't sure of herself at all. In fact, she very much wanted to kiss him again, and that thought mortified her. And worse, when she watched him lower his head with clear intent, she was already tilting her face up to his.

Then chaos erupted.

It all happened so fast, there wasn't even time to gasp, let alone utter a word of warning.

Mrs. Darden charged in, shrieking like a banshee, armed with their largest teapot. Then, all at once, the heavy porcelain came crashing down on Reed Sterling's head.

Chapter 11

"He walked off in more complete self-approbation than he left for her."

JANE AUSTEN, *Emma*

Part of Reed had always known that kissing Ainsley Bourne would be dangerous. Now he had proof. One minute he'd been wholly immersed in the sweet taste of her lips and the sumptuous give of her scolding mouth. And the next, he'd been waylaid flat.

He didn't know what hit him, but whatever—and whoever—it was took him down for the count. His eyes throbbed like they were going to burst out of their sockets, and the back of his head was warm and wet. Blood, likely.

He was never one to lose all sense of his surroundings, a lesson he'd learned as a lad. But as he lay on the floor, he didn't detect any threat.

Then again, it was a bit difficult to concentrate because someone was caressing him. Soothing fingertips sifted gently through his hair, and there was a warm cushion beneath his head. He drew in a contented breath, his nostrils catching the scent of rosehips and almond blossoms.

A strange sort of wonderment came over him. Was the *someone* Ainsley Bourne?

No. It wasn't possible—at least, not in reality—and yet, he could even hear the quiet reprimand in her voice. Though it was peculiar that it was not aimed at him.

"Mrs. Darden, for the last time, he was *not* attacking me."

"And what was I to think when I saw his hulking form in your office, hmm? How could I have known the pair of you were in the throes of—"

"No *throes*. There were no *throes* of any kind."

The caresser stilled the motions of her hands. And without her tender stroking, the throbbing pain at the back of his head returned tenfold and he fought back a groan.

"Did you hear that? I believe his breath fractured," said the slightly raspy voice that sounded suspiciously like Ainsley Bourne's. "Just look at his coloring. He may very well be a shade paler than before, and there will assuredly be a sizeable lump on the back of his head. Did you have to hit him so hard? I've never seen a man roll his eyes into the back of his head before, and I was barely able to slow his fall. What if he never awakens again?"

Even though his stuttered breath was unintentional, Reed enjoyed the results. Could it be that his prickly neighbor was truly smoothing her hands over his brow and along his temples?

It seemed so. And her delicate ministrations eased all his aches better than any tonic. Lying in her arms didn't do any harm to his ego either. In fact, he was already looking forward to reminding her of this moment in the weeks to come—every time she railed at him for not being properly attired or adhering to the strictures of society.

Apparently, Miss Bourne's skin wasn't the only thing soft about her.

"*Pooh*," the cantankerous cook muttered with disbelief. "It was just a tap to get his attention. I had brothers who suffered worse and they weren't half Mr. Sterling's size. He'll be fine in a trice. There's not a thing wrong with his coloring or his breathing. A fact you should know best considering how close you are to him. Not to mention how there wasn't a hair's breadth between the two of you before I—"

"Ruined our best teapot," Ainsley hastily interrupted. "How am I ever going to afford a replacement?"

Felled by a teapot? Reed nearly groaned again for the sake of manly pride.

The cook's outraged huff accompanied the clack and scrape of porcelain pieces sliding together. "Changing the subject doesn't alter the facts. Just what am I to tell Lord Eggleston, hmm? Dear me, I can only imagine how disappointed he will be to know that you've taken up with the likes of Mr. Sterling. If you're so interested in kissing all of a sudden, whyever don't you take up with a nice gentleman and marry him instead?"

"Honestly," Ainsley tsked. "Must you make it sound so sordid? I am not *taking up* with anyone, least of all a former prizefighter. It was a lapse in judgment. It will not happen again. And I would appreciate it if we kept this matter private. My uncle and sisters need never find out. The . . . event . . . you stumbled upon will never happen again."

"Mmm-hmm. You said that twice, you know. Looking at the way you're fussing over him, I have to wonder if you're trying to convince me or yourself."

The lap beneath Reed's head stiffened, fingers stalling midstroke.

"And what, pray tell, was I supposed to do after you tried to kill him? Leave him in a defenseless heap on the floor? You know I could not do that. I want to run him out of business, not murder him. At least, not today."

"*Stuff and nonsense.* It'd take more than a pot of tea to kill the likes of him."

At another mention of the teapot, Reed sighed inwardly in self-disgust. *Must they keep repeating it?* If his men ever learned of this, he'd never hear the end of it.

"For our sake, I hope so. I should not like to see either of us on trial for it would ruin the reputation of the agency. And reputation is nearly the only thing we have left. I have to hope that what I have observed of his even temperament remains to be true." She hesitated, a tense tremor rolling through her. "He doesn't seem to be the sort to call the guard or to hold grudges. Though one can never be too sure."

"No indeed. He's the sort to take matters—and willing neighbors, apparently—into his own hands."

"Oh, for heaven's sake," Ainsley muttered darkly, tapping her finger in an impatient tattoo against his temple. "I'm not going to discuss this any further. Now, if it wouldn't be *too* much trouble, do you imagine you could bring back a bit of toweling after you take the broken shards to the kitchen?"

"You expect me to leave you alone with him again?"

"He's hardly in a state to ravish me."

"Perhaps I'm more worried about what *you* might do to *him*," Mrs. Darden said with another huff. "Even so, I suppose *someone* has to see to the rug since Ginny is not yet back from market. Just try not to get too familiar while I'm gone."

The sound of her voice gradually faded beneath the fractious bustle of retreating footsteps and the faint clank and rattle of dishes.

Then, when all was silent, Ainsley Bourne expelled a slow breath. "I am seven and twenty, not some foolish young girl with her head in the clouds."

The stroking resumed. Reed felt a few gentle tugs as if she were twining the short wavy locks over her fingertips and he nearly found himself purring with contentment. He wouldn't mind staying right here for the remainder of the day.

Unfortunately, sooner or later, someone would discover that the front door was locked, thereby making the kiss Mrs. Darden witnessed all the more scandalous. And he still had an important matter to discuss with Ainsley as well.

"This isn't so bad, being petted by you. Remind me to get clobbered over the head every time I pay a call."

He didn't need to open his eyes to know that he'd startled her. He heard it in her gasp, felt it in the sudden absence of her touch.

"I thought you were near death." She slithered out from under him so quickly his skull hit the floor.

He groaned, grabbing the back of his head. Discovering he wasn't covered in blood but in tea, he groaned again, utterly emasculated.

As he sat up, the room spun in a blur of green walls and white casings. He took a moment to steady himself and focused on her smoothing her aubergine skirts in harsh, aggravated motions.

"And would you have mourned over my grave?"

"I would have dug the hole."

He'd wager she wished he was dead at the moment, rather than own up to the tenderness she'd exhibited. Yet even now she was anticipating his needs by pushing one of the pale upholstered chairs nearer to him with a faint little grunt of effort.

He felt the tug of a grin as he stood, bracing himself against the sturdy bronze frame. "Ah, Miss Bourne, I like sparring with you even more now."

"If you intend to say something rakish, then I won't hear it."

"Betrothed less than an hour and already you know me so well."

She stiffened. "You may leave now, Mr. Sterling. Again, I thank you for the use of your name, but my account with you is settled and closed."

"That remains to be seen."

"And what, pray tell, do you mean by that?" She hiked up her chin, hands on hips, brown eyes narrowed and frosty as barley in winter. "If this is about my clever attacks on your business and you think to find restitution from my lips, then banish the thought this instant. Simply because I allowed this one kiss to occur, doesn't mean it will happen again. In fact, I can say with certainty that it won't. I will never again endure any of your ruffian pawing."

Normally, he would have fired off an instant jab in retaliation. Exchange blow for blow. But he'd come to learn that her venom held more bite when she was putting up her guard.

He couldn't fault her for trying to gain a semblance of control after all the events that had transpired this morning—first with Mitchum's unwelcome call and then with Reed crossing another boundary between them.

In his own defense, however, Reed hadn't intended to kiss her. He'd merely wanted to rile her up to distract her from her worries. But then he'd touched her and his more honorable intentions faded.

What had made it worse—or better, he still wasn't sure—was witnessing the slow unfolding of desire in her face. The flush of her cheeks, the plump pout of her lips, and the inky darkness of her pupils spilling into soft brown all told him that she'd been curious, too.

And Reed was never one to pass up such a tempting opportunity.

His father had taught him to know when to hold back and when to strike.

Never rush, son. Wait for the perfect moment—your gut will tell you—but don't hesitate when you know it's right. If you do, you'll lose your chance.

While Dad might have been talking about angling at the time, Reed wouldn't have gotten this far in life if he hadn't taken every bit of advice.

"Ah, what tempting lips to guard such a waspish tongue." Reed's gaze dipped to her mouth.

She covered it with her delicate fingertips. "To you, I am *all* wasp."

"Then I am ever so fond of the way you sting, highness," he drawled, unable to resist a little more rakish goading.

"But as for *restitution*, I would not take payment from your lips. I much prefer your kisses free and unbound by restraint, as they were moments ago. And it's clear"—he continued over her sputters of denial—"that my retaliation against your first attack on Sterling's was just the right amount of enticement for you to hand them over."

She shook her head, adamant, color flaming in her cheeks. "You are wrong on *every* account."

"Is that all you have to say about my own clever counterstrike?"

"There is nothing to say because you did nothing. There was no trick—no piles of rubbish, no vulgar handbills delivered to my door, nor anything of the sort. I know, for I checked several times a day."

"And for days you expected something. You were constantly thinking about what I might do. Constantly thinking"—he grinned—"about me."

Her eyes widened, flashing with abrupt understanding. "You . . . you *devil*!"

"Not as easy to get rid of a thought as it is a handbill. Wouldn't you agree, highness?"

He should know, for he'd been thinking about her, too. Every day since their last encounter anticipation had gnawed at him, whetting his appetite.

This morning's interlude should have left him more than satisfied, and a bit smug, too. But he felt ravenous instead. Already hungry for the next taste, the next touch.

Forbidding as a goddess of war, she crossed her arms over her chest, the muffled tap of her foot on the rug keeping a solid, methodical beat. "I daresay you'll not recover so quickly from my attack today. Rumors do spread on fleeted foot, you know. Your sinful patrons will surely hear of the placards on your windows and think twice about crossing the threshold to your gambling establishment."

She was right. Her stunt this morning would cost him.

And it wouldn't be as simple to recover from as before. He'd likely have to plant more than a mere rumor of an old opponent trying to prod him back into the ring, but offer his patrons something more tangible.

"No need to worry about Sterling's. I'll always do whatever it takes to keep it in good standing."

At her frown in response, he lifted his shoulders in a controlled shrug. He didn't want to think about the tasks ahead of him when he had something more pressing on his mind.

"And what of your plans," he asked carefully, "regarding Mr. Mitchum?"

She paled considerably, the tapping of her foot falling still and silent. "The matter doesn't concern you."

"I've met his sort before and men like him don't seem to know how to leave well enough alone. He'll likely turn up again."

"Are you"—she swallowed—"trying to alarm me?"

Unmistakable vulnerability moved like a shadow over her milk-white features, snuffing out the glow from her eyes. When her wide-eyed gaze darted to the door, Reed's hands curled into fists. He wished he had Mitchum's neck in his grasp instead of the back of the chair.

What type of monster was Mitchum that the mention of his name could do this to the woman who so fearlessly confronted Reed on a near-daily basis?

Once again, he did not like the answers brewing inside his mind. He wanted to ask, but knew Ainsley wouldn't answer. She was too proud and too sharp-witted to do anything other than change the subject.

"I believe you prefer frank speaking. As do I." Even so, he gentled his tone before he continued. "Therefore, I will simply tell you that if you have need of more than just my name, you have but to ask."

Her attention swerved back to him. Speculation and mistrust knitted her brow as if she suspected he was a charlatan selling cure-alls from a portmanteau on the pavement. In all honesty, once the words were out, not even he was sure what he meant by them.

Was he offering to come and stand beside her if she beckoned, or . . . to beat Mitchum to a bloody pulp?

A warning shiver chased down his spine.

There was a reason Reed had only fought for prize money. Rage turned a man mindless, giving control over to an inner, bloodthirsty beast. Because of that, he'd vowed long ago never to fight a man in anger. And yet, in this moment, he wasn't entirely sure that he could keep that part of him chained if he ever stepped into the ring with the man who'd clearly done something to instill fear in Ainsley Bourne.

She broke the silence on an indrawn breath. "As I said, it won't be necessary. I'll inform my uncle of all that has transpired."

"All?"

Swift color returned to her cheeks and she carefully straightened her fichu. "The pertinent facts. I won't mention the betrothal pretense or . . . what followed. You needn't fear that my uncle will demand anything of you."

"You know," he began, "any woman might try to manipulate the situation to her own benefit. Perhaps as a next act of war."

There were a number of ways his arch nemesis could use this against him—by calling the guard, blackmail, threatening to tell the world that he was felled by a teapot . . .

"I should like to," she admitted. "But in all fairness, it would be grossly unsporting of me since I contributed to said events. At least, in part."

"Don't try to sell yourself short, highness. You *fully* contributed. I have your teeth marks on my flesh to prove it."

"That isn't possible. I never even—" She narrowed her eyes when he chuckled. "You are a cad and I detest you to your very core."

"Then all is as it should be."

She made no comment, but bent toward a stray fragment of white porcelain, hidden beneath a rosewood table. Reed spotted another piece of the infamous teapot. Moving the weighty chair back to its place, he picked up the shard.

Briefly, he recalled Ainsley mentioning to her cook that she could not afford a replacement. But surely it couldn't be true of someone who lived in such a fine house and burned beeswax tapers indiscriminately. Still he frowned. Where *had* all her servants been this morning?

Distractedly, he circled his thumb over the smooth-glazed surface. "I knew a man who came to my father's tavern on his off day each week—a butler for an old eccentric gentleman on a nearby estate. Mr. Adachi hailed from the Orient and he told me that, where he came from, men were hired to mend pottery like this with gold."

"That seems rather extravagant. Gold is too costly to waste on something broken. Not to mention, it would bring more attention to the imperfections."

"According to him, this practice—*kintsugi*, he called it—is a belief that history should not be something to hide, tossed in the bin, or even thought on with regret. There is beauty to be found in every journey, even the flawed ones."

Reed held out the fragment, but Ainsley did not take it. Instead, she stared at him with a quizzical expression, the inner workings of her mind held captive in her eyes. It was typical of her to keep her thoughts hidden. Not for the first time, he wished he could read every shift of her features as easily as a deck of cards or an opponent in the ring.

When she finally took the piece from him, she softly said, "I hope you're not too hurt."

"Nothing that can't be mended," he said, curling his fingers into his now empty hand. "And I'm sorry for your pot."

Her lips tilted upward at the corners, the light in her eyes returning. "'Tis a pity I do not have any spare gold on hand to mend it properly. I should like to see what design it would make. Though considering the hardness of your head, I do not imagine there is much left to salvage."

"And if it had hit *your* stubborn head, it would have disintegrated into dust."

At any other time, such jabs would have caused a heated argument. Instead, it brought smiles to both their faces as a strange sort of peace settled between them.

Then, silent for the moment—as if neither of them dared to break this new treaty—they left her office.

Walking along the corridor toward the stairs, he nearly forgot the reason he'd brought up the story about Mr. Adachi. "There's something we still need to discuss. You must employ a reliable butler and—"

He broke off at the sound of rapping on the door.

Stopping a third of the way down the stairs beside Ainsley, he saw the face of one of her sisters peer through the sidelights, squinting.

"Why is Jacinda knocking?" Ainsley's gaze skirted down the stairs and back to him. Her winged brows lifted in question, then dropped in abrupt understanding. And accusation. "Tell me you did not bolt the door. Tell me we were not caught kissing in my office with the house practically empty and the outer door locked as if . . ."

When she didn't finish, he filled in the blanks for her, every word punctuated by the continued knocking.

"As if I intended to put us both in the precarious situation of being discovered? Well, I didn't. I only meant to keep Mitchum away while we had an important discussion, which we have yet to complete. Now, I should like to propose—"

"Mr. Sterling, *please*," she interrupted, pressing a hand to her temple. "Your choice of words is not amusing in the least. Especially when we are about to be discovered and my reputation torn to shreds. The agency is already holding on by tenterhooks and this will surely be the end of everything that matters."

Perhaps now was not the best time to discuss butlers.

"We'll settle this matter a little later, then," he said, willing to compromise. "Point me in the direction of your servants' stairs and I'll slip away without anyone else the wiser."

But it was already too late. They went still as statues as the door opened and both Bourne sisters rushed into the house in a flurry.

Thankfully, Jacinda, the Duchess of Rydstrom, was busy pushing a pair of hatpins into her green silk bonnet when she said, "It is fortunate that I know how to put these to good use. Though I cannot fathom why the door was locked. Ainsley never leaves it locked."

The woman in question slid Reed an incredulous glare.

"Perhaps it has something to do with the mob outside of Sterling's," Briar, Lady Edgemont, said, peering outside one last time before closing the door, her white-gloved hand absently resting over the swell beneath her pink-striped dress.

Now it was Reed's turn to arch his brows in blame.

Ainsley merely pursed her lips in response, and damned if he didn't want to kiss her, right then and there. But he didn't. There was still a chance they could make their escape.

They both seemed to share the same idea. Turning in unison, he took her elbow, prepared to lead her back up the stairs.

Yet they hadn't made it a single step before she jerked to a halt and looked down. And blast it all if her dress wasn't wrapped around her shoe. Without a word, he quickly kneeled to untangle her, working as deftly and as silently as he could.

At the same time, the cook bustled into the foyer. She was coated in flour from head to toe, wiping it from her eyes with the corner of her apron, her ruffled cap awry.

"Mrs. Darden! What on earth has happened?" Jacinda asked.

"I couldn't say," she replied, up in arms. "Nothing is as it is supposed to be this morning. Broken teapot. A bit of toweling underneath the flour sack. The kitchen a disaster. And your sister—Oh! For the life of me I don't know what she was thinking to let that man inside."

"What man?" Jacinda and Briar said in alarmed unison.

Then together, they looked to the stairs. Catching Reed with a handful of Ainsley's skirts.

"Mr. Sterling!" Briar gasped, her hand flying to her open mouth. There was a muffled sound of a laugh before she continued. "Whatever are you doing to my sister?"

Ainsley batted his hands away and freed her own foot. "My shoe was caught."

"But what was he doing here *before* that?" Jacinda asked, her eyes narrowed with suspicion.

"We merely had another row."

"A *row* indeed." Mrs. Darden harrumphed.

Jacinda set her hands on her hips, watching him closely as he stood. "With the outer door locked?"

"That must have happened by accident," Ainsley answered again, her words edged with a note of warning, both toward the middle sister and to him when he deigned to offer his arm to assist her down the stairs. Ignoring him, she proceeded down, a step ahead of him the entire way. "And besides, Mrs. Darden has been here all the while."

"A perfect chaperone," Reed interjected, inclining his head toward the cook to demonstrate he held no ill will against her.

Though if her quick, agitated motions of brushing flour from her apron in his direction was any indication, *she* still held a grudge against him.

"I am thankful, sir, that I did not have to rush into my

dear girl's office and break a pot of tea over your head or anything of the sort."

He couldn't fight a grin. This entire interlude had turned into something straight out of Bedlam. "And for that I am truly grateful, ma'am."

"The back of your coat is wet, Mr. Sterling," came the duchess's disapproving voice.

Then her younger sister chimed in with an amused hiccup. "And your hair is damp, too."

"What can I say, other than it is London and it rains a great deal."

"It did not rain this morning."

"Yes it did, Jacinda," Ainsley said between her clenched teeth. "A brief, but drenching downpour. Now if you would step aside, I'm certain Mr. Sterling should like to be on his way."

"Always a pleasure," he said to the younger sisters and the cook. Then he faced Ainsley again.

There was still a matter of business to discuss—her need of a reliable man-at-the-door. But that would have to wait until she was more receptive. Right now she was glaring, the threatening chill in her eyes ready to freeze him into a solid block of ice.

He let his gaze drift to her lips, still tasting her sweetness on his tongue. "Miss Bourne, I look forward to our next . . . row."

And before he left to manage the hoard of gatherers in front of his hell, he had the distinct pleasure of seeing her blush.

Chapter 12

"A very little quiet reflection was enough to satisfy
Emma as to the nature of her agitation . . ."

JANE AUSTEN, *Emma*

Not an hour had passed before Ainsley was ready to
strangle both of her sisters. They had not been able to draw
a single breath without mentioning Reed Sterling. All she
wanted to do was forget about his . . . visit . . . and go about
the rest of her day, pretending that nothing had happened.
Was that too much to ask?

"It was just our usual row, nothing more," she said blandly.
Repeatedly.

Keeping to the same response seemed the wisest course
of action. Especially since Jacinda had an alarming knack
for interrogation. Her questions were so pointed that
Ainsley struggled not to shift in her chair and give herself
away.

"Perhaps a *row* was Mr. Sterling's excuse to come here,"
Briar chimed in with a dreamy grin on her lips. "Secretly,
what he really wanted this morning—and what he has
wanted ever since we moved here—was the chance to see
you alone and to kiss you."

Briar's ability to craft far-fetched scenarios nearly caused
Ainsley to break and admit the entire episode. Surely, what
actually transpired would seem tame and uninteresting compared to this.

"And his passion for you is the reason why he never wears a cravat, for he is always burning up with desire," Jacinda added with a well-timed waggle of eyebrows. This brought a hiccupped laugh from Briar and some sense to Ainsley.

Her decision was etched in stone. She would never, *ever* speak of what happened.

Likely, she would have to endure this ribbing for weeks to come. Perhaps even longer. And it was all Reed Sterling's fault.

He was the one who'd kissed her and caused all this up-heaval.

She still didn't know why he'd been so singularly focused. Had her name somehow made it to the list of sins he'd needed to complete by the end of the day? Perhaps the poster ordeal had interrupted his morning gluttony and he'd decided to feast on her instead.

Her breath caught on the vision her mind summoned. *Gracious!* What a scandalous—but intriguing—thought.

Well, whatever his intention, his method certainly proved successful. He'd breached her frosty exterior with melting kisses that she would not soon forget. If ever. She could still feel the warm pressure of his lips. Still feel the heat he roused to a smolder. Oh, how she wished she could snuff out these sensations as easily as a candle flame.

Her gaze drifted to the red cover of *Emma* on the console table near the door. The primrose was still there. Taunting her.

Even worse, she had two shards of a broken teapot in her pocket, along with the memory of her first pleasant conversation with Reed Sterling. The moment had been surprising and . . . well . . . nice.

But these were all distractions she didn't need. She couldn't waste time ruminating over a kiss when she had a business to manage and the pressing need to find a butler.

After this morning, it was clear she had to employ some-one to guard the entrance on the three days a week the agency was open. There could be no more leaving the door unlocked for her sisters.

Usually Mrs. Darden answered when someone called. But with her other tasks, it was simply too much for her to manage. Unfortunately, there hadn't been another option when they'd first opened the agency. And looking over the accounts now at her desk, there still didn't seem to be.

Their client list remained stagnant. With the high cost of living in London, renting this house, and the requirement to purchase food instead of growing their own, the family coffers didn't have the funds to house, clothe, and feed any more servants. And since it was considered bad form for *good ton* to work, they were forced to run their business under the illusion that they didn't require the money to do so.

Therefore they would simply make do as they had always done.

Her mind ran over the limited possibilities. Cutting back on paper, ink, and candles made the top of her list. Not to mention, they could use crow feather quills instead of the finer pens from the stationers, but her uncle had always been against this in the past.

Dear Uncle Ernest . . . Ainsley thought with a quiet sigh. She would have to tell him what happened. Some of it, at least, and without mentioning Mr. Sterling's involvement.

The less she spoke of her neighbor, the better chances she had of not blushing.

Ainsley left her office with no one the wiser. Her sisters had finished their teasing—for the moment—and were busily chatting about felicity in marriage and motherhood through the adjoining office door.

Uncle Ernest had returned a minute ago from his jaunt in the park, then disappeared into his office without a word. Likely he was jotting down a fresh sonnet for whomever he'd fallen in love with this morning. But Ainsley would have to disturb him.

Walking down the corridor, she spied a trail of yarn on the runner. Strange, but she didn't think Mrs. Teasdale was here yet this morning. After all, Rosamunde usually came directly into her office to chat about her knitting creations and the latest gossip.

Ainsley slowed her steps, feeling her brow pucker with worry. She hoped Mrs. Teasdale hadn't overheard any of her sister's teasing about Reed Sterling.

Through the crack in the door, Ainsley listened to Uncle Ernest, his cultured voice uncharacteristically harsh. "See here, woman. What's the meaning of this, barging into my office?"

"This is not an *office*," Mrs. Teasdale answered with a supercilious scoff. "Why, it looks more like a jungle with these potted palms and feather plumes around your desk. I'm surprised you're able to see anything."

Through the meager opening, Ainsley saw his lean form rise from the chair behind his desk as he tugged smartly on his gray satin waistcoat. Beneath thick waves of silver-sand hair, his lapis blue eyes narrowed at the woman who stood across from him, dressed in a garish magenta silk.

"Not that a person of your nature would understand, but it creates ambiance for my compositions. Which I was in the midst of writing when you so rudely barged in without so much as a knock. Now, if you please . . ."

"It looks more like you're just scribbling on a page. Find yourself in love with the first lady to bat her eyes at you this morning, did you?"

Oh dear, Ainsley thought with a sudden rise of amusement. Uncle Ernest was a gentleman in every regard. But when it came to his nieces, his poems, and his *affectionate friendships*—as he liked to call them—he was rather protective.

"The matter does not, and will not ever, concern you, madam."

"And my heart is fairly broken over the thought," Mrs. Teasdale answered, her tone dripping with honied sarcasm.

Ainsley decided that her conversation with him could wait until the verbal gunpowder cleared the room. Besides, she'd rather not have Mrs. Teasdale around for what she had to say about Nigel's call, and their need to trim expenses to hire a butler.

For the moment, she decided to head to the kitchen. Perhaps Mrs. Darden had ideas for cutting back on their food budget.

Yet, as she walked down the stairs, the thought of facing Mrs. Darden again so soon after she'd witnessed that terrible lapse in judgment sent heat rising to Ainsley's cheeks.

Though to be honest, kissing Reed Sterling had not felt terrible. It was quite agreeable, actually. *More than agreeable.*

The inextinguishable memory caused her stomach to flip and clench. Settling a hand over her middle, she did her best to quell the intriguing—but foolhardy—sensations.

"I would be better off to forget all about—*oof*!" She stopped short in a sudden full-body collision of breasts, stomach, hips, and thighs. She even hit her forehead on a chin. And not just any chin . . . "Mr. Sterling!"

"*Damn.* Are you hurt?" Reed asked, automatically securing her against him. One hand stole to the curve of her hip and the other reached up to rub that spot on her forehead in slow circles.

Pressed against a wall of thick muscle, Ainsley was unable to speak. He was so blessedly hard everywhere. Her soft curves and valleys molded against him in a seemingly perfect alignment. All the parts of her that had been slumbering for most of her life were now tingling and wide awake. In fact, they were flinging off the coverlet, fully alert, and ready for whatever might happen next.

Somehow, she managed to rasp, "I'm unharmed."

Apparently, he didn't believe her. His fingertips trailed from her forehead to her chin, tilting her face up for inspection. Then his attention veered to her lips. And lingered.

His indigo gaze simmered beneath the shadow of his lashes and her heart gave an excited leap. To make matters worse, her hands splayed possessively over the intriguing contours of his chest, warm and firm beneath his coat.

She was shocked by her responses, but couldn't seem to control herself. She only hoped he wouldn't notice.

One eyebrow inched upward and a slow grin curled his mouth on the nicked side as he leaned in to whisper, "Still not had enough of me today, I see."

Scalding heat climbed to her cheeks and she pushed free. Stepping back, her knees felt weak as peony stems and she had the mortifying impulse to return to his embrace.

Thankfully, she resisted. "Why are you here, again? I thought you would be busily scraping windows all morning."

The forbidding tone of her voice and the reminder of what they actually were to each other—enemies till death—doused the heat in his eyes. His grin faded and he released a slow breath. "I've hired a few urchins to do the labor, Miss Bourne. It may please you to know that your scheme has given them a better occupation than pickpocketing and begging on the streets."

In other words, he'd taken her trick and turned it into something good.

A perplexing rush of tenderness filled her.

"As you know, that was not my intention," she admitted, chagrinned. "But I am glad that you have given them an opportunity for honest labor, even if only for a day."

His brow flattened. "I've promised them continued employment if their work is excellent. It may surprise you that even common children yearn for a better life. Not everyone is so fortunate to be born into it. Doubtless, those who toil for their suppers are beneath your esteemed notice."

Ah, yes. She'd forgotten for a moment how privileged her life had always been. How she'd never had to worry about selling furniture from the house to purchase food at market and thread to mend her sisters' stockings. Or how society frowned on women with determination and the willingness to do anything to succeed in business. Those were only traits to be admired in men, after all.

She felt a migraine coming on, starting where her head had met his arrogant chin. And any tender feeling that might have glanced across her heart withered away like orchid petals after a hard frost. "It is strange how I do not see many of the hoi polloi enter your elite establishment. Are there no commoners who enjoy gaming?"

"I do not mark a person's birth against them."

"*Ha.* Do you not?"

He stiffened. "Many tradesmen—an ample number, in fact—have earned invitations."

"And those who are not so wealthy?"

She knew very well that he would not welcome anyone with an income as meager as her own, no matter what class the person was born into.

"No doubt they are working from sunup to sundown, ensuring that little Miss Highborn can sit in her office and play matchmaker."

Ainsley fumed at his presumptions, unable to speak for all the hateful words weighing down her tongue. Yet she did not bother to rail at him or to correct him. Instead, she smiled coolly, suddenly overcome with the perfect idea for her next attack.

It would be the best one of all.

She would send out dozens, if not hundreds, of handwritten invitations to attend a free supper at Sterling's. And the guests of honor, invited by Mr. Sterling himself—in a roundabout fashion—would be every commoner who visited the servant's registry.

She should like to see how his club fared once his wealthy patrons were elbow to elbow with the people who toiled in their kitchens and workhouses.

His eyes narrowed quizzically at her pleased expression as if he didn't know what to make of it. "Your two attacks have started rumors, you know. In fact, there's never been such a curious, eager crowd filling my gaming hell."

Of course, she thought with disgust, hating that all her work was for naught. Couldn't he have been inconvenienced at least?

"Is that so? Well, I'm simply delighted that you came here to tell me your news." She gritted her teeth. "I hope they all wore shocked countenances when you told them you were bested by a woman."

"I did not tell them of your involvement. Thoughtlessly, I kept it a secret."

She sputtered in futile outrage. "Surely someone has been able to figure out the party responsible. For heaven's sake, the handbills had our names printed on them!"

"And what did you want me to tell them? That the eldest niece of a respected viscount is so obsessed with running me out of business that she plays these little games—stealing into my club, sneaking over at the break of dawn—in the hopes that the entire *ton* will never think of my name without linking it to hers?"

Suddenly, the blood rushed out of her head. Ainsley was left with the dizzying understanding of what he was saying.

She'd wanted to make him appear soft. But she hadn't given a thought to how her actions could be misconstrued as a desire to gain his attentions. *Oh dear . . .*

"And you," she began uncertainly, "were able to turn it to your benefit convincingly?"

He nodded, his face stern with warning.

At once, she felt contrite . . . until he spoke again.

"Cease these attacks before there is nothing I can do to save you from yourself."

"To save me from—" She growled, actually growled, at the odious man. His arrogance had no limit! Hands on her hips, she leaned in, breath seething. "I will stop only when Sterling's is no longer across the street."

His gaze flashed with heat, drifting to her mouth.

For a single simmering instant, she knew he was recalling their previous quarrel. Her lips tingled with awareness. She was struck by opposing impulses—to either bite off his nose if he so much as twitched in her direction, or to kiss him senseless.

"It would be folly to continue on that path," he said in a low voice as if to himself. Then he shook his head and took a step back. "Regardless, that is not the reason I have returned. I am here to employ a man at your door. Since you have not seen fit to do so, then I am doing it for you."

Of all the nerve! She should have bitten his nose when she'd had the chance. "Who are you to demand anything of me? When I wish to hire a butler, then I will do so. I hardly need your assistance."

"I notice you don't employ any footmen either. Are you so against the male sex that you cannot stand them beneath your roof?"

She would rather prick her fingertip with a needle a thousand times than confess to Reed Sterling that she lacked the funds to hire more servants.

"You're being absurd. My uncle lives here, along with his valet." Though Mr. Hatman was a septuagenarian who spent most of his days napping in the dressing room. There had been times when she forgot him completely only to find him taking his evening meal with Mrs. Darden and Ginny in the kitchen. "Not to mention many male clients as well."

Unfortunately, the majority of those were also septuagenarians who'd applied initially, but hadn't gotten around to canceling their subscriptions. She'd even taken to looking over obituaries to mark clients off their list.

"Aye, that you do." He frowned. "And I've heard that these *gentlemen* have not always been shown to Eggleston's office as they ought."

She glared at him, wishing he was tied to a log pyre and she holding a torch.

"Are you honestly standing there, trying to tell me how to run my agency"—she stopped and made a hasty amendment—"how to assist my uncle in running *his* agency?"

Reed had the nerve to smirk as he crossed his superfluously bulging arms over his chest. "There is no need to pretend, highness. Not with me. We both know whose frivolous endeavor this really is, but that is neither here nor there. I've come to leave you with Mr. Finch during your business days until you employ a replacement for him. And if you would prefer to keep the association between us at a minimum, then I suggest you act with haste."

Only now did she hear voices coming from the little corridor that led to the kitchen—Mrs. Darden's chatter meeting Mr. Finch's familiar deep articulation. She could just imagine how Mrs. Darden felt about having an uninvited giant in her domain.

"You have overstepped, Mr. Sterling," Ainsley said, her words biting sharp. "I am my own lord and master and I'll not have the likes of you dictate what I should and should not do. You and I are nothing more than enemies. You hold no rights over me or my person."

"Of that I am fully aware," he muttered back, a muscle ticking along his jaw. "But just because you are stubborn all the way to your marrow, doesn't mean that you should also be a fool. Mark my words, Mitchum will return."

A strangled breath escaped her, a sudden chill creeping through her bones.

"You are resuming your scare tactics as a means of intimidation, I see. How base a creature you are, sir."

Ainsley felt like a cornered animal. She hated being handled in such a manner. And yet, his warning frightened her and she saw the sense in it. "Very well. Mr. Finch can remain, but only temporarily. The less I have to deal with any reminders of you, the better."

"In that, we are both in agreement."

It wasn't until Reed stormed back toward the kitchens that Ainsley was left feeling weaker. Strange as it was, she almost wished he would stay, because she always felt stronger when they argued.

Chapter 13

"Poor Mr. Woodhouse little suspected what was plotting against him . . ."

JANE AUSTEN, *Emma*

That afternoon Reed stood in the corner of his office, glaring at the stubborn creature on the top shelf of the bookcase. Keeping just out of reach, the cat had wedged herself in between the books, and was methodically pushing them over the edge, one by one.

"That is enough, Cat. Get down from there this instant."

The miscreant hissed at him and sent another book to the floor.

"You've already destroyed the ledger upon my desk. What more could you possibly want?"

And yet, Reed knew the answer.

Ever since the night of her escapade into the townhouse across the street, she'd started scratching him each time he called her *Cat* as if the name suddenly displeased her. Then he'd made a grievous error. He'd threatened to replace her ungrateful self with a little dog named Seymour if her temper did not improve. And she'd purred instantly.

Gritting his teeth, he shook his head and returned to his desk. "No. I will not give in to your childish tantrum. You will be called *Cat* and not—"

Another book went sailing, landing with a hard *thwack* on the wood floor.

"Damn it all. *Seymour* is not your name."

An instant later, she leapt down and then climbed onto his lap, nuzzling the underside of his palm with the top of her head.

"You are not Seymour," he said, though his tone had gentled.

The little manipulator purred in response and began to bathe the tips of his fingers.

Reed expelled a defeated sigh and scratched her tenderly behind the ears. "You have been very naughty today, Seymour."

"Meow." Her green eye glinted in triumph before she hopped down, swishing her tail all the way to the door. Just in time for Finch to appear.

"Stay back, you devil's spawn. I am in no humor to tolerate you today."

But Seymour went on her way without even pausing to taunt her nemesis. Finch eyed her warily as he shuffled into the room and sank down into one of a pair of claw-footed cigar-brown armchairs.

"You look as though you've recently risen from the dead, my friend."

Finch slid him a rueful glance. "Strange how it might seem that way, considering how I'd only slept a quarter hour when you sent a messenger to my door to have me work like a mule the entire day."

"Little Sally still cutting that tooth?" Reed asked, choosing to ignore the reference to the Bourne Matrimonial Agency. He needed a break from the constant reminders of Ainsley.

Her agency crowded the view from his windows.

Her scent had lingered on his clothes all day long.

And ever since their collision in the corridor, her soft, supple curves had left an imprint on his body that was driving him mad.

Hell, even his cat wouldn't let him forget her for a single moment.

"Sally is not as stalwart as her older sister had been." Finch dragged a hand over the purplish bruises of exhaustion beneath his eyes and pinched the bridge of his nose. "But at least we know she has a healthy set of lungs."

"This week will be different. For the first time in a long while, you'll share the same sleep schedule with your family. I've hired that large fellow we met at the tavern a month past." When Finch gave him a blank look, Reed supplied, "The one whose father was a tutor, though recently put in debtor's prison. Anyway, Mr. Pickerington will be watching the door. Temporarily. I sparred with him earlier and, while he has power, he lacks quickness—both in his fists and wits."

But testing Pickerington wasn't the only reason Reed sparred with him. He'd needed to expend his energy, to extinguish the heated, tumid tension that Ainsley Bourne had aroused.

"You think I'll only be across the street a few days, do you?" Finch asked with a dubious chuckle.

Frowning, Reed set aside his ledgers and tapped his index finger on the arm of his chair, settling back against the stiff leather. "It had better be."

There was too much at stake for him. And that was the main cog in the wheel turning Reed's foul mood. He was risking his own reputation—and Sterling's—to ensure that Ainsley was safe from Mitchum. After all, Reed couldn't always be there. He had a business to run. Yet when he'd offered her the services of his best man, she'd acted as if *he* was the villain.

He growled, his mood darkening.

"With no clients coming in, I don't see how they can afford to hire a man. A good butler would require a wage, sleeping quarters, livery, food, and whatnot."

"Of course, Eggleston can *afford* to hire one. I'm sure he hasn't simply because his eldest niece puts up a fuss about having men in the house."

Finch wore an inscrutable expression. "You seem to hold all the answers. So, I suppose, we'll just have to see what happens by week's end."

"It wouldn't surprise me if your replacement was hired by *day's* end," Reed supplied with certainty. "Other than your erroneous presumptions, how did it go? Did that ill-tempered cook threaten to beat you with her rolling pin?"

"Mrs. Darden and I have come to a better understanding. Since I could reach all the high places without a ladder, she gave me a feather duster and told me to make myself useful instead of standing about."

"I hope you set her straight."

"I started to, but then . . . well . . . she handed me a plate of scones and a glass of buttermilk." Finch lifted his giant hands in a helpless gesture when Reed's brow furrowed. "What? They were exceptional scones, and she said I could have as many of them as I wished. So I did. By the third plate and a sampling of an absolutely divine marmalade, we fell into amiable conversation. I cannot help it if she appreciates a man with a healthy appetite."

Reed stood, unable to tamp down an irritation that had nothing to do with the Bourne's cook. Stalking to the window, he glared across the street. "So now you're butler *and* maid?"

"Miss Bourne informed me that the other maids had the day off. Eggleston's valet, Mr. Hatman, seemed to be under the belief that there were no other maids. Though admittedly, he claimed not to spend too much time wandering around because of his rheumatism. According to him, his late father had been the butler at the viscount's country estate."

"I don't give a tinker's curse about the lineage of Eggleston's servants."

Finch closed his eyes, unaffected by the outburst. "I thought you might be interested to know that, until Miss Bourne took over the accounts, the servants weren't always paid. Apparently Eggleston's attentions have run more toward romantic ventures rather than to the fact that his land hadn't been prospering for years."

Reed held his tongue, refusing to reveal that the information bothered him.

Eggleston should have had a steward look after his estate, not burden his niece. Though learning this made it easier to understand why she was so used to managing things. Why she flatly refused to let anyone else step in. Even when it was for her own good.

"You may not be surprised, but I was," Finch said. "According to Mrs. Darden, Miss Bourne had only been sixteen years old when she and her sisters had gone to live with their uncle and began the task of running an entire household. I seem to recall *you* at that age. Your primary concern had not been managing the accounts of an estate, but more in managing the number of women you tupped in a single day."

Despite his fractious mood, a series of fond memories ran through his mind and a grin tugged at the corner of his mouth.

By sixteen he'd grown considerably. His scrawny body had filled out, lean and hard from his fights at university. Women of all ages and classes were giving him come-hither stares—from dairy maids on neighboring farms to the mothers of the same aristocratic prigs who'd tried to bully him—and he was more than happy to oblige them all. And often.

As a carriage stopped in front of the agency, adorned

with the Duke of Rydstrom's crest, Reed's attention returned to the matter at hand, and he quickly sobered.

"A girl of sixteen would not have been left the task of managing her uncle's estate. Mrs. Darden is simply doling out false praise through exaggeration. No doubt, Miss Bourne had been like any other pampered girl at that age, dreaming of finding a husband and having a home of her own."

"If that's all she wanted, then why didn't she marry Mr. Mitchum?"

Why, indeed. Considering how much she valued her reputation and was afraid to have her name sullied, the cause behind ending their betrothal had to have been great enough for her to risk the scandal. Great enough for her to cringe when a man lifted his hand.

"Whatever the reason, the end result is the same—Mitchum does not belong here," Reed growled. "As I said to you this morning, it was patently clear that she desires no reconciliation with him. But the blackguard will likely press his suit at least once more, until we make certain he understands just how pointless his pursuit would be."

Finch sat forward, perching his elbows on his knees, his fingers steepled beneath his professor's stare as if he were studying a thought-provoking subject. "Why do you suppose him to be a *blackguard*? Did Miss Bourne mention an incident between them?"

"No. It's just"—Reed hesitated, not wanting to reveal the whole of his encounters with Ainsley—"an instinct."

A sly grin alighted on Finch's mouth. "It is interesting how you frequently view the other men Miss Bourne comes into contact with as despicable. Not only her former betrothed, but I've heard you state before that the male clients are all lechers."

Unamused, Reed crossed his arms over his chest. "Whatever notion you have squirreling around in that gargantuan brain of yours, let it drop out your ears like a wasted nut-shell."

"If you insist. But I won't be the only one who wonders why you have sent your large and imposing friend to guard the door of the very woman who has plagued you since her arrival. A quiet brook of rumors needs only to fall over a few rocks before it turns into a waterfall."

Reed knew that only too well. When it came to gossip, men were as rapacious as vultures. Sure, they were sly at first, pretending not to listen or to care. Then, all at once, they would circle and swoop down on their prey, devouring it in great chunks.

And the news they currently feasted upon was the speculation of who might be goading Reed into a fight.

He'd already considered this at length. "We shall play it to the advantage of Sterling's. The story will be that you want me to call out Lord Savage, believing he is behind the recent mischief of handbills and placards. And I fired you because I didn't want you to lure me back into the ring. In retaliation, you chose to work nearby, in order to taunt me."

"From what I've heard, all it would take to knock you flat is a teapot."

The blow went straight to Reed's ego.

"If you so much as repeat that, I will drag *you* into the ring and knock out the rest of your teeth."

His friend chuckled. Clearly, he knew the threat was as empty as . . . well . . . a broken teapot.

"Damn it all," Reed muttered. He would never live this down.

Then Finch stood and his expression sobered as he shuffled to the door. "I know you are always looking to make a fortune, but this is a good deal of trouble to go through simply to keep Sterling's accounts in the black. Just how far are you willing to take this?"

"I'll always do whatever it takes to make Sterling's a success. Legendary."

"Ah, yes, the ever-imposing legacy you intend to leave behind one day," Finch said, leveling Reed with an all-too-perceptive look. "You know, there may come a time when you will not be able to put the interest of Sterling's above everything else."

Reed opened his mouth to respond, to tell his friend that a man had to seize whatever he could of this life. You never knew when it would be cut short. But Finch was already out the door. So Reed clenched his teeth on his answer, and his gaze shifted to the building across the street.

⁂

AINSLEY HAD forgotten about dinner at the Duchess of Holliford's this evening.

She stared through the open door of the townhouse to the carriage waiting on the lamplit street. Fear mortared the soles of her slippers to the foyer floor. She didn't want to leave. There was no telling where Nigel might be.

"We'd best not delay. You know how the duchess feels about dawdlers," Uncle Ernest said good-humoredly from the door, proffering his arm. Yet, when he looked at Ainsley, the smile he wore faded. "What is it, my dear? Are you unwell?"

Not wanting to worry him, she instantly straightened her shoulders and forced her feet to march forward. "Perfectly hale, just garnering my fortitude for the impending introduction our dear duchess has in store for me."

"Surely it isn't as bad as all that? Her Grace only wishes to see you settled and happy like your sisters." He patted her hand on his sleeve. "I should like to see the same. For you, especially."

The subtle strain in those last words drew her gaze to his solemn profile as he turned to close the door. He didn't need to elaborate. She already knew the reason.

It was because of that awful day in Hampshire. Which was the same reason she now held her breath as she scanned past the columns and topiaries, and down both lengths of the pavement. In fact, she didn't exhale until they reached the carriage and he handed her inside.

"Uncle," she began as the carriage jolted into motion, "I need to speak with you about a call I received."

She'd planned to tell him earlier, but shortly after his encounter with Mrs. Teasdale he'd left and hadn't returned until a little while ago. Though with her sisters around and Mrs. Teasdale lingering upstairs until after Mr. Finch had gone, it was for the best. She didn't want to involve her sisters. They'd never known of the events that led up to the end of her betrothal to Nigel. They could never find out either.

The idea of confessing the months of tolerating Nigel's demeaning comments and bruising grip—always concealed from others—was too humiliating to bear.

She was the strong one in the family. The one that everyone turned to in their time of need. And Ainsley intended to keep it that way. Not even her uncle knew the whole of it. He'd only borne witness to the worst.

Sitting across from him now, she told him about the unexpected visit, keeping her explanation brief. She mentioned only that Nigel had come to London to renew his addresses, and that she'd set him straight on that account.

Uncle Ernest looked toward the carriage window without a word, his aristocratic features stark in the shifting light and shadows.

"I have a friend who keeps a small home in Bath," he said after a few moments. "Since her husband died, she hasn't returned and I know the rent would not be overmuch. We could leave by week's end."

Ainsley knew that leaving would be her uncle's solution. Though after having mulled this issue over for hours upon hours, she had decided that she was far safer in London than she had ever been in Hampshire. Quite a strange notion, considering newspaper reports of pickpockets and cutthroats, along with the wastrels leaving the gaming hell at all hours of the night. And yet, she'd never felt threatened to venture outside, despite her close proximity to Sterling's.

Or perhaps, a voice whispered in the back of her mind, *you feel safer* because *of your proximity to Sterling's.*

She ignored the voice.

Holding herself firm against the sway of the carriage, she said, "I don't want to run again. Mr. Mitchum could find me in Bath as well. Or Whitcrest, if we lodged with Jacinda and Crispin. Or at any number of Briar and Nicholas's country estates. No, I think we had best stay here."

He looked back at her, bafflement marked in the furrows drawing his sandy gray brows together. "Does this have something to do with Mr. Sterling?"

She startled, her heart lurching. "Whyever would you say that?"

"Mrs. Darden told me that Mr. Finch had been in our foyer all day. Though the most I managed to get out of her was that if anyone could tell me what that 'dastardly Sterling' was up to, it would be you. Then she muttered something about the world going topsy-turvy and I left the kitchen, more confused than ever."

Ainsley did her best to feign disinterest in the topic, brushing her gloved fingers across her lap. "It's nothing really. Mr. Sterling happened to drop in this morning when Mr. Mitchum was here. Then after seeing Mr. Mitchum to the door, Mr. Sterling returned to offer the services of Mr. Finch until we could employ a butler."

She sucked in a breath, her side hitching on a twinge as if she'd strained something with that expurgated version of the story.

"It's peculiar that Mr. Sterling should care whether we

had a butler or not. Of course, the Duchess of Holliford has mentioned it a time or two. And I, well"—he shrugged sheepishly—"I may have fibbed a bit and told Her Grace that Mr. Hatman had taken the position. But when I tried to make it a truthful statement, my valet flatly refused on the grounds of preferring shoe polish to silver polish. Of all the absurdities."

"He is quite old, Uncle."

"Mmm . . . yes. I suppose we must hire someone. After all, it cannot bode well for us to have Mr. Finch in our foyer. He has a way of looking down at a man as one might to an insect on the footpath, right before he steps upon it."

Ainsley offered a nod of agreement, but was more bothered by the association to Sterling's than by Mr. Finch's imposing stature. Ever since her last two encounters with Reed, she knew it was imperative that neither she nor the agency had anything to do with the gaming hell across the street.

"I imagine," Uncle Ernest continued, casting her a hesitant glance, "that now is not the best time to mention the flowers and confections I had delivered to a new acquaintance today."

Ainsley sighed. "What's done is done. We will simply make do."

"I wish I had your level head about my own shoulders. You've always managed things so well. It is a wonderful trait to have, my dear. Ah, but your mother would have been so proud to see the fine woman you've become." Then he looked toward the window again, shadows settling in the hollows beneath his distant gaze. "Though she may not have been so pleased with my own efforts. I have not always been your finest protector."

Ainsley felt tears threaten, prickling at the corners of her eyes. She quickly blinked them away, refusing to relive the experience that was even more raw today than usual.

Then reaching across the carriage she squeezed his hand. "You have always been the best of uncles. Without you, we would never have been able to open the agency and help people avoid marriage to the wrong sort." Herself included.

He smiled wanly and gave her hand a pat. "I so wanted our little venture to be a smashing success."

"And it will be," she said, finding herself soothing his worries instead of the other way around. "I'll make sure of it."

She had a plan, after all. Today she'd written dozens of invitations for the servants' dinner at Sterling's. Tomorrow she would start interviewing butler candidates, finding the funds for the position somehow.

Soon, she would be rid of Reed Sterling's unexpected touches, melting kisses, and unwanted interference for good.

Chapter 14

"I have nothing to say against it, but that they shall
not chuse pleasures for me."

JANE AUSTEN, *Emma*

From the third-floor balcony, Reed surveyed the crush
standing shoulder to shoulder in the main card room of the
hell below. Men crowded around tables, the air thick with
shouts and cursing and the fog of cheroot smoke. Tempers
flared and purses jingled.

It was going to be an excellent night.

Even though it wasn't Ainsley Bourne's intention, her
first two acts of war—as she called them—had only helped
his business.

In the week since, he'd received dozens of requests—and
even bribes—to be put on the list. Not all were from the most
elite *ton*. Some came from those with padded pockets and an
eagerness to discover for themselves who dared to slight the
renowned prizefighter's manhood with their pranks.

He didn't care that they were snickering, betting on who
dared to insult him, and whether or not Reed would fight
again. That was precisely what he wanted.

There was more traffic than ever queued up outside his
door. So many carriages that the street was clogged with
whinnying horses and shouting drivers.

Grinning, Reed thought of Ainsley as he made his way
down the stairs. Unable to escape the noise, she would likely

stay awake all night, fuming *and* thinking of him. Whether she liked it or not.

"Haven't seen much of old Finch at the door," a man muttered as he passed.

"Mayhap you're looking at the wrong door. Someone told me that he's buttling across the street at the matrimonial agency. Heard he was seen through the window the other day with a feather duster in hand."

A series of guffaws rolled through the group.

Reed supposed that was his own fault. After all, he was the one who stationed Finch across the street. But what else could he have done under the circumstances?

He'd needed someone he trusted. Someone capable. Of course, all the men who worked for him fit that description. He'd even considered sending Raven. However, his handsome croupier was too much of a flirt for his tastes, always making women blush with just the flash of a grin.

Reed was certain that Ainsley didn't need such a distraction. So he chose the happily married Finch instead.

"I heard Lord Savage was the reason," another man said. "Apparently, Finch already opened a secret betting book for a fight between Sterling and Savage. That's what got him fired."

Reed paused briefly and slowly pivoted to face the men. Whenever he had the opportunity to pretend that he was bothered by Finch's absence, he sent a warning glare that had been proven to send men pissing their pants. This would keep feeding the pyre. And as long as the speculators weren't close to guessing the truth of why Finch was really across the street, then all the better.

To keep minds on the right course, he'd furthered interest by opening the betting books and putting down five hundred pounds against him ever entering the ring again. Which worked in his favor. It whetted the *ton*'s appetite, many calling for the man responsible to show himself and make a formal challenge.

He ventured out of the main hall and down the paneled corridor. Inside the bustling midnight blue roulette and piquet room, he saw Raven at the betting lectern in the corner, overseeing the cashbox and books.

"How are the wagers fairing?" Reed asked, keeping his voice low.

"Our *secret* book is filled—odds in your favor against Savage. They seem to think you have a score to settle and that you fired Finch in a fit of rage." Raven chuckled and shook his head, stirring the inky dark layers of his hair. "They're all idiots. Anyone who's ever watched you knows that you don't lose your temper. You're as cool as the stone in an icehouse."

"If it makes the men giddy as schoolgirls to think of me entering the ring again, then open up another secret book. Besides, it's only a matter of time before Savage issues a real challenge."

Reed turned to survey the room, seeing a few faces he didn't recognize. That was to be expected, he supposed, with the additional invitations he'd extended.

Yet for some reason, he felt unsettled by the pressing crowd, his senses on alert. "How was Pickerington doing before you came upstairs?"

"He'll never be accused of being a wit, to be sure."

"All the more reason for you to take him under your wing, teach him a thing or two. You have wits enough to spare. Even if you don't care to tell me how you came by all your worldly knowledge."

"There are some blokes you just can't teach," Raven answered, carefully dodging the enquiry. As usual. "I even warned Pickerington that there would be plenty of gents trying to filch their way inside, bribing him, claiming that

their name was left off the list by mistake, all sorts of tricks.
Then what does he do but get into a row at the door? So me
and Teddy went over to sort things out."

Reed was about to ask more but loud, sharp voices
coming from the next room drew his attention. Men angling
for a fight, no doubt.

He peered through the doorway into the hazard room,
where golden sconce light flickered against the red silk–
papered walls. But there were too many men swarming
about to spot the instigator. All he could hear were claims
of being cheated.

Here, in the depths of the hell, tempers ran more heated.

"Send to the kitchens for coffee. Clearly, it's past time
that a few of these gents had a cup or two," he said to Raven
before he ambled into the room.

Reed was familiar with soothing singed feathers. Some
men didn't know their limits and drank too much. Wagered
too deep. Of course, he wasn't a saint bent on keeping the
nobility from losing their shirts at his tables. Quite the opposite. He wouldn't mind if they were all beggared when
they left and begging him for a loan.

Even so, if there was going to be any bloodshed in his
gaming hell, then it would be in the ring upstairs. He'd open
up a new book and let the wagering commence.

Yet the instant he saw the man at the center of the uproar,
every hair on the back of his neck stood up on end.

Nigel Mitchum was here.

Damn that fool Pickerington for letting him slip through
the door!

"Is there a problem, gentlemen?" Reed asked, never
looking away from Mitchum, who appeared to be well into
his cups, cheeks ruddy, eyes bloodshot.

"And there he is," Mitchum announced with a loose-
jointed salute, "the man who would keep you well-liquored
in order to rob you of every farthing. I wouldn't be surprised

if he stole into your homes while you were keeled-over drunk underneath tables and bedded your wives."

"If he can stomach the sight of mine, then he's more than welcome to her," one man said, earning a roll of laughter. "Why do you think I'm here?"

"And mine's over at the faro table, likely losing my fortune. I'd pay him to take her."

Reed lifted his hands in a hapless gesture. "I'm afraid your hopes of offending someone are for naught, Mr. Mitchum. Perhaps you would do better at another club. I'll even pay the hackney driver to take you there."

"Of course, a bounder such as yourself couldn't be offended. You don't even mind taking another man's leavings, well used and still warm from his own pocket. At least, that's what you made me believe when we last met."

"Take care of what you say next, Mitchum," Reed warned, his glare causing the men nearest his target to sidle away.

Mitchum pressed a hand to his chest, trying to appear innocent, and clucked his tongue. "An undeserving threat, to be sure. Indeed, for I have done nothing but repeat what you inferred when you caught me *paying a call*—shall we say—on a certain lovely acquaintance we both share."

Mitchum's words intimated they had visited a harlot or courtesan, not a woman of virtue. The immediate congregation around them fell silent, eager as vultures at the sound of a death rattle. They were all waiting with baited breath for the barest hint of who this creature could be.

And if Mitchum so much as whispered Ainsley Bourne's name, her utter ruination would follow.

Wanting to quell the crowd's interest, Reed kept to his cool façade as he walked toward the blackguard, ready to haul him out of the club.

"There is but one firm rule at Sterling's," he said, his

voice low and deathly calm, "and that is we never besmirch a woman's honor. You, sir, have tread too close to that line and I must insist that you leave."

Either Mitchum was outrageously arrogant or fool enough to believe that Reed's threats were empty, because he skirted between a few more patrons. His eyes turned bright with the same cruel amusement Reed had once seen in Lord Bray's countenance. "And what does the lowborn son of a tavern owner know about honor? Did you learn it at university after your mother bedded her way into a better class?"

With a quick jerk of his head, Reed gestured to Teddy to escort him out. It was safer that way. Reed wasn't entirely sure he could do it without tossing Mitchum through the nearest window.

But Teddy wasn't quick enough.

As he took him by the arm and dragged him through the door, toward the stairs, Mitchum sealed Ainsley's fate with his parting shout. "Like mother, like son, I suppose. Shall we ring out a toast to the man of the hour—*Mister Sterling*—whose common neck was ensnared by the high-born matchmaker across the street?"

There were so many gasps at once that it might have cleared the smoke from the room. The crowd fell silent, the air punctuated by the absent tumble of bones on the felt table.

In the deafening stillness, he could almost feel every-one's thoughts bubbling at a low simmer, ready to spill over with one name on their lips. *Ainsley Bourne.*

They would be quick to call her a whore, too. Mitchum had seen to that.

Reed was surprised he'd heard anything above the din of blood rushing in his ears or saw anything other than the haze of red in his eyes. He'd never felt this close to murder.

In a flash, he knew what would happen—Mitchum's words would ruin Ainsley's reputation and make her an outcast. Not even the venerable Duchess of Holliford could save her from being shunned by society, driven out of London. And Mitchum wouldn't stop going after her. When a man like him set his sights on a victim, he would be determined to break her by any means possible. Lord Bray had proven this by dragging Mum back each time she'd tried to leave. And each time, he'd made it worse for her behind closed doors.

Reed knew that something had to be said to explain Mitchum's outburst. And there was only one thing he could think of.

Drawing in a deep breath, he pivoted on his heel and faced the crowd. Then pasting on a broad grin, he announced, "My happy secret has been unveiled before I could make a proper announcement. So, congratulate me, ladies and gentlemen and pour more whisky, for you are looking at a man about to be married."

It took a moment for the shock to settle and the agape jaws to shut. Then, with Raven strolling to his side and leading the cheer, an uproarious chorus of *Huzzah!* rose up to the rafters.

A fast line formed at the betting lectern, spectators ready to wager that the wedding would be in Gretna Green, and that Sterling would soon be a father.

Reed couldn't help but wonder how long it would be before his patrons went elsewhere for their entertainment.

Had he just struck the nail that would seal Sterling's coffin?

Moving into the corridor, he withdrew a handkerchief and surreptitiously wiped the sweat from his brow. When that was done, he stood in front of a large window that shone like mirror glass. Peering closely through the inky night sky, he spied a light across the street on the second floor, and his thoughts turned.

Raven came up beside him, only now revealing the shock in his expression as he scrubbed a hand over his face. "I wasn't expecting that. I don't think anyone was."

"It should make for some interesting wagers, I imagine."

"There's some talk starting in the other room. Men are saying that"—Raven hesitated—"if she was really yours, then you would have done something about it for the sake of her honor."

"And I did."

"But marriage? There might have been another way. Besides, the men are all itching for a fight, and just think of all the coin you could earn."

"A duel of honor—even if in a boxing ring—would have declared that she was mine to protect. Her reputation would have been tainted, regardless." And Reed would have fought a man in rage, even though he'd vowed never to do so.

"But, Sterling—"

"No," he interrupted firmly. "Now that it's all said and done, I don't want the topic of a fight between me and Mitchum broached again."

Raven expelled a breath of resignation. "You know, you were sort of . . . distracted in the moment. I'd wager that anyone would understand if you changed your mind."

"That isn't going to happen." Reed shook his head, a strange calm washing over him. He pointed to the gaming parlor. "Watch over things. I'm off to tell my bride-to-be the happy news."

Chapter 15

"... she soon felt that concealment must be impossible. Within half an hour it was known all over Highbury."

JANE AUSTEN, *Emma*

Ainsley was just beginning her nightly ritual of snuffing out the lights when a hard knock fell on the door. Her thoughts veered straight to Nigel.

She froze in the middle of the foyer, heart pounding in hard, panicked beats.

Then a softer rap came—just a tap on the glass—and a familiar drawl. "Highness, it's only me."

Relief rushed from her lungs so quickly that her breath bent the flame in the lamp she held. Though, almost in the same instant, her fear dissipated underneath a flood of irritation as she glanced at the clock.

"*Only* you? Only you would come to the door at midnight expecting to pay a call," she muttered, stalking forward in a swish of fawn-colored skirts. Wrenching open the door, she glared at his dark form and mismatched eyes. "Go away at once."

"Ah, such a sweet salutation. I am a lucky man, indeed," he said with a rueful laugh.

"It is late. Though I don't imagine someone like you would—" She broke off as he stepped inside and closed the door behind him. "Wait just a moment. I did not invite you in. And for your information, my uncle is upstairs."

"Good. He is the one I came here to see." Reed looked her over, expectation in his gaze, a smirk touching the nick on his upper lip. "Am I to try to conjure him or do you suppose you could inform him that I am here?"

"I won't disturb my uncle when he is in his library unless the matter is dire."

"I know you're used to taking charge, Ainsley, but I must speak with him directly."

The informal use of her name stunned her for a moment, the sound of it foreign to her own ears. He always called her *Miss Bourne* or, more recently, *highness*—both spoken with a degree of smugness. Using her given name was a breach of etiquette that suggested a mutual intimacy that was nearly as bold as . . . well . . . kissing her had been.

Heat flooded her cheeks. She fully intended to correct him, but he began toward the stairs without delay.

"Mr. Sterling, where do you think you're going?"

"The library, of course." He took the stairs two at a time, leaving her to storm after him in high dudgeon.

"Come back down here at once."

He did not stop but continued in long, floor-eating strides.

Apparently having heard the commotion, Uncle Ernest came out of the library, a book in his grasp with his finger tucked inside to mark the page.

At the sight of his visitor, his brows lifted then quickly furrowed. "Mr. Sterling, what is the meaning of this? It is too late of an hour to pay a call."

"Of that, your niece has so kindly informed me. However, the matter is of great importance and cannot be put off till morning."

Ainsley expected that propriety would win out over this oddly dramatic exhibition. But instead her uncle scrutinized Reed's countenance then summarily offered a nod.

"Very well," he said, returning to the room and crossing to the sideboard. "May I pour you a glass of port? I have a sense that I am going to require one. Ainsley, I have no water to add, but would you care for a glass?"

She crossed her arms, maintaining her skepticism. "Thank you, no. For a matter of such *great importance*, I should prefer to remain sober."

"As would I." Reed declined with a brief halting gesture of his hand before he pressed it against his black coat, seeming to wipe dampness from his palms.

It was only then that Ainsley noticed the agitation in his movements, the shifting from one foot to the other, the extending of his neck as if his snow-white cravat were choking him.

Wait a moment . . . was he actually wearing a cravat?

She'd seen him thusly attired before, but it was only during the first months of their acquaintance. Since then, she'd only seen him without. Yet with this part of him concealed, she couldn't seem to stop thinking about how accustomed she'd become to seeing the corded sinew of his throat, the bold jut of his Adam's apple, the dark hair rising from the open neck of his shirt and how it felt beneath her fingertips . . .

All terrible thoughts to have, standing in a room with her uncle present.

Suddenly, *her* palms were damp and she had to wipe them against her skirts. "Mr. Sterling, please, don't keep us in suspense. I'm sure the sooner we can be rid of each other the better."

"Oh, Miss Bourne," he said with a low, rueful laugh. "You are about to be thoroughly disappointed."

Uncle Ernest settled carefully down onto the tufted chair by the fire, his hand curled around his port glass as if the spindled stem were a lifeline. "At your earliest convenience, sir."

"Right. Straight to it." Reed stiffened, shoulders back. "I have come here to take your niece as my wife."

Ainsley gasped, the shock of his words taking ten years off her life. She must not have heard him correctly. Perhaps there was something in her ear like . . . like an elephant.

"Your—*what*?" And just in case she wasn't clear in her confusion, she continued inanely. "What?"

She wasn't certain how her uncle reacted because the room started to spin, growing dark and fuzzy. Listing slightly to one side she felt a familiar, solid wall of support beside her and a large hand molding to the inner dip of her lower back.

"Was that too abrupt, then?" Reed asked, his voice a teasing drawl in her ear. "Hmm, it seems so. Here, highness. You should sit down."

"I don't want to sit down."

But as she said the words, she felt herself sinking into a chair, likely the empty one opposite her uncle. Then before she was fully oriented, the firm smoothness of a glass against her lips.

"Take a sip," Reed urged gently. As she complied, his hand drifted to her nape, applying light pressure to the tautly wound sinew. "That's better. It will fortify you for what is yet to come."

There was more? Surely there could be nothing more outrageous than what he'd already said.

Drawing in a deep breath, she blinked. The darkness receded from the corners of her vision and the room slowed itself down, gradually wobbling to a halt like a spinning top left untended.

She watched Reed cross the room toward the escritoire to refill the glass. Then returning to her side, he paused to set the port on the wine table beside her uncle, who was studying him with a blank look.

Surely neither of them had heard correctly.

"Would you mind repeating yourself, Mr. Sterling?" she asked.

Reed cleared his throat, the flesh drawing taut with tension as one reacted when forced to swallow bitter medicine. "There was an incident which prompted my untimely visit. You see . . . Mr. Mitchum stole into Sterling's this evening and created a spectacle."

At once, her stomach dropped with dread. "What k-kind of spectacle?"

"A damning one," he answered, not looking at her. "He made a comment about my presence here the other day, remarking on our betrothal. Without thinking, I confirmed it."

Ainsley frowned. Something was missing from his story. She didn't imagine Reed ever said or did things without thinking.

Uncle Ernest sat forward, abruptly alert, but with confusion still corrugating his brow. "What's this about? Mr. Sterling has proposed before, and you agreed? You mentioned nothing of this."

"Because it was merely a falsehood meant to discourage Mr. Mitchum from calling upon me again. I had no intention—then or now—of it ever coming true. Mr. Sterling will need to claim it was all a farce."

She stared pointedly at Reed's hard profile but he didn't face her. He merely expelled a slow, patient breath as a tutor might to a child who did not understand her sums, keeping his focus on her uncle.

"The union would benefit us both, my lord. I could provide assistance to the agency and your family connections would elevate my position in society."

"The agency doesn't need your assistance," Ainsley answered, fuming. "And since when do you care about your position in society? You don't even like the aristocracy."

Irritation gave support to her legs. She stood, crowding him until he finally looked at her, his jaw clenched.

"True enough, but I thought it'd be the proper thing to say, since you are forever harping on propriety."

"I prefer that you keep to the truth."

"I am."

She scrutinized the set of his features coolly. Then a sudden swell of clarity swept through her and she realized what was happening.

She issued a huff of incredulity. "I see what this is about! Here you are, swaggering into our home, armed with the most ridiculous proposal, and it is only part of our ongoing war. Oh, you have retaliated most soundly, to be sure."

"War?" Uncle Ernest asked.

Ainsley nodded stiffly. "Yes, indeed. All of this is a jest, Uncle. You see, I declared war on Mr. Sterling because . . . well . . . I had to do something to stop his business from keeping our clients away. So I've been trying to ruin him, or at least force him to put his palace of sin somewhere else in the city. In turn, he has been quite cunning in his own reprisal. Do you know what he did after my initial strike? Nothing. Absolutely nothing. He is positively diabolical!"

Oh, she couldn't wait until he received his comeuppance with the servants' dinner.

Her uncle's brow furrowed in confusion. "You attacked his business and his response was to do nothing, and you've concluded that it was a means of subterfuge?"

"Indeed, because by not doing anything, he made me believe he was going to do something. He even confessed as much, the other day when we were alone in my—"

Ainsley stopped, feeling a rush of heat fill her cheeks. Reed crossed his arms over his chest and arched a smug brow at her.

Having a point to make, she hastened on, smoothing her hands down her pale skirts in quick, restless motions. "Well, that's not important. All that matters is that he will be leaving, now that I have discovered his true intent."

"Is my niece correct, Mr. Sterling?"

He inclined his head and she nearly expelled a breath of relief.

But then he spoke. "Every part, *except* the reason for this visit. What I said when I arrived is what transpired moments ago."

Ainsley frowned. He was playing a terrible trick. He had to be.

Uncle Ernest didn't seem to share her skepticism. Nodding contemplatively, he asked Reed, "And how do you feel about marriage?"

Ah-ha, she thought. This was the moment Reed Sterling—a man who vocally abhorred the notion of a sanctified union—would have to own up to his joke.

"I'm not averse to it," he said easily.

Ainsley sputtered. "That is a blatant falsehood! You are forever mocking this agency and its purpose."

"As I've said before, I just think a man should find his own woman."

"And drag her back to his cave, I suppose," she muttered under her breath, seething at the way the corner of his mouth twitched.

"Ah, so you are a romantic, then," her uncle said with a pleased smile. "I always suspected as much, what with the way you pay attention to every small detail at your club. A man has to have passion inside him for that."

"Uncle! Have *you* been to Sterling's?"

"Mmm . . . once or twice." He slid Reed a hesitant glance as if a secret were being passed between them. "I've been very fortunate at faro when Mr. Sterling deals the cards."

Ainsley rounded on Reed, pointing her finger. "You should have told me."

"Harmless fun, highness. I'd hardly beggar the uncle of my betrothed." The cad had the nerve to wink and her traitorous pulse hitched.

"We are *not* betrothed," she said in a flustered rush, the room unbearably hot all of a sudden. "And you are merely attempting to sidestep the accusation of your wrongdoing and, furthermore—"

"I had a sense there would be more. With you, there always is."

"—and furthermore," she repeated hotly, "if I were to ever marry, I would choose a gentleman who gave me the respect of requesting my hand because—as far as I am aware—it is still *my* hand, attached to *my* person, and therefore *my* right to give it if I so choose."

His grin faded. "That wasn't possible in this circumstance. Your name was tangled up with mine and there was no other way."

The conversation had now circled around to the beginning. They squared off, the air charged with frustration and conflicting perspectives.

Uncle Ernest, on the other hand, calmly sipped his port. He regarded her and Reed over the rim, then lowered the glass to the table. "Do you love my niece?"

Ainsley gasped, embarrassed. "Uncle, that is a most ludicrous—"

"I'd protect her, my lord," Reed said with all the emotion of a man awaiting the barber to extract a tooth. "And I'd keep her in a manner in which she is accustomed."

Then, like a strange dream from which she could not awaken, Uncle Ernest stood and extended his hand.

Reed shook it.

"Just one moment"—Ainsley wagged her finger at both of them—"you're speaking as if the decision has been made."

"Of course, my niece will have the final word, but I offer no argument." To make matters worse, her uncle continued as if he'd already predicted what decision she would make.

"The banns will have to be read this Sunday to quiet rumors, I imagine. Will you sit with us at church?"

"Whatever must be done," Reed replied.

"Good then. And afterward we'll retire here and speak of contracts."

"That is amenable. However, I want none of her dowry. Whatever monies and properties she has, she may keep for herself and use in any frivolous manner of her choosing."

"Very generous of you, my good sir. Isn't it, my dear?"

Ainsley didn't bother to speak. None of the words on her tongue were appropriate in front of her uncle, regardless. She merely glared at Reed Sterling, eyes burning with the hateful heat of a thousand suns.

So, in this farce, he would permit her to keep her dowry, would he? Quite generous, indeed. Even more amusing was the fact that she didn't have a farthing left of the original *immense* fortune of two hundred pounds. She'd *frivolously* given it all to debt collectors!

"Well," Uncle Ernest continued, clearing his throat. "I imagine the two of you have a good deal to talk about so I'll leave you to it. Good evening, Mr. Sterling."

"And to you, my lord."

While they were busy becoming the best of friends, Ainsley took her uncle's forgotten port to the escritoire. She needed distance between herself and the man she very much wished to murder.

Carefully, she poured the dark liquid back into the decanter—a surprising feat considering how she ought to be trembling with impotent rage. For the most part, her hands were steady. It was her mind that was quaking from this abominable turn of events. None of this was true. It couldn't be.

Behind her, she heard her uncle depart but knew that Reed was still there. Every fine hair on her nape and forearms seemed attuned to the palpable way he dominated the space.

"What exactly did Mr. Mitchum say that made you announce our betrothal *without thinking*?" she asked, not turning around. Instead she withdrew a handkerchief from her sleeve and dabbed at the crimson droplets that lingered on the rim of the glass and the neck of the decanter.

"It was more"—Reed hesitated—"the way in which he said it."

A cold chill tumbled through Ainsley.

Her stubborn refusal to believe him started to waver. She didn't want any of it to be true, but logic told her that Reed wasn't the type of man to craft such an elaborate falsehood. No matter how much she wished it in this circumstance. And perhaps that was at the root of it all. She didn't want to believe him because she was afraid to.

"Nigel always had a way of twisting things to suit his own purpose," she said quietly. "But I should like to hear the words, nonetheless."

Another pause came, this one even more alarming than the first.

Reed drew in a deep breath. "He intimated that you were . . . not chaste."

Ainsley closed her eyes. She could explain to Reed that her chastity had escaped intact by a hair's breadth, but it didn't truly matter. Her innocence had been lost that day all the same. "And how many people bore witness to this claim?"

"Enough."

At once, she felt exposed and vulnerable, as if every person at Sterling's this evening had been crowded into that tiny parlor and stood watching as she'd struggled to breathe from the force of Nigel's arm across her throat, leering at her bare legs as he wrenched her skirts higher.

Her hand shook as she splayed it protectively over her fichu. Beneath it, her lungs shuddered, a raw breath catching in her throat where an aquifer of tears waited, threatening to humiliate her further.

How would she ever recover? How would the agency?

"We'll make it right," Reed said, coming up behind her.

She turned and looked up at him with wide, wary eyes. "I don't know why you, of all people, thought to . . ."

"What? Tether myself to a prickly woman who wishes we'd never met?"

Ainsley nodded. But she was actually wondering why her enemy would go to such lengths to save her reputation. And this wasn't even the first time.

"I suppose it was better than hanging for his murder," he said with a shrug, his expression not unkind. He was making light of it. Yet there was an edge of grave sincerity in his voice that almost brought out those tears.

Slowly, he moved closer, a comforting heat rising from his body. She didn't even realize she was cold until then. A shiver coursed through her, chilling her all the way to her bones and, like a moth to a flame, she inched nearer to his warmth.

Then, as if it was the most natural thing in the world, he folded his arms around her.

For the sake of pride, she stiffened, fighting a sudden desire to burrow into him. "I did not give you leave to hold me."

"Didn't you?"

Gently, he tucked her in so that her cheek lay against his solid chest. Then his large, careful hands swept methodically over her back, lulling her into a strange sort of contentment.

Ainsley wasn't certain what to do, and so went still. This was unfamiliar territory. She was never one who sought an embrace. More often than not, she was the one who gave them. She'd held her weeping mother in her arms and also her sisters whenever they needed a shoulder to cry upon. But it had not seemed right for her to have done the same. She was the strong one, after all.

Yet, as she listened to the sure and steady beats of Reed Sterling's heart, she realized that she might have gone her entire life without knowing how splendid it felt to be held. Nothing more than a pair of strong arms offering a sense of security, without asking anything from her.

Well . . . other than my hand in marriage and the rest of my life, she thought wryly.

It still didn't seem real to her. Reed had offered up his own name for the sake of her own?

Surely, a man known for vice and virility would do himself no favors by claiming an attachment to the prudish spinster next door. So why had he done it?

She was too overwhelmed by all the events of the evening to formulate an answer. "You didn't have to protect my honor. I could have dealt with the ramifications on my own."

He didn't respond, but she felt the slow, hot press of something against the top of her head. A kiss?

With the tender gesture, she nearly gave in to the desire to relax against him. She felt her eyelids grow heavy, her breaths slow. It was disturbing how good it felt to be in his arms. Confusing.

How could it be that the man holding her was the same one she'd argued with on the pavement for nearly two years? It was like he was two different people . . .

The thought sent a sudden thrill of anxiety trampling through her and she tensed.

"It will all turn out well in the end. I'll make certain of it," Reed said, continuing his soothing strokes along her spine.

She squirmed away from him, her pulse frenzied from this half hour's upheaval.

"You're . . . different this evening," she said, eyeing him warily. And when he took a step toward her, she held up her hand and shook her head.

He instantly stopped, his feet planted on the carpet, but there was a flash of frustration in his gaze. "You've had quite a shock."

"That may be true, but I would prefer it if you treated me the same as you have always done. I would prefer it if you stayed the same. In the very least, you should be displaying a degree of irritated inconvenience by this entire episode."

If there was one thing she didn't trust, it was when a person's behavior ventured outside what was expected. Since the agency opened, she'd developed a set of skills, a keen sense for identifying the wrong sort. She could spot a philanderer or deserter before the ink was dry on the application. And her skin would crawl whenever she encountered the *charmers*. Like Nigel, they were the type who put on a grand show of being affable and enchanting, but were monsters in private.

Yet until this moment she didn't know how thankful she was that Reed Sterling had never pretended to be something he was not. Strange as it was, for all his wickedness and barbaric mannerisms, she'd found a sense of comfort in knowing what to expect of their encounters.

"That would prove pointless under the circumstances. Things are different now," Reed said, the flesh of his brow puckered.

She had the startling impulse to smooth the lines with her fingertips. To let his arms draw her closer and assuage her worries. Already her skin tingled in anticipation.

Clearly, she wasn't thinking straight.

She skirted past him and around the low-walled chiffonier, toward the corridor. "No, they're not and . . . and . . . you need to leave."

"You cannot shut the door on this as you would an unwelcome caller."

"I won't hold you to it." She began to pace the narrow strip of floor between the rug and the threshold. It was necessary to set things straight between them. "Our betrothal will be a mere pretense. In a few weeks, the *ton* will have forgotten all about it. After all, I've read that the king has been gifted a giraffe from the viceroy of Egypt. When the creature arrives, I'm certain that's all the news the papers will hold. And we will simply say that we've come to an amicable separation and no one will even care."

"My mum will care. She's been hounding me on this topic for so long that I don't recall if we've ever spoken of anything else."

She stopped and faced him, eyes wide with shock. *"Mum?"*

"Yes, highness. I have a mother," he said on an exasperated breath. "I did not, as you likely believe, sprout fully formed from Satan's tar pit."

She pressed her lips together, both amused and guilty. "Of course, I didn't think that. It's just so strange to hear you say *mum*. You've never spoken of her before."

"You and I haven't really had chats over tea, now have we?"

"No." She felt the tug of a grin at the notion. What type of scones would Mrs. Darden prepare for tea with the enemy? Something bitter and full of spice, no doubt.

"She'll want to meet you."

Her breath caught, a strange nervousness bloating her lungs as she wondered if his mother would even like her. "That wouldn't be wise, considering we won't be getting married."

His shoulders tensed, a muscle ticking along his jawline. "Is there someone else, then? Or is it that you would rather have had an aristocrat stand up for you?"

"Your actions this evening were far nobler than any man born of nobility might have been," she admitted quietly and saw him relax. "The truth is that I don't intend to marry."

"Come now, a matchmaker who has no intention of marrying?"

"Precisely."

"At all?"

"Not ever."

He seemed to consider this for a moment. Then those indigo eyes softened as they roamed over her features as if he saw something that required tenderness there. "But without marriage, how will you have that noisy life you miss?"

At first, she was confused. She didn't understand how he could know such an intimate thing about her when she'd never told anyone else. Then she recalled that night they were looking for his cat and how she couldn't stop her nervous rambling. *Bother.*

Peculiarly, the hand that no longer bore the scratch from his cat tingled and turned warm as if his touch had left an imprint on her. And only now did she become aware that they were standing within arm's reach once more.

She intended to take a step back, but her feet did not obey. "Are you saying that my husband would be a loud sort of fellow, clanging around my house?"

"No. He would give you children to fill it," he said with a low murmur of certainty.

If he had suddenly shouted the words, they would have been less startling.

Disconcertingly, she felt a sharp ache somewhere in her middle and a fluttering inside her chest as images flashed in her mind's eye. A girl giggling and skipping through the halls, then sliding down the bannister when she thought no one was looking. A pair of tousled-haired boys, one plunking away on the piano, the other holding a bunch of flowers freshly dug from the garden and with smudges of dirt on his cheeks beneath his mismatched eyes.

"I think you should leave now," she said in a rush. "In case you have forgotten, we are at war."

"You would still run me out of business? Bankrupt your own husband?"

"If that husband were you, the answer is *yes*." She tried to sound waspish, but failed miserably.

He had the nerve to grin about it all. She felt helpless against his devilish charm and nearly found herself grinning back. At least, until his gaze drifted to her lips.

Breathless, a thrill pulsed through her. "You shouldn't look at me like that. There will be no more pushing boundaries and . . . and . . . kissing between us. It will only confuse matters."

"Don't worry, highness. I'm not going to kiss you."

"That is correct."

"*You're* going to kiss me," he clarified with a rakish flick of his brow. "When you've mulled over our upcoming nuptials, and every doubt has been put to bed—"

She gasped at his audacity.

"Or *laid to rest*, if you prefer," he amended with a wicked chuckle. "Then you'll see that I'm right."

"We are *not* getting married. And I, most certainly, will not kiss you."

Yet, even saying the words caused her wayward pulse to quicken. She couldn't stop herself from remembering how it had been. How he'd opened her mouth with his own and slowly consumed her. Her tongue tingled, craving the taste of him again . . .

"Oh, you will. In fact, I'd wager you're already thinking about it."

Heat bloomed in her cheeks even as she shook her head in denial. "That is a bet you'll lose."

The snick on his upper lip and the erudite gleam in his eyes were both calling her bluff, but he didn't speak the words aloud. Instead, he inclined his head and moved past her, toward the stairs. "Sweet dreams, highness. I know that mine will be."

For a full minute, she stared at the vacant corridor, oddly displeased that he hadn't kissed her. She was irritated all over again. Mostly with herself.

Then she had the most troubling thought that, perhaps, there was more between them than a simple, straightforward animosity.

Chapter 16

"... every body was either surprized or not
surprized and had some question to ask ..."

JANE AUSTEN, *Emma*

"**Y**ou're *going to kiss me* ..."

Those taunting words had interrupted Ainsley's sleep all
night, waking her from several scandalous dreams.

In the first one, she'd taken him by the lapels and crushed
her mouth to his in the library. The following one took place
in her office. The next, out on the pavement. And finally, on
the stairs with her skirts tied around his hands.

This morning, she was exhausted, her nerves strung tight.

Yet at least she hadn't spent any time thinking about what
Nigel had said in front of the crowd at Sterling's. Dimly, she
wondered if that had been Reed's plan, to keep her from
worrying herself sick over the things she couldn't alter.

But no. It seemed far more likely that he was just devil-
ishly good at saying roguish things.

By now, half of London would have heard the news of
their betrothal. Hopefully, it would come as such a tremen-
dous shock—as it had to her—that whatever led up to the
announcement would quickly be forgotten.

She sat up in bed, yawning as she lit the taper on the bedside table. The absence of sunlight—as well as the clock on
her mantel—confirmed that it wasn't quite dawn. Even so,
there was no point in lingering beneath the coverlet when

she knew what scandalous tableaus lurked behind her eyelids.

Padding across the room to the washstand, she bathed with the chilled water from the pitcher. By the time she finished, she was fully awake and shivering.

But, too easily, her thoughts drifted back to Reed. All it took was the scent rising up from the jar of balm when she opened the lid. She recalled the comments he'd made about her softness, the low murmurs of appreciation. Then, as if trying to seal in his touch from days ago, she rubbed the silken essence of rosehips and almond blossoms from her palms to her elbows. She even brushed the cream over her cheeks and lips, too, thinking of his slow, burning kisses.

Her skin heated, her heartbeat quivering like a hummingbird's wings. In the oval looking glass, her face was now flushed, her lips full and darker, the deep hue matching the dusky rose of her nipples.

Experimentally, she rubbed balm there, too. Her skin ruched instantly, sensitive to the tentative brush. A strained gasp of pleasure shocked her, her stomach clenching sweetly.

She dropped her hands at once.

Pulse racing, she stared at the glazed-eyed stranger in the mirror and wondered what had come over her. She had never been one driven by passions. Those impulses led people to make rash, foolish decisions—the same way Mother had agreed to marry Father after having known him for a sennight. Too caught up in romantic fancies, she hadn't realized that he'd been pretending to love her. A scoundrel only telling her what she wanted to hear. He'd had no intention of stopping his philandering ways. And, in the end, he'd broken her heart past the point of mending.

Ainsley would never fall for such a trick. By the age of twelve, she'd already vowed to be far more rational. She'd used her parents' mistake to help her see the true nature of things between men and women.

Unfortunately, that hadn't stopped her from making her own dreadful error, but she was determined to use that experience to help others avoid such a fate.

The decision to marry should be made with a sound mind and a passionless heart. Any slight deviation from this could ruin one's life forever.

All at once, she was irritated. Restless. She glared at this strange new sensual creature in the looking glass. Then, stalking to the wardrobe, she slipped into a fresh chemise, stays, and a storm cloud–gray daygown, hoping the drab color would put her back to rights.

As was her habit, she went to the window to let in more light, forgetting it was too early. Even so, as she tied back the heavy drapes, she was welcomed by a soft lavender glow sifting in through the sheers.

Normally she could hear the noise of revelers at night before bed, and by morning she would awaken to the steady clamor of traffic, the sounds blending together into an indiscernible hum. Yet this early all she heard was the sedate clip-clop of a single carriage rattling down the lane.

Curious to see a sleepy, one-cart London, she parted the fall of lace. Her gaze drifted from the retreating scavenger cart on the wet cobblestone to the façade of Sterling's.

The windows were dark and slumbering. All but one.

Across from her, a light glowed, soft and golden. And on the window ledge within that room, sat the piebald cat she knew. Grooming herself, the unnamed cat paused in her ministration and turned her brindled head to stare back across the street. Then she set her paw to the pane as if she'd spotted Ainsley.

Smiling at this, Ainsley pressed her hand to the glass, too, but more so in a jest because she knew it wasn't possible that the creature was actually greeting her. More likely, her focus was on a raindrop, drifting down the other side of the invisible barrier.

Just as Ainsley was taking her hand away to finish dressing, a form approached the neighboring window in a few easy strides. The self-assured gate was so familiar it caused a jolt to rush through her. The pulse in her throat beat a hard tattoo. Then, before she could gather enough sense to slink back behind the curtains, Reed Sterling appeared.

Wearing only his shirtsleeves tucked into a pair of dark trousers, he gathered up the cat in his arms and cradled her against the broad expanse of his chest. He stroked her fur slowly, his lips moving as if he were crooning to her, his expression unguarded. In this light, he didn't seem like a man who'd used violence to make his fortune.

Ainsley did not mean to linger or to invade his privacy, but found herself entranced by this glimpse of him. Was this what he was like when no one was watching?

Well . . . no one other than her.

She should feel guilty for spying on him. And she did, of course, especially when her greedy eyes refused to look away.

The cat squirmed out of his grasp and returned to the window seat. This time, however, she placed both paws on the glass. In the next instant, Reed turned his attention to the view across the street.

Directly into Ainsley's bedchamber window.

She froze in place, hoping that her glass merely appeared like a mirror, reflecting the façade of Sterling's back to him.

But with the candles glowing behind her, she was not so fortunate. Leaning closer, Reed squinted. Then a slow grin curved his mouth.

At once, Ainsley became unaccountably aware of the silky balm she'd applied. Her skin was sensitive to every sensation—the feel of cambric against her taut nipples, the soft weight of her plaited hair hanging over her shoulder, the brush of muslin against her legs.

At the moment, she wore no stockings and no fichu. She

might as well have been naked. Staring back at him, she would almost swear that he could see every inch of her.

Crimson-cheeked, she staggered back beyond the sheer and untied the drapes, letting them fall in place. And as she struggled to catch her breath, she wondered how long Reed had known they shared a view. And how much he had seen of her.

At once, she started to fume. And it wasn't kissing Reed that consumed her thoughts.

She might very well have to kill him instead.

A SHORT while later, and fortified with irritation, Ainsley found Mrs. Darden and Ginny in the kitchen, breaking their fast.

With their schedules, it was a bit early for them to have heard the news. But doubtless there were servants aplenty in other houses nearby who were already scheming ways to pay a visit to this kitchen. So she knew that her beloved cook and maid should hear it from her.

Yet when met with the morning cheer and wishes that she'd enjoyed a good night's rest, Ainsley's mind drifted again to Reed and she faltered a bit.

Her reply came out in a strained rush. "And a good morning to the both of you. I slept well, thank you. And, just so you know, Mr. Sterling and I are betrothed."

She sucked in a breath, smoothed her skirts, and left it at that. After all, there was no reason to explain the circumstances, or provide any further details. Not when this entire debacle would be over in a few weeks.

A tense silence greeted her.

Mrs. Darden stood up from her stool and took her plate to the sink. Then, without a word, she pumped fresh water into a burnished copper kettle and set it on the stovetop. Hard. The fire below crackled and wayward sparks took flight.

Ainsley swallowed and saw Ginny nervously tuck a lock of brown hair beneath her ruffled cap. The maid cast a wary glance between Mrs. Darden and her, her copper-brown eyes going wide as pennies. Then she stood, too, and put a cloche over the bowl of gruel waiting on a tea tray. "I'll just . . . take this up to Mr. Hatman and give the two of you a moment. Um . . . congratulations, miss?"

"Thank you, Ginny."

As Ginny slipped out, Mrs. Darden stormed into the larder and came to the table with a crock of butter and a pint of cream. Then she went to the cabinets to take out a large earthenware bowl. It *thunked* down on the uneven work surface, rocking in a circular motion, the sound of it ringing like a warning bell.

"I can see that you aren't pleased with the news," Ainsley said. "But our betrothal was a matter of necessity."

Mrs. Darden stopped, a wooden spoon gripped in her fist, eyes flashing. "Did that scoundrel take more than a kiss, then?"

Ainsley startled at the assumption, then blushed. "No, of course not."

Mrs. Darden gave a sniff, muttering to herself as she stalked back into the larder. "I would have cut him to ribbons with my cleaver and put him in a stew. A man the likes of him certainly has gall, thinking he deserves one of my girls . . ."

Ainsley tried not to grin, but it was sweet the way their cook had always fussed and clucked over them. "It isn't as bad as all that. His intentions were actually quite honorable."

"If there is an honorable bone in his body then I'll eat a shoe." Mrs. Darden stalked back into the kitchen, her hard gaze narrowing over Ainsley's shoulder and to the sound of the door opening. "Speak of the devil. What do you think you're doing here, Mr. Sterling?"

Reed was here? Ainsley's heart leapt in her throat, her

cheeks still aflame from moments ago. He must have come straight here after . . . after he'd caught her ogling him in his bedchamber. Did he even have time to dress properly? The thought sent another rush of heat through her.

Stricken by wanton curiosity, she turned around to see for herself. Yet before she could, Mrs. Darden slammed a large sack of flour down on the table. A sudden plume of powder erupted in the air and instantly covered Ainsley.

Screwing her eyes closed, she coughed and began to wipe the flour from her own face.

"Allow me, highness."

Reed's low drawl sent her pulse on a harried path straight to her middle. Then he proceeded to clean her face with his handkerchief, his touch passing with care over her lashes. By the time she opened her eyes, his gaze was glowing with warm amusement.

"We keep surprising each other this morning, don't we?"

"How long have you known?"

The nick on his lip twitched as he continued his ablutions. "About our windows? Not nearly long enough. Though it's a pity you found a fresh fichu and put up your hair."

"And you took the time to dress properly. You even donned a cravat." She felt a strange spear of disappointment, along with a shameful desire to untie it and strip it from him as she had done in one of her dreams. "Though that mail coach knot isn't right for you."

His grin faded as he tucked in his chin to peer down at the waterfall of fine linen, anchored by a silver stud pin. "What's wrong with it?"

"It's too large. Perhaps a simple Oriental knot would be more suitable for someone with such a wide, muscular—" She broke off when she realized what she was saying and hoped the flour was hiding the color rising to her cheeks.

But then his grin returned. He leaned in close to whisper in her ear, "Your eyes have gone dark as coffee again. Betrothed only a few hours and you're already thinking of dressing me. Or is it *un*dressing me that's on your mind? Because if that is the case then I can certainly oblige—"

"Nothing of the sort. I'm merely wondering which knot would be the most effective in strangling you."

"You'd have to pin me down first," he said, brushing the handkerchief over the susceptible flesh of her lips. "Then again, I think I'd like that."

Mrs. Darden broke in and began slapping at his arm with a square of toweling until he released Ainsley. "That's enough, you heathen. Whatever wickedness you're speaking has no place in my kitchen. Now state your business and be off."

"Perhaps," he said winking to the cook, "I've come for you, Mrs. Darden. I've heard your scones are so fine that Mr. Finch is thinking about running away with you."

Forever weakened by the praises to her baking, her expression softened marginally. Still, she waggled a finger, though with little force. "I'll not fall for any of your charming ways. I can see the stripes on a snake a good distance away."

"Ah, but what harm is there in a mere garter snake? He only wants to rid you of the vermin that have stolen into the cupboard."

She eyed him shrewdly, hands on her hips. Then with a sigh of exasperation she went to the breadbox and withdrew a scone, handing it to him without ceremony. "You can have one leftover from yesterday."

Reed chuckled and inclined his head.

Though when his teeth sank into the golden pastry, his expression transformed from amusement to wonder. "Now I understand why Finch is so besotted with you. If I weren't already pledged, I'd drop on bended knee this instant."

Mrs. Darden blushed and waved her bit of toweling like a flag of surrender. "Go on with you now."

Ainsley rolled her eyes.

"I also came to invite my lovely bride-to-be to breakfast with my mother." Turning back to Ainsley, he flashed a disarming smile that sent her pulse skipping.

She wished he would stop teasing her. Why wasn't he taking the matter more seriously, instead of pretending to be unbothered by this turn of events?

"Since our courtship will only last until the news fades," she said quietly, "there is no need for me to meet your mother. It would be better if you went alone to explain the situation, I'm sure. And I will stay here to speak with my sisters when they arrive."

His grin turned sardonic. "Do as you must, highness, if it makes you feel better. I will see you again on the morrow for church. Shall I come here first and allow you to tie my cravat?"

"Only if you'd like it in the shape of a noose."

Then before he could say something roguish to charm a smile from her, she turned on her heel and went upstairs to clean up.

❧

REED ENTERED the narrow, three-story townhouse in Cheapside and headed up the stairs to see his mother. After years of enduring her nagging for him to marry, he was eager to deliver the shock of her life.

Drawn by the aroma of roasted meats and toasted bread, he entered the breakfast room that overlooked the rain-soaked garden below. Over the rim of her filigreed cup, his mother's eyes widened with pleased surprise.

"Good morning, Mum." He swept in and strode to the far side of the oval table and bussing her cheek before snatching a steak of bacon from her silver-rimmed plate.

She chided him with a cluck of her tongue. Dressed in a bright paisley morning gown and with her graying, brown-butter hair tucked into a lavender cap, she was the very picture of eccentric domesticity. "And what brings you here so early?"

Catching sight of her grin, he walked to the sideboard to fill his plate with more bacon, adding a mound of coddled eggs, kidneys, and a stack of toasted rye.

"Since you're forever complaining that you don't see me often enough, I thought I'd be welcome. But since I'm not . . ." Holding his heaping plate, he shrugged and looked to the door.

"Bah. You know you're always welcome. Why else would I have such a trough of food waiting?"

"Because you know the footmen fight over the scraps, and you like knowing that their bellies are full," he teased tenderly, sitting across from her.

There had been a time when she'd obsessed about his nourishment, during the year after his father had died. Sometimes they'd had nothing but turnip soup for weeks, the broth getting thinner day by day. Then she'd taken measures to ensure that there was food on the table by marrying that scum aristocrat.

Things hadn't turned out the way she'd planned. Not with her second marriage, or the third or the fourth. But at least they'd always had each other to lean upon. And Reed would make certain that his mother never felt the need to marry again, unless it was her wish.

"Keep feeding them as you do and they'll be too fat and lazy to be of use," he said with a grin around a mouthful of bread slathered in marmalade.

"Then give me grandchildren to feed."

This was the moment he'd been waiting for. Pushing his plate forward, he leaned back in his chair. "Which brings me to the reason for my visit."

She frowned. "Don't tell me you've got a bastard from one of those vulgar widows who frequent your club."

He clenched his teeth, wishing his mother did not know

so much about his business or his life. Besides, it had been a long while since his last tryst. "No. As a matter of fact, I'm getting married."

He waited for her eyes to widen with shock.

"Well it is about time," she said, instead, and more with scolding than with the glad surprise he expected. "By your age I already had a boy of fourteen running around and getting into mischief."

He expelled a sigh. "I've not been betrothed even a full day and you are already waiting for my house to be filled with children."

As the words left him, a warmth simmered in his blood as he imagined an infant in his arms, looking up at him with a pair of brownish-gray eyes.

Yet he didn't even know if Ainsley wanted children. Hell, he didn't even know if she would ever allow him in her bed. She was convinced they wouldn't need to marry at all, believing that the news would fade and she could end their betrothal without injury to her reputation.

He knew otherwise, of course. The same way he knew that reputation was what mattered most to her. In the end, there would be no other way.

So, for the time being, he was willing to be patient.

"And why not? You've got that big house in the country to fill, after all. And I've rooms aplenty for my grandchildren to visit. They can stay here, too, for whenever you and your bride want some time to yourselves."

He shook his head at his mother's romantic notions and laughed. "You don't even know who my bride is."

"Well it's Miss Bourne, of course," his mother said, giving *him* the shock of his life.

"Whatever makes you say that?"

"Because you haven't spoken of anyone else since the day you first met her. It was clear that she got under your skin straightaway."

He shifted in the chair, wondering what other secrets his mother was hiding behind that grin of hers. "You never mentioned your suspicions. In fact, I'm surprised that I haven't caught you visiting the Bourne Matrimonial Agency, chatting up Miss Bourne."

"Me, interfere? Never." Her brows arched with cagey innocence. "A mother always knows when to step away and let matters take their natural course."

Reed crossed his arms and narrowed his eyes, not believing her for an instant.

Chapter 17

"She had been extremely surprized, never more so,
than when Emma first opened the affair to her . . ."

JANE AUSTEN, *Emma*

"A Sunday afternoon walk through the park is always
lovely," Briar said from one side of Ainsley while Jacinda
walked on the other.

Ainsley clenched her teeth, sliding a glance to the gossip-
mongers they passed on the path. "It was bad enough that
the church had fallen deathly silent when the banns were
read this morning, but now we have become a spectacle for
the gawkers."

Yesterday she had told her sisters about the sham betrothal. They had taken the news surprisingly well. Of
course, Briar had become a little dreamy eyed. Jacinda,
on the other hand, had been prepared to investigate every
aspect of Reed's life, but Ainsley assured her that it wasn't
necessary. This would all be over soon enough.

Only now did she have her doubts.

Ever since this morning's announcement had rendered
the congregation mute with shock, she had a queer sense that
there would be no turning back. That, no matter what other
news swept in, the *ton* would not quickly forget this betrothal.

Was she still pinning her hopes on the arrival of the king's
giraffe to take the focus away from this entire debacle?

A giraffe, indeed.

"*I heard the nuptials are being forced by . . . circumstance.*"

"*And I've heard the affair has been ongoing for quite some time.*"

The statements came from a pair of busybodies who were looking their way and whispering behind gloved hands as they twirled their parasols. The saddest part was that they'd both been clients at one time.

Jacinda waved to them. "Lady Throckmeyer, how nice to see you. How is your daughter? After she eloped with your husband's steward, I've heard so little about her."

Lady Throckmeyer stiffened and quickened her steps along on the path, leaving Lady Baftig to catch up.

Jacinda smiled in triumph and said to Ainsley, "I'm only doing what you would have done for us. After Father left, you always said that the Bourne women never cower in the face of scandal."

"You did," Briar agreed with a squeeze of their linked arms. "And you also said that we were strongest when we worked together."

"I likely said that just to keep you on task when we had chores to complete. You were forever daydreaming, and Jacinda was always into mischief." Despite herself, a fond grin touched her lips.

"Nevertheless, you were right. Now that the banns have been read for you and Mr. Sterling, we will face the *ton* together."

"Well, I am glad to have you both at my side," Ainsley said.

"And this is where we shall stay," Briar said with a firm nod. "Can you believe that Lady Baftig had the audacity to pull me aside in the church vestibule, stating that her husband allowed her to wager on the month of your blessed event? She was actually hoping that I would provide some insight."

A spear of alarm tore through Ainsley. Unconsciously, her hand drifted to protect her midriff.

"Dear heavens, don't do that"—Jacinda sidestepped in front of her—"or we'll never sweep the rumors under the rug."

Realizing what she'd done, Ainsley made a show of brushing something from her blue muslin. Even Briar pretended to find something distasteful on her dress, wrinkling her nose as she pinched the invisible *thing* and tossed it onto the path.

Ainsley was immensely glad to have such wonderful sisters.

"As it is," Jacinda continued, walking on, "half the *ton* are sighing over tales of romance and chivalry."

Ainsley scoffed. "Then they are easily entertained. As far as I am aware, Mr. Sterling made his announcement after whatever that odious Mr. Mitchum said and that is all."

"There was a little more to it than that." Jacinda eyed her warily.

Off in the distance, Ainsley heard the chime of bells. Each toll seemed to reverberate through her bones. She should have known that Jacinda would not be satisfied until she knew all. Or nearly all.

There were things that would always remain a secret, if Ainsley could help it.

"Leave it to you to find out all the details," Briar said as she leaned in, expectation brimming in her glowing countenance. "Well, go on. Tell us."

"I don't know what Mr. Mitchum said before he was tossed out on his ear," Jacinda began, not realizing the relief she'd just given to Ainsley. "But I do know that one of Mr. Sterling's men escorted him in a hackney all the way out of town. And that isn't even the lion's share of the news."

"It isn't?" To Ainsley, this was news indeed. She had no idea that Nigel had been carted away.

Jacinda shook her head. "According to what Crispin's valet heard from the driver of Viscount Covingdale, there was a good deal of fuss afterward and mentions of a fight between your favorite gaming hell owner and Mr. Mitchum. Apparently, there are two—supposedly secret—betting books already filled with wagers on the outcome."

"A fight to defend your honor." Briar sighed, clutching her bosom. "How romantic."

Ainsley did not think so. She stopped on the path, waves of icy fury sluicing through her body as she clenched her fists. "The price of chivalry must be high these days."

So Reed had thought to rescue her, did he? More likely, he was angling to earn a fortune from the gamblers betting on a fight between him and Nigel. How convenient that he'd forgotten to mention it to her!

Well, she was about to tell Mr. Sterling to go to the devil. There was no possible way she was going to remain betrothed—even if only in temporary pretense—to a conniving wolf for a moment longer.

FOR AN hour outside the church, Reed endured pats on the shoulder, handshakes, and jests about marrying up in society. There were even a few snickers from men who wondered if Sterling's would become a tea parlor.

Standing beside Viscount Eggleston, Reed kept his expression neutral. He would never reveal that the sly slights against his common birth rubbed a burr beneath his skin, or that he was wondering if Ainsley felt that she was marrying *down*.

As for those who remarked on the fate of Sterling's, he let the force of his grip be the answer to that.

Even so, by the time they'd arrived at Eggleston's townhouse, his mood was fractious. He wanted to settle the contract quickly then leave to expend some pent-up aggression in a sparring session with Pickerington. But that wasn't to be the case.

Reed was in Eggleston's study no more than a minute before they were interrupted by a knock on the door.

Then Ainsley peered inside the room without sparing him a glance, her mouth set in a familiar stubborn line. He knew in an instant that he wasn't the only one affected by the congregation's reaction this morning.

"Uncle, might I speak with Mr. Sterling privately for a moment? If you would but wait across the hall, I intend to leave the door open. This won't take long."

A strained look passed between Eggleston and his niece. It was clear by the unusually long delay before he answered that there was an unspoken communication that Reed wasn't privy to.

Eggleston stood. "If you are certain."

"I am," she said quietly.

The instant they were alone, Ainsley turned to Reed and crossed her arms, her eyes frosty with haughty disdain. "Our pretend betrothal is at an end. I would rather be labeled a jilt and a . . . a strumpet than to have my name linked to yours."

He was a fool to think that the insults would end on the church steps.

Standing, he expelled a hollow laugh. "So, you would rather face ruination than taint your name with a commoner. I can't say I'm surprised."

"I'd never marry a man who would profit from my misfortune. You lied about your motives," she accused. "And I can only wonder how long it will be until you lie to me again."

Now he was a liar, too? This day was getting better and better. "As far as I recall, my only motive was to keep your name from being dragged through the gutter."

"Ha! A pretty sentiment, indeed, but I know the truth. I know all about your betting books and the fight you intend to have with Mr. Mitchum. I see now that you were nothing more than a chameleon last night when you *saved my honor*." She scoffed.

He stiffened, clenching his teeth. "I didn't lie to you. I don't know what you've heard but—"

"No. I refuse to listen to another word." She stalked to the door and gestured for him to leave. "I've dealt with enough of your kind to last three lifetimes. I have no use for charming liars who show one side to the world and a wholly different one in private. Whose moods shift without warning from agreeable to enraged—"

Her voice broke. She averted her face, the color draining from her cheeks.

At once, Reed knew this wasn't about him. Not entirely, anyway. And drawing closer, it wasn't contempt or anger in her eyes, but something more vulnerable. Fragile.

"Has a man raised his hand to you, highness?" he asked gently, needing to know once and for all.

She slid him a warning look. "We are not having this conversation."

"It was Mitchum, wasn't it?" he persisted. "He's the reason your betrothal came to an end and you fled Hampshire. He's the reason you flinched that day out front on the pavement."

Her expression was so stark, so wounded, that he could read the truth even when she didn't answer. Then, without warning, tears collected along the lower rim of her lids.

Reed found it hard to breathe, his chest tight. Reflexively, he reached out to soothe her, but she turned away, walking back into the room.

She stopped at the hearth, staring at the empty grate. "You may go, Mr. Sterling."

"If you're expecting me to leave you like this, then you'll have a long wait. You and I have more in common than you know, and I think it's time we knew a bit more about each other. Don't you?"

She quickly swiped at her cheek when he moved next to her. "I can see no point in it. We will be going our separate ways soon enough."

Oh, how wrong she was, but now was not the time to embark on that discussion again.

"Very well, then I'll begin," he said, swallowing down a rise of trepidation. "This scar on my lip is from the ruby signet ring of my mother's second husband when I was ten years old."

He shifted, uncomfortable as he waited for her response. His mother and Finch knew this part of his life, but he'd never trusted anyone else with a glimpse of his childhood. The thought of sharing it had always made him feel too vulnerable. Weak.

Ainsley glanced up at him with a start. "I'd always thought it was from a fight."

"Aye. But one-sided."

She searched his gaze. Her eyes were that same soft brownish-gray but now they glowed with fury in a way he'd never seen before. He could only describe it as *tender ferocity*. And, for an instant, he couldn't speak from the force of it washing over him. Through him.

"Only the vilest offal-eating maggot would abuse a child," she said with vehemence, as if seeing the boy he'd once been. "I hope your mother railed at him and cast him out."

"I lied to her about the cuts and bruises," he admitted. "Mum would've only blamed herself, and she'd suffered enough already."

"Did he . . . hurt her, too?"

Reed nodded. "It wasn't enough to make her cry, shouting that he'd married far below his station. No, he'd had to break the few possessions she'd collected—figurines and whatnots, given to her by her parents and by my father. Then he'd needed more—" He expelled a heavy breath. "He'd needed her to beg and cower."

She turned toward the empty hearth again, a visible shudder skimming over her as she clutched the folds of her fichu. "No wonder you detest the aristocracy."

"Not all of them."

He nudged her hand as if by accident. Then lingered, needing to know if sharing part of his past had been the right choice.

She didn't pull away. He took it a step further and turned his wrist, furtively sliding his palm against hers.

Her delicate fingers twined with his, held fast. "I know what you're waiting for, but I'm not certain I can be as candid. I've never spoken of it before and . . . well . . . I'm rather reserved in nature."

"You don't say."

She slanted him a look and squeezed his hand in gentle reprimand. He didn't mind at all, and caressed hers in return, rhythmically sweeping along the delicate inner curve between her thumb and forefinger.

"Mr. Mitchum was not the man he claimed to be," she said after a moment. Silence followed. Then she took a shaky breath and began. "At first, he was all charm and affability, eager to become acquainted with my family and to know my innermost thoughts and wishes. He even said he wanted the same things that I did—companionship and trust."

Reed noticed that she did not mention *love*. Why wasn't that at the top of her list?

"It all turned out to be a charade," she continued. "In fact, everything about him was false. In front of my family, he was charismatic and even-tempered. Yet in private—

after our betrothal was announced—he would brood, turning peevish and critical. At the least provocation, he would grab my wrist with undue force or pinch the skin inside my arm to reprimand me for a supposed slight to him. Fool that I was, I kept trying to please him only to find that my efforts were never enough. He always wanted . . ."

"More," Reed finished for her, the story agonizingly familiar.

"Yes. And it took me far too long to realize that I couldn't spend my life never knowing what to expect from my husband. Fearing the shifts of his moods. Yet by the time I'd had this epiphany, I'd already become a stranger to myself. That's when I decided to break our betrothal."

Reed felt a tremor pulse from her hand into his, and suddenly he felt colder, tension coiling in the pit of his stomach. "I have a sense you're not about to tell me that you immediately packed your bags and came to London."

"If only," she said, her voice strained. "We'd had plans to walk in the gardens with my sisters that day, but I asked my uncle if we might stay behind. Alone in the parlor, I told Mr. Mitchum that we were not suited. I even placed all the blame on myself, rather than risk wounding his fragile ego. But he seemed to hear the truth of what I was saying—that I could not bear a life with him. And I was a fool to believe that I had seen him at his worst.

"He altered again right before my eyes, cursing at me. Calling me the vilest names. Making up stories that I was a flirt and gave my affections to other men while I remained cold and sterile with him. He even seemed to believe these wild fabrications. Then he took hold of my shoulders and shook me hard enough to rattle my teeth. I stumbled back and—"

She slipped her hand free, resting it against her throat, below the frantic flutter of her pulse.

"You do not have to relive it if it is too painful," Reed said, unsure if he could bear hearing more.

She lifted her gaze, her expression so raw and vulnerable that he had to fight the urge to haul her into his arms. But he did not dare breech this boundary. Not unless she wanted him to. Instead, he opened his arms in invitation, needing her to know that he was here for her, no more no less. Then he waited.

It was the longest two seconds of his life.

Of her own accord, she stepped into his embrace. An instant tremor rolled from her body, through his. "I prefer that you understand, I think."

Gathering her close, he absorbed every tiny shiver, wishing he could do more.

"When I stumbled, he came down on top of me," she said in a whisper. "I tried to push free, but he seemed to be everywhere at once—his forearm bearing down across my throat, his hand wrenching up my skirts, his knee prying my unyielding legs apart. If my uncle hadn't charged in at the precise moment . . ."

She didn't finish. Instead, she buried her face into his waistcoat and broke apart on a sob.

The air left his lungs in a rush. His pulse raced. Reed felt as if he'd been there, watching it all. Helpless to stop it. Helpless to keep her safe.

He cinched his arms around her as if he could hold her tight enough to take it all away. And she burrowed closer, too, holding on to him as if she knew he would. If only he could.

Kissing her hair, he breathed in her sweet scent. He tried to hold back the fury he felt for Mitchum and the desire to hunt him down like a mad dog and rid the earth of him.

Yet even more powerful than that rage was the overwhelming admiration for the woman in his arms. After all she'd suffered, she'd never once given up. Never resigned herself to her fate.

Ainsley Bourne was a fighter, her will stronger than any opponent he'd ever faced.

"And then you came to London."

Sniffling, she nodded. "The very next day."

Reed recalled the exact moment he'd seen her, stepping out of a carriage well sprung with trunks, bandboxes, and portmanteaus. Looking down from his bedchamber window and through the veil of rain, he'd marveled at the way she'd taken charge, pointing from underneath a black umbrella, ordering the servants and the driver to discharge the luggage, while keeping watch over her sisters as they ventured inside the townhouse.

To him, she'd seemed like a little queen with her stiff, regal bearing and he was already set on despising his new neighbors.

Then she'd done something he didn't expect. Once her sisters were inside, Ainsley stood on the pavement and lowered her umbrella. She tilted her head back, closed her eyes, and let the rain fall on her face.

He'd been struck by her, fascinated in a way that he couldn't explain. And since that moment, he'd wanted to see her like that again, wholly unguarded and serene as the rain bathed her skin.

She was always going to be his, whether she knew it or not.

Reaching up, he lifted her face. He wanted to kiss away her tears, sip them from the thorn-shaped clusters of her eyelashes, drink them into his soul so he could take her pain away.

But, from the doorway, Eggleston cleared his throat.

Reed expelled a disgruntled breath. Instead of kissing her, he withdrew a handkerchief and gently blotted away all the lingering traces. Not wanting to give her uncle a reason to ask him to leave, he took one step back. Gradually, he heard the viscount's footsteps retreat across the hall.

Then, propping a shoulder on the far side of the mantel, he stared down at the ash beneath the cold grate. "And you were well rid of Mitchum for nearly two years. Pity that he didn't have the good sense to befall a fatal injury in all that time."

"I thought that he would have forgotten about me. After all, he'd proved often enough that I meant nothing to him," Ainsley said, her brow knitted. "When I'd heard he married, I never thought he'd look for me. Even so, I suggested to my sisters that we take our mother's maiden name as a measure of insurance. Of course, they do not know the true reason."

When she looked at him with expectation in her gaze, he knew she was asking him to keep her secret. Reed was moved by her trust in him. "I won't speak of it, or of anything between us."

She nodded in return. An alliance forged between them. And now was the time for her to understand that they had more than just a pretense of a betrothal.

"Before Lord Bray died, my mother and I stayed at the country estate while he amused himself in London. We spent days on end, weeks even, afraid of his return and kept vigil by the window. And likely"—he looked at her with discerning scrutiny—"kept too many candles lit at night."

"Am I that transparent?"

"Not nearly enough for my liking," he said honestly. "Ainsley, no one should have to go through their life looking over their shoulder, fearing what may be lurking around every corner. I would save you from that. But there is only one way."

A wry smirk lifted one side of her mouth. "I'm not entirely certain if you proposed marriage or murder."

Both. But instead of answering aloud, he reached out to tug her away from the direct view of the open door. Feeling her acquiesce without hesitation, he went further and pulled her against him. She yielded on a soft breath, her hands splaying over his waistcoat, her cheek resting in the crook of his shoulder.

"Was that a sigh of contentment, highness?"

"Of course not. You merely squeezed all the air from my lungs," she said, but he heard the smile in her voice.

"And I thought we were finally getting somewhere."

When his lips grazed over the top of her head and he breathed her in, he heard another contented sigh, but he didn't mention it.

"Whatever happened to Lord Bray?" she asked, her fingertip playing with a cloth-covered button.

"He died in a duel."

"I hope he was in agony for a long while."

Tilting her face up, he pressed his forehead to hers. "You and I are not so different."

"Reed," she said, sending a jolt through him from the intimacy of his name on her lips. "The idea of being at a man's mercy terrifies me. Everything I have would belong to him, and I've only just started to feel as if what I have, even my own person, belongs to me. That is why this has to be a pre—"

Before she could say pretense or pretend betrothal, or whatever else she concocted to keep the inevitable from happening, he interrupted. "Everything that you have is and will always be yours—your business, your dowry, and your person. I'd never force myself on you."

"But what about your life? Surely you must have a . . . mistress and any number of women fawning over you, and feeding your enormous ego."

At any other time, seeing Ainsley frown and hearing the sharp bite in her tone wouldn't have pleased him so much. Could she be jealous?

He lifted her hand, brushing his lips over the fine-boned

ridges of her knuckles. "I've been a wee bit too distracted by a certain neighbor who's declared war on my business to bother with any other women in a long while. And besides, when she marries me, I might earn a cease-fire."

"*Hmph.* I wouldn't count on that, Mr. Sterling." She stepped back, yet her fingers remained laced with his. For an instant, she stared down at their joined hands, her expression marked with inner confusion.

Reed tried not to grin. He'd gained a lot of ground today, advancing his troops toward victory, earning her trust bit by bit. But he didn't want to risk a setback, so he decided to give her time to mull over the inevitability of their future.

Bowing over her hand, he pressed a kiss to each of her perfectly rounded nails. He stopped when he reached her thumb. Noting its jagged edge, he tsked with affection. "You worry too much, highness. I could suggest a multitude of other uses for those pretty teeth and that sumptuous mouth."

Blushing, she slipped free and covered her hand with the other. "I'm certain I shouldn't care to hear any of them."

"Another pity," he said with a wink. "Of course, you could simply kiss your betrothed."

"I could. But I won't," she said with her usual hauteur. Yet, her eyes were soft and she made the mistake of biting her lip to hide a grin.

He chuckled as he strode to the door. "I suppose I'll simply have to settle for the kisses you blow to me from your window each night."

Ready for her swift denial, she surprised him by primly stating, "I suppose you shall, Mr. Sterling."

❧

LEAVING AINSLEY, Reed met Eggleston in the sitting room across the hall and closed the door. Seeing a slender writing desk ready with paper and ink, he dipped the quill and scrawled a figure. Then he handed it to Eggleston. "Draw up the contracts and put that down as her settlement, along with Harrowfield, my country estate."

"Mr. Sterling"—Eggleston balked at the page—"indeed that is a fortune! She would never agree to such extrava—"

Reed would give her more if he had it. "If I hang for Nigel Mitchum's murder, I want to ensure that she'll be a very wealthy widow and never have to put herself under a man's power again."

Chapter 18

"Little Emma, grow up a better woman than your aunt."
Jane Austen, *Emma*

The following morning, Ainsley held her fractious niece and paced around the office. Picking up various objects, she tried to distract Emma from crying, but nothing worked.

The agency was closed today. Nevertheless, that didn't stop a small influx of new applicants from arriving by post. It seemed that the Bourne matchmakers had mysteriously become *de rigueur*.

Then again, their sudden popularity might be due to the fact of the Season winding down and not that the *ton* had been waiting for the last Bourne sister to find a match. Ainsley refused to believe that it was because of her betrothal.

Regardless of the reason, they had work to do.

Briar sent a missive, stating that she would be late. But Jacinda popped in a short while ago for the new list, leaving Emma behind as she went to perform her usual investigations, vetting the potential clients to discover if they were the right sort or not.

Usually when the baby was here on the nurse's day off she cooed and played contentedly. But today, Emma was not pleased that her mother was away.

Ainsley's first failure in entertaining her niece was singing. It made Emma only wail louder. She didn't blame her. The off-key warbling even wounded her own ears.

Then she tried whistling the way Reed often did. Failure number two. A brief high-pitched sound was all she managed. And it was met with a peculiar baying from the neighbor's dog, through the open window.

Tickling and bouncing were failures three and four, and reciting Shakespeare's eighteenth sonnet was failure five. Emma tearfully despised being compared to a "summer's day."

"I know, dearest," Ainsley said, pressing a kiss to the baby's forehead. "There are days when I simply want to wail at the world, too. Best get it all out while no one thinks less of you for it."

As Emma continued to empty the Thames, Ainsley was beginning to fear that, among the many feminine accomplishments she did not possess—drawing, singing, and dancing at the top of the list—nurturing was one of them. Was there anything she was good at?

Hearing the click of her office door opening, she turned, expecting to see her sister. But it wasn't Jacinda at all.

Reed filled the doorway and her heart hopped beneath her breast. Her eyes greedily roved over his form, his muscular arms and chest encased in a green coat and buttery waistcoat, with his cravat tied in the Oriental knot she'd suggested. And yet, she wished he hadn't donned such proper attire for paying a call. She missed the sight of his throat and the open neck of his shirt. A shameful thing to admit.

"Mr. Sterling, whatever are you doing here?"

"At the moment, I can't recall," Reed answered, watching her with an alert intensity she'd never seen before. He looked as if he didn't know what to make of the vision before him. He even blinked. *Twice.* "I've never seen you with a babe before. Who is your visitor?"

With a handkerchief, Ainsley wiped at the drool collecting beneath the baby's pouting lip. "My niece, Emma. She's not in the best of tempers this morning. Nothing will dissuade her from telling me how miserable she is."

"She's likely cutting her teeth. Finch's daughter is enduring the same and he is having little luck as well. My mum knitted her a bizarre one-eyed doll that has seemed to help distract her. Does your niece have a doll, or even a rattle?"

He hesitated on the threshold, then stepped into the room.

It wasn't in him to leave someone floundering, and she smiled at this knowledge. "Yes, but no object holds her interest."

"*Hmm.* Have you tried bouncing her on your hip?"

"It only works for a short duration. I fear she realizes that I have no idea what I'm doing. I was never very good at providing comfort," she admitted with a regretful sigh. "When my sisters were little and they would suffer scrapes and bruises, I was there to dry their tears but also quick to assure them that what happened would mend. I'd even remind them of a previous scrape or bruise that had not left a permanent mark. What they required, I'm sure, was someone to coddle them for a while. Oh, but their tears would always burrow inside of me, making me feel just as wounded and helpless. Much like now."

Hearing her own words—though it was difficult over the wailing of her niece—Ainsley cringed inwardly. She hadn't meant to reveal more of her failings to him.

"Don't discount yourself too quickly," he said plainly. "From what I know of your sisters, they have fared well from your guidance. Both are intelligent, agreeable, and seemingly content with their lives. At least part of the reason for that is because they had you to give them strength when they needed it."

Ainsley's breath stalled in her throat. That was, perhaps, the most beautiful thing anyone had ever said to her. She didn't know how to respond.

Feeling inordinately shy all of the sudden, she tucked her head toward Emma and bussed her cheek. "Don't worry, dearest," she said, "when this is all over and you're able to eat Mrs. Darden's scones, you'll see that the pain was worth it."

Reed chuckled. "A truer fact has never been spoken. Especially the ones brushed with the divine honey glaze with almonds on top."

Ainsley should have known this about him. They'd been acquainted for so long, she should know everything about him. But, after the moments they'd shared in her uncle's study, this seemed very much like a new day. A fresh start.

"Those are my favorite as well," she said quietly, lifting her gaze when he came closer.

His nearness was as inviting as a warm fire on a cool morning. And when he spoke, his low uncultured drawl burrowed deep inside her, making her heart quicken. "Have you tried dancing with her?"

"I'm afraid that was another thing I was never good at. While Jacinda and Briar had lessons with a dancing master, I was seeing to my uncle's accounts."

"Perhaps you lacked enjoyment in the amusement because your teacher wasn't as skilled as he ought to have been," Reed said, misunderstanding. He held out his hand and, reflexively, she gave hers. "I, however, have been told that I am quite light on my feet."

She felt her lashes pinch together, her spine stiffening. "Have you, indeed?"

"Aye."

"And just *how* many women have showered you with such praise?"

"Enough." He grinned, a roguish light glinting in his mismatched eyes as he tugged her closer. "But I only want to hear it once more. From you."

"Well, you wo—*oh*—"

He turned her in a full circle, cutting off her diatribe in a breathless spin, her skirts swishing around her legs. Emma gurgled with a laugh, her drooling mouth curling up like a bow.

"The skill has aided me against many a sparring opponent," he said, guiding her into another twirl, making her giddy. "See? It's as easy as a country dance. And now we'll simply sway together as if we're her rocking chair."

With one hand still holding hers, his other settled on her waist with the baby between them, she felt a smile bloom on her lips, helpless against the insistent tug. "It appears as though you have the power to sweep even the smallest of women off her feet."

"Is that a compliment, highness? Or a confession?"

"Neither," she said instantly, her cheeks heating with color.

He flashed a wicked smile but made no comment. He simply swayed back and forth, keeping her body moving in time with his, her heart thrumming in a decidedly contented rhythm.

But Emma started to fuss again, gnawing on her chubby little fist.

"I think, perhaps, she is overtired," Ainsley said, brushing her cheek across her niece's downy tendrils.

"Then sing her a lullaby."

Ainsley issued a soft laugh. "I have already wounded her ears with my screeching this morning."

Drat! Why could she not stop telling him all the things that were wrong with her?

"I thought all debutantes possessed an array of accomplishments meant to entertain guests and delight their husbands."

Reed was teasing, she knew, yet it had always bothered her that she wasn't good at anything that mattered. She wasn't as crafty, nor did she know as many languages as

Jacinda. And she didn't possess a pinky's worth of Briar's innumerable talents. All she could do was write lists, add and subtract figures, and make the difficult decisions of how to run a household on a meager income. Nothing that she could demonstrate for the *delight of her husband*.

As she was pondering all her failings, Reed began to croon to her niece, saying, "Hush now, little one, and rest your head," his words gradually turning into a song, a low lullaby of sorts.

At once, Ainsley was entranced. The rich baritone was as silken as sun-warmed dew on tulip petals. She wanted to close her eyes and listen to him for hours. Emma must have felt the same. Gradually, her head sagged wetly against Ainsley's shoulder, her fractious grunts fading into sleepy, sweet-scented yawns.

Whenever Reed held Ainsley, he didn't only push past her boundaries but seemed to push some of his strength and certainty into her as well. In his arms, the doubts she'd always carried with her weighed nothing at all. And for that reason, she was sorry that the child had fallen asleep because then Reed released her and stepped back.

She felt the loss instantly. Left to stand alone, she was a cut flower without a vase.

A disturbing thought, indeed.

"I'll leave you now," he whispered, passing a gentle hand over the baby's auburn hair, and lightly over Ainsley's cheek. Then, moving to the doorway, he paused once more, as if she wasn't the only one who didn't want him to go so soon. His attention shifted to the red leather book lying on the console table. "A matchmaker's book for a matchmaker?"

If Ainsley had been paying attention, instead of allowing herself to be distracted by foreign notions, she would have remembered the flower tucked between the pages.

Too late, she saw the fringe of vellum as he reached for the book. She started forward, too, ready to hide it safely away. But in her clumsy haste, she knocked it loose.

The book fell back to the table, and the slip of vellum drifted aimlessly to the floor.

If it weren't for the baby in her arms, Ainsley might have thrown herself on it. Anything to keep Reed from discovering her secret.

But it was no use. Reed was already bending toward the fallen treasure, his fingers closing over the folded edge.

As he picked it up, he studied the pressed flower carefully. Then looked at her, head cocked in surprise. "Is this the same—"

"Don't be ridiculous. Of course it isn't."

A slow grin curled his lips. "I think it is, highness. I remember the little nick on the petal."

Without thinking, her gaze dipped to the nick on his upper lip. "It isn't what you think."

"Of course it isn't," he said, repeating her own words. Still grinning, he tucked the vellum carefully back inside the book. His pleased gaze flitted over her features. "Just in case you're wondering, now would be the perfect moment for you to kiss me."

She blushed furiously at his outrageous flirtation, temptation tingling on her lips. "I'm certain that moment came and went at least five minutes ago."

"Where is the key for your clock? I'm going to wind it back."

She refused to smile. "Why, again, did you come to call?"

"Perhaps I needed to see what fichu you were wearing today. I like this one—the netting is so fine I can see right through it." Ignoring her gasp, he moved closer and slowly reached up to tuck a loose tendril behind her ear. "Will you be wearing it when I return this evening?"

"This evening?" she rasped, a hot breath caught in her throat as his fingertips grazed the sensitive underside of her ear before he withdrew.

"Your uncle invited me to dinner on his way to the park. Didn't I mention it?"

But Reed did not wait for her to answer. He merely flashed a grin at her bemused expression and disappeared down the corridor. Not too far in the distance, she could hear him singing again.

On Richmond Hill there lives a lass,
More bright than May-day morn,
Whose charms all other maids' surpass,
A rose without a thorn.

THAT EVENING, Reed was surprised to find that he hadn't been the only one invited to dine. A little dragon was there as well.

If it weren't for the gray hair and wrinkles, the diminutive Duchess of Holliford might have looked like a child sitting in the armchair at the head of the table. Lifting a forkful of whitefish, she eyed him narrowly as if she suspected him of leaving bones in it.

But a child she was not. Nor was she addlepated with age, much to his regret. She was sharp-witted and insightful, yet also demanding in her need to satisfy her curiosity.

"I seem to recall a day when you paid a visit to me, Mr. Sterling," the duchess began when the next course arrived and a fresh silver-rimmed plate was placed in front of her. "It was shortly after the viscount and his nieces arrived, and you were determined to purchase this townhouse from me."

"I was, Your Grace."

Across the table from him, Ainsley lowered her napkin into her lap, her slender winged brows knitted. She looked lovely this evening, with her hair piled up into chestnut ringlets at the crown of her head. Candle flame from the chandelier bathed her skin in a creamy glow, accentuating her dark features *and* the way her lashes bunched together as she studied him with skepticism.

The duchess clucked her tongue. "Do not imagine that this arrangement will earn you the deed to the property. I am generous with my girls, but not with outsiders."

Outsiders? That was likely a polite euphemism for *commoners*.

"Isn't it possible that I would rather have Miss Bourne than a pile of bricks?" he asked simply. His focus on Ainsley, he saw the exact moment when color suffused her cheeks.

"Pay no attention to Mr. Sterling, Your Grace," she said in a rush. "He delights in saying the most outlandish things whenever the opportunity arises."

The little dragon eyed him shrewdly, nonetheless. "Pretty words, indeed, young man. Though time will be the best judge of things. It always is."

He inclined his head in agreement.

Then Eggleston, apparently liking Reed's declaration, smiled broadly and lifted his glass. "What a splendid time for a toast . . ."

After they all drank to the health and happiness of the bride- and groom-to-be, dinner resumed with less pointed queries from Eggleston, most regarding Reed's education and family. And he responded without elaboration, knowing that the duchess was weighing his every answer. Watching his every move.

He felt like a banker at the door of a vault, trying to hide the key from cutpurses.

"You must have seen a good deal of excitement at Sterling's," Eggleston said, chafing his hands together as he watched Mr. Hatman roll a linen-draped dinner cart into the room, presenting an elaborately molded brown pudding.

Distractedly, Reed watched as the elderly man lifted a shaky hand and proceeded to drench the dessert with fine spirits. A deluge of spirits, in fact.

"I have, indeed. Though perhaps those tales are not appropriate dinner conversation, my lord." Reed earned a warm look of approval from Ainsley.

Doubtless, she was unaware that such a small gesture sent his pulse hammering. Then again, it might also be the gown she wore this evening—an apricot-colored silk confection that reminded him of when he had seen the sleeve of her nightdress.

He hadn't been the same since.

"Though you must be concerned about your gambling establishment's future," the duchess remarked.

"Not at all, Your Grace. Sterling's is in the black."

"At the moment, perhaps," the dragon continued after a sip from her goblet. "However, there are rumors that the number of your patrons will fall considerably once you are married. After all, your fortune was made by men who were drawn to a basic male magnetism that they, themselves, did not possess. And a woman of good breeding has the power to polish away that tarnish those gentlemen find so enthralling."

Reed refused to shift in his chair or reveal that this same thought had been on his mind as well. Especially this evening before coming here.

Walking through his club, the crowd was noticeably thinner. He hadn't bumped a single shoulder. But he wasn't about to admit it to the duchess. Instead, he decided that a bland response was required.

Yet before he could speak, a fireball erupted in the corner of the room in a great *whoosh*. Gasps around the table followed. Hatman staggered back, waving a napkin. A brandy-soaked napkin.

It was only an instant before it went up in flames, too.

Ainsley and Reed both sprang into action. She assisted the bewildered Mr. Hatman into a chair. Reed doused one fire with a few stomps of his boot, and the other with a glass of water over the rippling blue flame. Eggleston crossed the room and opened the window.

Waving a silver tray to clear the smoke, he chuckled ruefully. "How did you like our *pudding spectacular*, Mr. Sterling?"

The charred, drenched pudding issued a final slow wheeze before the center dome collapsed into a puddle. "Is this a nightly occurrence?"

"Reserved for special occasions only." Ainsley coughed, but with a laugh and a full, heart-stopping smile.

Suddenly, he couldn't breathe. And it wasn't from the smoke either.

"We could all dive into the remaining disaster with our spoons," she rasped, "or retire to the parlor now. In a minute, I'll pop down to the kitchen and ask Mrs. Darden if she has a few scones left from this morning."

It took Reed a moment to respond. Her smile still had a firm hold on him.

But so did the duchess's warning.

He could imagine, too easily, how a life with Ainsley could change him, soften him into a man whose primary excitement was pudding fires and smiles. But no matter how appealing it was, he couldn't let it happen.

His goal was still the success of Sterling's, and he needed to make sure that Ainsley knew he wasn't about to change.

"A game of cards in the parlor sounds like just the thing," Reed said with a lift of his brow. "I could teach you how to play. Or is that too sinful of an amusement for a woman of good breeding?"

She paused in handing Mr. Hatman a glass of water and speared Reed with a cool look. "I know the rules and the object of many games, sir. If that is the way you wish to spend your evening, then I will have my uncle fetch the fish."

"Mere tokens? Afraid to play with real coin?"

She gave him a mysterious grin he'd never seen before. "I'm quite certain it would be best for you if we did not."

Reed was never one to back down from a challenge. A pity for his bride-to-be. Doubtless, she wouldn't like how this night played out.

AINSLEY LAUGHED at Reed's dumfounded expression as he stared at the pile of ivory fish on her side of the table.

Well, she had warned him, after all.

Following the first few unlucky hands of whist, Uncle Ernest and the duchess decided to repair to the sofa across the room and read poetry. Then Reed, with a sly grin, suggested piquet. And that was where it all began to fall apart. At least, for him.

His gaze slanted to hers. "You're either a Captain Sharp or were educated by one."

"Hardly." She scoffed. "We had few visitors to the cottage and spent little time in the village. In fact, the only reason I know the games at all is because I found a book in my uncle's library when we moved to his estate."

"Clearly, you've played quite a lot."

She shook her head and grinned impishly. "Not actually. The few times I practiced with Jacinda and Briar did not end well. They were unhappy—like you are now—and I was left bored. Card games are far too simple and I prefer more of a challenge. After all, if I'm going to spend my time on something, I should like it to be worthwhile."

He leaned in, staring at her intently as if he desired nothing more than to burrow into her skull and sift through the contents. "How did you do it, then?"

"I don't know what to tell you. I've always had a knack for numbers. I just seemed to know what cards you held, that's all."

Ainsley shrugged and rose from her chair, trying not to laugh at seeing him in such a state of bewilderment. She had set Reed Sterling on his ear and he didn't know what to make of her.

It was impossible not to grin. She couldn't recall having a jollier time in her entire life.

After bidding farewell to the duchess and her uncle, Reed followed her out into the corridor, brooding every step to the sconce-lit foyer.

At the door, he expelled an irritated breath through his nose and looked through the sidelights toward Sterling's. "Have you hired a butler yet?"

Taken aback by the sudden change in topic, her mood sobered somewhat. "I believe I've narrowed down my decision. Why do you ask? If Mr. Finch is tired of coming here, then . . ."

"It isn't that. It's just"—Reed raked a hand through his hair—"*hang it all* . . . I don't want him to know how soundly you've bested me. This clobbering was even worse than the teapot."

Laughter bubbled out of her in an uncontrolled flow of joy. She tried to stop it by cupping her hand over her mouth, but then her eyes watered, giving her away. "It will be our secret, then."

Watching her, Reed's expression softened. He drew near and lifted a hand to her face, collecting the wetness from her lashes with the pad of his thumb.

At his warm touch and the heated look in his gaze, her breath quickened. The remaining mirth was trapped in her body, humming like a bumblebee caught in a night-blooming flower, waiting to burst free of the petals.

"I would rather take something else," Reed said in a low

drawl. His gaze dropped to her mouth as he put his damp thumb to his lips, tasting her. "But I'm waiting for you to give it."

That unrepentant rogue made it impossible to breathe, or to think of anything other than leaping into his arms. And she wanted to so badly her body ached. Her own gaze strayed to his mouth, craving the scalding press of his flesh to hers.

But down the hall, she could hear the duchess and her uncle in conversation, readying to depart. Ainsley could imagine how shocked and disappointed they would be to discover her in the throes of kissing—even more so than Mrs. Darden had been.

Ainsley expelled a long, frustrated sigh and quickly opened the door. She practically shoved him out onto the pavement. "Good night, Mr. Sterling. Pleasant dreams."

Reed stared back at her, the gold glow from the foyer glinting over that smoldering ember in his iris. Then he grinned at her wickedly, the way the devil might when he knew someone was close to succumbing to temptation.

"When it comes to you, highness, all of my dreams are scandalous."

Shamefully, she wanted to hear more. Wanted to ask him to describe one in detail. But before she made that mistake, she closed the door sharply and leaned against it, her heart beating like a heathen's drum.

They would both be better off to leave certain curiosities to the safety of dreams.

Chapter 19

"A few minutes were sufficient for making her
acquainted with her own heart. A mind like hers,
once opening to suspicion, made rapid progress."

JANE AUSTEN, *Emma*

Reed watched from the window of his office the following
morning and saw the exact moment when Ainsley spotted
the primroses on her doorstep.

She stalled on the threshold and stared at the cluster for
the longest moment as if she didn't believe they were there.
Then she smiled. And he smiled, too.

*Highness, you will have to work all the harder now to
prove that our little encounters have meant nothing to you.*

Ainsley glanced across the street, her focus on the door
to his gaming hell, perhaps waiting for him. Then, apparently
believing that he wasn't going to make an appearance, she
slipped outside and gathered the plump bouquet he'd tied
with a crimson ribbon, bending her cheek to the buttery
blossoms. Before she went back inside, she wavered on the
threshold, uncertainty in her posture.

Then shyly, she pressed her fingertips to her lips and
looked once more at Sterling's.

"Damn it all, it's true," Raven muttered beside him.

Reed nearly jumped out of his skin. "How long have you
been standing there?"

"Long enough to see that you've gone soft and moony-eyed." Raven shook his head in disgust.

Reed snatched the ledger from his grasp. "The tallies from last night?"

"Yes. But the numbers aren't good."

"We've had slow nights before. Nothing to be concerned about." And yet, skimming the figures, Reed was concerned.

"There've been other rumors," Raven continued with an ominous pause. "It seems that Mitchum fellow didn't take your invitation to leave London, after all."

Reed clenched his fists, his knuckles popping. "Where is he, then?"

"He made a friend of one of your enemies. The last man you ever fought, in fact."

"Lord Savage?" When Raven nodded, Reed cursed, incredulous. The marquess refused to let go of that fight, harping that the match had been rigged by someone who'd slipped him a sleeping draught beforehand.

Savage had taken sour grapes and made vinegar with them.

"For the past two nights," Raven began, "Savage has been hosting exclusive parties and fights in his ballroom. And guess who's the main attraction? His new friend, Mitchum. Undefeated, too."

What was Savage up to this time?

For a full two years after their fight, he'd called Reed a coward, challenging him whenever they'd met on the street. But Reed had earned the money he'd needed to open Sterling's. There'd been no reason to fight again.

Glowering down at the ledger, he dropped it onto the surface of his desk. The strangest part was, before the fight, he'd actually thought Savage wasn't that bad of a fellow . . . for a blueblood.

"There's more," Raven said, sifting a hand through his dark hair, his gray gaze hesitant. "And you're not going to like it."

"No. I don't suppose I will, considering how I'll have to beat you senseless before I get *all* the information out of you."

Raven—usually so sure and cocky, proclaiming to know that Reed was coolheaded—took a step back. "According to one of the girls at Miss Molly's, there's even talk of Lord Savage shopping around for a place to put an exclusive club. Only, he says that Sterling's will be vacant as soon as you become"—Raven hesitated—"Mr. Matchmaker."

So that was the banner Savage was waving now, then?

Reed expelled a slow breath. Calling a man a coward was one thing. At least it kept the patrons interested in seeing if there would be retaliation. But this?

"Very well. We'll see what happens tonight. If nothing changes then I'll host a lottery again. That worked before."

Raven shook his head. "I dunno if a lottery will be enough. Seems to me that the only solution is for you to fight again. With you sparring Pickerington and all, that's what everyone's expecting. It might be the only thing that'll bring them back. And for most of us," he said as he made his way to the door, "Sterling's is the only family we have."

As Raven left, Reed turned to the window. There was so much at stake, not only for himself but for everyone around him.

Yet, his primary thoughts centered on Ainsley. He'd come so far in earning her trust, knowing her better, day by day. She was afraid of letting him get too close, of letting him inside her life, and especially her heart. And he knew without a doubt that she would never marry him if he stepped back into the ring.

Reed hoped that Raven wasn't right. All Sterling's needed was a good turnout this evening and everything would be back on course.

"AND THERE she is, the bride-to-be," Mrs. Teasdale announced from the doorway of Ainsley's office, clutching her hands to her bosom. "Hard at work on planning your nuptials?"

The mere idea of Reed caused Ainsley's stomach to lift, tilting toward her lungs. It had been happening all day, distracting her. She was never on task for more than five minutes before she caught herself thinking of him. And twice, she'd even sighed as if her lungs had sprung a leak. Such a nuisance.

Even now her gaze strayed to the full bouquet of primroses on her desk. All but one. She'd taken a nick-petaled blossom and pressed it into a book in her bedside table, the crimson ribbon tucked in between the pages.

"Actually," she answered, forcing her gaze back to the stack of papers on the desk, "I have been inundated with subscription renewals from former clients all day, in addition to interviewing potential butlers."

"If you're undecided, I could help. Always willing to lend a hand, dear. Especially now that you're getting married—*oh*, what a happy event." Mrs. Teasdale clapped her fingertips together as if it were her own wedding.

Ainsley kept the conversation on a more productive track, steeling herself against the power of the primroses. "I think we shall hire Mr. Clementine. Although thirty-seven is somewhat young for this station, he's a staid fellow and comes with impeccable references. Jacinda vetted him already, and Briar finds him affable enough."

"I hope he's a comely and virile young man, then. That'll keep your uncle from swaggering through the halls as if he's heaven's gift to the world of females. He spends so much time writing those awful poems that they've ruined his vision." She dusted her hands together and walked over to the forgotten tea tray. "Collided straight into me in the kitchen as if I weren't even there. Then, instead of apologizing like a gentleman ought, he made a fuss about some big to-do on the street holding up his carriage and keeping him from an appointment."

Ainsley felt a grin tug at the corner of her mouth, but kept it to herself. "You don't find my uncle handsome?"

"Oh, well, he's fine enough to look at, I suppose. That is, if you're partial to blue eyes and all that wavy silver hair. But if you've seen one pair of blue eyes, you've seen them all. Two of my husbands had blue eyes. As for myself, I've lost a taste for them." She made a face as she lifted the lid to the teapot and peered inside. "Why, this has gone cold and murky. How long has it been here?"

Ainsley glanced at the clock with a start. It was much later than she thought. When Uncle Ernest had popped his head inside a moment ago, she hadn't paid any attention. But come to think of it, he had said that he was escorting Miriam Canfield through the park and hoped to share an early supper—which usually meant that he would be home rather late.

But now she eyed her visitor with curiosity. "Since this morning . . . What brings you here so late in the afternoon?"

She sniffed. "I didn't come at all last week. Thought you might have noticed."

"We all noticed, Mrs. Teasdale, that was the reason I sent a letter to your house, enquiring about your health."

"And mighty kind of you. Such a sweet girl." She smiled broadly. "So you're marrying Mr. Sterling, at last. I knew this day would come. There was always a bit of a spark between the pair of you."

Ainsley's lungs suddenly felt like a butterfly conservatory, each insect taking flight at once. "I believe it was mutual loathing you sensed."

"*Bah*, that's just passion working its way to the surface. If you ask me, when a body spends part of her days thinking about matchmaking and part of her days thinking about the rogue across the way, then something has to come of it. And it did, at last. I'll bet you'll have a babe on the way before the year's through."

"Mrs. Teasdale, please." The pen in Ainsley's hand blotched the application. Instant heat rushed to her cheeks. Though she would never admit it aloud, her mind had wandered to what it might be like to have Reed's child, more than a time or two. "The banns have been read, but it will be a long while—years and years—before we actually marry."

And perhaps not even then.

She'd mulled it over quite fixedly and decided that she liked Reed a bit too much to marry him. Affection and passion muddied one's thinking. And since her thoughts were constantly focused more on Reed than on the agency, she was clearly not in the proper state of mind to make any lasting decisions.

After sharing those dreadful moments of her past, she'd felt a burden lift. It was a secret she'd carried too long on her own. And hearing the story of what he endured as a child, she knew that he understood.

Only Reed could have made her feel safe instead of vulnerable. Sheltered instead of unguarded. She'd never felt that way before.

It was terrifying.

If she gave her heart to Reed, then he would have the power to shatter it beyond repair. She shivered at the thought, thinking of her mother.

"*Years and years?* No, indeed. He wouldn't have asked you if he didn't want to marry you straightaway. A virile man like him could only bide his time for so long, you know."

Ainsley looked down at her cup and saucer, her thoughts as brackish as the tea. In all honesty, she didn't know how

Reed felt about marrying her. Was it just that he was willing to take a wife? Any wife? Or did he genuinely like her?

It would be so much simpler if the lending library had a book on him . . . with illustrations. *Mmm . . . now there's a thought.*

She cleared her throat, trying to keep her musings properly attired. "If you must know, Mr. Sterling was merely being gallant when he announced that we were to marry."

Mrs. Teasdale grinned slyly. "*Gallant?* An *oaf* like him? That is what you called him, isn't it?"

"I was mistaken about that. He's actually . . . well . . . he's actually quite gentlemanly when he chooses to be."

He could also be wicked to the core.

Proof of that were all the scandalous dreams he'd caused. Dreams that went beyond the realm of mere kisses. Last night, she'd even dreamed of watching him undress through the window, then stripping out of her own clothing for him before rubbing balm on herself. And she'd awoken in a pulse-pounding frenzy, perspiration collecting beneath the bedclothes, her skin taut, breaths panting.

Embarrassed to think of it now, she took a hasty sip of tepid tea to cool her blood.

"Well, that's just fine, indeed," Mrs. Teasdale said, eyeing her with a grin. "I'm glad all that talk of war is behind you and there'll be no more tricks."

Ainsley suddenly choked, spewing tea all over her desk. She stood up, coughing and sputtering.

There was one more trick, but she'd forgotten. The dinner for the servants and laborers at Sterling's was tonight!

"What is it? You look like you've had a fright."

"You came in through the kitchen, did you not? Was there a great deal of traffic on the street?"

"More hackneys, horse carts, and men on foot than the eye could see."

Oh dear. "Mrs. Teasdale, I just remembered a plan of attack I put in place last week."

Ainsley crossed the room and walked briskly down the corridor. Then, from the library window, she parted the curtain to peer outside.

An abashed laugh bubbled out. "I don't think Mr. Sterling will be very happy about this."

Chapter 20

"Her heart was in a glow, and she feared her face might be as hot."

JANE AUSTEN, *Emma*

Ainsley kept watch at the library window. Her first successful attempt at ruining Reed Sterling was working.

"Drat it all," she muttered, worrying the corner of her thumbnail.

Well into evening, the crowd on the street below had not lessened. Common laborers piled into Sterling's by the droves, while dozens of fine carriages moved on without stopping.

Slipping back, she grabbed fistfuls of brocade and closed the drapes. She only wished that she could shut out the stirrings of guilt, too. This was certainly a sorry way to repay Reed for all he'd done for her.

If it hadn't been for his suddenly announcing their betrothal, the agency would have been ruined. They certainly would not have received so many applications and renewed subscriptions by post. And worse, it was becoming clear that the problem mightn't have been Sterling's close proximity, after all. Perhaps, the *ton* had been waiting for her to marry.

On a heavy sigh, she turned from the window . . . and saw Reed standing at the library door.

Her guilty heart lurched, her hand flying to her throat. "Mr. Sterling! You startled me."

A candelabra sat on the low bookshelf between them. Pale light slanted over his hard-set features, intensifying the harsh shadows and the warning look in his eyes. "I'm surprised you didn't invite the circus."

"They refused the invitation," she quipped, trying to hide a nervous tremor that ran through her.

"Do you know how much this is going to cost me? How many of my patrons will never return?"

She swallowed. "You could simply send the others away."

"If you were in my place and saw scores of people— their faces filled with more than hunger but with eager delight at the prospect of gaining admittance to your fine establishment—could *you* send them away?"

Put that way, no. And admittedly, she had known, even when she'd plotted this trick, that he couldn't have done so either.

"If it makes a difference," she hemmed, "this was all in place before you announced our betrothal."

He flung out his arm in an infuriated gesture. "Yet you purposely kept this scheme from me as if you still saw me as the rubbish next door and not a man who deserved your respect? I could have prepared for this, Ainsley."

The hard edge of anger in his voice twisted her stomach into a tight knot, and she placed a hand over it. "We were at war."

"Are we still?"

Her throat dry, she didn't answer.

He heaved out a gust of breath, and rolled his head back against the door, lifting his face to the ceiling. "And now you're acting skittish with me. That is just splendid."

"It's my nature to be wary when confronted with an ill-tempered man."

"Perhaps with others, but not with me. You've always been different with me."

But Ainsley had never seen him this way, tension emanating from every pore with an underlying edge of desperation. "I think you should go."

"Damn it all, Ainsley. I'm not going to raise my hand to you!"

"I know that," she shouted back in defense.

Then she took in a deep breath and looked closer at the man across the room, at his pained expression. Sterling's meant everything to him. He'd fought for it and now his life's work was being threatened. He was cross, even angry, and rightly so considering what her subterfuge likely cost him. If the same had been done to her, she wouldn't have hesitated to rail at him and even do worse things, like plot against him.

Yet he had never done a thing against her.

"I know that," she repeated, her voice softer, soothing. She took a step forward—*two, three.* "Speak your diatribes and have them out. I will not deny you the chance of voicing your irritation when I was the one who caused it."

He raked a hand through his hair and said as if to himself, "I'll likely have to fight again to bring it back."

"You're not that man any longer. I couldn't look at you the same if you were."

"And how do you look at me?"

Her cheeks heated and she couldn't answer directly. "I'm sure that this little act of subterfuge won't end up being all that terrible."

A single brow arched in doubt.

"You'll see," she assured him, skirting around the chiffonier to stand in front of him.

"Are you finished with war, then?" he asked on an exhausted breath, holding out his hand in offering. A peace treaty.

Slowly, she nodded and slipped her fingers into the warmth of his palm. Then, rising up on tiptoe, she pressed her lips to his.

Shocked by her own actions, she instantly withdrew.

But Reed tugged her back in a sweet collision of bodies—breasts, stomachs, hips, and thighs. Unmistakable pleasure escaped her on a gasp, her hands splaying over his black-satin waistcoat.

"I told myself I wasn't going to kiss you again." His raw gaze swept over her features. "Not unless you asked me to. Not unless you finally admitted that we are more than enemies."

She opened her mouth to apologize for her trick. He didn't give her a chance.

His hand slid to her nape. "But right now, I don't give a damn about that. After the day I've had, I need to forget about everything else. And all I want is a long, slow taste of your lips."

Ainsley's pulse leapt in hard, excited beats. She lifted her face.

Still his actions were cautious, his movements slow and careful. It took forever before he eased his mouth over hers. Then, feeling the warm pressure, she nearly sagged with relief. She'd needed this, too. She'd been craving this—*him*—for days.

Yielding in that same instant, she slipped her hands over his shoulders, her fingertips weaving through his dark silky strands. Reed growled, a low gruff sound of approval. It seemed to unleash a new part of him.

This kiss turned reckless, demanding. A searching frenzy of hot, panting breaths and lips sliding edge to edge. Tongues tangled in open-mouthed tastes to satisfy the gnawing hunger that had plagued them for days . . . weeks . . . months . . . or even longer. Dimly, Ainsley wondered if every encounter, if every argument, had been leading them here. As if this close-quarter conflict with Reed was what she'd wanted all along.

Only he seemed to know that part of her had been asleep. Only his searing kisses could awaken this strange, wondrously unfamiliar passion lurking inside her. And she was fully alert now, fitting her body against his.

Her breasts ached. A tight coiling settled deep inside her midriff. She rubbed against the solid contours of his body, needing to understand how he was put together and why he felt so blessedly good. It was like having her very own resource of learning—a living, breathing, circulating library.

He pulled her closer, his hand sliding down her spine to the dip in her lower back and further down, gripping the curve of her bottom. She should be shocked by the intimate gesture. But she was too immersed in this new field of study. She wanted to know everything. As if he sensed this, he lifted her higher, rocking his hips against hers, drawing out her helpless mewl of pleasure.

But then a sudden, startling awareness caused her to go very still.

She knew what this part of him was.

All at once, he was too close. Too big. He was every bit the prizefighter she knew he'd once been.

Pulling back, he kissed the corner of her mouth, breathing hard. His eyes were glazed with passion and hunger, but there was also gentle understanding. "Ainsley, I'm not going to hurt you."

He lowered her to her feet. His embrace was still firm enough to be comforting, but light enough to allow her to escape.

It surprised her that she didn't attempt to move away. Standing between his widespread legs, she couldn't reconcile her need to be held by him with the opposing impulse to run away to her bedchamber and bolt the door.

Reed lifted his hand to her cheek, his gaze following the tender stroke of his fingertips. His expression was marked with the same fascination he always had when they touched, telling her without words that he was marveling at how soft she was. "And I'm certainly not going to take you, here, in this study. Not even if you begged me to."

Ainsley stared up at him in wonder, at the warm drowsy look in his mismatched eyes, and came to the most startling awareness. She trusted Reed Sterling. Implicitly.

She never thought she would be able to feel that way about a man in her entire life. And this realization was even more alarming than the idea of losing her heart to him.

At the thought, that organ lurched upward, weightless, and she swallowed to keep it where it belonged.

"*Beg you*, indeed." She tried to issue a haughty sniff, to put a barrier back between them.

But Reed was having none of that. His head bent lower and he grazed his lips along the edge of her jaw, nibbling the underside.

"Oh, highness, don't tempt me to prove you wrong."

A jolt of pure, inexcusable pleasure raced through her. Yet when he pressed kisses down her neck and reached the tender place that Nigel had once bruised, she stiffened again, her throat constricting. Even though the wound had healed long ago, the memory lingered.

She sensed a change in Reed, too, in the way he held his breath, his hands skimming up and down her back until she gradually relaxed. And then he kissed her throat.

His lips followed a horizontal line at the very base, soothing her, dissolving away all the bad memories and replacing them with new ones.

The heated urgency that brought them together a moment ago now transformed into a slow unfolding. Something even more potent than desire.

Before she was even conscious of moving, her head tilted

back to allow him better access. His lips grazed over her flesh without hurry, building the intensity between them.

A pulse settled low and heavy in her body. She clutched the hard mounds of his shoulders, her fingertips biting through the wool as he laved the vulnerable niche. Was it possible to die from pleasure?

He paused at the edge of her fichu and breathed in deeply. "You cannot know what this scrap of fabric does to me or how it controls my thoughts. Such wicked things, these fichus."

"Take it off," she rasped, the hoarse plea in her voice foreign to her own ears. She felt the curve of his lips against her skin.

"Not yet, highness."

He kept this barrier, but his mouth nudged between the silken gathers to kiss the vulnerable skin beneath. She felt the delicious scrape of his whiskers, the warm press of his lips, the nudge of his nose as he drew in her scent. His hands slid up her ribs, forming a new cage around her, fitting just beneath the heavy swells of her breasts, his thumbs teasing her with slow sweeps against the underside of her flesh. The heat of him penetrated layers of muslin and cambric as if she wore nothing at all.

Her nipples grew taut, aching. She couldn't bear it. She wanted to strip off her clothes and free them. Rub balm into them. Anything.

A frustrated sound tore from her throat. *"Please."*

Reed's hand drifted up over the mounds, inch by inch. Finally, he cupped her. Shamelessly, she pushed her aching flesh into his palms, wanton and begging. Dear heavens, begging! And she didn't care either. She wanted him there—*yes, there*—where his thumbs were passing over the crests in wicked sweeps, his callused flesh catching on the muslin.

Lost in high-strung pleasure, she drove her fingers through his hair and pulled his mouth to hers, kissing him with fervor, her tongue tasting the seam of his lips, the spice and heat of his breath. She felt so unreserved with him—practically unhinged—but it didn't matter. He understood her better than anyone ever had.

He lifted her against him again, their bodies perfectly aligned, his hips pitching forward to give hers purchase. She clung to him on a gasp, welcoming him into the throbbing niche, tilting, sliding intimately.

Angling her head, he kissed into her open mouth, nudging her tongue with his, as if taunting her to retaliate. And when she did, a guttural groan vibrated in his throat. He kissed her deeper, harder. The silken slide of his tongue in the dewy heat of her mouth matched his slow, mesmerizing pelvic undulations.

Every pulse point hummed. The low insistent coiling grew more intense with every rock. She felt restless. Tingly. It was too overwhelming.

She broke the kiss, pressing her cheek against his, panting.

"A little more, highness," he urged, grazing his mouth over hers.

Clinging to him, she closed her eyes, hips hitching reflexively. "Something's happening to me."

"Let down your guard," he whispered, his low drawl curling through her, making her tremble.

Ainsley's mouth turned back to his, seeking and frantic. Desperate, fractured sounds rose from her throat. She needed something more, but she didn't know what it was. So she took his lower lip between her teeth and suckled it, then licked into his mouth, feeding on him. And he bore it all, holding her wriggling body securely.

Reed gripped her bottom, steadying her in one place, never ceasing his methodical motions. Her entire focus centered there—*yes, there, right there*.

"That's it, highness. Hold on to me. I'll take care of you . . ."

All at once a cry surged from her lips, raw and foreign.

Her body jerked, lurching in rough spasms like ice breaking apart after a long winter. Scalding pleasure washed through her in lush, pulsing waves that went on and on and on.

She sagged against him, his hold fierce, almost crushing. But she loved it. Anything less wouldn't have been enough.

Gasping for breath against his neck, she wished he didn't have a cravat in the way. "Hold me," she rasped, needing to be closer still. "Tighter."

When he did, her body clenched sweetly in response, drawing out a series of smaller tremors.

For a long moment, she wasn't even sure what happened. Then gradually awareness crept in. She recalled spying certain texts on the subject of pleasure paroxysms—or *le petite mort*, as the French called it—only she hadn't known what it was.

At least, not until now.

And if the smug curve of his mouth and the devilish glint in his eyes were any indications, he knew, too.

Ainsley's cheeks flushed. A wave of embarrassment hit her, full force, and she covered her face with her hands. "Don't look at me like that. This is all your fault."

He chuckled. "I would readily take the blame, but you were very much a part of it. Very much, indeed."

"Cad. If you hadn't invaded my dreams with your wicked promises, this never would have happened," she said without venom, confessing it into his shirtfront.

"It could be worse."

"I don't see how. I'm mortified. Though I couldn't seem to help myself. Everything just felt so . . . and you were so . . ." *Wondrously hard*, she thought. "I didn't want it to end. Part of me still doesn't."

Abruptly, he set her apart, the position forcing her to stand on wobbly legs. She kept hold of him. And with her gaze already lowered, there was no disguising the hard, heavy angle filling the fall front of his trousers.

Unexplainably, she was more intrigued by the shape of him than afraid. Splaying her hand over his waistcoat, she drifted lower.

"Highness," he warned softly, taking her hand in his and lifting it to kiss her palm. "Don't make it impossible to keep my promise not to take you here in the library."

Thrilled, but abashed, she pressed her lips together and looked up at him through her lashes. "I did not mean to tempt you. I was simply . . . curious."

"Be curious all you like after we are married."

"About that. I must insist that we do not rush too—"

He kissed her quickly, soundly. "Argue with me about this next time."

Reed didn't give her a chance to say any more. He left her standing there, alone in the library, her thoughts helplessly drawn to the idea of arguing her point with him. Listing the reasons that they shouldn't rush into anything. But he, scoundrel that he was, would likely convince her otherwise.

She was already looking forward to it.

Chapter 21

"Leave shame to her. If she does wrong, she ought
to feel it."

JANE AUSTEN, *Emma*

Reed stepped out onto the pavement in front of Sterling's
the following afternoon, prepared to cross the street and
argue with his favorite enemy.

Of course, he had no dispute to settle with Ainsley today.
He rarely ever did. He'd always let matters between them
take their natural course, just as they had last night.

He grinned, his blood stirring as he recalled her soft cry
and sweet shuddering body. She was so close to being his,
to truly accepting that they would be married regardless of
circumstance, that it was almost impossible to stay patient.

Distracted, he didn't hear someone hailing him until
his view of the townhouse was blocked by a thorough-
bred. Looking up past the gray stallion, to the rider in buff
breeches and a green coat, Reed wished he hadn't bothered
to stop.

Lord Savage tipped his hat over his blond head, a smirk
cutting through angular features. "Just the man I came to
see."

"I haven't got time for more of your pointless challenges."

"Too busy playing Mr. Matchmaker to have a chat with
an old friend?"

The moniker grated on Reed's nerves. "We were never friends—a fact I distinctly remember since our days at university."

Savage swung a Hessian behind him and descended to the pavement, standing toe to toe with him, one hand on the reins. "See, that's the thing of it all. If it hadn't been for me and the others, then you wouldn't have become the man you are today."

"Favors surpassed only by a hangman offering a shorter rope," Reed gritted. "And I've already repaid you by giving in to the fight you wanted."

The only reason he'd fought Savage at all had been because, in school, his insults had been tame compared to the others. He didn't remark on Reed's parentage, but kept to foolish everyday things like mocking a response he'd given during an exam or jesting that his arms were too long for his body. Almost good-natured ribbing, really. They might have been friends of a sort if not for all the times they'd bloodied each other's noses.

The marquess hiked his pompous cleft chin. "That's not the way I remember it. Our prizefight never ended."

"You were staggering around, mumbling to yourself. All I had to do was push you down to the mat and you stayed there for the full count."

"There it is! At last, you admit that you didn't finish the fight."

Reed glanced around to the gawkers who'd formed around them. "You weren't yourself."

"So you took *pity* on me?" Leaning in, Savage's voice dropped low with warning, green eyes flaring. "You made me look weak, and that is something a man cannot forgive. I demand satisfaction."

"You'll go to your grave never having it. Those days are over."

There was too much at stake for Reed to consider boxing

as an option to save Sterling's. Ainsley had made herself perfectly clear last night.

He intended to leave Savage there on the pavement before they drew any more of a crowd, but the marquess dared to take hold of his arm.

"I shouldn't be too hasty to dismiss me this time. Perhaps you haven't heard, but I have a new venture and it's taking the *ton* by storm."

Reed shrugged free. "I know all about it."

"Of course you do. Your urchin spies are everywhere," he said, matter of fact, then arched a brow. "I've taken in a foundling myself, you know. A certain Mr. Mitchum."

"If I were you, I'd send that one back to the gutter where he belongs. Nothing good can come of keeping him."

Savage shrugged. "I'm not certain that's entirely true. Mitchum claims to have been acquainted with your Miss Bourne. I don't know the particulars yet, for he's a sly sort who knows how to reveal just enough to hold a listener's interest, but I'll find out soon enough. It won't take much. He is an overblown peacock, after all, with ideals full of grandeur and empty pockets. But he's a good fighter. Perhaps you'd even like to have a go at him in the ring."

"Not even if you paid me," Reed said, fists clenched. He fought to keep his expression neutral, but with the mention of Mitchum it was nearly impossible.

The marquess eyed him shrewdly. "Hmm . . . I have a sense that, if you had it your way, you'd fight him even if I *didn't* pay you. Just think of the crowd you could gather. From what I've heard, you could certainly use it. So then what's stopping you? Could it be that Miss Bourne disapproves of your fighting, even at the detriment of Sterling's?"

"Don't you have somewhere else to be—a corset fitting with your tailor, perhaps?"

"You haven't lost your sense of humor, old friend. But you might have lost your edge." Savage laughed as he mounted his horse. "Love makes men so pathetic! I ought to know. Just be sure that the woman you love doesn't slip a sleeping draught into your drink before our fight."

"*We* aren't going to fight."

Savage flashed a grin. "The exhibition I'm holding tonight will guarantee far more gentlemen at my house than your hell. Therefore, I have a feeling you'll change your mind soon enough . . . *Mr. Matchmaker.*"

Reed glowered at the retreating horse's arse, his heavy thoughts turning. Just what was Savage planning?

❧

REED WALKED through Sterling's that night. The cardrooms were occupied by only a handful of loyal patrons, but rumor had it that Savage had quite the hoard.

He stopped in the first-floor hall and faced the window, his frown reflecting back to him. All day long, he'd been tense and uneasy. He couldn't shake it. He didn't like Savage's association with Mitchum.

"Your cat is a peculiar creature," Finch said with a laugh, his large frame coming into view. He gestured with a thumb aimed over his shoulder toward the stairs. "I was just in the kitchen when she came up to me, meowing over and over again, tilting her head this way and that. It was like she was trying to have a conversation."

"Perhaps she was welcoming you back," Reed said absently.

Today had been Finch's last day at the agency and tomorrow, Clementine—another of Reed's men, though Ainsley did not know it—would start.

She wouldn't approve if she knew that he'd handpicked her butler, but Reed would do anything to keep her safe. He'd even posted a man around the perimeter of the townhouse, ever since the day he'd first met Mitchum. Tonight was Teddy's watch.

"Highly doubtful. That devil's spawn didn't even attempt an assault," Finch said. "She just sprinted off, leaving through the kitchen window. And I see you glowering, but I'm certain she'll turn up like a bad penny. Much like your friend Savage always manages to do."

The mention of the marquess caused Reed's shoulders to tighten, his nerves on edge. Their earlier conversation still clanged through his mind like a warning bell.

"Sterling's will fare well once again," Finch said, misunderstanding. "Savage will become bored with his new pet."

"And in the meantime, Mitchum is being petted and praised and touted as a champion by London's elite gentlemen?" Reed scrubbed a hand over the knots gathering at the base of his neck. "That kind of adoring attention can affect any man. Yet for one solely ruled by his ego, it can be dangerous. I worry that it will only make him crave more."

"Then fear not," Finch said, "for I just heard from Raven that Savage is stepping into the ring himself tonight."

Ah. So that's what he'd planned. "He's trying to whet the *ton*'s appetite for a fight between us."

Finch slanted him a look. "Agreeing to it seems the obvious solution. Simply demand that the match be held here, then your patrons will flock back to the nest by droves."

Reed couldn't fight, not when Ainsley was starting to let down her guard with him.

"I don't like the timing of it all," Reed said. "It's too convenient. First Mitchum comes to pay a call on Miss Bourne, then makes a scene here, and now I'm supposed to believe that he is still in London because he has aspirations of being a boxer?"

"Granted, it does reek of suspicion. However, at least you know that Mitchum is better occupied now. From what I recall, Savage was a severe taskmaster upon himself. Rest assured, he'll keep Mitchum far too busy to cause you trouble."

An uneasy shiver chased down Reed's spine. His gaze strayed out the window to the townhouse across the lamplit street, where Teddy was circling to the back of the house.

"But trouble is brewing nonetheless."

THE BOURNE Matrimonial Agency had been flooded with potential new clients today. The dream that Ainsley and her sisters had embarked upon nearly two years ago was within reach.

She should have been thrilled by the turnout, eager, and focused. But instead, she'd been absentminded all day, easily distracted, sighing, and simply not quite herself.

Instead of focusing on the pertinent facts during an interview, she'd found herself asking the oddest questions. *Do you whistle? Are you fond of dancing? How do you feel about parlor games?* And the applicants were eager to share their answers.

Ainsley never fell into easy conversation with a client. She was straightforward and impersonal. All she wanted were the facts. Then after the application was complete, she typically stated with measured authority, "The agency will strive to find a match based on the information provided."

Today, however, she found herself chatting and laughing. Then, to make matters worse, she actually concluded an interview by saying, "We're going to help you find the love of your life."

Insanity!

Ainsley had opened her mouth and somehow Briar had fallen out.

Though in her own defense, it had been difficult to concentrate on anything since last night. Her mind careened to Reed when she least expected it. She caught herself smiling at odd moments throughout the day, too. Grinning like an escapee from Bedlam.

Proof was the reflection in the darkened window glass of her office. A blush tinged her cheeks and a dreamy brightness shone in her eyes. She'd never seen such an expression on her face before.

Was this what love was like?

If it was, she wanted no part of it.

Letting the curtain fall, she turned away and began to pace, gnawing on the corner of her thumbnail.

She didn't want to be in love with Reed. Her mother had loved a man, past the point of reason. Past the point of seeing that she still had a life to live and children who needed her. Ainsley never wanted to lose all sense of what mattered.

Her efforts for the agency had been positively worthless today.

Well, it had to stop. No matter how exciting Reed was to kiss, how safe she felt in his arms, or how diverting it was to argue with him, she refused to fall in love. She was too sensible.

Lowering her hand to her side, she tucked these errant thoughts away. She wouldn't even give them credence.

In love with her betrothed? *Ha.*

Head firmly on her shoulders, she left her office and headed toward the stairs. It was time to begin her nightly ritual of snuffing out the tapers, floor by floor. Though, with her uncle away at the Duchess of Holliford's, she would leave the foyer lit as she always did.

Ainsley had begged off from this evening's dinner, claiming a need to file applications and plan the wedding breakfast. The truth, however, was that she didn't feel at all proper enough to sit at the duchess's table. Not after last night. The duchess would take one look at her and see her for the wicked and wanton creature she'd become.

Even now, her face heated with a blush at the memory. And part of her—she was ashamed to admit—hoped he would return again this evening and find her alone. Crossing the foyer, she peered through the sidelight glass and gazed at the façade of Sterling's, sighing like a starry-eyed debutante. *Pathetic.*

Noticing that the number of carriages stopping was considerably smaller than it had ever been, a pang of guilt churned in her stomach. This was her fault. And knowing that he cared about his business as much as she cared about hers, she had to make it right.

Distracted, she didn't even see the cat on her doorstep until it meowed at her.

Ainsley reached for the doorlatch, then hesitated.

Reflexively, her thoughts went to Nigel, even though it made no sense. After all, she knew that he was escorted from London by one of Reed's men. He certainly wasn't waiting on her doorstep. But a shiver raced down her spine, nonetheless.

Ever since his unexpected visit, she'd made a habit of checking to ensure the doors were locked, several times a day. There was no such thing as being too careful.

It was dark tonight. There was no moonlight to fill in the shadowy places between her door and the lamplit pavement ahead. She squinted into the gloom, cupping her hands around the window. Then, seeing nothing amiss, she opened the door.

The scruffy creature scurried inside, wending around her skirts. She looked up with a blink of her one good eye and proceeded to meow over and over again, and each time with a seeming degree of urgency.

"Well, good evening to you," Ainsley answered with a laugh, bending to pick her up. But the cat was having nothing to do with that and darted upstairs instead, slipping away in a white blur. "If you're here for a dish of cream, then you'll have to join me in the kitchen. There'll be no hiding in my bedchamber again."

Shaking her head, Ainsley closed the door, then locked it before heading up the stairs.

Since she had already closed the office doors, it took only a quick look down the first corridor to see that the cat was nowhere in sight. She was just heading toward the library around the corner when she heard a faint creak from below. Knowing that Uncle had given Reed a key to the door, she wondered if the sound was her betrothed coming after his cat.

She looked down toward the foyer below, but didn't see him. Or hear him, for that matter. Whatever had caused that sound stopped.

A peculiar chill swept down her spine as she studied the sconce light shining against the marble floor. There were no mysterious shadows, and every niche and furnishing was illuminated.

Chafing her hands over her arms, she told herself she was being foolish. Then she walked on toward the library.

The open archway glowed warmly from the light of a small fire in the hearth and the lamp she'd left burning. She planned to while away the hours this evening by reading Shakespeare's sonnets in search of an answer to the questions that had been stirring in her mind and in her heart.

Although, if she was to the point of turning to poetry for guidance, then she suspected her heart was already lost.

A peculiar noise halted her musings. She couldn't quite place it, but it sounded like wood clacking together, like chair legs bumping underneath a dining table. It made no sense. Since Mrs. Darden had gone to bed an hour ago, it had to be the cat getting into mischief.

Or it was Reed coming inside. Perhaps, she thought with a grin, in his haste to see her, he'd knocked into the umbrella stand in the foyer.

In case that was it, she called out, "We are up here, Mr. Sterling. Your cat is putting me on a merry chase again."

Walking around the chiffonier that bisected the room into two parts—the library and the sitting nook—she checked beneath both chairs. Though knowing how much the cat enjoyed a spot on a window seat, she stepped over to the corner and pulled the drapes back. But the creature was not there.

Since she had not heard Reed call out in answer, Ainsley comprehended with disappointment that her first assumption was likely correct. She was alone and the cat had caused something to tumble off a table or shelf. However, once she found the cat, she could return the bundle to Reed. And that thought cheered her.

Tuning her ear to any noise, she listened for the cat. The air was still aside from the crackling flames behind her. And something about the responding silence caused her stomach to twist nervously.

She hesitated before taking another step toward the corridor. Perhaps she had imagined the sounds?

No. She knew the difference between a creaking house and footsteps. Only the old Ainsley had second-guessed herself.

Nigel's constant manipulations and truth twisting had made her doubt herself. For a time, it had been so dreadful that she'd hardly been able to decide what dress to wear on any given day, worried that the color would bring a chiding comment about her complexion, or that the shape of the gown would make her look dowdy, as he'd often said when they were alone. Yet in front of her family, he'd told them that it was Ainsley who'd worried that she looked dowdy, making it seem as though she'd been seeking a compliment.

Thinking about Nigel sent a fresh chill slithering down her limbs.

Reed will come soon for his cat, she thought, chafing her arms. Then, steeling herself, she walked back into the corridor.

She stopped with sudden dread, greeted by a tunnel of darkness. Every sconce light had been dowsed.

The corridor yawned before her. She was standing in the only light, her shadow a ghostly figure beside her.

"Reed?" she called out, a tremor in her voice.

More than anything, she needed to hear his voice telling her not to worry.

"Not quite, Ains."

Chapter 22

"She could not speak another word.—Her voice was lost; and she sat down, waiting in great terror . . ."

JANE AUSTEN, *Emma*

Nigel emerged from the blackness, the flickering light catching eerily over his twisted grin.

Ainsley drew a breath, refusing to panic. She was a different person now, stronger than she'd ever been before. "I—I believe I made myself perfectly clear during your last visit. I am betrothed to another man. There is nothing to discuss."

"You made a fool of me," Nigel said, his voice sure and calm.

He'd subjected her to months of verbal and physical abuse, and yet *she* was trying to make a fool of him? Of course he would see it that way. Doubtless, he couldn't even fathom that she might deserve respect and compassion instead of cruelty.

Fortunately, she knew that all men were not like this. While her uncle had always been an example of kindness, it was Reed who'd proven that, even with a tough exterior, a man could be surprisingly gentle and caring. A man could be precisely who and what he claimed to be.

Feeling more self-assured than during their previous encounter, she stiffened her spine. "That was not my intention. Now, if you would leave . . ."

"A man doesn't easily forget that," he said. "Nor have the villagers. Those common people have nothing better to do than give me sideways glances, and whisper snide comments under their breath. And my parents haven't forgotten either. They don't allow a single day to go by without reminding me of the mistake I made by letting you get away."

"But you married someone else. Surely, they—"

"You left me no choice."

He took a step closer, and she took a step back, her harried pulse climbing.

The low light revealed a swollen discoloration near his left eye. On closer examination, she also noticed his cravat was wrinkled, the cuffs on his gray coat smudged with dirt. And his waistcoat was missing one button.

It gave her a shock to see him on the far side of his usual, impeccable standards. He looked as if he'd recently been in a fight.

"It's because of what you did that I had to marry in haste," he continued. "And my father, the youngest son who'd inherited nothing, couldn't forgive me for marrying a poor vicar's daughter. Not when I had the daughter of a baron in the palm of my hand—quite literally, if you'll recall."

Ainsley's stomach turned at the crude remark. "As a *daughter*, I would not inherit anything either. Besides, my father has already acknowledged his illegitimate son."

"You still don't understand," he said with a condescending smirk. "My aim was always much higher. You and your sisters are the only surviving relatives of a viscount, and since you're the eldest, it will be *our* son who will inherit. Our son who will live in the finest house, and my blood will be in his veins. I'll be the sire of generations of viscounts to come."

"You and I are never going to have a son."

"Do you know," he continued conversationally, deaf to her resistance, "my wife's death was actually a gift to me.

Another chance, as it were. Because I knew that you were here in London, still unmarried. Still waiting for me."

Ainsley shivered. The gleam in his gaze caused her to step back, her confidence faltering. He always had a way of twisting facts to concoct these wild fabrications and then convince himself of their validity.

"I'm marrying another man. The banns have been read," she said emphatically, desperate for him to see reason, once and for all.

"Ains, I can see straight through your excuses. I always could. Remember that day in the parlor, when you were all soft and squirming beneath me? You'd played coy, but I knew you'd been waiting a long time to have me all to yourself." He tsked. "And when your uncle interrupted us, you only pretended offense."

"That isn't true."

He took a step inside the room. His movements were slow enough that it shouldn't have been threatening, and yet the subtlety seemed almost snakelike. As if he were waiting for the right moment to uncoil and strike.

An icy finger of panic skated down her spine. Her gaze darted past his shoulder to the darkened corridor and she wondered if Mrs. Darden would hear her call out.

"It's no use to scream," he said, eerily reading her thoughts. "I locked the door to the garret, where Ginny sleeps, and I propped a chair underneath the handle to Mrs. Darden's door. Mr. Hatman's too old and frail, and barely makes it down the stairs as it is. So you see, even if they heard you, they wouldn't be able to do anything."

"We have a b-butler now," she stammered, grasping at straws, hoping to stall him as she skirted around the chiffonier, putting the low bookshelf between them.

"Who arrives tomorrow," Nigel said with a self-satisfied shrug. "I've been in London a bit longer than I let on. Long enough to know the mornings when Ginny goes to market. When Mrs. Darden leaves the kitchen door on the latch to run a batch of scones next door. When your uncle dines with the Duchess of Holliford, and how late he'll stay there tonight. We won't be interrupted this time. And don't worry, I have a carriage in back waiting to drive us to Gretna Green so my son will be legitimate."

Ainsley swallowed down a sour rise of bile, trying to regain a sense of calm. "Nigel, you're not speaking rationally. Think about what you're saying."

He smiled, eyes alarmingly bright. "Remember that sportsman I hired to teach me boxing? Well, he introduced me to Lord Savage. And you know what he said? He said that I could be a prizefighter."

She didn't answer, believing that this was one of the many times he didn't require a response. All he really wanted was to hear the sound of his own voice. So she focused on trying to figure out a way past him.

If she could make it to the window, then she could scream out across the street. Someone outside of Sterling's would hear her. And Reed would come.

And yet, if she went deeper into the room, then it would be easier for Nigel to trap her here.

"Aren't you listening? You know I hate to be ignored."

She nodded, forgetting that he wanted her undivided attention, regardless of whether he was listening to her or not. "I'm glad for you."

"Don't condescend me. That's how you always made it harder on yourself." He shook his head and gestured wildly. "And here I had the plan to do this properly and marry you first. Once we're wed, everyone will realize that you only left Hampshire because you were trying to make me chase after you, and that you wanted to make me jealous by pretending to be engaged to Sterling."

"It isn't a p-pretense," she stammered in a rush. "In fact, he'll drop by any moment to fetch his cat. He—he won't like to find you here."

From the sneer curling his lip, she realized that was the wrong thing to say.

"I'd like that. I'd like him to catch us together, to see you squirming beneath me, to know where I've been." He snickered. "I'm going to be the man who took Sterling's woman. He thought he could toss me out of his club without fighting me? Well, by the time this is over, I will have done what no other man could do. I will have bested the great prizefighter."

Ainsley tried to push down the panic threatening to freeze her in place. She focused her thoughts on Reed instead, remembering all the times he'd held her and soothed her.

At once, her senses cleared. Her gaze flitted to the candelabra standing on the edge of the chiffonier. A plan to get out of this room quickly formed in her mind.

Attempting to reason with someone like Nigel was a waste of time.

"I won't scream," she lied softly, hoping to calm him. "We can talk about this."

"There's a good girl. Now, come over here. I don't want to waste time chasing you around furniture."

Ainsley's fingers lightly skimmed the polished surface of the low shelf as she stepped around to the other side. But her progress was slow, her legs shaking like dahlia stems in a storm.

"Are you planning to become a prizefighter?" she asked, knowing that all things *Nigel* was Nigel's favorite subject.

He hiked up his narrow chin. "I could. I've even been the premier fighter at Lord Savage's townhouse these past two days, all the men cheering me on, ladies batting their lashes, hanging all over me like I'm a king." He laughed, his expression dripping with self-satisfaction. "You're jealous. I can see it in your face. Well, if you're a right proper wife and do as you're told, you might be able to keep me away from the temptations of London."

"Is that where you were this evening? Lord Savage's, I mean." She glanced to his eye, noting the color had darkened, the flesh more swollen than before.

It was always a risk, pointing out a flaw in his appearance, but she hoped it would only encourage him to keep talking about himself and become so distracted that he didn't realize what she was doing.

Lifting a hand, he frowned, wincing as he tested the raw flesh. Then he noticed the dirt smudged on his cuffs and straightened sharply, tugging on his sleeves. "I caught a man sniffing around your garden and took care of him. He won't be dragging anyone out of Sterling's club for a long time, I should think."

Ainsley felt a jolt of alarm at the news. What had Nigel done? And if one of the men from Sterling's was in the garden, had he been sent over by Reed to fetch the cat?

Did that mean Reed didn't plan to come here, after all?

Her stomach fell with cold dread, sending shivers through her. Unable to hear any more, Ainsley lunged for the candelabra.

But so did Nigel. Her hand grasped the heavy silver base just as his covered hers in a punishing grip, digging into her tender flesh and bones. A pained whimper escaped her.

He grinned in triumph, his eyes flashing in the light, crazed. "You see. That's what I—"

Ainsley shoved hard. The motion caused the flames to sputter. Then she drew in a deep breath and blew with all her might. Droplets of hot wax peppered his face.

Nigel shouted, eyes screwing closed. His hand released hers as he sought to wipe the wax from vulnerable skin. "You worthless cow! Oh, you are going to pay for that."

Ainsley raced from the room and down the dark corridor, memory guiding her steps. Rounding the corner, she ran to the faint glow of sconce light rising up the staircase opening, and filtering down from the tapers burning in the second floor hall.

Freedom was only a few steps away. If she could just make it to the stairs . . .

But in the next instant she found that the stairs to the foyer were blocked. Chairs were piled sideways, stacked high and interlocked in a barricade. That must have been the noise she'd heard earlier—Nigel preparing to trap her inside!

"You're not going anywhere, Ains," he called, his voice echoing down the corridor. Coming closer. "You'll never be too far from my reach."

THERE WERE a dozen tasks waiting for Reed, but he found himself at the window again. He'd been drawn to this view even more than usual tonight.

He couldn't explain the reason, but something about it unsettled him.

The dim reflection in the glass revealed Raven's form striding toward him and Reed glanced over his shoulder. "Any news from Teddy?"

Raven stopped beside him. "Last report was that he was heading into the garden to have a look."

He knew that Teddy, more than anyone else, would be thorough, investigating every shadow. Then he'd give a report, every half hour, to let Reed know if he needed someone to take over. "And how long ago was that?"

"The top of the hour."

The standing clock in the corner showed that it was half past. Teddy should be making an appearance on the pavement any minute now.

"But I have a report of another kind," Raven continued, a dark glower settling over his features. "It has to do with Lord Savage. Apparently, he decided to enter his own ring this evening. And when word spread through the hazard room, we lost a dozen more patrons."

Reed cursed. "Well, I hope Savage and Mitchum beat each other to a bloody pulp."

"He isn't fighting Mitchum. Savage is welcoming anyone who has the bollocks to put up his fists."

"Then where's Mitchum?"

"In the crowd, I s'pose."

Reed shook his head, tension clawing at his neck. "No. He'd need to be at the center, lapping up the attention. Send a runner to the man I have watching Mitchum. I need to know exactly where he is."

THE SERVANTS' stairs were just ahead. Ainsley could make her escape. But knowing that Nigel had a carriage waiting out back—and likely a driver he'd hired to assist him with her abduction—made her too leery of falling into a trap.

She couldn't risk it.

Thinking quick on her feet, she sprinted *up* the stairs instead. He wouldn't expect it, and that might give her just enough time to make it to the window and scream for Reed.

She had complete faith that he would come for her. Or perhaps, it was the only hope she could cling to.

Yet on the second floor every sconce was lit, flooding the corridor with light. If Nigel were to come up here, it wouldn't take him any time to find her.

Needing to disorient him, she pinched out the flames of each sconce, slowly immersing herself in darkness. Then she locked bedchamber doors, collecting keys in her fist. Hopefully, he would be fooled into thinking that she'd sealed herself inside.

Everything she did was to give Reed a little time, because he would come for her. She chanted the words inside her mind like a mantra. *Reed will come for me.*

He would surely recall teasing her about her overuse of candles and her responding explanation that she had a system. So when he would look at the agency tonight, he would notice that the lights were mismatched.

He had to notice. She was pinning all her hopes on him.

At last, she made it to her own bedchamber and locked the door. The only light came from the streetlamps below, sifting in through her open drapes.

She flew to the window. Setting her hands on the frame to lift it, she pulled with all her might. It wouldn't budge. She tried pushing the edges to crack the seal. Still, nothing. The rain and heat had likely warped the wood, making it swell in the frame.

But she couldn't stop trying. Sterling's was only a single pane away.

Frustrated tears gathered in her eyes as she dug in with her fingernails, straining until they chipped and broke, her fingertips raw.

A door rattled not too far away. Nigel had come upstairs.

The next sound she heard was a shriek of splintering wood and then a hard *boom* that vibrated the floor. He must have kicked the door inward.

"You know I detest childish games, Ains," Nigel called, his voice agitated above the beat of hard-footed steps. "I'll break down every door! I'll find you. Don't think I won't. And when I do, I'm not going to be pleased. I was going to make this nice for you, but not anymore."

Another loud shriek and boom as a door fractured open and crashed against a wall. He was getting closer.

Ainsley flattened herself against the wall and stared at the door in the faint light. Then somehow, even with her heart thudding with dread in her ears, she heard a plaintiff meow.

The cat! She'd forgotten all about her.

Dropping to her knees, she peered underneath the bed and spotted one green eye glowing in the shadows.

"Shh . . . it's going to be fine. Just stay there," she whispered, wishing she could hide beneath the bed as well. But the space between the rails and the floor was simply too narrow.

On her knees, she scanned the room, looking for a hiding place.

The wardrobe? No, it would be the first place he would look, surely. And behind the screen would do no good either, for her shoes would show beneath it.

Her shoes . . . This gave her a thought. Slipping out of them, she positioned the toes to peek out from beneath the curtain. If he came in here, perhaps he would cross the room and think he'd found her. That might give her enough time to slip away. That was, if she was hiding someplace near the door.

Or nearer, she thought, spying the cedar chest at the foot of her bed.

Carefully, so the hinges would not squeak, she lifted the lid. Inside was one of her mother's gowns and a fur-lined winter mantel, and not much else. It wasn't a very large chest. When she was much younger, she used to slip inside when she would play hide-and-seek with her sisters.

Ainsley wasn't sure that she would fit now, but she had no other option than to try.

Hastily, she pulled out the clothes and set them on the floor, then she stepped inside. Hunkering down, she squirmed, arranging her legs and hips in a cramped, uncomfortable position. But it worked. Then she picked up the clothes and covered herself.

However, it wasn't until she heard the door rattle and Nigel's gruff explosion into the room that she realized she might have sealed herself in her own coffin.

REED WAS restless and uneasy, waiting for the report from his runner.

Attention fixed on the townhouse, he studied the windows, his gaze searching from one to the next. Some were darkened, and some glowing with their usual light. Nothing too odd, considering how Ainsley kept the sconces lit until she was ready for bed. And yet . . . something niggled at the back of his mind, gooseflesh raising hairs on his arms.

He looked again.

This time, he noticed that the ground floor was still lit, but the first floor was dark. Most of the second floor was, too. All but one.

That wasn't like Ainsley. For as long as he'd been looking across the street, he'd seen those windows all aglow until— systematically, floor by floor, from bottom to top—she doused the lights.

A cold breath rushed out of his lungs. Seeing Raven on the stairs, he called out, "Get Finch and Pickerington."

Chapter 23

"I know what you mean—but Emma's hand is the strongest."

JANE AUSTEN, *Emma*

"I've found your hiding place," Nigel said in a cruel sing-song as he entered her bedchamber.

Buried inside the cedar chest, Ainsley felt the bump of hard-footed steps growing closer and she struggled not to make a sound. Then she heard a hollow sound of a wooden door clacking open.

Her wardrobe. She was glad that she hadn't chosen to hide there.

"Ah-ha. Now I see you! Shivering behind the curtains, hmm?" A muffled clatter followed, the wrenching of drapes from the heavy rod. "Damn it all! I'll tear this house down room by room. I know you're here. You're not clever enough to elude me."

She had to get out, but she was frozen in terror, too afraid to lift the lid and try to dart away.

Reed would see the lights, Ainsley told herself. He had to. He noticed everything.

And yet, small doubts were creeping into her foggy mind. What if he didn't see her windows? It was rather arrogant of her to think that he spent any time watching the agency, thinking of her. For all she knew, she was the only one who looked across the street day and night, thinking of him.

And what if Nigel was right? What if she would never truly escape him?

"I bet you're hiding under the bed. I'll have you on top of it in short order. I'll cut every scrap of clothes from your body with my boot knife. And then I'll teach you a lesson you won't soon forget."

A knife! Ainsley sucked in a breath. Had he brought a knife because he planned to kill her if she didn't cooperate?

She was starting to hyperventilate, her breaths coming up short. The cedar air grew hotter by the second. Darkness threatened to swallow her whole.

"What's this . . . a cat?"

Ainsley jolted. She wanted to burst out of this chest to help the creature. But she was afraid that she wouldn't be able to keep either of them safe. All she could do was hope that the cat would flee the room and save herself.

Nigel snickered. "You're the most pitiful looking—*Argh!* Bloody hell! Get off!"

Staggered steps clomped around the room. "Bleeding cat, get off my head! Stop scrat—*ah!*" The stumbling continued. A heavy thump hit the chest. Then Nigel's rants seemed to come from the floor as if he'd fallen. "Damn you beast! I'll kill you!"

Then all at once, a high, keening wail pierced the air.

The room fell eerily silent.

Ainsley sucked in a breath, tears stinging her eyes. *No, no, no . . .* Not that precious cat. The creature had been through too much misery to meet an end like this. She deserved a long, happy life, not a cruel act of fate.

Gripping the woolen mantle tight, Ainsley tried to muffle the choked anguish of her tears as she sobbed, wishing that she'd been half as brave.

That cat had lived more of a life than she had ever dared.

In one way or another, Ainsley was always hiding herself to keep from being hurt. Shutting away her feelings.

Making excuses that she was being responsible rather than impulsive and uninhibited.

The simple truth was that she had stuffed herself in a cedar chest a long time ago.

But Reed had challenged her to show herself, drawing her out bit by bit. Teaching her that she didn't have to be afraid.

Ainsley wasn't ready to die without ever having lived. She wanted more. Wanted to collect moments and memories by the bunches, to press them between slips of vellum in the book of her life. And one day, when she was ancient and grizzled, she wanted to sit beside Reed, hold his hand, and look through the pages with a smile.

~

REED WASN'T expecting to find an elderly man—dressed in a nightgown and brandishing an umbrella—in the foyer of the agency. The man was as ghostly white as his stocking cap but what his cloudy blue eyes lacked in sharpness they made up for in ferocity.

"I'll take you all. I served in the regiment under General Wolfe."

Reed didn't wait for conversation. He began searching every room on this floor.

"Be at ease, Mr. Hatman," Finch said, ducking his head as he came inside. "We're here to see that Miss Bourne is safe. That's Mr. Sterling and this is Raven, and Pickerington will be coming through the back. We'll need to let him in."

Reed returned to the foyer. "Where is she? Where is Miss Bourne?"

Mr. Hatman lowered his weapon and looked up the stairs. "I'm not sure, sir. I heard some terrible noises—a man's shouting and knocking around. Ginny heard it, too. But the door to the garret had been locked and it took a lot of force—and time, I'm afraid—to open it. We heard someone on the stairs when we were coming down. By the time we reached the bottom and saw the open kitchen door, everything was still as a churchyard. Then we heard Mrs. Darden shouting from her room, and saw the chair locking her inside. She'd heard the shouting, too, and hard footsteps running past her door. Now she and Ginny are upstairs, still searching. Don't you worry. No one will get past me. I served in—"

Someone screamed from above.

Reed jolted and ran to the stairs. Taking them two at a time, he shouldered through a blockade of chairs at the top.

Then he found Mrs. Darden in her frilly nightdress and ruffled cap. She was standing at the end of the hall, just beyond the offices, her face pale and twisted in anguish.

"A knife, Mr. Sterling," she sobbed, pointing to the rug at her feet. "And there's blood on it. What do you think happened?"

Nigel Mitchum, Reed thought. Icy terror rushed in his ears, drowning out whatever else the cook was saying.

Like a madman, he began searching offices, tearing through them one by one. Then the parlor. He sprinted down the next corridor to the library. That was where he found an upended candelabra on the floor, broken tapers, spatters of wax. But no blood.

The blood . . . He tried not to think the worst. Instead, he focused on the search. He would tear this house apart to find her.

Dashing up the stairs, he saw the horror of doors splintered open, the contents in the chambers ransacked.

Ainsley must have put up quite a fight. The thought tortured him.

Halfway through the bedchambers, he came upon the maid, startling a cry out of her. But by the looks of her tear-shredded face, she'd already been sobbing a good deal.

"Have you . . . found her?" he asked, unable to speak Ainsley's name aloud, fearing it would break him.

Ginny covered her face in her hands. "There's blood in her room."

Her muffled words sent Reed into a blind panic. He charged into the last bedroom at the end of the hall, wild-eyed and bloodthirsty. The wardrobe door hung by one hinge. The drapes in a heap on the floor. The screen broken. He was going to kill Mitchum.

Then Reed saw the blood on the floor.

His heart stopped. He couldn't breathe. His eyes fixed on the small, dark puddle in front of the hearth and the thin, ragged trail leading to the door.

In a rage—in agony—he howled, head back, the bellow ripped from the center of his soul. His fists hung useless by his side. What good were they to him when he hadn't been here to protect her?

Why hadn't he been here sooner?

"You came."

Reed heard the soft rasp behind him and he turned slowly.

He didn't trust his eyes at first. As if in a dream, he blinked, watching a figure sit up inside a chest, clothes falling to her lap, hair tousled and tears streaming down her cheeks.

Then Reed moved without thinking. One instant he was near the hearth and the next he was clutching her body, his hands fisted in her gown. On a shudder, he buried his head in her neck, breathing her in, making sure she was real.

"You came for me," she said, her voice hoarse.

She was alive. She was here. He said her name over and over again, like a prayer that men chanted when they were broken down to one single hope.

Wrapping her arms around him, her face wet, she began

to pepper him with fevered kisses. "I knew you would see the lights in the window. I knew I couldn't be wrong. Couldn't be the only one drawn to the window at all hours."

He held her face in his hands, kissing every exposed inch, still making sure she was really here. "You're never wrong, highness. But it took me far too long to get here."

He couldn't stop thinking about what she must have suffered, the terror, the broken doors, the blood—

He began a new frantic search, his hands cataloguing every limb and curve. When he reached her ribs, she sucked in a breath. He dropped to his knees. Then, prodding further, he checked for any signs of blood, a tear, a puncture. But he couldn't find one. "Are you hurt?"

A stifled, squeaking sound escaped her. "Other than being ticklish, no. You, however—with your wild eyes, disheveled hair, and pale face—appear as if you've come from battle."

He stood again and held her close. "This is no time to jest."

"I am unharmed but"—she stopped, her expression haunted—"I heard Mr. Mitchum attack your cat."

"So that's the reason for the blood." Reed closed his eyes and tucked Ainsley's head against his chest.

"You haven't found her?"

He didn't want to think about the trail of blood, or Mrs. Darden's gruesome discovery near the servants' stairs. "Not yet."

"She was very brave," Ainsley whispered.

He pressed a kiss to her hair, lingering. "And so were you."

When she shook her head in mute response, he had to argue. "Throughout it all, you kept your head. I saw the candles in the library, the locked bedchamber doors. You outsmarted him at every turn. There isn't any other person, man or woman, who could have been as brave and clever."

"I kept thinking of you"—she smoothed her hand over his cheek, her eyes soft—"trying to summon the strength you always give me when we're together."

Reed kissed her then, so overwhelmed that he couldn't think straight. And she kissed him back with equal fervor.

Their bodies fused together in a desperate, incendiary embrace. Whatever barriers remained between them burned away.

Her lips parted, welcoming the desperate plunge of his tongue. His hand slid down the ripe swell of her bottom, lifting her against him, reveling in the supple crush of her breasts, the inviting heat of her sex. She hitched against him, cinching her arms tightly behind his neck, issuing soft, wanton murmurs. Angling her hips, he let her feel how he ached for her, how he would have died if he hadn't found her in time.

Then he lowered her to the edge of the bed. All he could think about was how much he needed her. How much he wanted to fill her body, over and over again, to make her his once and for all. He looked at her flushed face and brushed rich, glossy tendrils from her cheek, his fingertips tracing her kiss-swollen lips. He'd imagined her like this too many times to count, with her dark eyes glazed with passion.

Lifting her arms, her hands slid to his nape, drawing him down to the bed. "I knew you'd come for me."

Reed hovered above her, his mouth and body ready to claim . . .

Then her words sank in and awareness hit.

What in the *bloody hell* was he thinking? She had just survived a horrifying ordeal and was lucky to escape with her life, let alone unharmed. And so he had the brilliant notion to take advantage of her when her wits were addled?

Reed muttered an oath and straightened. He looked around at her disordered room, and to the door opened to the hall. Not too far off, he saw the maid cast an uncertain glance over her shoulder then pivot back the other way. Even so, it was clear by the blush on her cheeks that she had caught them kissing. And very nearly a great deal more.

"We cannot stay here."

Ainsley sat up and slipped her hand in his. "Shall we go to Sterling's, then?"

"You're asking me to take you to . . ." He stopped. Clearly, she was not herself. The Ainsley he knew would never set foot in his *den of iniquity*.

From experience, he knew that surviving a dire encounter often made people susceptible to excitement and rash behavior. His mum usually had gone on a tidying-up frenzy after Lord Bray left the house, stripping linens, rugs, and draperies from every room until she wore herself out from exhaustion. And sometimes men acted strangely after a fight, especially when unexpectedly victorious.

The hard thumping of the heart and rapid blood flow through the veins tended to make a person feel impervious and ready to celebrate, never thinking of consequences. They wanted only to bask in the glow of their triumph.

A survivor's euphoria.

Reed looked at Ainsley with fresh eyes—her flushed face, the pulse fluttering wildly beneath the delicate line of her jaw.

"We're not going to Sterling's. Mitchum hasn't been found yet and I have to take you someplace safe and far away. Do you understand?"

Her cheeks drained of color, her gaze darting over her shoulder. "Do you think he's still here somewhere?"

"No," Reed assured her. "I imagine he heard the servants. And since he couldn't find your clever hiding spot, there was nothing else he could do but leave."

For now. Reed was certain he would make another attempt.

Ainsley clutched his hand tighter. "I won't feel safe unless I am with you."

Sinking to his knees, he kissed her palms tenderly. "That cannot happen, highness. Should anyone discover that you spent a night with me before we are married, your reputation would be in tatters."

He turned her hands over to kiss her fingertips, but saw that every one of her nails was broken, chipped, and cracked as if she'd been through a war. Muttering an oath under his breath, he vowed to kill Mitchum slowly. There would be much agony and wailing and pleading.

"In case you haven't noticed, I'm a complete disaster, reputation and all," she said softly and bent to press a kiss to his temple. "Mr. Mitchum made it clear that he wanted people to know."

Doubtless, Mitchum wouldn't have cared if she was compromised in front of witnesses. Perhaps that was even what he wanted—a way to force her hand. *To force her . . .*

Reed's blood began to boil again and it took every ounce of control he had not to run out the door and hunt that man down.

"He may be telling someone this instant," she continued, closing her eyes as if defeated. "His nature is to spin his own heroic tales. Once the *ton* learns of the attack, there will be nothing of my reputation—or the agency's for that matter—to salvage. By morning, Mr. Mitchum will have succeeded in fiction where he did not in truth. And I"—she paused on a fractured breath—"will never truly escape him."

"You will. I'll make sure of it."

She studied him closely. "How? By unleashing that dark fury I see in your eyes?" Lifting her free hand, her fingers brushed the disorderly locks away from his forehead and shook her head, her soft eyes pleading. "If his actions bring out violence in you, then he will have succeeded all the same."

Reed knew she was right. But that left him only one option. "If you come with me, highness, there will be no turning back. No lengthy betrothal. You will leave as Miss Bourne and return as Mrs. Sterling. Are you prepared for that?"

In response, she took his face in her hands and pressed her lips to his.

Chapter 24

"How much more must an imaginist, like herself,
be on fire with speculation and foresight!—
especially with such a groundwork of anticipation
as her mind had already made."

JANE AUSTEN, *Emma*

Ainsley reclined in the portable tub, the steaming water a
magic potion for relaxation. How could it be that fear and
anxiety weren't eating her alive after such an ordeal?

The first time she'd packed up and escaped Nigel, she
hadn't been able to sleep for a week. She'd been constantly
worried about her uncle and sisters, not wanting them to
suffer because of her. Spent endless hours ensuring that
their lives were in perfect order.

She'd never revealed how it left her fragile, exhausted,
and soul weary.

This time was different. She wasn't facing any of it alone.
For the first time in her life, she could lean on someone
strong, and share her thoughts and fears.

Sinking deeper into the water, she rested the back of
her head over the louvered lip of the tub. It felt luxurious,
decadent—not just the bath, but the fact that she could
have a nice long soak and know that Reed was in control of
things beyond the door.

He'd taken charge in London as well. After stuffing a few
things in a satchel and leaving his men with instructions,

Reed had whisked her off, traveling to wherever they were now. It was strange to realize that she didn't even know the name of this hamlet, where they'd stop next, or what they'd eat or drink. Quite unlike her usual self.

Yet she was merely content to be with him. She'd even slept for most of the journey, dozing in his strong arms, unworried.

It was only when Reed had left the carriage that she'd roused, startled that his comforting warmth was no longer surrounding her. Alone and alarmed, her first instinct had been to call out for him. He'd instantly appeared at the carriage door, proving that he was never far from her side.

Taking her hand, he'd explained that they'd arrived at an inn to rest, but would be off in a few hours again. Then, in short order, he'd paid for two meals, two rooms, lodging for his driver, and a change of horses.

She had not seen him since. Though given the fact that she was in a steaming bath, it was for the best. A giggle bubbled out at the thought.

Ainsley *never* giggled. It was absurd to do so, especially at a time like this. Yet she couldn't summon any of her usual worry, not about Nigel, her reputation, or how the townhouse and agency would be set to rights in her absence.

And she knew the reason why—Reed Sterling. The man she would soon marry.

There was no use denying it. No more lengthy betrothal. *No more hiding,* a voice whispered at the back of her mind, reminding her of the realization she'd come to inside the chest. *Her coffin.*

Only now did her heart beat in a harried rhythm. Her breaths quick and short. The firelight in the hearth seemed to grow cool and dim.

Then her mind conjured Reed and, all at once, the panic subsided.

She exhaled a deep, calming breath. Her skin was still

chilled, but the room was brighter. Her thoughts sure and steady.

Rising from the bath, she stepped out. After drying off with a flannel, she applied the balm that Reed had so thoughtfully packed. He'd also grabbed her hairbrush, the nightdress from beneath her pillow—though how he knew it was there, she would have to ask him later—and her mother's ballgown from the cedar chest. Likely he did not know that such a garment was hardly fit for traveling, but she wouldn't complain. He was doing everything he could to take care of her.

I'm marrying Reed Sterling, she thought with a dazed grin, slipping her arms into the soft cambric of her nightgown and then over her head.

It surprised her that she was not overwhelmed with trepidation. And there was no part of her that felt weaker by this realization either. In fact, though it seemed counterintuitive, she felt stronger knowing that she could depend on him instead of managing things on her own.

How odd.

And instead of fretting and mulling her thumbnail to the quick, she felt a pressing need to live a fuller life. To fill her remaining days and years with more than a sense of purpose.

She wanted her family to be happy and for the Bourne Matrimonial Agency to be a whopping success, of course. But, most of all, she wanted Reed. Whenever she reached out, she wanted her hand to find his. Whenever she lifted her arms, she wanted to be swept up in his embrace. And whenever she closed her eyes, she wanted to taste his kiss.

What she didn't want, however, was to let fear rule her anymore.

If Nigel had intended to terrorize her so much that she thought only of him and stopped living her life, then he would be disappointed.

A hesitant knock fell on the door, breaking through her musings.

A small feminine voice asked, "Ma'am, if it isn't too much trouble, Mr. Sterling would like to know if you're ready for your dinner."

"You can inform Mr. Sterling that I am not hungry," she said, smiling to herself, the ruffled hem of her nightdress swishing over her toes. She knew Reed would dislike this answer, and could just about count down the seconds until she heard another—

A hard rap of brutish knuckles fell on the door, and she nearly laughed.

"Ainsley," Reed said, weary exhaustion in his tone, "you have to eat something."

"I don't believe I shall, Mr. Sterling." Oh, how she loved to argue with this man.

Smiling, she sat by the fire and began to brush her damp hair, letting the heat from the flames dry the chestnut locks into burnished waves. Beyond the door, she heard a murmured conversation, Reed's gruff drawl loud enough that she could hear him send for her meal, regardless of her wishes.

The quick patter of the maid's footsteps retreated, but not his.

The floor creaked beneath a heavy boot. "Are you decently attired?"

"I am covered, though—"

The door clicked open, scraping in the crescent groove worn into the floorboards. Reed stepped in. His expression was hard and weary . . . until he looked at her, sitting in front of the fire in her nightdress.

"—not properly."

Normally, she would rush to cover herself, to put as many barriers between them as possible. But seeing the flicker of the firelight glow hotly in his indigo eyes roused her curiosity. What was he going to do now—cross the room and take her in his arms? Kiss her senseless? Show her all sorts of wicked and wonderful things?

Her pulse leapt excitedly.

Slow and thorough, his gaze swept over her. High color slashed the crests of his cheeks. She'd seen this look before and knew he was thinking of kissing her, and perhaps a good deal more . . .

Yet for reasons beyond her understanding, he shifted, restless. He averted his face to the bathwater, then to the bed, and last to the window.

A bashful rogue? Oh dear, this was the last thing she expected from him.

"You're not dressed," he chided, his voice deep and hoarse. Even so, he made no move to depart.

She grinned. Rising from the chair, she crossed the room. And while standing within arm's reach of him, she unfolded the red coarse-woven blanket resting at the foot of the bed and wrapped it around herself like a shawl.

"And you're not wearing your cravat. Dare we stand in the same room?"

Peculiarly, her usual sense of reservation was absent. However it seemed to have infected Reed, instead.

"Three of a clock in the morning is not the time for teasing, highness." He scrubbed a hand over his drawn face and through his damp hair, firelight glistening in the dark strands, making her fingers itch to run through them. "I need to make certain you are well rested and fed so that you're thinking clearly later this morning."

In other words, he was not convinced that she was thinking clearly now.

Ainsley wanted to tell him about her epiphany, but knew that this wasn't the right moment. Besides, he likely wouldn't believe any words of a romantic nature coming from her.

They had been at war for too long. Their two factions would require time to adjust to this new treaty. Therefore, she would be patient and bring him about gradually.

"Very well," she consented. "I shall have broth."

"You'll have a full dinner. I've ordered a chicken, a pork pie, mutton, green peas . . ."

"Good heavens! Am I supposed to eat all that, or is there a trencherman army encamped in the stable yard?" She went over to the window and rubbed her hand in a circle over the cool, foggy glass, making a show of peering outside before she lifted her brows at him.

He shrugged, kicking the bedpost with the toe of his boot. "I wanted you to have your fill of whatever took your fancy. We've only dined together once, and I don't yet know what your favorites might be."

Glimpsing this sweet, uncertain side of his nature, Ainsley's heart nearly burst. What else would she learn about him if she kept peering closer?

"I like everything," she answered conversationally. "Well, except for asparagus. I detest that awful vegetable. Whenever the duchess serves it, I have to find clever ways of disguising that I haven't eaten any."

His mouth gave way to the first grin he'd had throughout this entire ordeal. And when she saw that snick winking at her, it warmed her. "I don't like asparagus either."

"Then we shall hope our feast is free of the abominable stalk."

"*Your* feast," he clarified, turning toward the door.

"You're not staying?" When he shook his head, she took hold of his arm, adding hastily, "Then how will you know if I've eaten a single morsel?"

"*Highness,*" he warned, hesitating on the threshold.

The blanket chose at that instant to slip from her shoulders. Reed's gaze flicked down the length of her, all the way to her bare toes peeking out beneath her hem, then took a slower path back up to her face, heating along the way.

She sensed he was weakening a bit, or perhaps that was just her knees. They'd gone a bit wobbly. Arguing with him always did this to her, only she hadn't known what it was before.

She dared to take a step closer. Reaching out, she plucked at the cloth-covered button on his coat, looking up at him through her lashes. "Is it too much to ask for you to stay a little while longer?"

He swallowed, his hands flexing and unflexing at his sides as if he wanted to put something in his grasp. *Her?* She hoped so. He was looking at her lips as if he might devour them.

Instead, he bent down, grabbed the blanket, then wrapped it around her again. Yet he lingered in her breathable space, her lungs filling with his familiar scent. Then he lowered his head and—

The maid knocked on the door, the moment lost.

In quick succession, three servants entered, toting empty pails in each hand, and set about emptying, drying, and removing the tub. Then during all this, another set of servants brought a small round table and a pair of stools, along with a great quantity of food.

By the time it was all in place and the circus of servants had gone, Reed seemed to have resigned himself to dining with her. Better yet, with the fire toasty and the room so snug, he even started to shrug out of his coat. But then he paused, uncertain.

"By all means, continue," she said, her voice slightly hoarse as her greedy gaze spied a hint of rippling muscle beneath the fine linen. It had been a long while since she'd seen him in his shirtsleeves. "I believe there are rules on propriety about this sort of thing. Simply put, it is much preferable for a man to remove his coat than to allow perspiration to dampen his brow."

She was lying through her teeth. Though she must have sounded haughty enough to be convincing, for he stripped out of the garment and hung the coat on the peg behind the door. Now, if only she could think up a rule about removing one's waistcoat . . .

"Is something amiss with my buttons, highness?"

Her gaze shot up to his, her cheeks flushing with guilt for mentally undressing him. "I thought I noticed a loose one. I would be happy to mend it for you."

She was positively diabolical!

He ran an absent hand down his torso, testing the thread tension, and shook his head as he lowered down onto the stool opposite her.

Drat.

At first, Ainsley could hardly concentrate on the food. But then, after tasting the scrumptious roasted lamb and salted potatoes, she was suddenly ravenous. The red wine was delicious and full-bodied—a far cry from the watered-down libation she was used to drinking—and it pooled warmly in her stomach, humming through her veins.

She was more at ease. Here she was, in her nightdress, flush-cheeked and alone in her room with Reed, and she wasn't thinking about propriety.

Her boundaries had fallen away, parting like the shroud of Lazarus when she'd opened the lid of the chest and saw that Reed had come for her. It was such a powerful thing—to feel as though she truly mattered to him. That he wouldn't have simply turned around, walked away, and never looked back.

So much warmth filled her heart that it was nearly impossible not to move over to his side of the table and sit in his lap. And he made it more difficult by always touching her. Reaching across to fill her plate, he would pause to nudge her lace sleeve out of the way, or tuck a lock of hair behind her ear. And each time he put another spoonful of food on her plate, she pretended to bat his hand away, *accidentally* tangling her fingers with his, softly chiding him for fussing over her.

Would this be how they would spend their lives together?

She'd like to think so.

As the night drew on, they chatted about an endless array of topics, from what they both disliked about boiled chicken—the floppy, slimy skin—to tales of what it had been like growing up in their small villages.

Ainsley enjoyed hearing about the patrons who'd come to his father's tavern. Though it didn't escape her notice that his childhood stories ended when he reached the age of ten.

"Your eyes crinkle at the corners whenever you mention the tavern," she said with a fond smile of her own. "You must have been happy then. It's no wonder you chose a similar occupation to your father's—providing food and drink and respite to whomever walks through your doors."

"I come from a long line of men and women who labored with their hands to make a life for themselves," he said proudly, but there was an edge to his voice, as if he thought she meant to slight him.

So she quickly said, "I find hard work of any kind admirable."

He nodded absently and took a gulp of wine, but said nothing more.

She didn't want their conversation to end there. She needed to know all about how he became the man he was. Therefore, she altered the topic. "You know, my uncle speaks of his days at university with such fondness, I often wish that I could have gone. I'm not much for listening to lectures, mind you, but I'm certain I would have enjoyed the libraries. What was your experience like?"

The light of mutual contentment in his gaze shuttered closed.

"Challenging."

And that was all he gave her. Apparently, this was a tender subject, too.

Ainsley didn't give up. She told him more about her life, talking about the number of disagreeable tutors she and her sisters had had, recounting tales of Jacinda's mischief-making—which had caused at least two of them to leave before they'd fully unpacked their satchels.

Gradually, Reed opened up to her again, offering more enticing glimpses of his life.

The food was left forgotten as he told her of his own escapades as a lad. With a slow grin, he admitted to giving his mum a few gray hairs, and trying her patience.

Listening to his tales, Ainsley was a bit envious. She'd only flirted with the idea of rebelling. At least, until she'd declared war against her neighbor.

"I'm looking forward to meeting your mother," she said honestly. "I only wish you could have met mine."

"Do you think she would have approved of me?"

Ignoring the dubious lift of his brow, Ainsley thought for a moment. "Actually, yes. Both she and my uncle shared similar traits, always eager to be swept away by romance. I have a feeling that my mother would have found you quite dashing."

"And your father?" Reed dropped his napkin on his plate, the flesh of his brow furrowing. "Come to think of it, is he someone that I should ask for—"

She shook her head. "Lord Frawley is not part of my life. We were unimportant to him. Invisible. Doubtless, if you ever happened to meet him and mentioned my name, he would only stare blankly at you."

Abruptly, the wine lost its pleasant warmth. Perhaps trying to unearth commonalities they shared wasn't the best idea.

Yet when she set down her glass, Reed reached across the table and took her hand in his. "Highness, if he has chosen not to be in your life, then he has only robbed himself of knowing one of the finest women in the world."

His tender sentiment stole Ainsley's breath.

"We don't need to speak of our pasts anymore this evening," he said, brushing his thumb along the small protrusions of her knuckles. "Besides, we have enough things in common that you've no need to look for more."

"That wasn't what I was doing," she argued, and his brows arched with skepticism.

Unwavering, he held her gaze. "We'll be good together."

"How can you be sure?"

"Because we're both stubborn and determined and hate the idea of failing. But, most importantly"—he paused to draw a breath—"when we set our sights on a goal, we put our hearts and souls into reaching it."

Her throat felt tight, her heart lodged there. She swallowed. "It seems we have a good deal in common."

"And there's more, too," he said, his voice dropping lower as he turned her hand over and traced the sensitive lines of her palm.

Yet, before he could describe the *more* to her—which she believed had something to do with how well their bodies fit together when they kissed—another knock fell on the door.

The servants had frustratingly impeccable timing.

A short while later, their dinner was cleared away and the servants gone. Moving to the open door, Reed reached for his coat.

At the thought of him leaving her alone, an unexpected spike of fear tore through her. "Surely, you're not going to go now."

"You need your rest. I saw how many times you tried to hide a yawn behind your napkin. You're exhausted, as anyone would be after all you've been through."

She didn't want to think about it, especially not in the dark, alone in an unfamiliar bed. When she was awake and in control, she could keep her thoughts here in the present, and looking toward the future she hoped to have with Reed. But there was still part of her that feared her unconscious mind would be quick to put her back in that nightmare.

"I don't feel sleepy, no matter what you say." In that same instant, a huge yawn overtook her.

Reed chuckled and teased, "I'll tuck you in, if you like."

There were nights when she'd had scandalous dreams of him saying things like that, but this circumstance wasn't what she imagined.

All she had to do was tell him that she was afraid and he would feel obligated to stay with her. But she didn't want that. She needed him to stay because he wanted to.

"If I am tired, then I have you to blame for pouring the wine too heavily and keeping the fire too warm," she said with feigned terseness. "Not only that, but I have a terrible pain in my neck because of you. After the way you held me in the carriage, I can only manage to turn my head at an awkward angle. Now, the only way I could sleep is if I were put in the same position."

Reed looked to the tiny bed and back to her and frowned. "Highness, if you are asking me to lie down with you—"

"*Asking you*, indeed. You're a wicked man. Of the two of us you've been the only one to speak of tucking me in that bed." She sniffed, hoping he did not see through her pretense. "But I refuse to be cross with you after all you've done. And besides, we are getting married. Therefore, I shall allow you to hold me until I fall asleep. Just five minutes, or so."

THREE TORTUROUS hours later, Reed left Ainsley's side. He'd never been so exhausted or aroused in his entire life.

It had not even taken her five minutes to fall asleep, but he couldn't bring himself to leave her. Her bluster was all an act. Proof of that was the wide-eyed fear in her eyes when he'd moved to the door. So, he'd stayed.

He'd held her in bed, her warm body snuggled enticingly against him. Her sweet scent filling his every breath. For hours.

He'd soothed her with caresses along her back, brushed away the wispy hair that fell across her cheek, and traced the hand she'd splayed over his chest, but nothing more salacious. Not even when—in her sleep—her leg curled around his, her unbound breasts pressed invitingly against his side, and the heat of her sex called to him like a siren's song.

Each time he'd dozed for a minute, he'd wakened to a raging erection, his hand drifting to her sweet bottom and his hips unconsciously angling toward hers. The soft, needy sounds she made in her sleep only made it worse.

Now, leaving her room, he was in agony. He'd never ached like this before. Walking with a normal stride was impossible. His bollocks were squeezed so tight they might have been in a vise. It was clear that he would have to take himself in hand if he was going to survive any more time with Ainsley curled up beside him. Or he was likely to lose his mind and take *her* inside the carriage.

At the thought, another hard-seated surge nearly crippled him. He jerked at the fastenings of his trousers, the weight of his cock springing free, stiff as a guidepost. Then, at last, he—

"Rain's a coming, sir," his driver said with a jarring rap on the door. "We should get a foot under us soon if we want to avoid washed-out roads."

Damn and bollocks. Reed gripped the rearing beast and shoved it down, shifting uncomfortably as he refastened his trousers, calling back through the door. "Very good, Mr. Smith. Miss Bourne and I should be down shortly."

"Oh, and a missive arrived with the Earl of Edgemont's seal."

The special license, Reed thought, glad to have that matter settled. He knew he could count on Edgemont. The earl was one of the better aristocrats—slow to temper and quick to laugh. A right solid fellow. "Just slide it under the door, thank you."

Reed walked over to the washstand to splash water on his face. He gave himself a quick shave, hoping that by the time he finished making himself presentable, he'd have his ardor under control. Then he donned a cravat, tying it in the Oriental knot he'd practiced. And even pulled on a fresh coat before marching across the hall.

His knock was harder than he'd intended. A lot of things still were.

After a moment, she opened the door. In her nightdress, she looked sleepy and rumpled and far, *far* too beddable.

He gripped the doorframe, breathing in rosehips and almond blossoms and losing his mind.

"Rain is coming. We'll marry without delay." He frowned, not sure that made sense. And from the ragged, almost desperate, sound of his own voice, he might as well have added, *"Now, here in the coaching inn. Beside that little bed."*

It was not the most romantic of proposals, by any means. If he'd had all his faculties in working order, he would have given her a flower and dropped to bended knee.

Damn it all, why had he not thought of that? She deserved to be wooed with flowers and confections and whatever else besotted fools were supposed to give the woman they loved.

"Since it hasn't been three weeks from the reading of the banns, I presume you've obtained a special license?" she asked with her usual pragmatism.

Then her lips curved in a smile as if she knew that it drove him positively wild whenever she spoke to him all prim and proper.

Helpless, he caught himself listing forward, drunken with lust, until he was forced to steady himself. "I have . . . or, rather, your brother-in-law has. And I have a ring as well."

He'd purchased it the day after he'd announced their betrothal, combing through dozens of rings at the jewelers until he'd found the right one. He could have bought the largest ruby and the most vulgar emerald he'd ever seen, but that was not the Ainsley he knew. Instead, he found something elegant and modest and forthright, like her.

"Then it is all arranged," she said, her cheeks tinged pink. "You've been rather busy. So, I suppose I shouldn't dawdle."

"No," he said inanely, already imagining her stripping out of her nightdress. Seeing her bite the corner of her mouth drove him to the brink of madness. It was all he could do to keep himself on this side of the threshold.

She turned to close the door, but hesitated. Her gaze shyly met his. "I should like children . . . if that is agreeable."

He stared down at her, hoping he didn't look as uncontrolled and hungry as he felt. He would give her a child nine months from the day—*from the minute*—if she asked. But he would not rush her. He was nothing if not patient. Even if it killed him.

"Aye. I'd like that."

"Then it seems, Mr. Sterling, you are about to have a wife."

Before he could force himself to move away from the door, he reached out and caught her by the waist. Pulling her flush against him, he kissed her soundly, then set her back on her feet.

Chapter 25

"His wedding-day was named."

JANE AUSTEN, *Emma*

In a tiny church standing in the quaint hamlet of Knightsbury, Ainsley and Reed spoke their vows with the steady solemnity required of the moment. They held each other's gazes as he slipped the most perfect gold band on her finger, and she became his lawful wife.

The elderly vicar patted Reed's shoulder and said, "I never thought I'd see this day, lad."

Only then did Ainsley realize that Reed had brought her to someplace familiar to him. This was not simply a random church, but a destination.

"I knew you wouldn't believe it unless I were here in the flesh." Reed unleashed a broad grin, tucking her against his side as if it was the most natural thing.

The vicar's cheeks creased in a smile, his attention settling on her. "Mrs. Sterling, your husband's as good as they come, but a mite mischievous from time to time. Most of my gray hair came from him and the way he'd—"

Reed cleared his throat. "I'm sure my wife"—he paused for a breath and glanced down at her, something akin to shock and wonder in his expression—"I'm sure my wife doesn't want to hear the stories of the youth who ran wild here."

"I wouldn't be too certain, *husband*," she said, simply because she could and liked the sound of it. "Perhaps I should like to hear every single one."

The vicar laughed. "Yes, indeed. I knew it would take a strong woman to rein you in."

Reed didn't take offense, but turned toward the open window where the hard patter of rain swept in with a cool breeze. "Pity, it appears the storm will delay those stories. We'll have to depart at once to make it home."

Home. Ainsley liked the sound of that word from his lips. It held such quiet promise.

When they arrived a half hour later, Ainsley instantly liked the look of *home*, too. At the end of a flagstone walkway stood a shingled cottage with a whitewashed door and window trim, and a fieldstone chimney poking out of the thatched roof. Such a quaint little cottage. It seemed to represent the softer side of his nature that she'd grown so fond of.

Reed didn't leave her much time to admire its exterior, however. He whisked her from the carriage and out of the driving rain, setting her on her feet inside the cozy space.

Watery gray light shone in from a pair of cheerful box windows nestled inside the bare horsehair plaster walls. The hardwood floor was tidy and flat, adorned with a round speckled rug in the entryway. Standing in the center of the room was a trestle table topped with wide planks, gray and age-worn. There was a snug little alcove in the one wall, guarded by yellowed curtains on either side. And above it was a little loft, with a wooden ladder that reached the floor.

"Is this where you lived with your mother?"

"And my dad, aye," he said with a nod, staring down at her with a sense of expectation radiating from him. "Will this be tolerable?"

"It's lovely."

Her declaration earned a surprised lift of his brow. She was hoping for a kiss, but he left her to stand in the one-room cottage alone as he helped the driver.

Unfastening the cloak from around her shoulders, she hung it on a mantel peg to dry, and set about lighting the fire. It took only a spark of flint before the dried kindling and tinder bundle hissed to life beneath a stack of slender logs.

She dusted her hands together and crossed the room to a small square nightstand beside the bed and found linens inside. There was a patchwork coverlet in faded blues and yellows, along with sprigs of lavender tucked in between each layer.

Ainsley pulled the bedclothes out to air, but found they weren't musty in the least. Therefore, she made the bed, tucking the linens around the mattress and laying the coverlet in place. Then, surveying her work, she thought about her wedding night.

A tiny cold spear of trepidation ran through her.

Stepping back to the fire, she held out her hands to warm them. Would Reed be a gentle and patient lover? Would he kiss her breathless? Rouse her to shuddering pleasure?

Of course he would. Likely all he would have to do was simply look at her in that smoldering way of his and her blood would simmer. And she would welcome the warmth, she thought.

Wondering what was keeping him, she stepped to the window. Through the sheeting rain, she saw Reed wave to the driver and heard the jangle of rigging as the carriage trundled away.

Reed paused underneath the overhang guarding the threshold to shake the water from his hair and stomp the mud from his boots. She skirted around the corner as he stepped inside and stood next to a large basket tied with a blue ribbon and two satchels.

Then he closed the door behind him and her nerves leapt in a harried jolt.

They were alone now. Man and wife.

"The roads should hold out long enough to see him to the stables," he said, struggling to shrug free of his sodden coat.

She moved to help him, turning him around with a little nudge of her hand as if they'd done this dozens of times. "Are the stables far? I didn't see any from the road."

He gave her an amused glance, but complied. "Near enough."

It took a few tugs before she could even pull the garment from his shoulders, the sleeves turning inside out down the length and girth of his arms. But her progress halted at his wrists. "You're going to have to unclench your hands or I won't be able to finish."

"Then you're going to have to take what's inside them."

"Oh, I didn't realize you were holding—"

She gasped as he unfolded his fingers. There, carefully nestled in both palms, were violets. For a minute she simply stared at them without moving. Her heart and lungs made her feel buoyant as if she could float up the rafters.

"They're no primroses, of course," he teased in a low drawl that sent warmth burrowing through her, "but I saw them near the downspout and they were about to get swept away by the rain."

She reached for them, her fingertip brushing the velvety petals, and quietly said, "I like violets, too."

Their gazes met, held for a moment . . . until he glanced over her shoulder to the freshly made bed.

He quickly turned his attention to the rafters. "I think there's a cup on the mantel that might make a vase of sorts, and there's plenty of water. Smith and I put pails out to collect the rain."

Taking the flowers, she swept toward the hearth. His reaction to the bed had her feeling shy and uncertain. Had making it look neat and welcoming been too bold of her? They were man and wife, after all. Surely, he didn't expect them to spend their first night together laid out on the table.

At the thought and the image it conjured, her cheeks turned hot—at least four different shades of red—and she kept her face averted as she arranged the blossoms.

When she finished, she believed that the little violets drooping over the edge of a brown earthenware cup made the prettiest bouquet she'd ever seen.

Reed came up beside her and held his hands out toward the fire, his gaze on the flowers. "That looks nice. Homey."

"It does, indeed. Thank you," she said. "My sisters and I used to put violets on endive and eat them."

His brows knitted together but a smirk played on his lips. "You're not going to eat your wedding bouquet, are you?"

"Only if that basket of food from the vicar's wife is full of asparagus."

"If that's the case, then I'm taking the biggest violet for myself."

She set her hands on her hips and grinned at her husband—good heavens she liked the sound of that, even if only in her thoughts. "Not if I have anything to say about it."

His eyes darkened, smoldering and hungry as he gazed down at her. Her lips tingled, ready for his kiss and curious about what would follow. In fact, she was fairly obsessed with the thought, needing to have all the information to put her mind at ease.

But he turned away abruptly. Then, picking up the basket, he placed it on the table. "Let's see what we have then."

"I don't mind if we wait."

He glanced down to where her hand rested against her midriff. Beneath it, dozens of little knots were forming, waiting to be untied.

"Not feeling well?" he asked.

"A bit of nerves."

Automatically, he took a step toward her and laid his hands on her shoulders, trailing them down in a soothing caress. "You don't have anything to fret over, highness."

"That may be easy for you to say but I don't know . . . well . . . what comes next."

"What do you mean, when we return to London?"

She shook her head, fighting another blush. "No. I mean here, between us."

When he still looked at her as if he hadn't a clue, she expelled a frustrated breath. She glanced to the bed and then back to him. Was he going to make her say it aloud?

Apparently so. "The . . . consummation of our marriage."

He jerked his hands away so fast she might have been a burning coal.

A wash of color slanted across the bridge of his nose and cheeks, and he cleared his throat a few times before he finally spoke. "We should wait until we are more ourselves. Perhaps a rest after our long journey would set matters aright."

Until we *are more ourselves?* It seemed that *he* was the only one not acting like himself. Not one bit.

Normally, she was the reserved one between them and yet she very much felt in need of a shepherd's crook to prod him along. Where was the rogue bent on kissing her brainless?

"Very well. Since sleeping seems to be your answer for every issue, we'll have a lie down and consider it later." Then, with a little verbal nudge, she added, "Which side of the bed would you prefer?"

He swallowed and pulled at his damp cravat. "I'll sleep in the loft. You take the bed."

Apparently, the bashful rogue had returned. Ainsley hoped this wasn't a permanent condition.

Though in the back of her mind, she couldn't help but wonder if there was a different reason behind this recent alteration in his behavior. Did he regret marrying her?

Chapter 26

"... people may not think *you* perfection
already.—But hush!—not a word, if you please."

JANE AUSTEN, *Emma*

Ainsley couldn't take another moment of silent musings
in the bed, and neither could her thumbnail. All she'd been
able to do for the past hour was worry about the reason Reed
seemed so altered.

She could understand if the pressure of their pretend betrothal and then hasty marriage had finally overtaken him.
Perhaps he had been more inclined to a lengthy betrothal
instead. Perhaps he wasn't prepared to be saddled with a
wife so soon. Could he be considering an annulment?

When that startling thought took hold, Ainsley sat up.
She was past the point of mulling.

Needing an answer, and refusing to wait any longer for
him to make an appearance at the bottom of the ladder, she
wrapped the coverlet over her shoulders and climbed up to
the loft.

She caught him lying on his back with his arms folded
behind his head, staring blankly at the rafters, his big body
filling the small space.

"Ah-ha," she said, startling him with a jolt. "Just as I
suspected, you aren't sleeping at all."

He bolted upright, his expression guilty. "I might have
just awoken."

"I would have heard your breathing alter. Instead, I just felt you thinking."

"Is that so?" He arched a brow and settled back against a makeshift bolster—one of the coarse-woven wool blankets from the carriage and another spread out beneath him.

"Yes, you emit tension in waves whenever you are puzzling over something," she said distractedly as she stared at his long trouser-clad legs crossed at the ankle, his bare feet exposed.

She blushed at the intimacy of such a sight, noting their large and sturdy size, and how they were dusted with dark hair. Balanced on the rung, her own feet were bare, too. Her stockings and even her outer dress and fichu were drying by the fire. So were his coat, waistcoat, and cravat. Though considering that he'd seen her in her nightdress, she didn't think it too scandalous for her to be in a worsted petticoat, stays, and chemise. And besides, she still had the coverlet.

At least . . . until she climbed up higher and the patchwork barrier slipped free.

He stared at her fixedly, his gaze scorching a path along her throat, and over her breasts as if she wore nothing at all. Her skin reacted to this, her nipples drawing taut.

Then he turned his head and scrubbed a hand over his face and shifted uncomfortably. "You shouldn't be up here with me."

She felt the sting of his rejection like salt in a fresh wound. "If you regret our marriage and desire an annulment, tell me at once."

"Not at all. But if that's what *you* want—"

"No," she said quickly. "I'm just trying to understand your obvious reluctance to be near me. If it is because you find my kisses . . . awkward and . . . um . . . unpleasant, then . . ."

He expelled a rueful puff of air, a laugh that bruised her ego.

Yet he surprised her by angling toward her, his fingertips resting against her cheek. "Ainsley, if your kisses were any sweeter, softer, or more arousing you would incinerate me into a pile of ash."

Even though his tone was grave, the pleasure of his words tunneled through her in a burst of sunshine warmth.

"Then why aren't you kissing me?"

"I fear I could not stop once I started."

She studied his countenance carefully. "Truly?"

"Aye." He withdrew his touch and frowned. "And the last thing you need is to be ravaged by your brute of a husband."

Normally those words would have given her pause. But her husband was not a brute. And frankly, the thought of being completely, thoroughly ravaged by Reed Sterling made her positively giddy. So she shimmied around his feet to the other side of the loft.

"Don't smile at me like that, Ainsley. It only makes me want to kiss you all the more. And stop moving closer. No, don't curl up beside me either," he warned, his nostrils flaring on a deep breath. "Damn, but the scent of your skin drives me to madness." His arm snaked around her, his wavering resistance vibrating in the thick ropes of muscle. "You're not yourself."

"Or perhaps, I'm more myself than I've ever been before." She peered closely at his mismatched eyes, finding disgruntled disbelief. "To convince you that I am of sound mind, should I scold you? Wag my finger, perhaps? Remark on every one of your flaws?"

"Something of that nature," he muttered, but there was a smile in his voice as his hands roved up and down the lengths of her bare arms, winnowing out tingles of sensation with every pass.

If she was going to let her barriers down with Reed, then she would have to tell him the truth and stop hiding behind her usual reserve.

Drawing back—albeit marginally, for she didn't want to lose this cozy spot—she wagged her finger. "Mr. Sterling, whyever are you still dressed in your shirtsleeves? Don't you realize that I've spent far too much time imagining you without them?"

He blinked, clearly shocked. She was, too. And when he didn't respond immediately, she averted her face, feeling utterly naked.

Reaching out, he gently took hold of her chin and looked into her eyes. "Have you?"

She swallowed, certain her cheeks had gone seventeen shades of red.

His mouth curved into a slow, wicked grin. "Tell me all the naughty things you've been thinking about me."

"You first," she croaked.

"Oh, so many things. Hmm . . . where to start?" He laughed, a low roguish sound, and ran his fingers along her plait, drawing it forward, passing the ribbon-tied end across her lips and then his own. "I suppose with this. I've thought of you with your hair draped over your shoulder—"

"That doesn't sound too scandalous."

"—and what it would be like unbound, falling over me like a silk curtain, with you gazing down at me. Your bare body rising and falling over mine," he concluded softly, painting a breathlessly risqué picture with his words.

"You have a much better imagination than I."

"Perhaps because I've been thinking about it a while longer," he said wryly, slowly wrapping the coil of her hair around his wrist.

"For how lon—"

He tugged gently, bringing her mouth to his.

Reed claimed her lips with such tender possession that she forgot all about her question. All she could think was *at last*, and surrender to the sublime mingling of their flesh, tingles dancing over her skin. They should have been doing this all along.

With every taste, she lost more of her inhibitions. Forgot about her reservations. Rising to meet him, her hands splayed over his chest, and suddenly the kisses were not tame at all, but hungry and searching.

He cinched his arm around her waist, lifting her higher until she was half-sprawled, one leg draped over his, her petticoat inching upward until the soft wool of his trousers grazed her bare skin. It felt so decadent, so wanton, that she gasped. Taking advantage, he stole into the heat of her mouth, sliding and curling his tongue wickedly against hers.

Such a naughty rogue, she thought, practically purring. And he was all hers.

She suckled his flesh, feeding on his deep guttural grunt of approval as his hands skimmed over her body, into every dip, every curve. He tugged gently on the coil of hair in his grasp and tilted her back. His open mouth grazed the underside of her jaw, nipping along her throat, laving the tender pulse fluttering beneath the susceptible flesh.

She would have been embarrassed by the sounds she was making at any other time. But right now, she was lost to pleasure and unable to get her fill.

Reading her thoughts, he pulled her fully atop him. And she whimpered as her body slid over his hard contours, her hips settling perfectly onto his, and hitching sweetly. She didn't think a kiss could feel any better, until his hand drifted down her back to the curve of her bottom.

He tilted upward at just the right angle to draw out a desperate, needy mewl. She wanted to keep him right there, forever. But he had something else in mind. His deft fingers flicked over the buttons at the back of her petticoat until she felt the garment sag.

Ainsley rose up, looking down at the hungry, glazed look in his eyes and argued, "See here. I still haven't seen you without your shirtsleeves."

With a speed she never would have believed unless she'd seen it herself, he pulled the linen over his head and let it sail to the floor. And . . . *oh . . . my . . . heavens* . . . he was magnificent. His broad chest was furred and thickly mounded, the line of his clavicle fading into thick ropes of muscle at his shoulders, and his abdomen ridged on either side of the tapered hair trailing down past his navel.

She made an inarticulate sound of appreciation an instant before he captured her lips again. He kissed her deeply as her greedy hands explored and gripped the firm, sloped contours of his shoulders, the unfathomable girth of his biceps, and the taut sinew along his back. She wanted to feel every inch of him.

He seemed to have the same notion and rolled her onto her back. He was impossibly strong and powerful, his large hand following every line, fitting every curve, and coasting down to the hem of her petticoat—

Then all at once, the air turned cold on her legs. It was hard to breathe. She stiffened, remembering that far away day in the Hampshire parlor with Nigel.

Reed pulled back, breathing hard, his eyes dark with desire. "Highness?"

"It's nothing," she said, swallowing down the memories, trying to ignore them. "Just kiss me again."

He pressed his forehead to hers, the heavy thud of his heartbeat filling her palms. Then tenderly, he tucked a lock of hair behind her ear. "You're scared. You had a bad memory, didn't you?"

She hesitated to respond.

Yet, with the way he looked at her, he already seemed to know. There was no point in pretending. Not with him. He knew her worst, most vulnerable moment.

"Oh, you don't know how much I wish it never crossed my mind again. But when I felt the cool air on my legs, I just . . ." She blew out a breath.

He pressed a kiss to her cheek. Keeping her against his side, he rolled to his back, his breathing still rough and labored. "It's only natural to be afraid. I knew better, and I should have been more patient."

Frustrated, her hand fisted over his chest where she rested her head, listening to the driving thud of his heart. She was so full of wanting that her own heart was going to burst. There was so much longing in her that she was desperate to put an end to it, her body restless.

She had a sense that if they weren't able to overcome this, here and now, they never would. And she would be trapped forever with those painful memories instead of with something to replace them. "I'm not afraid of you."

"I know."

"And I want to be with you . . . as your wife."

"We have time for that," he said with gentle, unnerving fortitude, his hand skimming down her bare arm, toying with the fallen tapes.

"But I don't want to wait." She knew she sounded like a petulant child, but it couldn't be helped. This was too important to remain unsaid. "I'm tired of always waiting. Sometimes I feel as if I've spent my whole life waiting."

"For what, highness?"

She didn't know what the answer was until it fell from her lips. "For this, I think. To be here with you."

He stared fixedly at her for a moment. Then a slow, warm smile curved his lips, but he didn't say anything. Instead, he leaned in and pressed his lips to hers.

This kiss was slower, patient—such a simple thing, really—and yet it left her breathless. It was as if he'd just told her a secret. Her heart thumped warmly, her blood quick to simmer once more.

"Perhaps if I knew what to expect, then I wouldn't be nervous. Whenever I'm unsure or have a question, I go to the lending library to see what I can learn."

"I shouldn't be surprised," he said fondly, his fingers playing lightly along her back, her nape, driving her to distraction. "But if I tell you everything I want to do to you, I imagine you will become even more nervous. I have a very long list, you see."

"Tell me. Imagine that you're writing a book on the subject and I'm just an avid reader."

"Highness, you're not making this any easier. Now I'm thinking about you reading such a book, following every word with the tip of your prim and proper finger, then your tongue flicking over the pad to turn the page."

Emboldened, she brushed her fingertips into the springy hair, pretending to read the firm muscles, line by line, pausing at the flat discs of his nipples and watching them pucker against her touch.

"You are a fascinating subject," she whispered, loving the warm feel of his flesh, the crisp hair as she continued to *read* all the way to his navel. Looking up at him through her lashes, she saw him watching her with a hot, glazed look in his eyes. "Tell me just what I need to know so that I can be prepared."

He stared at her for a long moment, deliberating, debating. Then, at last, he said, "Lower your hand."

She swallowed, disconcerted by a battle between nerves and a shameful degree of curiosity. And, of course, the curiosity won.

Splaying her hand, she followed the tapered trail of hair that led to the waist of his trousers. "Here?"

"Lower," he said, his voice tight with strain.

She obeyed, riveted by the large outline beneath the fall front, angled from his waistband to the mound between his thighs. She skimmed lower still, settling over the thick ridge, feeling him shift against her palm.

He choked out a groan. "Aye, there."

She trailed down the full length, marveling at the hardness, the heft. And he was hot there. Attempting to curve her hand around him, her own body responded with coiling warmth.

"That," he said through clenched teeth, "is the part of me that will be inside of you."

Ainsley pondered this and drifted lower, and lower still. Comprehending what to expect, however, didn't assuage her nerves.

"Surely not *all*," she said, her brow puckering. It would never work. "Though perhaps, the trousers are impeding my understanding. I'll need to see what you look like beneath the wool."

Inquisitive, she flicked open the first fastening.

"Wait." He stalled her hand. "Not yet. I don't think I can bear it."

"If you are shy or worried that I won't like the look of you, I'm sure I will. You are exquisitely formed in every other way."

He issued a choked laugh. "You are about to unman me, wife. And I would much rather spill my seed with my cock buried to the hilt inside you."

"Oh." She blushed, her body clenching, feeling oddly empty. "Is that how you refer to your . . . um . . . phallus?"

Living in London, she'd heard the bawdy word many times, and like any respectable woman she'd turned a deaf ear to it. But now it was different. Spoken in his gruff drawl, she felt an illicit thrill race through her.

He sobered, his expression chagrinned. "It was crudely put and I should learn to speak more delicately."

"No, indeed. It was not a reprimand. I should rather refer to your . . . cock as you do." She flushed at least five hundred shades of red, she was sure.

"Damn," he said, his head falling back on another groan.

"I should never have mentioned it, for now I want to hear your sweet, proper lips say that vulgar word whenever we are alone."

"It isn't too vulgar. At least, not when you say it."

He hauled her fully on top of him, then kissed her again, so soft and gentle that it nearly brought tears to her eyes. He was assuring her by slow degrees, telling her she was safe, that she was desired. That he would take care of her.

A rush of tenderness overwhelmed her. It was so powerful that it shook her, leaving her heart open and raw.

And she didn't know what to do with the deluge of emotion flooding from the flayed organ beneath her breast. So she gave it to him in wild, frenzied kisses, fitting her body to his, seeking that perfect alignment that they'd found before. And she found it again, hips tilting, rubbing. "I want to kiss you all the days of my life."

Reed didn't answer with a similar declaration. He growled, a low and primal sound. Shaping his hands over her skull, he kissed her with so much passion that she trembled from the force of it.

This time, when she felt the hem of her petticoat inch higher, exposing her legs, she was eager for the cool air to relieve the sweltering blood humming through her veins. And she wanted to hurry him along. She was tired of boundaries between them.

Straddling his hips, she wiggled, ridding herself of the garment, while he took care of her stays and chemise with a scoundrel's efficiency. Then all at once, she was bare before him.

The rainy gray light illuminated every inch of her milk-white flesh. His hungry gaze missed nothing, resting first on her teardrop-shaped breasts, the left slightly fuller than the right. Then he drifted to the midriff that was neither flat nor plump but some degree of softness between, and finally on the dark thatch of curls that guarded her sex.

She felt more shy than she ever had in her life. Perhaps she was too hasty in deciding *completely* against boundaries.

She tried to wrap her arms around herself.

"Please don't," he whispered, a pained breath shuddering out of him. "I've thought about you for so long, I just want to look."

Her dusky nipples pebbled under his scrutiny, her stomach clenching. "I'm not symmetrical. In fact, I'm a bit—"

"Perfect," he interrupted. Lifting his hands, he cupped the heavy swells, and her breath came out in a squeak. "And mine."

The possessiveness in his statement did terrible things to the rhythm of her heart. She should be ashamed of how it thrilled her.

His thumbs dragged over the tender crests, drawing the rosy flesh tighter still. She covered his hands on a gasp, her hips hitching against his. Her breasts ached, heavy and ripe like fruit ready to fall from the tree. With each teasing pass, a spear of pure pleasure quickened the deep pulses in her body.

He rose up, taking a pale swell to his mouth, and she clung to his shoulders, watching as he brushed his lips across the vulnerable peak, his breath warm and soft. Then he sealed his mouth over her.

Ainsley gasped as he suckled her flesh, laving her. Reflexively, her hands clutched his head. And she wasn't sure if she wanted him to stop . . . or to do this forever.

Forever, she swiftly decided, arching her back, giving herself over to each tender tug and the tight coiling building inside her. And when he stopped, she whimpered in protest.

"Patience, highness," he crooned, flicking his tongue over the eager tip. "There are rules about these things."

She would have smiled if her body wasn't ablaze with need. "Rushing is acceptable in certain situations. Such as crossing the street or leaving a house on fire."

"Is your house on fire, highness?"

"Yes! Yes!"

He chuckled, navigating a slow, scorching path to her other breast. Clearly inclined to torture, his mouth coasted unhurriedly along the underside of her breast. He took his time, her body aching. Breathless and desperate, she whimpered, fisting her hands in his hair.

Then, finally, he took her into his mouth and she cried out. Joy and ecstasy rolled through her in waves. Her hips nestled his. A pulse throbbed, heavy and insistent, compelling her to seat herself fully on that heavy bulge.

Reed issued a gruff grunt, his head falling back, eyes squeezed shut. "You are going to be the death of me."

Her knees pressed against the coarse woolen blanket as she kissed his throat and dipped her tongue into the salty, hollow niche at the base, humming with delight at her discovery. "Not until after I've had my fill of you, and that will be a long time from—"

He took her face in his hands, interrupting her with a savage kiss. This felt like more than a *claiming* but a surrender as well. His next words proved it.

Breaking their kiss, he gazed at her, never wavering. "Whatever you need, I will give it to you."

Ainsley's heart fluttered. Reed's virility and strength did not come from his brawn or from forcing his will onto others. It was something born into him and shaped throughout his life. And, like always, he was willing to wait for her decision.

Another terrifying rush of tenderness filled her, gathering wetly in her eyes, pounding hard in her chest. She knew what it was now, but she was afraid to say the words aloud. So she simply said, "I only want you."

And then she kissed him.

He made a sound deep in his throat and it vibrated into her, setting the rhythm of her heart. Their bodies undulated, his hands coasting along her back, around the cage of her ribs, brushing her breasts, her stomach, and lower still until his fingertips found the dark curls, and drifted to the dewy heat between her thighs.

It surprised her that embarrassment didn't make her want to stop his exploration. Not even when he slid one finger down the damp seam of her flesh and back up again, teasing her open on a strained whimper. The touch so good she could hardly breathe.

Closing her eyes, she felt him delve deeper, his fingers honey slick, his callused thumb circling the tautly furled nub of flesh. For someone who had never been particularly passionate, she certainly adapted quite well to this strange new person emerging from within her. Such a simple touch and she no longer cared about being exposed to him. All that mattered was how he made her feel.

She gave herself over to it, her own fingertips gliding absently over his bare arms. Instinctively, her body started to move against him, searching for that shuddering release. Helpless mewls rose from her throat. The tight coiling sensation gripped her and . . .

He stopped and withdrew his hand.

Disoriented, she blinked down at him, his color high, a wild look in his eyes as he ripped open the fastenings of his trousers. A thick shaft of dusky flesh reared out through the opening, the base surrounded by a thatch of dark fur. Staring at him, she was both alarmed and fascinated.

"I can stop," he said in a murmured rush, then repeated himself twice more, his declaration sounding like a mantra. "We don't have to go further. I want you to feel safe with me."

"I do, you ridiculously wonderful man." And she reached out to touch the hard, enthrallingly silky length.

He stiffened, his lungs working like a bellows. She felt a tremor roll through him at her tentative grasp. And when she gripped him fully, his breath fractured on a groan, his blood surging beneath her palm.

She felt a stirring of feminine power as she stroked down the length of him. "Do you like that?"

"Aye," he rasped.

"And what about this?" Her hand went up, drawing out a glistening bead of dew at the top. Experimentally, she slid her thumb over the tip to the intriguing slickness.

On a groan, he put a hand to her nape and kissed her, drawing her body down until she was splayed over him, eager and pliant. His furred chest teased her sensitive nipples, making her wriggle against him. And there was a sense of urgency in the way his body shifted beneath her.

Suddenly she felt a hot, hard pressure nudge her entrance. She didn't instantly welcome the thick intrusion, or the burn of her flesh stretching to accommodate his girth. And Reed, too, must have had his doubts for he cursed and grunted and withdrew from her completely. His breath stalled. Then he entered the clutch of her body with excruciating slowness, wedging inch by inch. But again withdrew.

Though, stalwart as he was, he repeated this several times until she began to anticipate each shallow thrust and retreat. Gradually, her body warmed to his methodical, velvet strokes, her own hips moving to meet him. She sighed into his mouth, her fingertips twining into his hair.

Yet while she was delighted by this new stirring of arousal, he seemed near death.

A guttural sound of agony caught in his throat. And just as she was starting to feel guilty—though not so much that she would ask him to stop—he took firm hold of her hips, thrust upward, and drove in deep. Impaling her.

Ainsley cried out, her hands curling into fists. She'd

known it all along—he was just too big! Too much. She tried to wriggle away.

He held her against him, his voice pleading on one long strained breath, "Please don't move, not yet, not yet . . . you feel too good and I just couldn't bear it."

She went still at once and tried to catch her breath. It was impossible with his thick flesh wedged so deep. Her unyielding body constricted around him, pulsing, pushing. And yet, gazing down at him, she noticed his drawn expression, his shallow breaths, his struggle to maintain control.

It was strange to see him this way. So unguarded. So undone. She wasn't the only one vulnerable in this moment. In fact, *she* was the one over him. A position of control, keeping him locked inside. Reflexively, her body clenched on this knowledge, wrenching a stuttered breath out of him, his eyes squeezing shut.

They stayed like that for a moment more, then her pain ebbed, replaced with a feeling of supreme fullness that made her anxious to move. Of course, a very good and dutiful wife would never think of moving when her husband begged her not to. But perhaps she was a bit too used to warring with him to listen completely. She couldn't seem to stop her instinctive desire.

She shifted, inching upward to lessen the unending pressure.

"Ainsley, please."

She inched back down, feeling her body stretch as he filled her again. There was raw tenderness, but no pain. Well, at least, not for her.

Her husband, on the other hand, groaned, neck arching, hands flexing on her hips.

"You've always had far too much power over me. And now that I know what it feels like to be inside you, I will be putty in your hands for the rest of our lives."

Her lungs cinched tight on his admission. "You shouldn't say such things."

"I didn't mean to say it aloud. See what you do to me?"

She was only beginning to, and stared down at him in wonderment. How long had it been this way between them? Yet the answer didn't seem important anymore. All that mattered was that they'd finally made it here.

Lowering down over him, she pressed her lips tenderly to his. In turn, he kissed her, his hips rocking rhythmically beneath hers, the length of his hot flesh sliding slow and deep. Her body gripped around him in a tight, wet embrace. It was amazing how two people who had been enemies, until recently, could move together as one. She never knew she could feel this close to someone, to feel his heart beat in time with hers, to feel his thoughts inside her mind as they searched for the same goal, exploring each other and losing themselves in every pleasurable moment.

He shifted beneath her, arching at an angle. Their bodies rubbed in two places at once. Now it was her turn to gasp. Intimately joined, that pulsing throb kicked with a lush jolt. Beneath her mouth, she felt the nick on his upper lip curl smugly.

"Do you like that, highness?" he teased, arching up to move against that same spot over and over again.

She wanted to say something in return, to match him quip for quip, but she was too busy dying. That's what it felt like. Her heart beat so fast and her body clenched so hard that she was certain she would erupt like a kettle under pressure.

She couldn't stop the moans from spilling out of her throat. He drove into her, deeper and deeper still, kissing her as if he knew death was near and these were the final moments of life.

All at once, that tight coiling inside sprung free. Her body jerked. She jolted over him. Stars flashed behind her eyes, a universe erupting inside her in millions of tingling sparks. Unending spasms pulled on his flesh, clenching him tight. Then he broke, too, filling her in violent shudders, her name ripped from his throat in one exalted shout.

Ainsley sagged over him, their bodies slick with perspiration. His skin tasted of salt as she ran kisses over his shoulder where she'd inadvertently marked him with her teeth.

She panted, "I thought we . . . were both going . . . to die."

"We did," he said with a smile in his voice, his hands coasting over her bare skin, and she felt herself starting to doze. But before she fell asleep, with his flesh still buried deep inside her, she thought she heard him say, "I'm sure this is heaven."

❧

THEY DOZED for an hour or more, until the sky grew dark beyond the windows. Reed had gone down to add more logs to the fire a short while ago, and now, lying in the loft, he watched the flames fill the room in warm golden light, and gild the curling tendrils of Ainsley's dark hair.

His wife. He could scarcely believe it, and her response to their circumstances had surprised him in the best possible way. He'd never been more content in his life—and he never imagined he'd feel that way in this tiny cottage.

In fact, he'd kept the property only to remind him of where he'd begun and to see how far he'd come since. Harrowfield—his true country house—was a mile up the lane and large enough to fit two dozen cottages within its walls, and adorned with such furnishings that even the Duchess of Holliford would be impressed.

He'd brought Ainsley here, in part, to bring her out of whatever daze she'd been lost in. He was sure that the moment she saw these poor accommodations she would instantly rail at him and start shouting that she wanted an annulment. Not that he wished for such, but he just wanted the assurance that she was fully aware of the journey they had both embarked upon.

That plan, however, quickly fell to the wayside when she climbed up to the loft. And somehow, she'd pulled him into a dream and they had both become lost in a daze together.

He hoped they never awoke from it.

Bare beneath the blanket, she stirred, snuggling back into the nook of his body. In turn, he kissed her shoulder and moved his hand from the lush curve of her hip to the warm soft flesh of her stomach, thinking about their future together. "Are you hungry?"

"Famished," she admitted sleepily. "But I don't want either of us to move."

He nuzzled her neck. "Not move at all?"

"Oh, perhaps a little wouldn't be too terrible." Arching for him, she exposed the side of her throat and sighed when he kissed her there. Then she covered his hand that rested over her midriff, her fingertips lightly caressing. "Do you think your child is growing inside of me this very moment?"

"I'm not certain, but I know a way we could give it better odds." He pulled her closer, letting her feel the hard jut of his arousal against the firm cushion of her bottom.

She responded with a gentle nudge and a smile in her voice. "Is that so?"

Chapter 27

"Emma was almost ready to sink under the
agitation of this moment. The dread of being
awakened from the happiest dream, was perhaps
the most prominent feeling."

JANE AUSTEN, *Emma*

A woman should enter into marriage with a sound mind
and a passionless heart. And yet, somehow, Ainsley had
fallen in love with her husband.

There was no other way to explain these tender, turbulent
feelings. Even from that very first meeting, she'd experienced
the most peculiar tingles beneath her skin like water agitated
to a simmer. She hadn't understood the volatile reaction then.
But now . . . she wondered if she'd loved him all along.

The notion sent a lance of fear through her.

From the loft the following morning, she heard Reed
singing outside the cottage. His robust baritone and bawdy
lyrics made her blush. Although after yesterday and last
night, she was surprised she still could.

Oh, the things he'd done to her—scandalous, delicious
things. Especially that second time. Proving his infinite
patience, he'd touched and caressed her endlessly, taking
his time to bring her to that desperate, breathless frenzy.
Lost in the throes of passion and torment, she'd scolded him
for being far too thorough. But her slow-handed husband

had only laughed, low and wicked, and then sent her over the edge as he shunted deep.

Even now, hours later, she could still feel his hands on her, and the aftershocks from the many times he'd made her quake. Her body clenched on the sweet memory, craving him.

She sighed like a simpleton in love.

Wrapping a blanket around herself, she made her way down the ladder, her movements revealing tenderness in places that she never even knew existed. Then her thoughts returned to last night and she smiled again.

Perhaps love wasn't too frightening. After all, at least he wasn't the type of man who hid things like other families or maniacal tendencies. Reed never hid behind pretense. He was precisely the man he claimed to be. Nothing more. Nothing less. Her heart would be safe with him. Wouldn't it?

Padding over to the fire, she considered the answer. It reassured her to know that he possessed qualities like loyalty, honesty, and respect. And she could never have fallen in love with a man who kept things from her or who didn't understand her nature.

Suddenly, this terrible brimming love wasn't so terrible after all. Perhaps she could trust her heart to make a sound decision.

She felt like whistling, hoping her tune would blend with his. Pursing her lips, she blew a contented stream. But all she'd managed was a pathetic little squeak. And that was when Reed opened the door.

Shirtless and glorious, he carried a pail of water in each hand. His brow arched rakishly as his gaze perused her form, from tangled head to bare toes. "Are you puckering your lips for a kiss, highness? I am ever-eager to oblige."

Absently, he kicked the door closed behind him and crossed the short distance to her, setting down the pails an instant before he gathered her in his arms.

"I was attempting to whistle." She gave a half-hearted

push against his shoulders, practically purring as his warm hands stole inside the blanket to the dip of her waist, the curve of her hip, coasting over the swells of her bare bottom—

She leapt back and clutched the wool around her. "You are too bold for the bright light of morning."

This did not deter him in the least. He only grinned and stole a kiss. "But this is the best time of day to see you, all rumpled and flushed. I should have added this to my list of fantasies. You look rather fetching in a blanket. Then again, as I recall, you look rather fetching out of it as well."

He eased his mouth over hers, tasting her in slow, deep pulls. Shamelessly, she sagged against him, his furred chest teasing the tender peaks of her breasts, his hands gliding beneath the blanket, bringing her to swift arousal.

Yet when he ventured to the apex of her thighs, teasing the dark curls, she drew back once more. "I have not bathed."

"That is why I brought in water."

He began nibbling the underside of her jaw, pulling her flush. His woolen trousers abraded her naked skin, inviting her to rub against the heavy bulge beneath the fall front. And before she could control it, her hips tilted toward him.

"Then allow me a bit of privacy and perhaps then . . ."

"Let me take care of you," he whispered, his lips trailing down her throat.

He parted the blanket to find the full slope of her breast, drawing the tight crest into the warmth of his mouth. Her breath shuddered and she wove her hands through his hair. Unheeded, the blanket fell to the floor.

He lifted her, walking back the two steps to the trestle table, then lowered her bottom to the age-smoothed surface. "Hold on to the edge, and stay just like this."

Body simmering and mind in a sensual fog, she watched dazedly as he dipped his hand into the water. "I thought you were going to take care—"

She sucked in a breath as he cupped his dripping hand over her sex.

"Oh, that's cold."

"Is it?" he asked, slyly teasing the seam of her heated flesh, the callused pad of his finger drawing out a quiver of anticipation.

Wordless, she nodded as he fondled and nudged between the passion-swelled flesh to the vulnerable throbbing bud. Turning her head, her lips sought his. She tasted his smile as the tip of his finger circled her. He was, indeed, taking care of her. Already close to the edge, she whimpered into his mouth.

But he withdrew, and bent to dip his hand back into the water. Then he repeated those slow, torturous ministrations. "Still cold?"

"Yes. Yes," she said, shivering with need, her eyes closed. She wasn't even sure what the question was.

"Then let me warm you."

His mouth grazed her throat, nipping lightly along the way down, before he feasted on one breast and then the other. Leaving her panting, he roamed lower still, trailing over the soft rise of her stomach.

It wasn't until she felt his shoulders against her inner thighs that she opened her eyes and saw him kneeling in front of her.

Embarrassed, she tried to close her knees, to cover her sex with her hands. "Wh-what are you doing?"

He pressed a kiss to the top of one thigh and then the other. "Shh . . . Just relax and think of this as part of your new bathing ritual."

Taking her hands, he parted them like a curtain. Then, before she knew what he was about, he leaned in to press his mouth to her sex.

She nearly choked on a gasp, her hands flying to his head to push him back. "But you cannot . . . that is . . . you should not."

The scoundrel was undeterred. He licked her so slowly that she could feel the texture of his tongue, the heat of his mouth, the vibration of his throat when he murmured appreciative noises. "Mmm . . . You're so soft and sweet and wet, I'd like to stay here for hours. Make a meal out of you."

"You"—she swallowed, feebly attempting to push him away—"shouldn't."

"Are you asking me to stop, or are you being shy?"

She thought for a moment, considering. She didn't want to be too hasty. "It's just . . . well that's a place where we . . . where you and I . . . and it's for the purpose of . . ."

"Pleasure?"

"Procreation."

He gave another slow lick, the flat of his tongue exciting every nerve at once, jarring the pulse at her sex into an insistent throb. "But doesn't this feel good?"

"It feels . . ." She watched him in bashful fascination, her legs widening of their own accord, heat spreading in waves over her skin. "Scandalous."

He chuckled, nipping her playfully. "Then perhaps you should tell me what part of my body is allowed to touch this sweetest part of yours. That way, we won't have a misunderstanding in the future. What about my fingers?"

He demonstrated. Her body clenched around the blunt tip of his finger, welcoming the slow, thick slide all the way to his knuckle and then out again. Breathlessly, she said, "Yes, yes, your finger is good. Quite good."

"And my lips?"

"Mmm-hmm . . ." was all she could say as he swept back and forth over her tautly furled flesh.

"And what about my tongue?" He sealed his mouth over her, his clever tongue swirling around the heavy wanton pulse.

She could only gasp a response, her head falling back.

Then twining her fingers in his hair, she allowed—no, *encouraged*—him to do the most wicked, wonderful things. She didn't know what he was doing to her, but she never wanted him to stop.

Reed bathed her for endless minutes. Lifting her knees to his shoulders, he sampled the tender swollen flesh until her cries reached the rafters. The pleasure was so intense, she feared it would break her apart.

"Let go, highness," he urged, his voice hoarse and needy. "Lie back. Let me have you. All of you."

She lifted her hands free of his hair and began to dip toward the table, but something stopped her. The thought of lying on her back, vulnerable and exposed, without any control, sent a spear of trepidation leaping inside her chest.

So she stopped halfway and groped at his shoulders. "I—I need you inside me."

Giving in to her wishes, he stood. She grabbed desperately at the fastenings on his trousers, freeing him. And without hesitation, he pushed inside her eager, aching body, the sudden thick invasion a blessed relief.

Closing her eyes, she clung to him as he drove in deeply, on and on, until helpless spasms racked her, ripping his name from her lips. Then he jolted once—*twice*—filling her with violent liquid pulses.

It took a long moment to catch their breath. All the while, he smoothed his hands over her face, tucking away strands of bedraggled hair, soothing her. Then, with his flesh still wedged inside, he took her mouth and kissed her with infinite patience.

"Just so you know," he said softly, "I'll only take what you're willing to give. And I'll wait as long as you need me to."

Apparently, he'd noticed her hesitation. And while she offered a nod in response, she was afraid he was in for a very long wait.

Worry niggled the back of her mind, making her wonder if, perhaps, she didn't feel completely secure. While she knew Reed would never let anything happen to her, now that her heart was involved, there were new risks she hadn't anticipated.

What if he tired of her? What if she never mattered to him? What if he walked away without ever looking back?

A cold shudder seeped into her bones at the thought.

Picking up the blanket, he draped it over her shoulders and kissed her forehead. "How about I make tea for us, hmm?"

"No, no. I'll make the tea . . . with the other pail of water, of course." She clutched the blanket around her and slipped down from the table, feeling the slick of him between her thighs. She would clean up when he left, she decided, and quickly skirted to the side. "I'll rummage through the basket and make you a fine breakfast."

"Is that so?" He grinned, but there was a distinctly dubious lift of his brows.

"I'll have you know that I've helped Mrs. Darden on many occasions. Why, I'll have a feast prepared in no time at all. Do you think you can manage to find an occupation out of doors for a few minutes?"

"That depends."

Ainsley nearly set her hands on her hips, but didn't dare risk losing the blanket. "On what?"

"On whether or not you're going to cook naked."

She blushed all the way to her bare toes. Then, taking his shirt from where it dried by the fire, she pushed it into his hands and shooed him out the door.

Once he was out of sight, she bathed in earnest and donned the wrinkled dress she'd worn yesterday and the day before. She was a frightful sight, to be sure. And without a looking glass in the cottage, she wasn't sure what her hair looked like after she brushed it out and pinned it up in a twist.

However, since it wasn't something she could alter, she set about making a hearty breakfast. While she might not be able to *let go* completely, she could at least fill her husband's stomach.

Foraging through the basket from the vicar's wife, she found a round loaf of rye bread, a mincemeat pie, a pudding crock, and other prepared foods. There was a pint of cream and a bowl of fresh eggs as well.

It had been quite a number of years since she'd helped Mrs. Darden in the kitchen, but Ainsley believed she could make a decent batch of coddled eggs and toasted bread.

As she cracked the eggs and dropped them one by one into the empty pot hanging over the edge of the fire, she started to think about her new role as a wife.

Perhaps, during the agency's slower times, they could return here. This cottage would be a welcome respite from their busy London lives. And should they become blessed with children, their laughter would fill this cozy space.

Resting a hand over her midriff and lost in this dream, Ainsley forgot the reason she no longer helped Mrs. Darden in the kitchen.

Or rather, why Mrs. Darden no longer allowed Ainsley to help her.

Smoke rose from the uneven slices of bread near the fire *and* from the pot, the acrid smell of char wafting in the air. Using the hem of her dress, she took it off the hook and laid it on the hearth stones. Then she stared down at the disaster. *Another failure.*

How had the bottom turned black and crispy so quickly while the top was still pale and runny? And why was toasting bread so bloody difficult? Every single slice had caught fire.

They were still smoldering when Reed walked inside.

Hesitating on the threshold, he took in the carnage at a glance. His brow furrowed as he looked to an errant flame erupting from one of the slices on the hearth ledge. Then the corner of his mouth twitched and he chafed his hands together. "I'm famished. What have you . . . cooked for us, hmm?"

"Toasted bread." And because of her overeager aspirations, there was nothing left of the loaf.

He walked over and peered into the pot, speculating over the contents. Before he could ask, she supplied, "Coddled eggs."

"Ah. Well, I'm certain they'll be delicious."

Ainsley felt a mortifying prickle of tears at her failure. "How dare you be kind and polite. You're supposed to be goading me into an argument. Why, next you'll likely offer to eat every morsel."

His eyes went wide as saucers and he swallowed. "Let's not be too hasty. I was merely showing my support."

"Well . . . stop." She swatted at him as he crowded closer, and her hands came to rest on his shoulders. "It only makes it worse. I cannot cook to save my life, or yours, apparently. And I cannot even whistle."

"Now, now, highness. Everyone can whistle."

She shook her head and demonstrated, issuing a hard-fought, pathetic little chirrup. "See? It's clear that I'm not good at anything that matters."

He slid his arms around her waist and tugged her against him, their bodies aligning perfectly where he was hard and she was soft. "I happen to know you're good at a number of things."

"I was talking about being a wife."

"So was I," he leaned in to whisper, grazing the underside of her ear, "and I'd say you're rather exceptional at being *my* wife."

A confusing jolt of pleasure fluttered inside her at the possessiveness in his statement. She prided herself on being an independent thinking woman, and yet there was something alluring about having him think of her as *his*. And the way he looked at her and held her made her thoughts turn inside out, her pulse galloping.

Likely she would never be able to balance the accounts with him in the room.

Distracting her, he nipped the corner of her mouth and murmured, "The secret to whistling is knowing where to put your tongue. Give me yours, highness, and I'll show you."

Chapter 28

~

"Those were the words; in them lay the tormenting
ideas which Emma could not get rid of, and which
constituted the real misery of the business to her."

JANE AUSTEN, *Emma*

The following day, Reed walked with Ainsley down the
lane, her soft hand twined with his. He lifted it for a kiss,
hardly able to believe this day had actually come—he was
happily married to Miss Prim and Proper. "I think you're
going to like the surprise I have for you."

He tried not to sound too proud. But it wasn't every day a
man was able to show his wife just how far he'd come in the
world, making his way with his own two hands.

"I feel as if we are attending a masquerade," she said
with a glance to her teal satin gown and voluminous skirts.
"I am overdressed for a stroll, and yet quite underdressed
as well."

His gaze dipped admiringly to the creamy swells fairly
spilling over the ruffled edge of the low-cut bodice. "You
look rather fetching."

"I seem to recall you saying that as you pretended to
assist me with the buttons up the back," she muttered, clearing her throat with tender reproof.

"It isn't my fault if that color makes your skin look good
enough to eat." He grinned as her cheeks flushed pink in

the sunlight. "And besides, I would give you dresses enough to fill ten wardrobes, and enough fichus to blanket all of London, if you so desired."

"I possess all that I need. Besides, my clients at the agency would think I'm putting on airs."

"Perhaps you won't always be at the agency."

"Will you have me playing hostess at Sterling's?" Her brows arched, a smirk toying with the corner of her mouth. "Or, now that you know my proficiency for numbers, will you have me keeping your books? I could, you know. I know how to stretch a farthing."

He chuckled. "Raven keeps the books for me. And besides, if I had you at Sterling's, it would fall to ruin."

Her steps slowed and she frowned. "I was in earnest when I told you my tricks are over. And I hope you know that I would do anything within my power to undo the damage I've done to your business."

"Highness, I only meant that, with you near me, I would be too distracted to stay on task. Even now, I cannot seem to keep myself from sweeping in for a quick kiss," he said, demonstrating and earning a shy smile. "What is past is past. We are different now—I, a married man and you, my lovely whistling wife. Come on, then. Let's hear that splendid music you make."

"Do you really think it's splendid?"

The piercing, off-key sounds she'd produced long into the evening hours had made him happier than any man could stand to be. "As I said, it's all a matter of knowing where to put your tongue."

She narrowed those pretty brown eyes, her sooty lashes crowding together. "Why do I have the notion you made a bawdy jest?"

"I have no idea," he said, all innocence. "Perhaps you're still thinking of all the wicked things you did last night with that shockingly skilled tongue of yours."

She blushed scarlet then burgundy. "I was only trying to see if I could please you the same way that you . . . Oh, stop grinning at me, you wicked man."

Unable to control the impulse, he tugged her into his arms and kissed her again, his hands cradling her face, tilting her, tasting her. He would never get enough of her mouth. Not for as long as he lived.

Last night had been about more than just the pleasure she brought to him. It was about seeing another side of her.

They'd been lying together in the loft—at her request because, apparently, she liked how cozy it was—and she'd asked about the scar on his arm. When he'd told her the story about the carriage house and Lord Bray and Finch, she'd pressed her lips there. Then wordlessly, she'd slipped out of her nightdress, and climbed over him, pressing tender kisses all over his face and his body, her unbound hair falling over him like silk. She'd explored and tasted him, shyly suckling his tumid flesh into her warm mouth.

And yet, in those endless, passionate moments she'd done more than arouse and pleasure him. She'd given herself, little by little. Releasing her inhibitions bit by bit. He hoped that he wouldn't have to wait long before she trusted him unreservedly.

He wanted to obliterate Nigel Mitchum from her mind, and to let her know that she was safe. That she could be free with him.

"Reed," she said, pulling her lips from his, breathless, her gaze soft and sleepy. "Let's go back to the cottage."

He nearly tossed her over his shoulder, and sprinted back toward home. But then he reminded himself that the cottage was not their home, even if she'd made those tiny four walls more welcoming than he could have known was possible. Because of her, the cottage had become a wonderfully euphoric place that he would visit often in his memories. And perhaps, in the years to come, they would take a stroll down the lane and *reminisce* beneath that tiny thatched roof.

"We aren't going back," he said, gesturing with a nod up the lane, "for we have almost arrived at your special surprise. It's just up the way."

She exhaled her impatience but dutifully looked ahead, the sunlight turning her eyes to amber gems. "I don't see anything other than a monstrously large house. We must be on the grounds of some local lord's estate and will soon be accused of trespassing if we go further."

"Thankfully, the owner of Harrowfield does not mind our trespassing."

"Oh?" Her brows arched. "Are you acquainted with him?"

Reed laughed, a mixture of eagerness and pride swimming in his veins. He couldn't wait to show her inside, to let her see the fruits of his labor.

Reaching down, he took her hand again and brought it to his lips. "Aye, and so are you. In fact, you're married to him."

⚭

AINSLEY LOATHED surprises, and this one was no different.

In all the time that she'd known Reed, he'd never mentioned a country manor. And now she was wondering what other monumental things she didn't know about her husband.

The notion made her uneasy.

"You've been quiet this past hour, highness. Aren't you going to tell me what you think of it all?" Reed asked as they climbed a wide mahogany staircase.

With her thoughts worried and distracted, it was difficult to absorb the vastness of the rooms, the vaulted ceilings trimmed with plaster molding, and windows enough to overlook the view of the considerable grounds from every angle.

There were Turkish carpets, fine furnishings, and oil paintings, and . . .

"It's lovely. Unexpected and overwhelming, but lovely," she admitted on a heavy breath, her hand gripping the polished rail.

"Aye." He grinned proudly. "Remember that eccentric baron I mentioned, whose servants would come to my father's tavern on their off days? Well, this was his until he passed away a decade ago. The house sat empty for a time, giving me the chance to win a few more fights, open Sterling's, and then buy it for myself."

She glanced at his fists and tried to swallow down her uncertainty. "Why did you never mention this before? And for that matter, why did you not bring me here straight from the church?"

He offered a half shrug. "Because you weren't yourself."

The landing at the top of the second floor hosted a little sitting nook framed by a window before the corridor split off in two directions. It was quiet here, their steps muffled by a red-and-gold runner. But her thoughts were not silent.

She studied his profile as they walked down a paneled corridor, arm in arm. "So you've said. But that does not explain why you chose the cottage of your childhood, instead of the home where you live whenever you visit the country."

Though, for as long as she'd known him, he'd spent nearly every day at Sterling's.

"If you must know, I thought the cottage would bring you to the realization that you actually married me."

"I knew it the moment it happened. I was there in the church, if you'll recall." Ainsley tried to keep the terseness from her tone, but if the tightening of his forearm beneath her hand was any indication, she failed.

She didn't want to argue, especially after spending these euphoric two days together, but she had to make sense of it all. "Then what about after we established that I was of sound mind—why not tell me then, hmm?"

"If *I* recall, we were otherwise engaged. It didn't seem to matter in those moments."

His quickness to dismiss her query pinched her already too-tender feelings. "Surely, you expect things like honor, trust, and honesty from me. You wouldn't want me to hide anything from you."

His keen indigo eyes fixed on her, a muscle ticking at the hinge of his jaw. "It is a house, not a deception. I wasn't keeping a secret from you, so banish those dark musings I see stirring in that frosty gaze."

Ainsley stared back at him, hard, thinking his request was impossible. Didn't he know her at all?

However, because Reed had never proven himself to be a deceiver, she decided to give him the benefit of the doubt. She tried her best to quell the uneasiness brimming inside her.

Seeing the alteration in her demeanor, Reed leaned in to kiss her cheek. "There. We're making progress already. Our first married tiff and it is all swept under the rug."

The only problem was, whatever went under the rug would have to be dealt with sooner or later.

They walked on toward a long narrow room, papered in a cheerful yellow, with dormer windows set into the slanted ceiling, and a view of the lush gardens below.

Reed tugged her fingertips playfully. "Aside from my *apparent* oversight in not telling you about my house the day we first met—"

"*Or* the day we married," she muttered.

"—what do you think of the place?" He gave her a wry sideways glance. "Can you see yourself here for all the years of our lives? That is, if we do not manage to kill each other first."

She felt a grin tug at the corner of her mouth. "It is quite grand."

"Just grand enough, I should think."

"Mmm . . ." she mused with a nod, looking around at all the gleaming surfaces, the cloying scent of turpentine and beeswax polish in the air. There were a number of servants who lived here, at least two dozen had been lined up to greet them when they'd arrived. "It will be a great deal to take on, however. Especially if the agency continues to increase our clientele, and I don't see why it shouldn't. Many of my days will be occupied in London, overseeing accounts, just as yours will be at Sterling's. I'm sure I'll be able to manage, but it will take time for me to build a rapport with the house-keeper, to learn the names of all the servants, keep track of their duties and salaries and off days."

"You needn't concern yourself with any of that. I have a steward and fine housekeeper who keeps everything spit spot. Not only that, but, Mr. Adachi—the butler for the gentleman who'd once lived here—is still here. He practically runs the place for me since I spend most of my time in London."

She looked at him, bewildered. "Then what would *I* contribute?"

"Oh, perhaps you would like to decorate this room." He pulled her into his embrace, his hand settling into the small of her back to pull her flush against him, and nibbled on the underside of her jaw. "I thought it would make a nice nursery. It has space enough for more than one or two beds."

The idea of having his children, of holding them in her arms, warmed her. Yet she was chilled by the way he presented it. An undercurrent of tension skittered through her veins, trapped and looking for an outlet.

So here was this enormous manor house and she would have no part in managing it, other than choosing decorations?

Did he expect her to spend her days frittering around the house arranging flowers, and pushing one child in a perambulator in the garden while another was growing in her womb—and to repeat the process until they'd filled every room in the house? Was that truly all he wanted from her?

When Reed arranged to marry her, had he given thought to how their lives would fit together? Or did he merely want a broodmare?

He could have married any woman for that.

And perhaps that was at the crux of her worries—that she didn't matter to him.

"Of course, you could choose any room you'd liked for the nursery, if this doesn't suit," he said, misunderstanding her knitted brow.

It used to unnerve her to think of his uncanny ability to read her. She even imagined that he understood her as no one had ever done before. But now she wondered if he'd ever truly seen her at all.

She pasted a smile in place. "It is a pretty room, and it would make a nice nursery."

"Then if you are too tired to see the rest of the house, we can finish our tour later."

"No, I am not tired, just lost in thought. This was quite the surprise, after all."

"A good one, I hope." He looked at her eagerly and she responded with an automatic nod, wanting to please him. "Then I should like to show you my favorite room next."

Ainsley tried to set her mind at ease as they walked down the stairs and through a series of corridors. She knew she shouldn't be troubled by her thoughts. After all, their union was not of a romantic nature. And yet . . .

She wanted assurance that she was special to him in some way. That he wouldn't have done all this for just anyone. But the truth was he'd never confessed any deep feelings, not even during their most intimate moments.

She supposed that was her unhappy answer.

"Here it is," Reed said with a sweeping gesture, "the music room. We'll have many a party in here, gathered around the piano with lots of singing, and I can open the rooms for dancing as well. We could invite our friends, or have your sisters and their families over. As our own family grows, our sons and daughters will be married here and you shall arrange the perfect wedding ball."

At once, she felt wholly inadequate. The flaws in her nature had never felt so insurmountable before.

She couldn't hold in her confusion a moment longer. "*Parties? Balls?* I've confessed to you that I don't sing or play. I don't dance well or draw. And the pointless, polite conversation required at parties is not my forte either. Is that what you want in a wife? Some perfect creature with nothing better to do than embroider pillow slips and pluck at harp strings?"

And would he have wanted any woman in his bed as well?

"Then practice whistling, it matters not," he said, his voice edged with tension. "Ainsley, all I'm offering is the life you might have had if you hadn't moved to London. I'm giving you the freedom to have whatever life you wish."

"And if I wish to live in London?"

He issued a rueful laugh, scrubbing a hand over his face. "Then I'll fill this manor with rabid wolves and buy a townhouse in London. Would that make you happy?"

"You're not taking this seriously. After all, I have a business to run."

"If you say so."

"And what do you mean by that?"

"Only what I've said before—that *somehow* men managed to find brides before the Bourne Matrimonial Agency existed."

A rush of panic flooded her veins. Surely, he didn't expect—wouldn't demand—her to give up the agency. It was more than a mere business. It was her family. Not just her uncle and sisters, but the memory of her mother lived there, too. Her presence was in everything they did.

"What we do for our clients is important," she said, her voice thread thin.

"So important that you spend your time sabotaging Sterling's?"

"I apologized."

"And I accepted," he said through his teeth. "Unfortunately, your apology won't bring back the patrons whose opinions about Sterling's exclusivity have been forever altered. So now, I will have to fight again to bring them back."

She looked down at Reed's hands with dismay, remembering how he'd told her the reason he'd stopped fighting—because he had slow hands. Pugilism was a dangerous sport. From what she'd learned by reading the papers, the practice of using mufflers on the hands had lent itself to men hitting each other in the head. And some had even died from taking too many blows.

"Stop looking at me like I'm a monster, Ainsley. I've already told you that boxing matches are about endurance not violence. Don't you trust me, yet?"

"Does a broodmare need to trust the man who purchased her at auction? That's all I am to you, after all," she spat, daring him to deny it.

He didn't. In fact, she wouldn't even know he'd heard her if she hadn't seen him flinch ever so slightly before he faced the window.

"Well, I certainly hope you haven't made up your mind," she said.

He offered a curt nod. "I have. The match will be between myself and Lord Savage."

"You're not even going to discuss it with me?"

"The matter is of necessity."

A swell of guilt churned inside her, mixing with the panic, hurt, and frustration. This was her fault.

She looked around at the house and all its grandeur. He likely spent a fortune on its upkeep from month to month. "The agency is doing better. If all goes well, then my position will provide enough income for you to keep Sterling's. I know how much it means to you."

He slid her a dark look. "I'm man enough to take care of my own wife."

"You needn't see it as an insult. Think of the money as a dowry of sorts, as any gentleman would expect when marrying."

"In case you've forgotten, I'm not a gentleman, highness. Just a man, and a common-born one at that."

She huffed in frustration. "Yes, as you keep reminding me. Pointlessly, I might add. I know who I married, and it wasn't a pugilist."

"Oh, but it was. Look down your nose all you like, but I earned money with my own two hands. Whatever it takes, I intend to do the same until the day I die."

She blanched, suddenly visualizing Reed's lifeless body in a coffin. Tears pricked her eyes. She could lose him when their lives were just beginning.

How was it possible that she'd finally fallen in love, only to have such a fragile thing threatened to be stripped away from her?

"If it matters to you"—*if I matter to you*—"I don't want you to fight anymore."

"There's no other way."

"Because Sterling's will fail? Or is this more about manly pride and your need to prove yourself to your patrons?"

He didn't answer, though a muscle ticked along the hard edge of his jaw.

Ainsley laid a hand against her bare throat, wishing she'd worn a fichu today. She felt vulnerable without it. "And when will this fight happen?"

"Upon our return."

And he never thought to mention this to her, either.

Somewhere along the way between London and Knightsbury they'd become intimate strangers to each other.

"Very well then. We should return as soon as possible. That way you can take care of what matters most to you."

His fists clenched at his side. "We have a good amount of daylight ahead of us and Smith can have us home by nightfall."

❧

THE JOURNEY to London was fraught with silence. The two of them occupied opposite sides of the carriage, and stared—unseeing—out opposite windows.

Reed thought he'd glimpsed the shimmer of wetness against Ainsley's lashes, but she'd turned away too quickly, settling into the corner of the carriage with her eyes closed. Even so, he'd wanted to haul her into his arms at least two hundred times and tell her that everything would be fine in the end.

But that would be a lie.

He didn't know how it was going to end. He'd thought enough had changed between them that they could move past the things that had always kept them apart.

Not anymore.

Obviously, they were destined to live on opposite sides of the street.

Glancing across at her now, he saw that she'd drifted to sleep, her head lolling awkwardly to the side, her back wedged into the corner. She had one hand on the cushion, but the other rested over her midriff as if she was thinking of the child they may have created together.

Drawn to her side by a force he could no more deny than his own name, he moved to the other bench. With care, not wanting to disturb her, he tucked her against him so that she could sleep more comfortably.

Resting her head on his shoulder, she stirred but didn't awaken fully, and murmured, "Are we home yet?"

"Not yet, highness," he said softly, pressing a kiss to her head.

Chapter 29

"No; do not pity me till I reached Highbury . . ."
JANE AUSTEN, *Emma*

It was late into the evening when the carriage arrived in London. Neither Ainsley nor Reed mentioned the fact that she had slept in his arms for the latter half of the journey. And she would never admit that she'd been only pretending to sleep for the past hour or more.

Instead, they entered the townhouse together, a tense silence between them.

Mr. Clementine opened the door and greeted them with a respectful bow and felicitations on their marriage. Before Ainsley could utter a word or enquire about the household, Reed pulled him aside and asked all the questions that had been waiting on her tongue. Used to seeing to these matters herself, it was difficult to stand apart as if she were a stranger in her own house.

Even so, she kept her ear to the conversation, unwilling to be shut away.

In short order, she learned that repairs had been made, the painting around the door trim completed today, the two new maids were efficient, and the footmen were ever-so-grateful to be given the opportunity.

In the brief exchange, it became clear that Reed had hired men who'd attended the dinner she'd plotted—back when she'd still intended to ruin him. Though once more he'd found a way to turn her trick into something good.

This gave her a glimpse of the man she thought she'd fallen in love with, further confusing her turbulent thoughts.

Hearing the shuffle of footsteps on the stairs above, she turned to see Uncle Ernest rushing down in his pale blue banyan and slippers, his silver-sand hair mussed, his lapis-blue eyes wet.

Before she could utter a word, he pulled her into his surprisingly strong embrace, a tremor rolling through him. "My dear, Ainsley, I am so overjoyed to see you that I can hardly put it to words. I've been distraught since discovering what happened and my regret is insurmountable. I should have been here when you needed me."

"No," she said, returning his fierce embrace. "It wasn't your fault at all. You couldn't have known."

"I am grateful that Mr. Sterling arrived and set matters aright. Had he not been—"

"Mr. Sterling has been generous to us during the ordeal," she interrupted.

"And you have married," her uncle said quietly, his uncertain gaze flitting from Reed to her. "Are you . . . content with your situation?"

Well, there is little I can do about it now, she thought wryly.

Yet, with all things considered, it was better that she'd married Reed. What did a broken heart matter when she had the agency to manage?

"Yes," she lied after a moment, only then realizing that Reed's conversation with Mr. Clementine had concluded and her husband was now standing off to the side, waiting.

Uncle Ernest turned to him and shook his hand, expressing all manner of gratitude until Reed cut in that they'd had a long day. Understanding, her uncle left them to sort out a matter of their own—the sleeping arrangements.

Briefly, Ainsley wondered if Reed would leave her and go to Sterling's instead. But then, without a word, he gestured for her to precede him up the stairs. They walked together in the strained silence that seemed like a permanent fixture between them.

The corridor was filled with the muffled sounds of their footsteps and the unmistakable, too-sweet odor of new wood and fresh paint. The scent always reminded her of the last days she'd lived in her childhood home, with her mother's coffin in the parlor. And looking into her own bedchamber, her gaze settled on the chest at the foot of the bed.

A chill stole over her and she rubbed her hands over her arms to warm them.

"He won't return," Reed said quietly, standing near enough for her to feel the heat from his body, tempting her to draw closer. He even angled toward her as if expecting her to take a step.

Doubtless, he would enfold her into his strong embrace. But she resisted, needing to rely on her own strength instead of his. Rebuilding the barrier between them seemed the only way to protect the susceptible organ beneath her breast.

After waiting a moment, Reed expelled a breath. "I posted men outside before we left, and they're working together so there won't be any chance of being blindsided."

"And have you any news on Teddy?" she asked, having learned that he was the one who'd given Nigel the bruised eye.

Reed nodded. "The doctor said that, fortunately, Teddy's head was harder than the brick that felled him."

A brick? It shouldn't surprise her that Nigel had resorted to any means to win.

She looked again into her chamber. It had been scrubbed and polished, every surface gleaming warmly in the firelight, every piece of furniture repaired to look as if nothing had happened.

Then her gaze settled on the new rug that lay on the floor, where the blood had been. "Do you think the servants ever found the cat?"

"Mr. Clementine just informed me that she was found at Sterling's. Injured, but alive," Reed said softly.

Ainsley felt tears prick her eyes, again, overwhelmed with gladness. Without thinking, she nearly reached for his hand, but stopped herself in time.

Reed expelled a slow, even breath. "She has always been a fighter."

"Perhaps we could see her tomorrow, unless"—Ainsley hesitated—"you intend to go to Sterling's tonight to see her and to take care of your business."

"Finch and Raven are managing the hell in my absence. With there being so few carriages out front, they do not have need of me. And since I want to look over the town-house, regardless, I intended to remain here."

He didn't ask her preference, she noticed. Her spine stiffened. At the very least, he could have discussed it with her. But this was only another reminder of how little her opinion mattered. "You may choose from any of the guest rooms."

Indigo spheres hardened to marble, a muscle ticking along his jawline. "Then I will take the one nearest yours. That way, if you have need of me, I shall be close by."

"I'll fare well on my own. I've done so before," she said curtly, then stepped into her bedchamber.

The instant the door closed, she sagged against it. Then all at once, a sob broke free. She stifled it with her hand. But the terrible ache she'd been holding back for so long broke through the dam and escaped in a deluge down her cheeks.

Rᴇᴇᴅ ʜᴀᴅ his hand wrapped around her door handle for a full five minutes. In that time, he didn't hear her stir a single step, but saw her shadow linger below the door. He imagined her on the other side, doing the same as he, waiting. Debating.

But in the end, neither one of them moved to reclaim the ground they'd made at the cottage.

Theirs was now a war of attrition.

Chapter 30

"Matrimony, as the origin of change, was always disagreeable . . ."

JANE AUSTEN, *Emma*

If yesterday had been the longest day of her life, then last night had surely lasted two lifetimes.

Ainsley had not slept at all, so she dressed early and made her way downstairs. She knew that Mrs. Darden would give her far more information about how the household was faring than Mr. Clementine had offered to Reed.

After being smothered with affection by Mrs. Darden and Ginny, and patted on the shoulder by Mr. Hatman, Ainsley had met the new servants and found them to be amiable and eager. Dotty and Bea were sisters who shared the quirk of finishing each other's sentences. Ralph and Ben did not speak very much at all, but were square shouldered and ready for their tasks.

They were the servants that she would have chosen, if given the opportunity. Yet another commonality she shared with Reed—along with stubbornness.

Her stomach growled as she entered the paneled breakfast room. It had been yesterday morning since she'd last eaten. They'd stopped at the same coaching inn for a change of horses and a meal, but with her thoughts in turmoil, she hadn't eaten a morsel, much to her husband's displeasure.

Even now, looking at the heavy steaks, kidneys, and eggs on the buffet, she lost her appetite. Nevertheless, she was pragmatic enough to know that she needed something, and settled for a slice of toasted bread.

Ainsley looked at the perfectly golden hue with a rueful grin, recalling her own foray into the world of toast making. And in that precise instant, Reed strode into the room.

Always alert, his gaze instantly swept over her form, glancing at her plate. For an instant, their eyes met and held.

Knowing that they were sharing the same memory of the ruined breakfast and the scandalous bath that preceded it, her cheeks saturated with heat.

Abruptly, she turned back to the buffet.

"Did you sleep well?" he asked from beside her.

"Splendid," she lied. "And you?"

"Not splendid."

She shifted from one foot to the next, unable to think of a suitable reply. So instead, she motioned to the door and began her excuses. "I usually eat in my office and work during these hours, so I'll leave you to enjoy your meal."

He slid her a dubious look. "Ainsley, there is no reason to avoid each other. We have matters to discuss, and the sooner they are settled the better."

She hiked her chin, her vertebra aligning one by one. "It was not a tactic of avoidance. I truly do eat in my office each morning."

"Then perhaps," he said through clenched teeth, "you can make an exception this time."

Before she could respond, Briar swept into the room in a flurry of pink and let out a gasp. "You are home, after all. When I didn't find you in your office just now, I became frantic with worry all over again."

See? Ainsley thought as she arched her brows at Reed. "You needn't have worried. All is well, as you can see for yours—*oof*!"

Briar leapt forward and embraced Ainsley, nearly knocking the plate from her grasp. It would have fallen, too, if Reed had not rescued it from her hand in time.

"I'm so glad you are home and safe and sound," Briar murmured into Ainsley's fichu. Then she drew back and searched her gaze. "But all is not well. It is clear to me now that you have been putting on a brave show for quite some time. You never once mentioned that Mr. Mitchum was so . . . changeable. That must have been the reason you ended your betrothal. Yet you needn't have kept it to yourself. I have two perfectly good ears, even if one has a brown mark from Jacinda burning it with the curling tongs."

Ainsley was not used to being scolded by her youngest sister, but understood that it was meant with affection. She was about to say as much when Jacinda suddenly rushed in. And, spotting Ainsley, stopped abruptly.

"You weren't in your office and I thought—" Jacinda broke off, her panting breaths coming up short. Then she, too, launched herself at Ainsley until both of her sisters where squeezing the life out of her.

Of course, Ainsley used the opportunity to cast a haughty look to Reed, who rolled his eyes to the ceiling and shook his head. After filling his own plate—and hers, she noted—he sat down at the table, just as Briar's husband, Nicholas, strolled in carrying a tray overladen with steaming scones. One already in his mouth.

The Earl of Edgemont bowed to Ainsley and said, after he swallowed, "I'm glad to see you looking so well, *Mrs. Sterling.*"

Her cheeks heated instantly at the name, the two cottage days flashing in her memory on a hot blur. She didn't dare look at Reed this time. "Thank you. And I'm grateful for your assistance as well."

Without his help, they would have had to drive to Gretna

Green to marry and there would have been no saving her reputation. No honeymoon at all. No happy memories.

Surreptitiously, she watched as Reed shook his hand and began talking with familiarity. Before Nicholas married Briar, he'd frequented Sterling's and they'd developed a friendship. Even so, Nicholas was reluctant to share any of the scones with his new brother-in-law. Then again, he rarely shared them at all. So it surprised her all the more when he let Reed take two.

The Duke of Rydstrom was the next to join their party, strolling in with a cooing Emma in one arm and . . . a plate of scones in the other.

Mrs. Darden must have known there would be a ravenous horde to feed this morning.

Crispin inclined his head and looked at Ainsley with brotherly affection. "I'm glad to see you have returned. If you had been gone another day, my wife was determined to hunt for you and ensure that you were well."

Proof of this was in Jacinda's wet eyes before she blinked her tears away and smiled. "But you are here now and I no longer have to plot how to drag out all the information from that Mr. Finch who stubbornly kept it to himself. He was going to talk no matter what."

Knowing her sister's determined nature, Ainsley laughed and slyly slipped out of the embrace. "Of that, I have no doubt. But as you can all see, I am here, and well, and we have no need to discuss it further."

"And you are married now, to *Mr. Sterling* of all men!" Briar exclaimed, then cast a hasty look over to the table. "Which is wonderful, of course. Jacinda and I have known for quite some time that our sister fancied y—"

"You should break your fast to keep up your strength, Briar," Ainsley interrupted, focusing her gaze on Briar's swollen middle.

Jacinda, with mischief glinting in her gaze, added too quickly, "That's true. Ainsley was forever going on and on about your cravats, or lack thereof. But I see you actually do own one."

"Jacinda, please. It is hardly proper to discuss a gentleman's attire at the table."

"Then it's good that I'm not sitting at the table yet," she said with impish delight as she scooped up her daughter and teased a giggle out of her, effectively quieting Ainsley's response.

Though it mattered little if she'd planned to chide her sister or not because in the next instant the breakfast room became even more crowded.

Mrs. Teasdale breezed in and—shocking everyone— swept Ainsley into a dancing, happy embrace.

But then an ever greater shock came when Reed suddenly stood and said, "Mum? What are you doing here?"

A beat of silence followed.

"Mum?" both Briar and Jacinda said in unison, brows lifted.

Now Ainsley looked to Reed who appeared to be just as dumbfounded as she was. Then to Mrs. Teasdale, she said, "Mr. Sterling is your . . . your . . ."

"My sweet boy. My Lancelot," she said, rushing across the room with her hands raised as if she fully intended to take his face in her hands.

"Lancelot?" Nicholas asked, choking on a bite of scone until Briar patted him on the back. *"That* is your given name?"

"Lancelot was my father. I've always gone by Reed and my mother knows this," he said, leveling the woman in question with a firm shake of his head.

"But if you're Reed's mother, then why did you encourage me to start a war with him?" Ainsley asked, confused.

"Mum," Reed chided, indignant. "Ah. So that's how the handbills made it inside. I should have known."

Rosamunde quirked a grin and issued an offhand shrug, the gesture only now familiar to Ainsley. Why hadn't she noticed the similarity before?

"Well, I was tired of waiting for something to happen. When it came to Miss Bourne, you were always so—"

"Now isn't the time," Reed interrupted his mother.

Mrs. Teasdale's grin went wide and she held up a finger. "But I have one more surprise for you . . ."

She bustled out of the room, and returned with a basket. Then, lifting the paisley blanket from the top, she slowly revealed the contents.

Ainsley's hand flew to her mouth on a happy sob as she spotted the white-and-gray fur and heard a plaintiff *meow*. She turned her wet eyes to Reed and saw that he was smiling with tender affection as he walked around the table toward his cat.

"Careful now, she's still hurt. Doesn't move around very much. But a friend of mine who owed me a favor stitched her up and gave me laudanum to keep her calm."

Reed gently stroked her fur and received a sleepy lick on the hand in return. "I knew she was a fighter."

"Yes, your Seymour certainly was. Mr. Finch found her behind Sterling's and took good care of her until I came."

"Finch did that?" Reed arched his brows and issued a disbelieving laugh.

"Seymour?" Jacinda asked, her brow puckered as she looked from the cat to Ainsley. "Isn't that the name you called Mr. Fluffington? That's a peculiar coincidence."

Ainsley's gaze met Reed's, a warm current traveling between them.

He shifted from one foot to the other and issued an offhand shrug. "That was the only name she liked."

Ainsley hardly knew what to think.

Briar laughed with a cheerful hiccup. "Oh dear! Ainsley, you know what this means, don't you? If Mrs. Teasdale hired us to find a bride for her son, then . . ."

Jacinda laughed next. "Oh, this is too much! You railed at us and yet you did precisely what you said you'd never do—you married a client!"

Chapter 31

―⌣―

". . . this sweetest and best of all creatures, faultless
in spite of all her faults . . ."

JANE AUSTEN, *Emma*

Once the others left the breakfast room, Reed was alone
with his mother, the food cold on the buffet and on his untended plate.

At least Ainsley had eaten something before she'd left.
She and her sisters had taken Seymour and the basket up
to her office. And after good-natured ribbing from his new
brothers-in-law about his matchmaking mother, they also
left.

Reed stared at his mum, incredulous. "All along, you've
been sneaking in here and I never knew."

"A mother will resort to any means to see to her son's
happiness. Oh, and I had a time of it, to be sure," she said
around a mouthful of scone, then a quick sip of tea. "At
first, I waited until I knew you weren't watching through
your windows to catch a glimpse of Ainsley. Only when you
decided to sleep would I come in through the front door. But
as time grew on, and you kept to your vigil—"

"I was not keeping a vigil," he muttered, embarrassed at
having been spotted.

"—longer and longer each morning, I had to resort to
coming in through the kitchen. And a fortnight ago, I nearly
ran headlong into you and Mr. Finch, which would have

upset the entire applecart. But I shimmied up the servants' stairs just in time."

"You plotted against me."

"*Against* you?" She laughed affectionately and touched the tip of his nose. "It was all for your benefit. You should be thanking me for my interference, goading her into war. Though frankly, it was less my doing and more yours, with the things you said to her."

"Trust me, Ainsley can give back as good as she gets, all on her own."

His mum absently brushed crumbs from her lap. "If you ask me, you've always been too patient for your own good. No doubt you would have waited for her forever and I wouldn't have any hope for grandchildren."

Reed didn't bother to tell her that the prospects weren't favorable in that regard. The last thing he wanted was her scheming again. Knowing his mother, she would board up the doors of every bedchamber but one, forcing Ainsley and Reed to sleep in the same room. Which wasn't a terrible idea, come to think of it.

He had missed his wife last night, already accustomed to her soft warm body fitting perfectly against his. He missed her scent, too. Every breath that wasn't rosehips and almond blossoms was wasted. Lying in the dark, he'd invented thirty-seven excuses to knock on her door and enter her room, but he'd used none of them.

Perhaps he *was* too patient for his own good. Because all he wished to do right this instant was dash up the stairs, pull her into his arms, and kiss her until he tasted her sigh of surrender.

Then he'd lock the office door and do every wicked thing he could to make her love him.

"Your father would have liked her," his mum said, staring into her cup. "He was fond of anyone with a lion's share of determination. I believe he instilled that in you as well."

"Aye. Dad always said to do whatever I could to make my biggest dream come true."

His mum looked up and smiled, looking years younger in the golden morning light. "He was right. But dreams are about more than finally achieving them. It's what you do to keep them alive that matters most."

Reed knew she wasn't talking about Sterling's. "Some things are a bit more complicated."

"Not when it comes to love."

The instant she said the words, Viscount Eggleston appeared in the doorway. He took one look at her, pivoted on his heel, and strode back out. Then somewhere, further down the corridor, he sneezed.

"That man is a nuisance on the entire female population," she said, her voice raised as if she hoped to be heard by the object of her ire.

Reed chuckled. But his thoughts were tucked inside a cozy cottage, where for two days he'd been lost in the best dream of his life.

"You have a faraway look about you," his mum said, reaching over to pat the top of his hand. "You're brooding over something."

He didn't bother to deny it. "Aye."

"Well, by the blush on Ainsley's cheeks every time your eyes met this morning, I would say that you made some progress on your honeymoon."

"*Mum,*" he warned.

She tutted. "I'm not asking for details, boy. All I want to know is, will it be enough to gain me grandchildren before next spring?"

He pretended not to hear her.

After handing his mum into a hackney, Reed was about to cross the street and check the books, to see how Sterling's fared in his absence. But he couldn't leave Ainsley alone.

According to his latest report from Finch, there had been no sign of Mitchum.

Reed knew better. Vermin like Mitchum never went away voluntarily. They just crawled into a hole and waited for the right time to catch you unawares.

An uneasy shiver scratched down Reed's spine at the thought.

Without delay, he went back inside the townhouse, strode up the stairs and directly to Ainsley's office.

He peered inside and caught her fussing over Seymour, pressing a kiss to the top of the scraggly head. Leaning against the doorway, he half wondered if she'd let him linger in this spot all day. "I can take her, if you like."

His wife looked up from the basket, eyes bright, lips almost curving in a smile. "I'd like to keep her, if that's agreeable."

"I wouldn't want her to be in the way."

"She won't be. And besides, if Jacinda can be here with a babe on her hip, I can certainly manage . . . Seymour." The last word was only a breath, but potent enough to tinge her cheeks with color.

It was the first sign of her defenses weakening.

Reed decided to see if he could gain a little more ground. "And if I'd like to check in on her throughout the day?"

Ainsley bit the corner of her lip. "Unless I'm with a client, I see no reason you shouldn't."

It was as good as an invitation.

Reed was about to leave, with the promise of his return between them. But just as he turned away, he discovered he was not the only man at Ainsley's door.

Lord Hullworth approached from the stairs and Reed planted his feet.

The *ton* considered the bronze-haired Hullworth to be London's most elusive bachelor—a man with a triple threat of fortune, handsomeness, and title. He was also on the exclusive list at Sterling's, though seldom came. But when he did, he was always reserved, playing only a few hands of faro before ending his evening early.

The instant the marquess's pale gaze alighted on him, Hullworth inclined his head. "Sterling. I hear congratulations are in order. Please accept my best wishes for you and your bride."

"Thank you, Hullworth," Reed said, his brow furrowed. "Did you come here specifically to deliver this message?"

"Lord Hullworth is a client of ours," Ainsley interjected. She crossed the room and shook hands with the marquess—the clasp lasting a bit too long for Reed's tastes—then smiled up at him. A bit too brightly.

Hullworth grinned back. "I've been too absent, I fear. But with my sister's social calendar, I've been hard-pressed to find a minute for myself."

In other words, Hullworth—in the only apparent minute he had—came here to see Ainsley.

Reed stood beside his wife and slipped a hand to the small of her back. Ainsley slid him a look of warning, but he didn't budge.

Issuing a huff of exasperation, she turned her attention to Hullworth. "I imagine Meg is quite popular in her first Season."

"Yes, and much to my own dismay as well as to Daniel Prescott's, I should think. But the besotted lad is determined to wait for her to sow her oats. I only hope she is quick about it," Hullworth said. "Opportunity doesn't always present itself when most convenient."

Reed growled, earning glances from both parties.

Then Hullworth's eyes widened and he took a step back. "I hope you do not mistake my meaning for a flirtation. I was referring to a girl I once knew in my youth. The one who got away, as it were."

"Ah." Realizing his error, Reed inclined his head. But to ensure there were no doubts left between them, he added, "Then I hope *my* wife will be able to assist you in finding one of your own."

"Which would be a simpler task," Ainsley began with a tight smile over clenched teeth and a nudge of her elbow into his ribs, "if you would leave my office . . . *dearest*."

"I'll return later to check on our Seymour," Reed said, glad to note that the mere mention of the cat's name thawed the frost from Ainsley's eyes.

Now if only they could forget about all the obstacles between them.

Chapter 32

"The pain of his continued residence in Highbury,
however, must certainly be lessened by his marriage."

JANE AUSTEN, *Emma*

Until today, Reed had no idea how much work Ainsley
actually did.

She was never still for a single moment. A constant stream
of new clients flooded in and out of her office. And in the few
seconds she was by herself, she had a pen in her hand, marking papers and ledgers, scrutinizing applications, comparing
lists, writing letters, and whatnot. She fielded questions from
the new maids, settled a dispute between Mrs. Darden and
the chandler over the price of candles, and spoke with each
and every client with calm assurance, stating that she would
do her utmost to find the perfect counterpart. She managed the
house, paid the accounts, and did it all without faltering.

There weren't many men—or perhaps not even a single
one—who could accomplish so much.

She spied him watching her in the hall and crossed her
arms. "What do you think of our 'game,' Mr. Sterling? Our
'frivolous endeavor'?"

"It's more involved than I imagined," he said honestly.

"Other than parish vicars, there really isn't another ser-
vice like ours." Even now, she was in motion, turning on her
heel and disappearing into her office.

Apparently knowing that he would follow, she continued. "After my mother's experience, I knew it was necessary."

"You've never told me of that. All I know is she died when you were young."

Ainsley faced the escritoire, pouring two cups of tea. "Yes, of a broken heart. Our father had been instructed to marry a young woman from a respectable family. Any woman would do. Mother, on the other hand, had married for love, too blinded to see the truth. Or to accept the fact that he was never going to be the man she thought he was. On her deathbed, she asked me to look after my sisters and to ensure that they didn't make the same mistake."

"And you were just sixteen?"

When she nodded, he thought of the heavy burden she'd carried all this time. It was a large responsibility to take care of two younger siblings and manage a house when she'd been practically a child herself.

He should have known that everything Finch tried to tell him had been true. Yet Reed had stubbornly wanted to believe she'd led a privileged life, even after witnessing evidence to the contrary on their honeymoon. Ainsley had dived right in to making the cottage a home, cleaning, making beds, washing their laundry at night and hanging it by the fire. And a spoiled debutante wouldn't have tried so hard to cook something edible.

Now he wished he'd eaten every burnt morsel.

"What about your father . . ."

"If you're asking if Lord Frawley suddenly swept back into our lives, the answer is no. Oh, he'd returned briefly before Mother fell ill—long enough to lift her hopes—then left again, taking our dog with him."

Reed darted an incredulous glance to the basket holding their sleeping cat and then back to her. "He took your Seymour?"

"You needn't sound so shocked, it was a long time ago, after all."

"There should have been someone to step in to take care of you."

"We took care of ourselves, which made us all the stronger. We also have Uncle Ernest, who dotes on us exceedingly." She paused, glancing to the red leather book on the table near him. "And our mother never truly left us."

Reed laid his hand on the book, turning it to see that fringe of vellum peeking out. He was more honored than he could express that his nicked flower was tucked between the pages.

"I think," he said quietly, "our mothers would have liked each other."

Her mouth curved in a wistful smile. "Indisputably. They were both romantics, cut from the same cloth—or stitched from the same skein, as your mother would put it."

Hearing voices in the hall, he knew they were about to be interrupted. But there was one more thing he had to say before he left.

"I was wrong, you know."

"Of course you were," she said with that teasing rasp he loved so much. "But which specific instance do you mean?"

He stepped closer, holding her gaze. "This matrimonial agency is not a frivolous endeavor. What you do is essential for many people."

He leaned in and stole a kiss from her stunned lips, then left her to do her work.

It was nearing half past four when Ainsley lifted her head to see Reed stride into her office, carrying a tray. He frowned when he looked down at the plate of cheese and fruit he'd brought earlier.

"You said you'd eat something."

Her heart quickened at his show of surly concern. "I didn't realize the hour had grown so late. Why aren't you at Sterling's this evening?"

She was eager for him to leave, but only because she had a plan in place to make amends for ruining his business.

This morning, before her brothers-in-law had left, she'd pulled them both aside and begged a favor. Abashed, she'd explained to Crispin and Nicholas what she had done to ruin Sterling's reputation, and how unforgivably successful she'd been.

Of course, her plan wasn't *all* for Sterling's sake. She had selfish reasons, too. Knowing that Reed intended to fight again, she wanted to offer another option. The idea of seeing him hurt tied her stomach in knots. And if it was because of something she had done, she could never forgive herself.

Thankfully, her brothers-in-law both agreed to send missives to their acquaintances. Tonight, she would discover if it helped.

"I am, but I wanted to ask you something," Reed answered, still frowning with disapproval at her untouched plate.

She resisted the urge to roll her eyes. Then, rising from her chair, she came around to the side of her desk and picked a plump grape off the vine. Popping it into her mouth, she chewed slowly, relishing the sweet burst. A droplet escaped and she darted her tongue out to capture it.

Mismatched indigo eyes watched her fixedly, heating by degree. He took a step closer. "You are forever distracting me."

Ainsley was tempted to eat another grape. She would eat them all if he continued to look at her like she was *his* feast.

In that moment, she nearly forgot the reason they'd left Knightsbury and returned to London. At least, until he spoke again.

He cleared his throat. "If you could have anything you wanted, what would it be?"

Love, she thought instantly. *Unconditional, soul-searing love. To matter to you. To be your first thought in the morning and last thought at night.*

But just thinking the words brought a prickle of tears to the outer corner of her eyes. So instead of saying that, she looked down to the tray again and pretended absorption with the cheese, cutting a slice with the slender knife. "For the agency to be a roaring success, of course."

He nodded, but looked strangely disappointed and pensive. "I thought that's what you'd say."

"Why?" She put down the knife, her appetite vanishing again. "What would it be for you?"

He stared at her lips, then her eyes. "To give you whatever you want."

Then he left her, making her wish she would have told him the truth instead. What might have been his answer, then?

Chapter 33

"Emma was sadly fearful that this second
disappointment would be more severe than the
first."

JANE AUSTEN, *Emma*

Sterling's was an absolute crush. Walking from one card-room into the next, he was swimming upstream, the flow of bodies always pushing against him. It seemed that every man who'd ever received an invitation was here—one hand on a brimming goblet and the other on a bulging coin purse.

The red hazard room pulsated with men dressed in their finery, sweating and cursing, laughing and cheering, and losing their shirts.

It was the best night Sterling's had ever had.

With Pickerington at the door, Finch came up beside Reed and cuffed him on the shoulder. "I cannot understand what you could be brooding over, Sterling. Why are you not mingling with your rich guests and crowing about the fight you will win against Savage?"

"I have been," Reed said in automatic defense. "This is a capital night."

"And yet you speak the words with the same cheerful intonation as a man set before a band of pirates armed with blunderbusses."

The truth was, he'd been having second thoughts about the match ever since he'd left Knightsbury. "What do you think Trudie would do if you ever took up fighting again?"

"Box my ears," Finch said. Then his expression turned serious. "She'd likely pack up the girls and move to Plymouth with her mother."

Reed nodded thoughtfully. "I bet she would."

"From your expression, I gather that your new bride is equally opposed to pugilism?"

Before Reed could offer a reply, Raven pushed his way through the crowd and handed him a pristine white calling card. "Did you actually extend an invitation to this bastard?"

Reed read the single name in the black letters: *Savage*.

"His lordship is in your office," Raven supplied coolly, appraising Reed as one did a stranger in a dark alleyway. "He specifically asked not to cause a spectacle. Wants to speak with you in private. Claims it's an urgent matter . . . 'between friends.' Havin' tea with Savage on Sundays, Mr. Matchmaker?"

Reed grinned darkly and cuffed Raven's shoulder. "Just for that, I'm going to tell my wife and her sisters that you're looking to marry. They'll arrange so many teas with proper young ladies that you'll beg me to end the torment. And speaking of tea, did you take that parcel to my wife?"

Raven nodded but looked stricken and pale. "You wouldn't really do that to me, would you?"

Turning away to shoulder through the crowd, Reed left him to ponder his fate.

AINSLEY STARED down at the parcel with dismay. From the post stamp in the corner, it had come from Knightsbury. Reed must have intended to give it to her when they were still at Harrowfield.

Drat! Why did he keep doing this to her, making her love him more and more?

Her eyes misted over as she picked up the once-broken teapot from the day he'd first kissed her. Now the shards were lovely works of art, refitted together with seams of shimmering gold. And beneath it in the straw lay a card that read: *Proof that all things can be mended. R.*

She noted that it wasn't signed, *With all my love, your husband.* Or even, *With great esteem and affection.* No. Instead, it was just *R.*

Placing the teapot back inside the crate, she swiped a tear from her cheek.

Could all things be mended?

She tried not to put so much pressure on the outcome of tonight, but failed miserably. If Sterling's was a success, then Reed wouldn't have to fight. And she would never have to think of him being hurt, or worse . . .

Needing a distraction from her thoughts, she busied herself with locking up the offices for the evening. But when she returned to hers, she saw that it wasn't empty.

"Mrs. Teasdale," she said with surprise. "Or rather . . . I'm not sure what to call you any longer."

"You could always call me *Mum,* but given your reserved nature, *Rosamunde* would be just as nice, too," she said, smiling up from the knitting in her lap, needles clacking away.

"Thank you, Rosamunde."

As Ainsley sat at her desk, she studied her mother-in-law with fresh perspective. She'd gone through a terrible ordeal with her second husband, yet she was kind and caring. Not only that, but she still found a reason to love. Married four times, and she wanted another chance.

The woman might very well be batty, but she was batty in the best possible way.

"Besides, my full name—Rosamunde Sterling-Wilcox-Teasdale-Stilton—is something of a mouthful."

"What brings you here this evening?"

She offered a half shrug. "A feeling, I suppose. Can't explain it. I just had the need to be close by. So I came for a chat with my favorite daughter-in-law. Have you ever thought about knitting, dear?"

"No, I can't say that I have. I don't think I'd be very good at it." Ainsley eyed the misshapen bundle of red yarn and tried to imagine what it might possibly become.

"Well, that's not the point of it," Mrs. Teasdale said with authority. "Knitting is like love, you see. It doesn't have to be perfect. It just has to be yours. Give it everything you have and something will come of it."

Ainsley stared, dumbfounded by her mother-in-law's insight. It was uncanny how she said the most peculiar things but turned them into brilliance.

"So, I see you're looking over my son's application."

Ainsley started, and guiltily covered it with her hands. "Oh, I was simply . . . going to . . . put it away."

Rosamunde smiled down at her knitting. "I suppose you're wondering why I kept my answers so vague."

Name: Lancelot
Interests: helping people
Beliefs: some good, some bad
Income: a fair amount
Property: yes

Ainsley traced the page with her fingertip, the corner of her mouth curving fondly. The answers, while ambiguous, were oddly accurate. "I presume it is because you wanted to keep it a secret?"

"Partly," she agreed. "But mostly I just wanted a reason to come back and get to know you. After all, I had an inkling that you were going to marry my son. Of course, I didn't think it would've taken this long."

"But you've been coming here for a year," Ainsley said,

surprised. "How could you have thought I would marry your son all that time ago?"

A mysterious grin alighted in her eyes. "Call it mother's intuition."

"Well, you're very good."

"That's what I keep telling that boy of mine. Never underestimate the power of a determined mother. Now, do you think my first grandchild will like a red muffler or a blue one?"

"Oh, I . . . um . . . I'm not sure."

"I'll make both. You never know. After all, Reed's father had a twin, and these things tend to skip down the line like a flat stone on a pond."

Ainsley blushed, wanting to change the topic. "Did Reed always want to become a pugilist?"

"I'd say that boxing found him," Rosamunde said. "Had a terrible time in school. Those highborn boys weren't very kind at all. But Reed never gave up. Every day he got a little better and a little stronger. Now some mothers might have worried that their son wanted to be a better fighter to hurt people—especially after what he'd been through—but not him." She shook her head and sat up straighter, pride in her gaze. "Always had a gentle soul. In fact, I think part of him felt a little sad after every victory."

"Then why did he do it?"

"Because he could never be dependent on anyone other than himself. Even though I offered him a settlement, he refused to take a farthing from Lord Bray's estate. He took *a loan for his education*, he'd said, then paid it back, right and proper. To him, that money was tainted—a reminder of how people treated you when they thought you were nothing but common rubbish. When they thought you didn't even matter."

Tears gathered in Ainsley's eyes. She knew a bit about how that felt.

How many times had Reed raised his defenses, labeling himself as common born? She hadn't paid it any heed because it was never something she thought about.

In case you've forgotten, I'm not a gentleman, highness. Just a man, and a common-born one at that.

Clearly, it mattered to him. Yet, she'd never told him, unequivocally, that it didn't matter to her. And when she did, she hoped that he wouldn't need to fight to prove himself anymore.

ENTERING HIS office, Reed saw Savage standing at the window. "When I extended an invitation, I thought I'd find you in the center of the hazard room, demanding a fight at the top of your lungs. And I was going to grant your—"

"Don't toy with me," Savage said without facing him, "not when I'm this close to letting everything fall apart for you. I was fully prepared, mind you, to stand back and laugh at your complete societal annihilation. But my bloody conscience brought me here, instead."

"What *are* you talking about?"

On a strained exhale, Savage turned away from the window. The flickering light from the single taper on the desk cast eerie shadows over his face, making him look haunted.

He raked a hand through his pale hair. "Apparently, Mitchum is touting a twisted tale, marking you as the villain for absconding with his intended, Miss Bourne."

"The blackguard can spin as many stories as he likes. I know the truth," Reed said with surprising calm that belied the rushing of blood in his ears at the mention of Mitchum.

"He's also saying that he came to London to contest the banns."

"No one would believe that if they saw what he did to the townhouse."

"Yes, but you were too thorough, keeping it all quiet for the sake of her reputation." Savage pointed an accusatory finger. "Anyone who knows the truth won't dare speak it for fear of inciting your wrath. Hell, the only reason I know it is from your man *Teddy*. Who, by the by, cannot tell a lie to save his life. You really ought to be more choosey with your foundlings."

Tension built at the nape of Reed's neck. "It's Mitchum's word against mine and I have men who will vouch for me."

"Men you pay a salary to will hardly matter. Once word spreads, most gentlemen will be on his side. He's quite convincing when he wants to be. He has proof as well. A church leaflet with his name and hers, announcing their nuptials. And worse. . . . Mitchum claims that she is carrying his unborn child."

"That is a lie," Reed growled, slamming his fist down on his desk.

"I suspected as much, considering that you've been watching over Miss Bourne for nearly two years." He clucked his tongue and shook his head. "I've always found your patience unnerving, you know. At school, you never came after any of us, no matter how many insults we'd sling your way. I can't speak for the others, but I never gave a fig about who your parents were or weren't. I just wanted you to fight me. After all, it was my father who killed Lord Bray. You knew that, and yet you never came after me to settle the score."

"Believe me, your father did my mother and me a favor."

Savage blinked. "So the rumors were true. Is that why you never unleashed that rage I saw lurking in your eyes?"

Reed nodded absently.

"You bastard. You might have said something and saved me years of guilt."

Ignoring him, Reed paced the room. "Hasn't Mitchum done enough to her?"

"It's you he wants. A proper fight. He has it in his head that he'll be the one to defeat the great Reed Sterling."

Reed glared at Savage. "I wonder who fixed that notion into him."

"What purpose does it serve to cast blame ex post facto? And you could have warned me that he's insane."

"I believe I did." Reed scoffed. Then, lost in thought, he muttered absently, "But you were always foolhardy, and just as overzealous with your left hook."

"Bloody hell." Savage shook his head. "Well, the point is, you'll have to fight him."

"No, I won't. I'll make it disappear." *I'll make him disappear, too.*

"There are too many people who've heard his rants. They are likely on their way now."

In that precise instant, Finch stormed into the room. "There's a mob gathering out front and it's being led by—"

"Mitchum." Reed stalked to the window. Sure enough, that prig was standing on the pavement. Crossing the room, he was eager to tear into the blighter. "He's not going to get away with this."

Finch took him by the shoulders. "That won't settle an issue of this magnitude."

Reed didn't care. Mitchum was going to pay one way or the other.

"You must demand satisfaction," Savage added quickly. "If you don't, you may as well kiss Sterling's farewell. No man would respect you enough to walk through your doors. Not only that, but your wife would become a pariah."

At that, Reed stopped.

Finch's hands fell from his shoulders. "I'm afraid Lord Savage is correct. While you may be able to recover Sterling's in time—with enough boxing matches and lotteries—the Bourne Matrimonial Agency would cease to exist."

The agency and her family were all that mattered to her. And *she* was all that mattered to him.

Clearly, there wasn't another way. Reed looked to Finch, resigned. "You'll stop me from killing him, won't you?"

His friend nodded gravely.

"Very well," he breathed. "Bring in Mitchum. We'll have this out, once and for all."

Chapter 34

"If I loved you less, I might be able to talk about it more."

JANE AUSTEN, *Emma*

Rosamunde was just attempting to teach Ainsley how to knit when Uncle Ernest rushed by her office door. A moment later, she heard the sounds of porcelain smashing.

She lurched to her feet, hurrying into the corridor. The door to his office was ajar, light flickering from within. Then came another crash just as she came upon the scene of chaos. "Uncle!"

Both urns were shattered on the floor, plumage scattered. A disarray of papers and broken pens littered the floor. An armchair overturned. And Uncle Ernest looked like a madman, wrenching open the drawers and letting them collapse, unheeded.

"Where is my sword?" he shouted, color rising to a beet hue. "It wasn't in my bedchamber. Mr. Hatman assured me that it was downstairs. And that cad isn't going to get away this time."

Ainsley blinked, thoroughly confused. "Mr. Hatman, a cad? What could he have possibly done?"

But her uncle didn't hear her. He continued his frantic search, muttering under his breath about honor and justice and doing whatever he must to protect his family.

Rosamunde swept past her and entered Bedlam. Without

uttering a word, she stood toe to toe with him, took his face in her hands, and kissed him soundly.

Uncle Ernest tipped back on his heels, owl eyed. "What's the meaning of this?"

"You were off your rocker," Mrs. Teasdale said with a light pat to his cheek. "Something had to be done."

He drew in a breath, his color returning to normal. "Well . . . thank you . . . Rosamunde."

"My pleasure." And then she kissed him again before taking a step back.

Ainsley shook her head, the last minute of her life leaving her more than stunned. Her uncle seemed to be equally perplexed. "Why are you looking for your sword?"

His attention swerved to Ainsley. "I have some distressing news that has to do with your husband and Mr. Mitchum. My dear, you may want to be seated for this."

Ainsley didn't sit. She stood on her feet and faced the news directly. Even so, her knees wobbled as her uncle told her about Nigel's lies and the accusations he'd fired upon Reed.

"They are having a duel of honor in Sterling's boxing ring as we speak."

She forced herself to be pragmatic. No matter what her wishes were, Reed had to fight. Whether it was for her honor, his own, or for the sake of Sterling's, it didn't matter. The match was happening, regardless. "But there's one thing that I cannot understand. Why were you looking for your sword?"

"I couldn't bear the thought of Mr. Mitchum walking away without justice. I've heard he's a rather formidable opponent."

A cold chill washed over her and she shivered to the soles of her feet.

"You're frightening the poor girl with all this talk." Rosamunde tutted, stepping around the carnage in the room to take hold of Ainsley's hand. "My son is an exceptional fighter. Lightning quick, they used to say."

Panic rushed in Ainsley's ears. He wasn't fast any longer. And Nigel would use that to his own advantage.

"There's no need to fret, my dear," Uncle Ernest said, coming up beside Rosamunde. "After all, Mr. Sterling has your heart and there is nothing that gives a man greater power."

But Reed didn't know that he had her heart. She'd never told him that she loved him. Loved everything about him . . . Even the prizefighter he once was.

Chapter 35

"I may have lost my heart but not my self-control."
JANE AUSTEN, *Emma*

His house. His rules. His challenge to fight Mitchum for the sake of honor. So then why didn't Reed feel in control?

He pushed through the crowd, bumping shoulders, his focus on the ring straight ahead. No one would know that his usual sense of calm assurance had abandoned him. His palms were sweaty, his ears ringing.

Mitchum was already there, dressed like a dandy in his blue-frocked coat and high-necked cravat. The younger son of a blueblood, trying to look the part. He had a pair of sycophants cooing over him as well—one taking the coat from his shoulder, and the other offering a spoon of snuff.

Mitchum took a quick snort and pinched his nose before slowly rolling up his sleeves to the elbow.

Reed wasn't about to pretend this was a gentleman's fight. So he stripped his shirtsleeves over his head and tossed them to the floor, standing bare chested.

The crowd went silent for a breath in an almost comical pause. Reed would've laughed, but there was no humor in this moment. The simple truth was, Nigel Mitchum was ruining his life.

Ainsley would lose everything if he didn't fight. And she would never forgive him if he did.

There was no way to win at all.

THE SCENE at Sterling's was a foul nightmare of perspiring men pressed together, shoving, shouting, and cursing. Ainsley could hear grunts and the sickening wet slaps of hand to body blows.

Men were already chanting. "Hit him, Sterling! Give him a solid facer."

While many others were cheering for Mitchum to "Bloody 'is nose—that's right! Crack 'im in the ribs!"

She tried pushing through the crowd, but never got far enough. Thankfully, she spotted Mr. Finch towering over everyone else. She flapped her arms to get his attention.

"You should not be here, Mrs. Sterling," he said when he came to her side.

"I have to stop this madness before it's too late."

"It isn't a sight that any woman would want to see."

"Well, it's good that I'm not just *any woman*, then. I'm his wife," she said proudly. "Now take me to him."

In order to get through the crowd, Finch had to pick her up like a child, an arm locked around her waist. By the time he pushed through to the ring and set her down, Reed was bloodied and bruised. And in his expression, she saw resignation. He seemed to be holding back.

Nigel took advantage, pummeling him, blow after blow.

"Stop this!" she shouted. "Stop this at once!"

No one heard her. She kept trying, pushing in front of the cheering horde, waving her arms. But Reed didn't even look her way. She had to get his attention.

Desperate, she swept under the ropes and into the ring. Yet standing at the far side, he still didn't look at her. Which, she supposed, was for the best since he had someone hitting him. But she had to tell him before it was too late for her words to make a difference.

So she did the only thing she could think of—she rushed up to the fight.

Confronting her own nightmare, she tried to pull Nigel away, grabbing fistfuls of his shirt. But he didn't even budge, or seem to know she was there at all. She shouldn't be surprised. He never had before. The only thing that mattered to Nigel was Nigel. She'd always hated that about him. His poor little fragile ego couldn't bear to think about anyone other than himself, his appearance, and how everyone saw him.

If only she had a large mirror to put in front of him. It would distract him for hours. Aside from that, humiliation was the only other way to defeat a man like—

Her breath caught on an epiphany. Suddenly, she knew just what she had to do to stop the fight.

Stepping back, she drew in a deep breath for courage, and then . . . pulled down Nigel's trousers. Since his arse was so flat and flabby, it took little effort.

The crowd exploded in laughter. Nigel stumbled back, legs tangled. It was just the opportunity she needed.

She skirted in front of Reed and took his battered face in her hands, blood seeping from a cut on his brow and another from his lip. "*What* are you doing?"

Reed blinked a few times then grinned at her, almost drunkenly. "I'm not fighting, highness. Not really. You see, I listen to every word you say."

"The first time you decide to do as I ask and this is what I get? Insufferable man."

She growled, tears flowing down her cheeks while simultaneously drying up in the steam of her exasperation. Stripping a handkerchief from her sleeve, she began to wipe his face.

"It was the only way I could win the prize I really wanted. You, just you."

Ainsley wanted to throttle him. "And now you're bleeding. Didn't you think for a moment that, perhaps, the reason I didn't want you to fight was because I couldn't stand the thought of you being hurt?"

"I have a hard head. Did you like the teapot?" He smiled wider, causing his lip to bleed more.

"Stop that," she said, fussing over it. "Weren't you thinking about what you'd be leaving behind if something worse happened to you before I got here? Take Seymour, for instance. Who will look after her?"

"I imagine you'll do a fair job of it."

Ainsley wasn't getting through to him. He still looked dazed. So she tried a new tactic. "And I suppose you'd expect me to raise little Lancelot all on my own."

His breath caught and he blinked, his eyes gradually clearing. "You are not naming my son Lancelot."

"With you gone, who would've stopped me, hmm?"

He shook his head, scrubbing a hand over his face, and eyed her reprovingly. "Your own good sense, I should hope."

"Well then, what if my second husband would have been a gamester, spending your fortune before being carted off to debtor's prison. Where would I be then?"

Reed took her by the waist, jaw tight. "What *second husband*?"

At last, he was back.

"You don't actually believe, now that you've awakened me to passion, I could simply bury all my desires. I would need a man who . . ."

He crowded her, his feet on either side, her skirts bunching between them. "What kind of man, highness?"

"You, just you," she said fiercely, using his own words. "I love you far, far too much to ever give you up."

Then, rising up on her toes, she kissed him. The sea of men watching cheered and bawdy comments ensued, along with a few whistles. Her reputation as a respectable matchmaker might be in tatters by the time she finished, but that didn't matter.

"Now," she said, drawing back on a breath, "I want you to fight him. And, more importantly, I want you to win."

Reed was about to say something—an argument by the look of his flattened brow—but then Finch shouted.

"Sterling! Get down!"

Ainsley turned as Reed grabbed her. In the same instant, she saw Nigel holding a flintlock dueling pistol. And when the shot rang out, she screamed.

Chapter 36

"What totally different feelings did Emma take
back into the house from what she had brought
out!"

Jane Austen, *Emma*

Reed dove to the floor with Ainsley curled beneath him,
the shot ringing in his ears.

He clung to her, his hands roving over her back, her arms,
her torso. She was doing the same, her soft hands clutching him. He studied her face, her tight grimace, hearing a
pained groan from her lips.

No . . . no . . . no. Not her. But where was she hit? He
started his frantic search all over again.

Then softly she said, "You're so heavy."

He stilled over her, panting every breath. "Are you hurt?"

"I don't think so. Are"—tears flooded her eyes—"you?"

"No." Though the truth was, he wasn't sure.

Every sense was solely focused on her. She was so small
beneath him, so fragile. He grasped her hands, kissing
them. Then the sounds of the club started to filter in. Dozens
of shouts merged together.

Raven's voice penetrated the melee. "He's down!"

Then Finch bellowed, "Take the pistol!"

Reed slowly turned his head, and he saw who was hit.

Savage was down, gripping his shoulder, blood pooling
on the floor. He scowled at Reed, growling, "You're a pain

in my arse, Sterling. Don't you even know how to win a fight when all my coin's on you?"

The crowd started to close in to aid Savage, obscuring Reed's view. Flicking a glance past them, he saw Finch wrenching Mitchum's arms behind his back. Normally, Finch's meaty grip and strength could subdue any man. But Mitchum was wild-eyed and writhing like a madman, sinking lower and lower to put the giant at a disadvantage.

Trouble was brewing.

Reed started to rise, keeping Ainsley tucked beneath him.

Then all at once, Mitchum leapt up, hitting Finch in the chin, knocking him off balance for a second.

But that was all it took.

He slipped free, darting to the outskirts of the room toward the door.

Without hesitation, Reed sprang to his feet. Barreling through a line of patrons, he cut across the room.

They faced off on either side of the stairs. Then Mitchum came at him on a yell, shoulders down to charge.

Reed set his feet apart, hauled back, and landed one single punch.

That was all it took.

Mitchum stopped cold. The whites of his eyes rolled to the back of his head and, stiff as a board, he fell to the floor.

LATER THAT night, and standing near the washstand in her bedchamber, Ainsley fussed over Reed, dabbing the wet toweling over the cuts on his face. "This one on your brow has closed. However, if you don't stop smiling, the one on your lip will never heal."

And because he was such a compliant and patient man, she rose up to press a kiss there. He responded by edging closer, his hands gripping her hips, aligning their bodies.

"I'm afraid I cannot do that," he said, trailing his mouth

to the underside of her jaw. "This is the best prize I've ever received from a fight."

"Which part, being bludgeoned or nearly shot?"

It had been hours since the fight, but she still shuddered to think about it all.

She was thankful that Lord Savage had only been grazed in the shoulder and stitched up by a surgeon. But even more grateful that Nigel had been carted off in leg shackles and irons. At the very least, he would be transported for his crimes and she could finally put it all behind her.

"You forgot to mention having kissed me soundly in front of an entire gaming hell. Surely, that was breaking a rule."

"I was forced by circumstance."

He grinned again. "I hate to tell you, but your actions today have ruined your chances for ridding St. James's of Sterling's. Those who thought my wicked character might be tainted by a prim and proper wife now believe it is the other way around. My patrons are more loyal to me than ever."

"A strange tale, indeed, for I heard the opposite—that the Bourne Matrimonial Agency has secret ways of bringing devilish rogues to heel. My clients are more loyal to our cause than ever."

When he reached that sensitive place beneath her ear, she abandoned the bath for the moment, and wrapped her arms around his neck.

"But that isn't even the prize I meant," he said, nuzzling.

"It isn't?"

"I was talking about you. You're all I've wanted from the first moment."

"Hmmm . . . You've been reading my uncle's poetry," she teased.

Pulling her flush, his lips pressed softly to her temple, her cheek, then her lips. He lingered sweetly in a familiar way that made her think he was telling her a secret. And when he looked at her, that secret was also in his eyes.

"One day, nearly two years ago, I looked out the window and saw my new neighbors moving into the townhouse across from me," he began, holding her gaze. "I wanted to laugh at all the fuss and bother, but then I saw this woman lift her face to the rain. It only lasted an instant, but there was something so fragile and serene in her that she called to me like nothing else had ever done before. I couldn't explain it at the time but I felt a gnawing emptiness inside. I'd worked hard for everything I'd possessed, and yet I'd never absorbed a single moment completely the way she had done. And I was captivated by her."

Ainsley's heart began to race, her lips parting. "Who . . . who was she?"

A slow smiled curled his lips, telling her to be patient. "I knew that if I could get close enough to her, she could teach me how to absorb every small moment. And I was right. Whenever we met, time slowed down, noises faded, the constant driving voice in my head went quiet, and all that was left was her.

"And she's smart, and adamant about the rubbish on her doorstep," he continued, his low drawl burrowing deep inside her. "She can flay a man alive with one lash of her tongue. And she's so beautiful that it makes me ache to stand close to her and not touch her." His hands skimmed down her back, loosening the fastenings of her dress, exploring her skin with unfathomable gentleness. "And even from the first day, whenever she looked at me, her eyes would go dark as coffee and I wondered for the longest time if she was feeling the same way, but hiding it better."

"She was," Ainsley whispered, tears clogging her throat, blurring her vision. "It sounds as if . . . as if you loved her."

He took her face in his hands, collecting her tears, kissing them away. "And I will for all the days of my life."

She sniffed and threaded her fingers through his hair, fitting her body against his. "Pretty words, Mr. Sterling. But a man proves himself with his actions."

"Then perhaps I shall employ lengthy measures to prove myself."

Tilting up her chin, he took possession of her lips, the kiss unfolding slowly, leaving no part of her unclaimed. His hand roved down to her bottom, lifting her, seating her against the hard ridge beneath the fall front of his trousers. And she arched, cradling the hard ridge of his sex with the softness of her own.

"I love you. Every part of you," she whispered fiercely, sliding her mouth along the ridge of his jawline, taking his earlobe between her teeth. "The tender parts. The fighting parts. The maddeningly patient parts . . ."

"The wicked parts?" He rocked against the low, liquid throb in her body.

A tremor rolled through her on a gasp, a promise of the quake to follow. "Especially the wicked parts."

Wasting no time, he crossed the room to the bed and set her on her feet, deftly stripping her out of her dress and undergarments.

His hungry, mismatched eyes roamed over her naked body and he breathed in deeply. "Lie back, highness. Let me have you."

She did so without hesitation, her arms above her head. "What are you going to do with me, Mr. Sterling?"

The nick on his upper lip winked at her when he grinned.

Epilogue

"What years of felicity that man, in all human calculation, has before him!"

JANE AUSTEN, *Emma*

Seven Years Later
August

Matthew slouched down on the grass and sighed with the exhaustion only a six-year-old could feel when being kept from the new pony at the stables. "Why are we giving flowers to Mum? You already gave her one this morning, like you do *every* morning."

"Because they make her smile," Reed said, tousling his son's brown hair. "Now, pick one of those pink stonecrops by your feet."

"I'm bringing her a perfect violet," Arthur said, his blue eyes squinting at the petals of the flower he just picked before tossing it to the ground and reaching for another.

Reed glanced down to the carnage of not-quite-perfect blossoms and chuckled. "Those are geraniums. And your mum likes them even if they're rough around the edges, son."

Apparently, Arthur disagreed and tossed another to the ground.

The twins were identical in every way except demeanor. Their natures were split evenly between those of their parents. Where Matthew was rowdy, Arthur was reserved.

Matthew would occasionally sing a bawdy tavern song—
which he may have overheard purely by accident—while
his brother could not carry a tune in a two-gallon pail but
could win any card game with his eyes closed.

Together they could argue the bark off a tree. But they
could also conspire mischief like master criminals. The
twins were a force. And no children had ever been loved
more, Reed was certain.

"The only reason Arthur called them violets," Matthew
said in singsong, "is because he thinks that's the color of
Arabella's eyes."

"Do not."

Reed looked from one to the other. "Do you mean your
Uncle Raven's daughter?"

Matthew answered for his brother. "He wants to marry
her. He even wrote her a poem, the way Granduncle does
for Grandmum."

"Did not."

"Did so. I saw it tucked beneath your pillow. You compared her eyes to violets and her lips to strawberry tarts."

Arthur stiffened and faced Reed, pointing a finger at his
smirking brother who lounged back on the grass with his
arms folded behind his head. "Dad, as the eldest, I demand
my own bedchamber. I will no longer endure the nonsense
of this child."

"I'm only twenty minutes younger."

"And clearly, an entire lifetime of wisdom apart."

Knowing this was serious to his eldest child, Reed did
his best not to laugh. Resting a hand on Arthur's shoulder,
he said, "We'll talk to your mother about it. Come on then,
let's go inside. Matthew, do you have a flower yet?"

Grunting, the younger twin swiped absently at the low
shrub before he slowly lumbered to his feet as if he were six
hundred years old. "I still don't see why Mum needs more
flowers when it's the perfect day for riding the pony."

"Because she deserves something special to press in a remembrance book."

"But why?"

"You'll see."

Inside, Reed quietly opened the bedchamber door and peered inside. Soft golden light spilled through the window over Ainsley, sitting up against the bolster pillow. Her face glowed, her chestnut hair falling in a plait over her shoulder. And when she smiled at him, his heart beat in a contented rhythm. It happened each time without fail.

Every day, Reed marveled at how much he loved her, then the next day he would love her all the more.

Crossing the room, he pressed his lips to hers, breathing in the sweet scent of her skin, her soft hand caressing his cheek. Then he bent to kiss the tiny forehead peeking out from the bundle on her lap, and wondered dimly if a man could die from such happiness.

"Are you ready for visitors, highness?"

"Of course," she whispered, her voice a little raspier than usual after the long morning's efforts.

Their boys came in a slow procession, both of them holding their flowers outstretched in their fists.

"Come and meet your sister, my loves," she said, peeling back the blanket just enough to reveal the tiny head covered in dark, wispy curls. "What do you think of her?"

Matthew frowned. "She looks old, like the Duchess of Holliford."

"You're not supposed to say it even if it's true," Arthur added, nudging him with his elbow.

Ainsley laughed softly. "You both looked wrinkly, too. That's just how babies are for a few days. Just wait. In a little while, she'll blossom and be just as pretty as the pair of you."

"Mum," Matthew said, rolling his eyes but with a crooked grin on his lips.

Arthur peered closer, considering. "She is sort of scrunched together like a flower bud. What do we call her?"

"Hmm . . . I was thinking of naming her after a flower," Ainsley said, lifting her gaze to Reed. He nodded, having a sense of what she would say.

But the boys were too eager to share their thoughts first. "You should name her Galahad, like my pony."

"What about Geranium or Daisy? At least those are both flowers," Arthur said.

"He actually wants her to be called *Violet*. Don't you, Arthur?"

"Well, Galahad is a stupid name even for a pony."

"Boys," Ainsley said softly, lifting her finger to her lips, the baby squirming in her arms. Then she slid a smiling glance up to Reed. "Such a noisy life you've given me, Mr. Sterling."

And you've given me the best life, he thought. Better than he'd ever imagined.

They lived in Harrowfield during the summer months and each winter at Christmastide. The Bourne Matrimonial Agency was closed during that time, too, with most of the *ton* away at their own country houses. However, that did not stop the influx of applications by post, or the local villagers dropping by to see if his wife could find them their perfect match.

As for Sterling's, it was not the legendary gaming hell that he'd once imagined it would become. It was more a gentleman's club now, but Reed still gave boxing lessons upstairs on occasion. He didn't mind at all.

His dream was still the same, only now, he was able to look at his true legacy and watch them grow, day by day.

Standing with his family, he felt something brush against him and saw a scraggly cat wend her way around his trousers. A bit grayer in patches than she used to be, she blinked up at him and sank her claws into his leg. He reached down and picked her up.

"I think someone else is curious about the newest member of the family," he said, stroking her soft fur. "Seymour, I'd like you to meet"—he paused, holding his wife's gaze—"Primrose Sterling."

Keep an eye out for

Lord Holt Takes a Bride
The Mating Habits of Scoundrels, Book 1

The first in a charming, witty regency series about three friends who set out to write a primer on the marriage habits of aristocrats to help other debutantes avoid ruin . . . but discover more than they bargained for when it comes to scoundrels!

Coming Spring 2020

THE SMYTHE-SMITH QUARTET BY
#1 *NEW YORK TIMES*
BESTSELLING AUTHOR

JULIA QUINN

JUST LIKE HEAVEN
978-0-06-149190-0

Honoria Smythe-Smith is to play the violin (badly) in the annual musicale performed by the Smythe-Smith quartet. But first she's determined to marry by the end of the season. When her advances are spurned, can Marcus Holroyd, her brother Daniel's best friend, swoop in and steal her heart in time for the musicale?

A NIGHT LIKE THIS
978-0-06-207290-0

Anne Wynter is not who she says she is, but she's managing quite well as a governess to three highborn young ladies. Daniel Smythe-Smith might be in mortal danger, but that's not going to stop the young earl from falling in love. And when he spies a mysterious woman at his family's annual musicale, he vows to pursue her.

THE SUM OF ALL KISSES
978-0-06-207292-4

Hugh Prentice has never had patience for dramatic females, and Lady Sarah Pleinsworth has never been acquainted with the words *shy* or *retiring*. Besides, a reckless duel has left Hugh with a ruined leg, and now he could never court a woman like Sarah, much less dream of marrying her.

THE SECRETS OF SIR RICHARD KENWORTHY
978-0-06-207294-8

Sir Richard Kenworthy has less than a month to find a bride, and when he sees Iris Smythe-Smith hiding behind her cello at her family's infamous musicale, he thinks he might have struck gold. Iris is used to blending into the background, so when Richard courts her, she can't quite believe it's true.

JQ4 0916

At Avon Books, we know your passion for romance—once you finish one of our novels, you find yourself wanting more.

May we tempt you with . . .

- **Excerpts** from our upcoming releases.

- Entertaining **extras**, including authors' personal photo albums and book lists.

- Behind-the-scenes **scoop** on your favorite characters and series.

- **Sweepstakes** for the chance to win free books, romantic getaways, and other fun prizes.

- Writing **tips** from our authors and editors.

- **Blog** with our authors and find out why they love to write romance.

- **Exclusive content** that's not contained within the pages of our novels.

Join us at
www.avonbooks.com